VAULT

DAMIAN A. WASSEL
PUBLISHER

ADRIAN F. WASSEL
EDITOR-IN-CHIEF

NATHAN C. GOODEN
ART DIRECTOR

TIM DANIEL
EVP BRANDING DESIGN

REBECCA TAYLOR
MANAGING EDITOR

DAVID DISSANAYAKE
DIRECTOR OF PR & RETAILER RELATIONS

IAN BALDESSARI
OPERATIONS MANAGER

DAMIAN A. WASSEL, SR.
PRINCIPAL

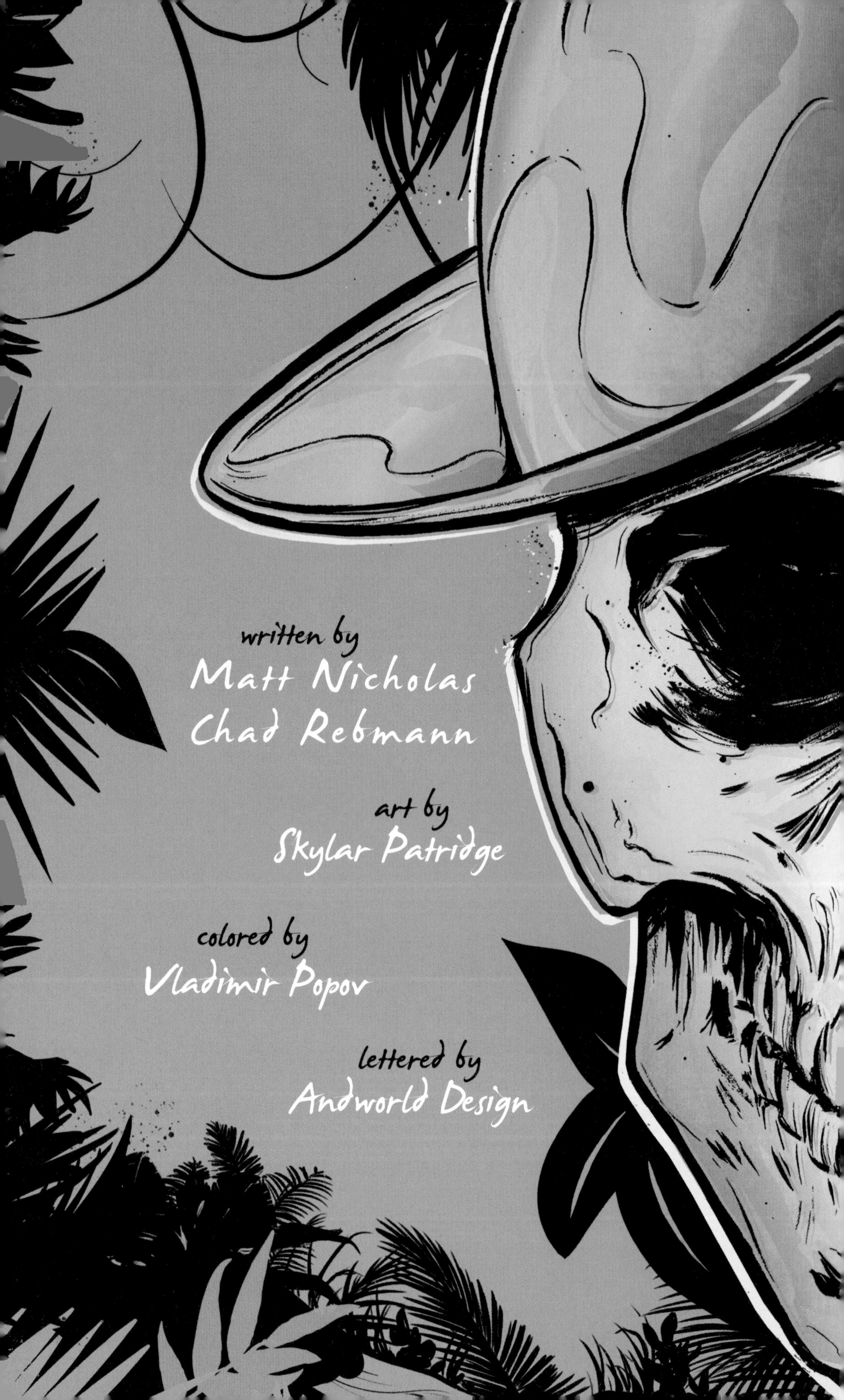
written by
Matt Nicholas
Chad Rebmann
art by
Skylar Patridge
colored by
Vladimir Popov
lettered by
Andworld Design

Vault Comics Presents

RELICS OF YOUTH

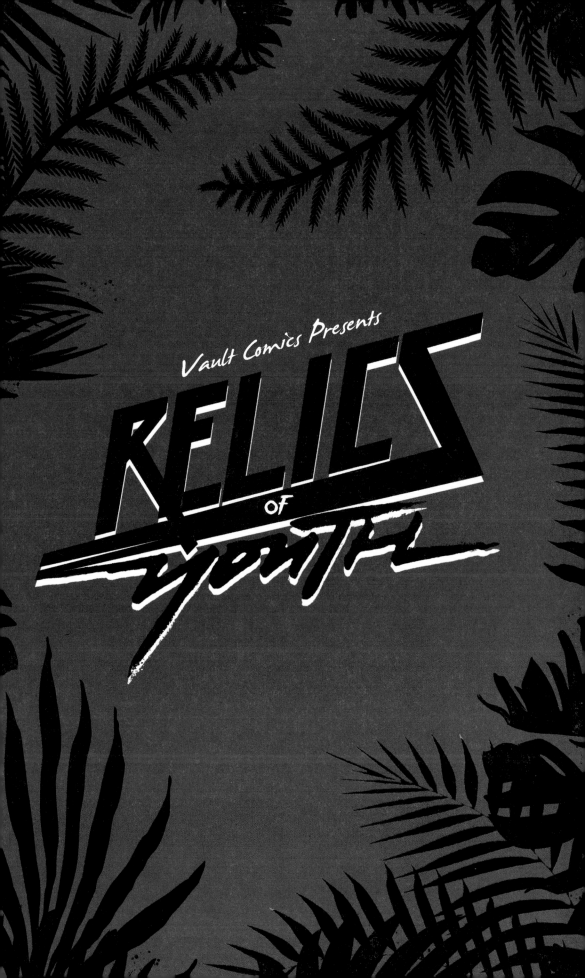

CHAPTER
ONE

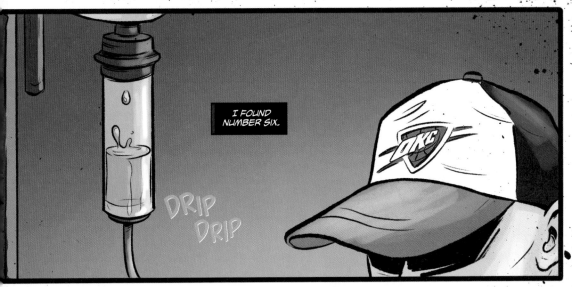

I FOUND NUMBER SIX.

DEREK FORGE.

A QUICK CHAT ON THE PHONE AND I COULD TELL HE WAS *LEGIT.*

AT FIRST, WE TALKED ABOUT A BUNCH OF B.S., ABOUT OKLAHOMA, SCHOOL...

THEN HE MENTIONED THE ISLAND...

I COULD HEAR IT IN HIS VOICE.

THE FINAL CONFIRMATION CAME WITH A PIC OF THE *TATTOO.*

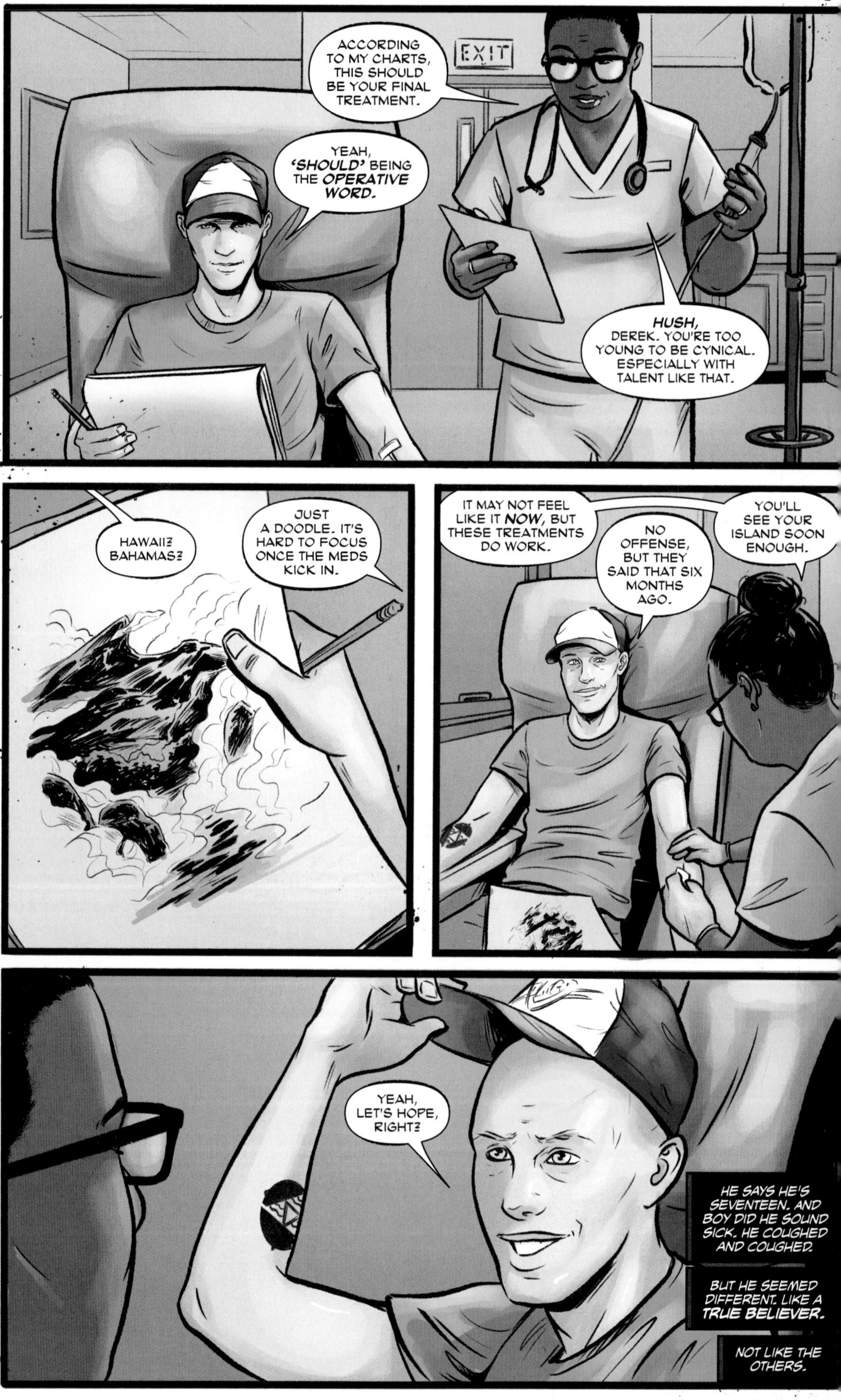
EXIT
ACCORDING TO MY CHARTS, THIS SHOULD BE YOUR FINAL TREATMENT.
YEAH, 'SHOULD' BEING THE OPERATIVE WORD.
HUSH, DEREK. YOU'RE TOO YOUNG TO BE CYNICAL. ESPECIALLY WITH TALENT LIKE THAT.
HAWAII? BAHAMAS?
JUST A DOODLE. IT'S HARD TO FOCUS ONCE THE MEDS KICK IN.
IT MAY NOT FEEL LIKE IT NOW, BUT THESE TREATMENTS DO WORK.
NO OFFENSE, BUT THEY SAID THAT SIX MONTHS AGO.
YOU'LL SEE YOUR ISLAND SOON ENOUGH.
YEAH, LET'S HOPE, RIGHT?
HE SAYS HE'S SEVENTEEN. AND BOY DID HE SOUND SICK. HE COUGHED AND COUGHED.
BUT HE SEEMED DIFFERENT. LIKE A TRUE BELIEVER.
NOT LIKE THE OTHERS.

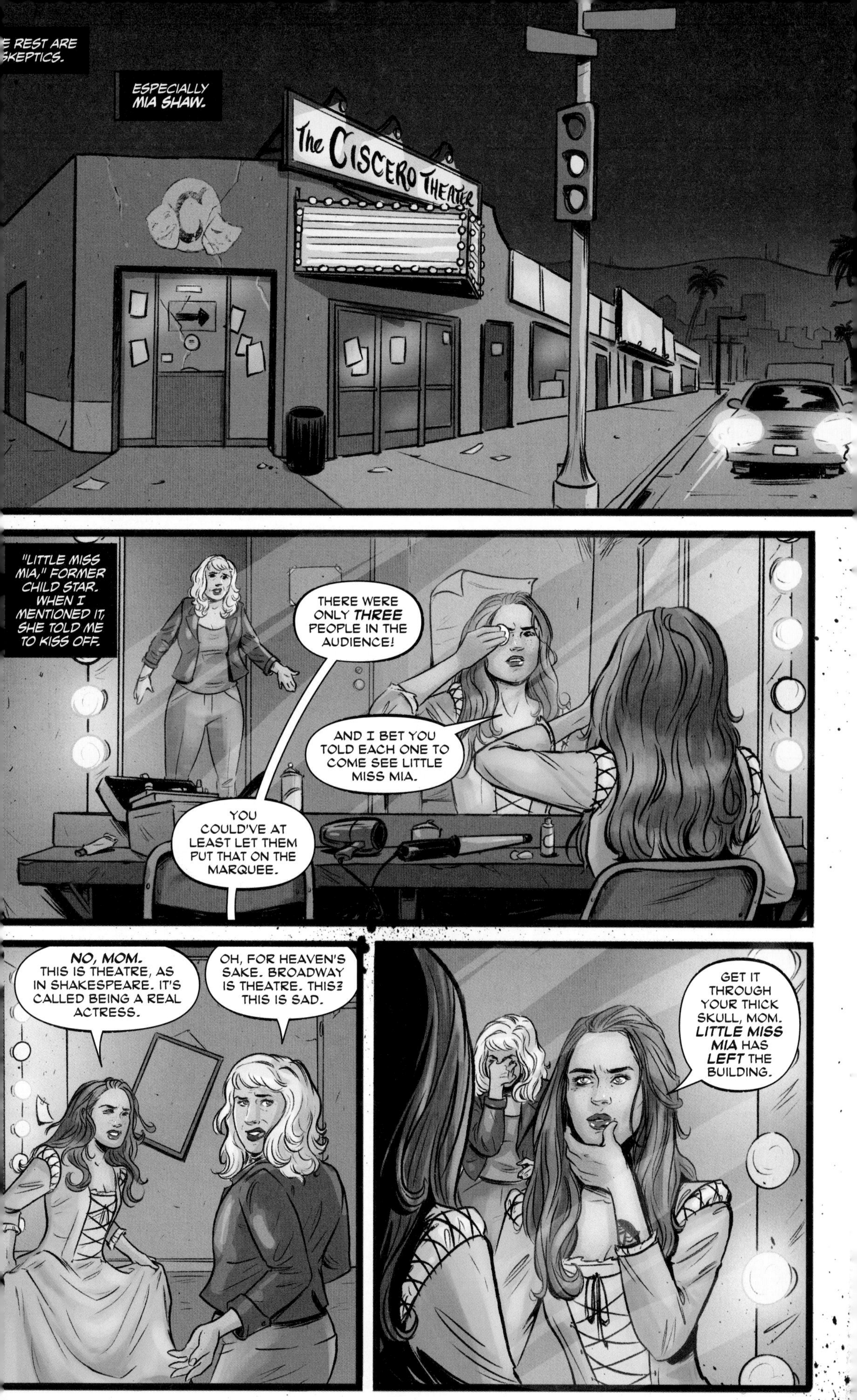
E REST ARE
SKEPTICS.
ESPECIALLY MIA SHAW.
The CISCERO THEATER
"LITTLE MISS MIA," FORMER CHILD STAR. WHEN I MENTIONED IT, SHE TOLD ME TO KISS OFF.
THERE WERE ONLY THREE PEOPLE IN THE AUDIENCE!
AND I BET YOU TOLD EACH ONE TO COME SEE LITTLE MISS MIA.
YOU COULD'VE AT LEAST LET THEM PUT THAT ON THE MARQUEE.
NO, MOM. THIS IS THEATRE, AS IN SHAKESPEARE. IT'S CALLED BEING A REAL ACTRESS.
OH, FOR HEAVEN'S SAKE. BROADWAY IS THEATRE. THIS? THIS IS SAD.
GET IT THROUGH YOUR THICK SKULL, MOM. LITTLE MISS MIA HAS LEFT THE BUILDING.

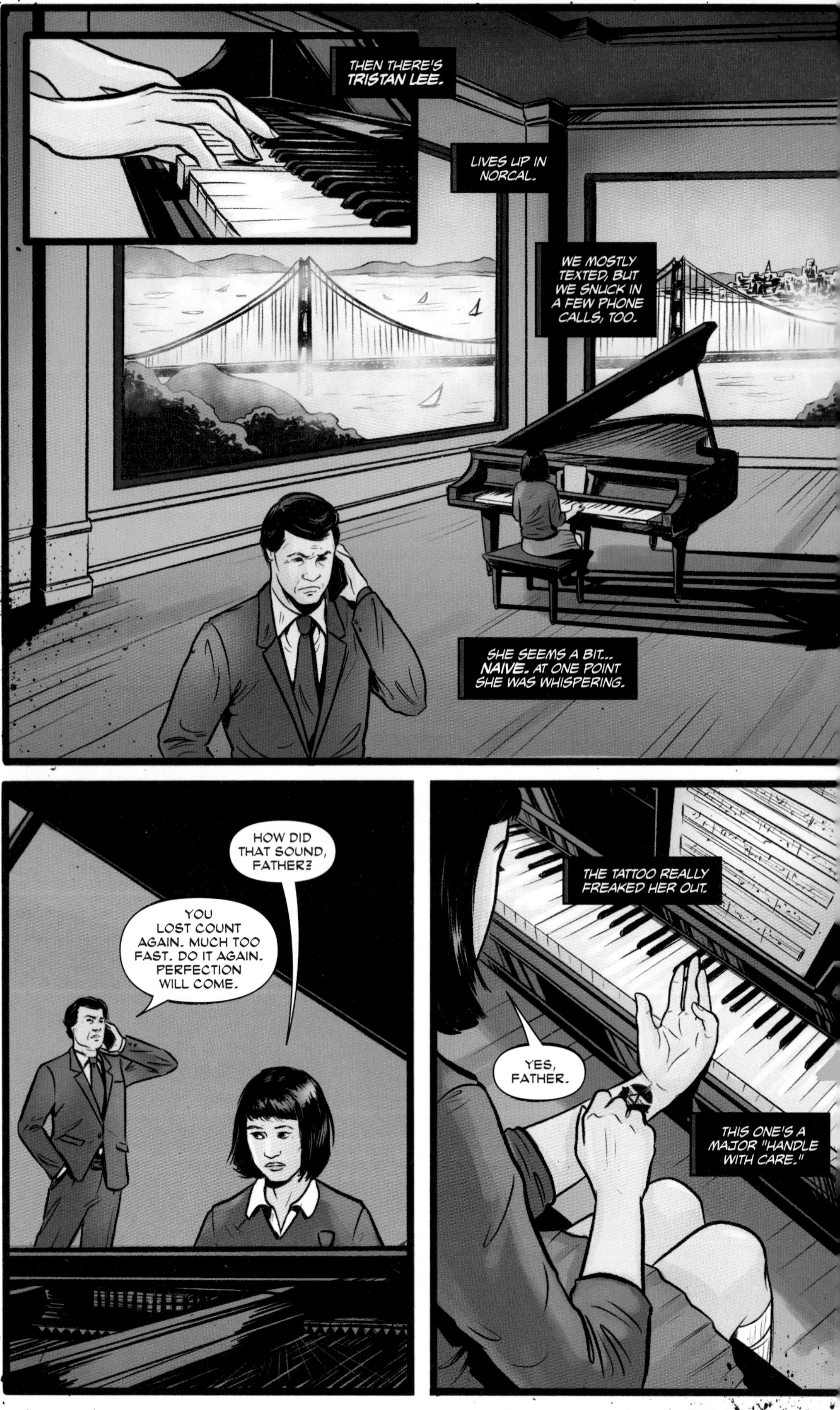
THEN THERE'S TRISTAN LEE.
LIVES UP IN NORCAL.
WE MOSTLY TEXTED, BUT WE SNUCK IN A FEW PHONE CALLS, TOO.
SHE SEEMS A BIT... NAIVE. AT ONE POINT SHE WAS WHISPERING.
HOW DID THAT SOUND, FATHER?
YOU LOST COUNT AGAIN. MUCH TOO FAST. DO IT AGAIN. PERFECTION WILL COME.
THE TATTOO REALLY FREAKED HER OUT.
YES, FATHER.
THIS ONE'S A MAJOR "HANDLE WITH CARE."

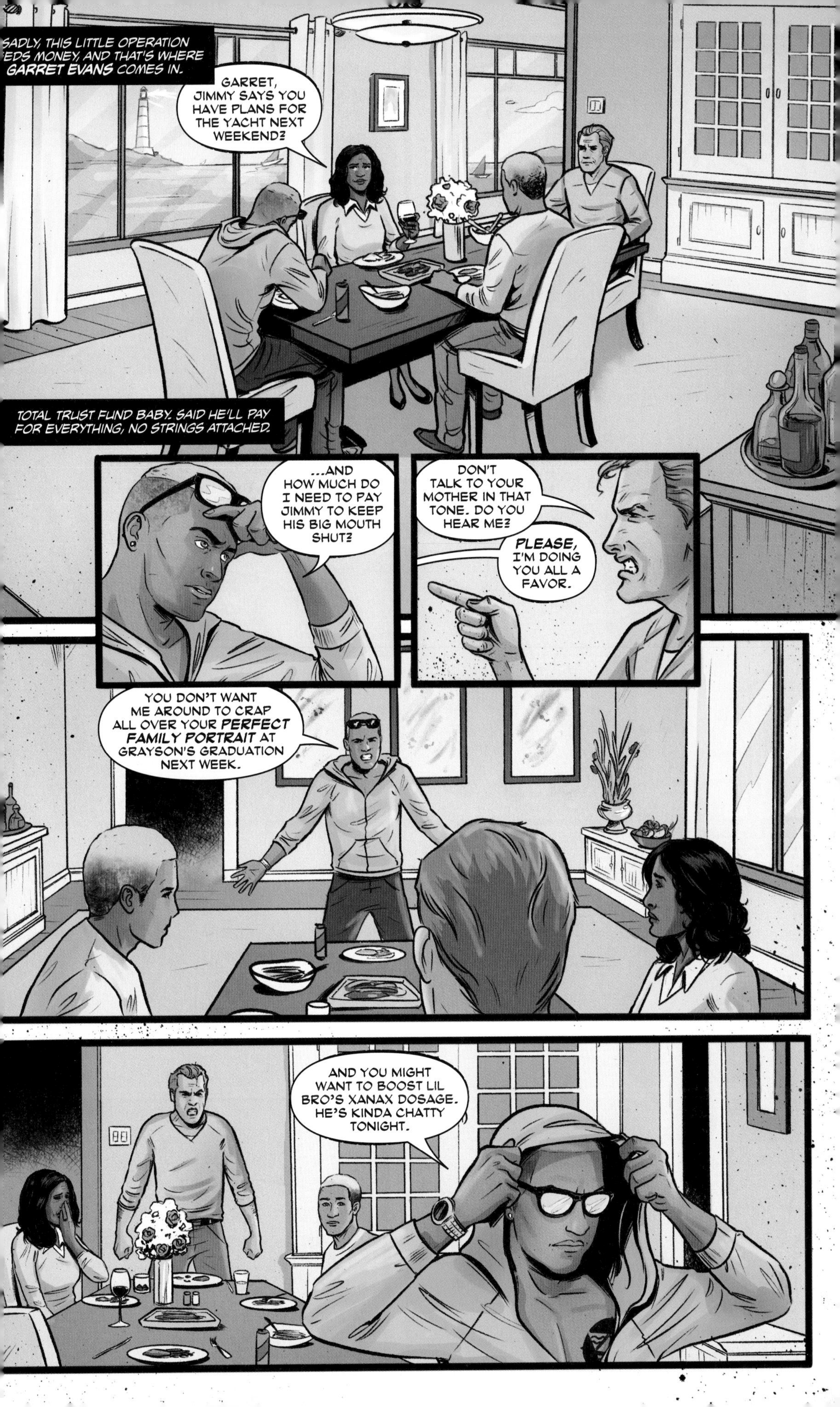
SADLY, THIS LITTLE OPERATION
EDS MONEY, AND THAT'S WHERE
GARRET EVANS COMES IN.
GARRET, JIMMY SAYS YOU HAVE PLANS FOR THE YACHT NEXT WEEKEND?
TOTAL TRUST FUND BABY. SAID HE'LL PAY FOR EVERYTHING, NO STRINGS ATTACHED.
...AND HOW MUCH DO I NEED TO PAY JIMMY TO KEEP HIS BIG MOUTH SHUT?
DON'T TALK TO YOUR MOTHER IN THAT TONE. DO YOU HEAR ME?
PLEASE, I'M DOING YOU ALL A FAVOR.
YOU DON'T WANT ME AROUND TO CRAP ALL OVER YOUR PERFECT FAMILY PORTRAIT AT GRAYSON'S GRADUATION NEXT WEEK.
AND YOU MIGHT WANT TO BOOST LIL BRO'S XANAX DOSAGE. HE'S KINDA CHATTY TONIGHT.

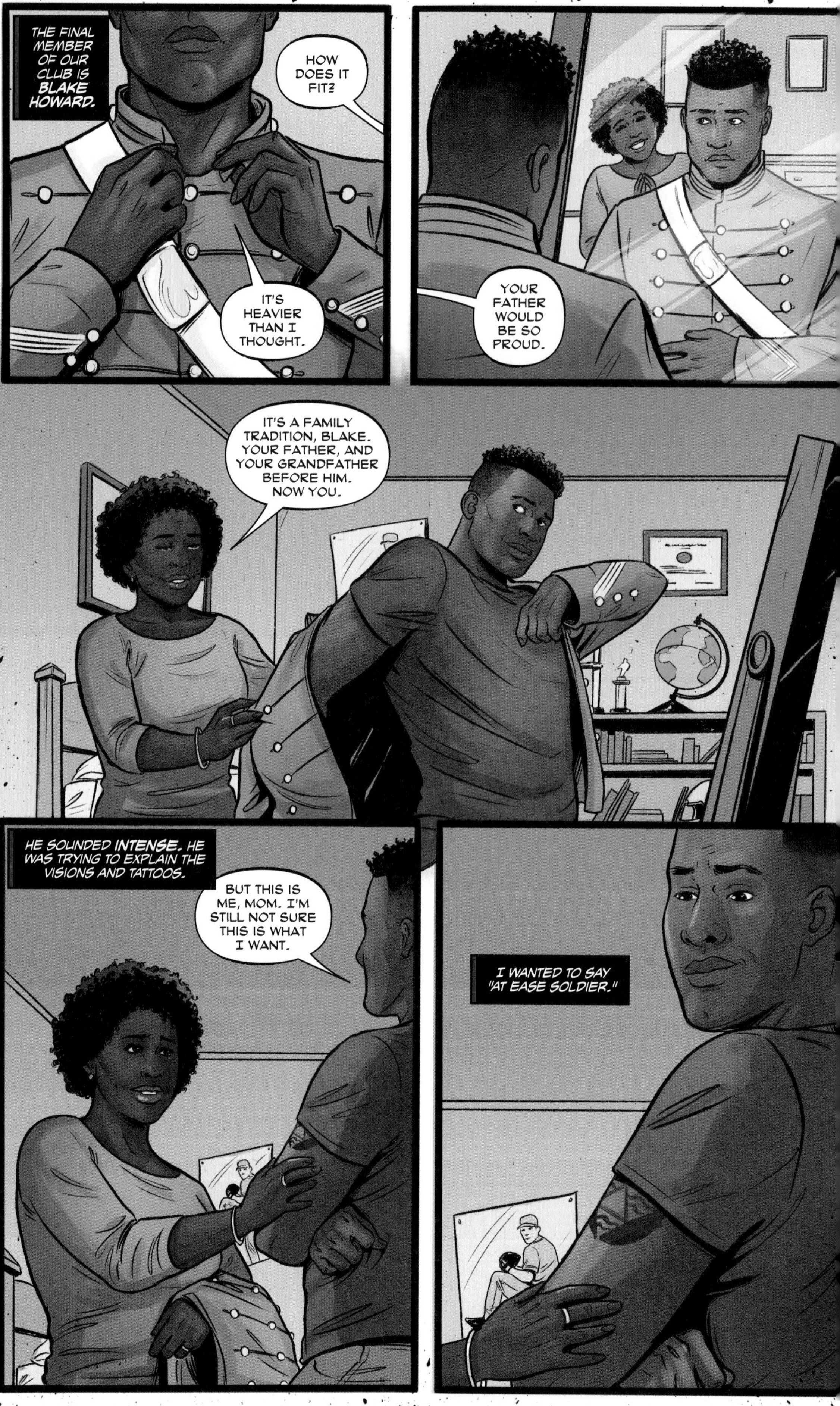
THE FINAL MEMBER OF OUR CLUB IS BLAKE HOWARD.
HOW DOES IT FIT?
IT'S HEAVIER THAN I THOUGHT.
YOUR FATHER WOULD BE SO PROUD.
IT'S A FAMILY TRADITION, BLAKE. YOUR FATHER, AND YOUR GRANDFATHER BEFORE HIM. NOW YOU.
HE SOUNDED INTENSE. HE WAS TRYING TO EXPLAIN THE VISIONS AND TATTOOS.
BUT THIS IS ME, MOM. I'M STILL NOT SURE THIS IS WHAT I WANT.
I WANTED TO SAY "AT EASE SOLDIER."

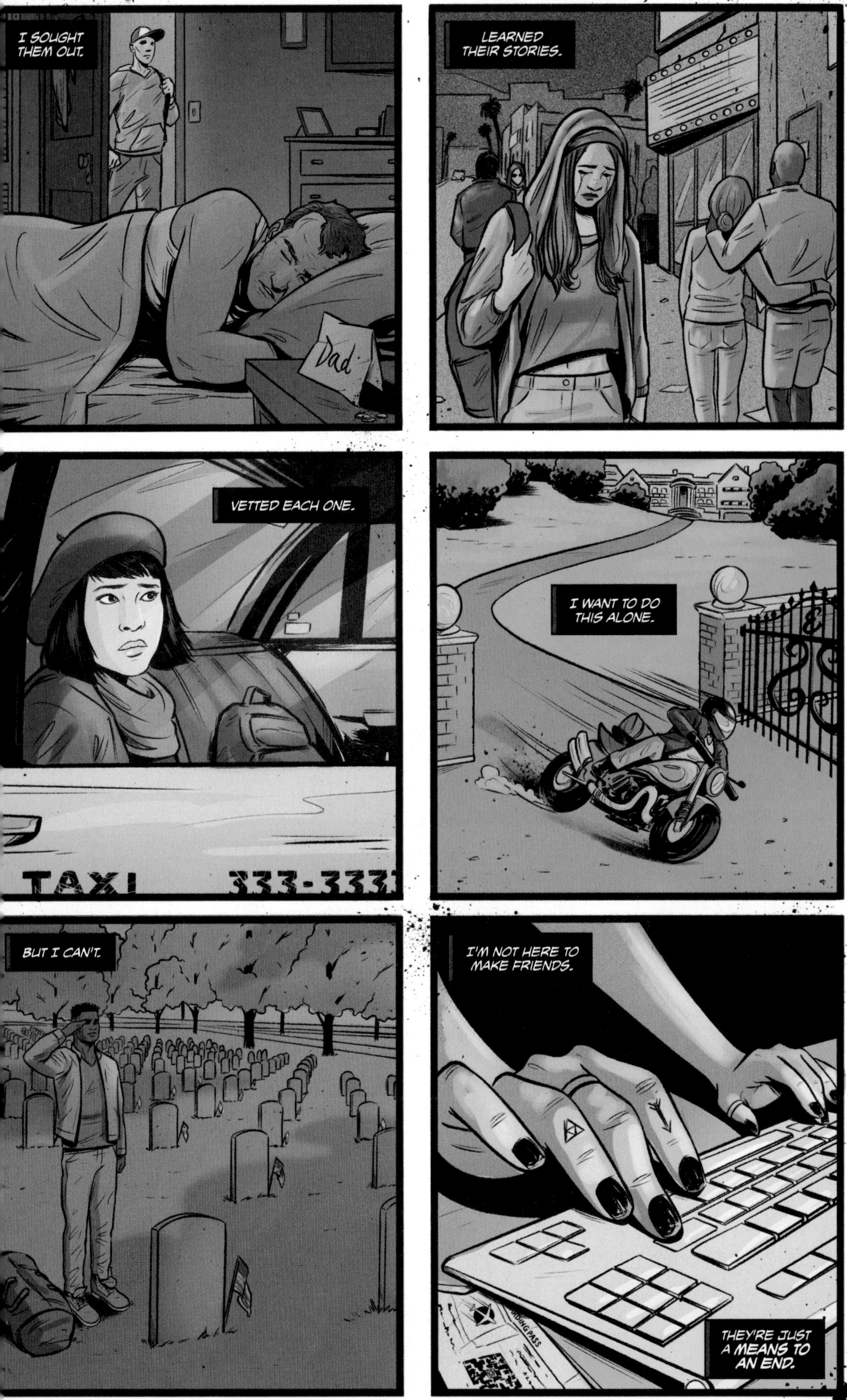
I SOUGHT THEM OUT.
Dad
LEARNED THEIR STORIES.
VETTED EACH ONE.
TAXI 333-333
I WANT TO DO THIS ALONE.
BUT I CAN'T.
I'M NOT HERE TO MAKE FRIENDS.
THEY'RE JUST A MEANS TO AN END.

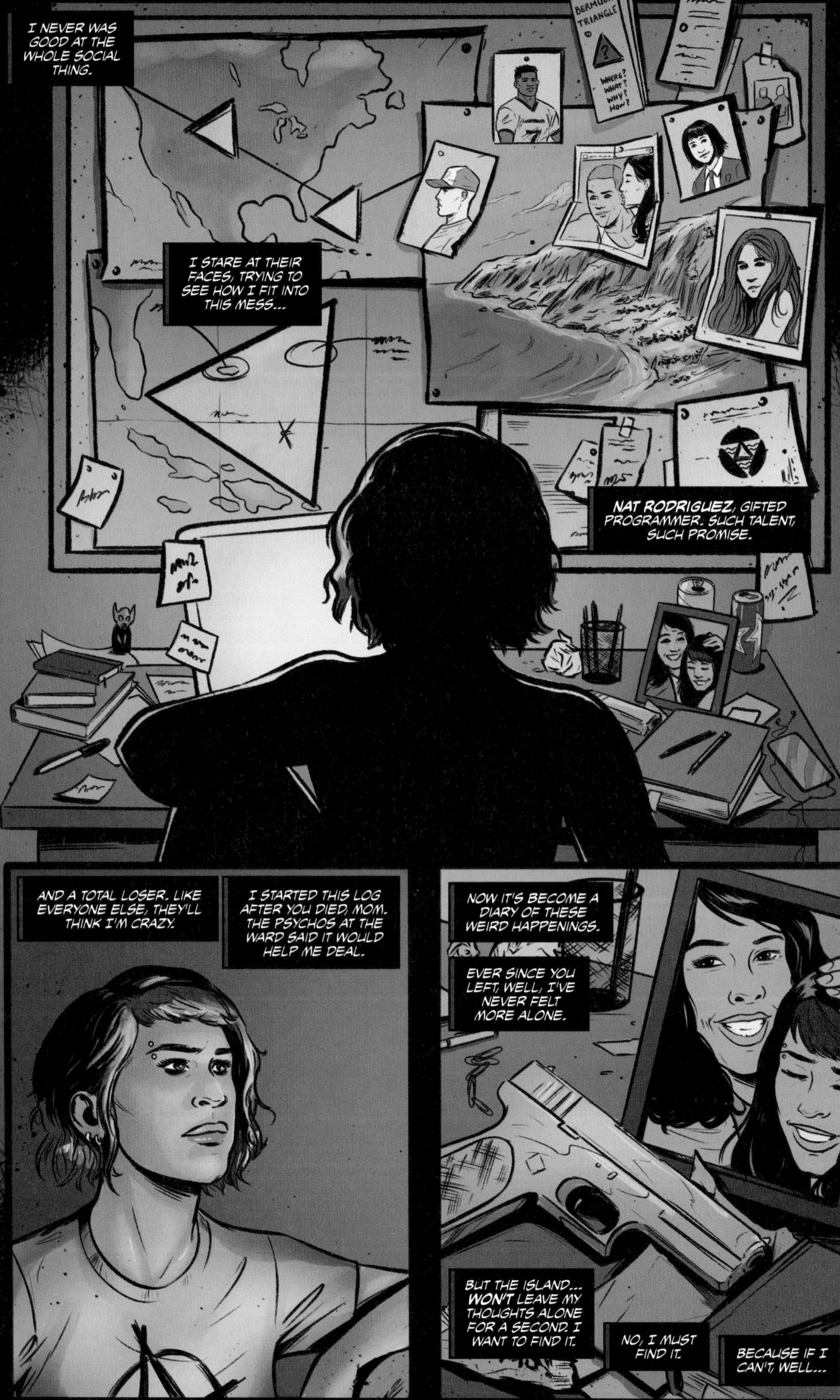
I NEVER WAS GOOD AT THE WHOLE SOCIAL THING.
THE BERMUDA TRIANGLE
WHERE? WHAT? WHY? HOW?
I STARE AT THEIR FACES, TRYING TO SEE HOW I FIT INTO THIS MESS...
NAT RODRIGUEZ, GIFTED PROGRAMMER. SUCH TALENT, SUCH PROMISE.
AND A TOTAL LOSER. LIKE EVERYONE ELSE, THEY'LL THINK I'M CRAZY.
I STARTED THIS LOG AFTER YOU DIED, MOM. THE PSYCHOS AT THE WARD SAID IT WOULD HELP ME DEAL.
NOW IT'S BECOME A DIARY OF THESE WEIRD HAPPENINGS.
EVER SINCE YOU LEFT, WELL, I'VE NEVER FELT MORE ALONE.
BUT THE ISLAND... WON'T LEAVE MY THOUGHTS ALONE FOR A SECOND. I WANT TO FIND IT.
NO, I MUST FIND IT.
BECAUSE IF I CAN'T, WELL...

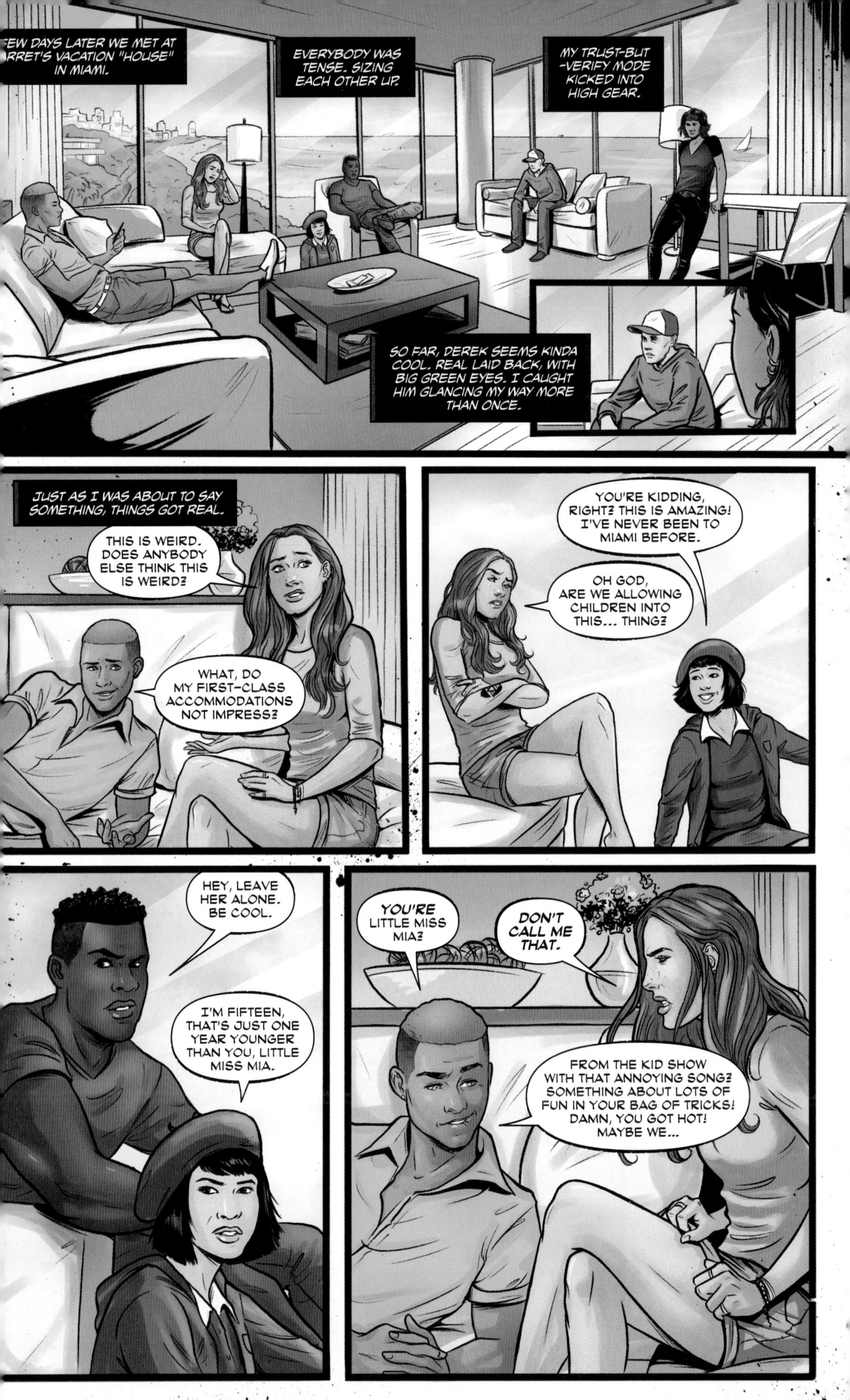
FEW DAYS LATER WE MET AT
ARRET'S VACATION "HOUSE" IN MIAMI.
EVERYBODY WAS TENSE. SIZING EACH OTHER UP.
MY TRUST-BUT -VERIFY MODE KICKED INTO HIGH GEAR.
SO FAR, DEREK SEEMS KINDA COOL. REAL LAID BACK, WITH BIG GREEN EYES. I CAUGHT HIM GLANCING MY WAY MORE THAN ONCE.
JUST AS I WAS ABOUT TO SAY SOMETHING, THINGS GOT REAL.
THIS IS WEIRD. DOES ANYBODY ELSE THINK THIS IS WEIRD?
WHAT, DO MY FIRST-CLASS ACCOMMODATIONS NOT IMPRESS?
YOU'RE KIDDING, RIGHT? THIS IS AMAZING! I'VE NEVER BEEN TO MIAMI BEFORE.
OH GOD, ARE WE ALLOWING CHILDREN INTO THIS... THING?
HEY, LEAVE HER ALONE. BE COOL.
I'M FIFTEEN, THAT'S JUST ONE YEAR YOUNGER THAN YOU, LITTLE MISS MIA.
YOU'RE LITTLE MISS MIA?
DON'T CALL ME THAT.
FROM THE KID SHOW WITH THAT ANNOYING SONG? SOMETHING ABOUT LOTS OF FUN IN YOUR BAG OF TRICKS! DAMN, YOU GOT HOT! MAYBE WE...

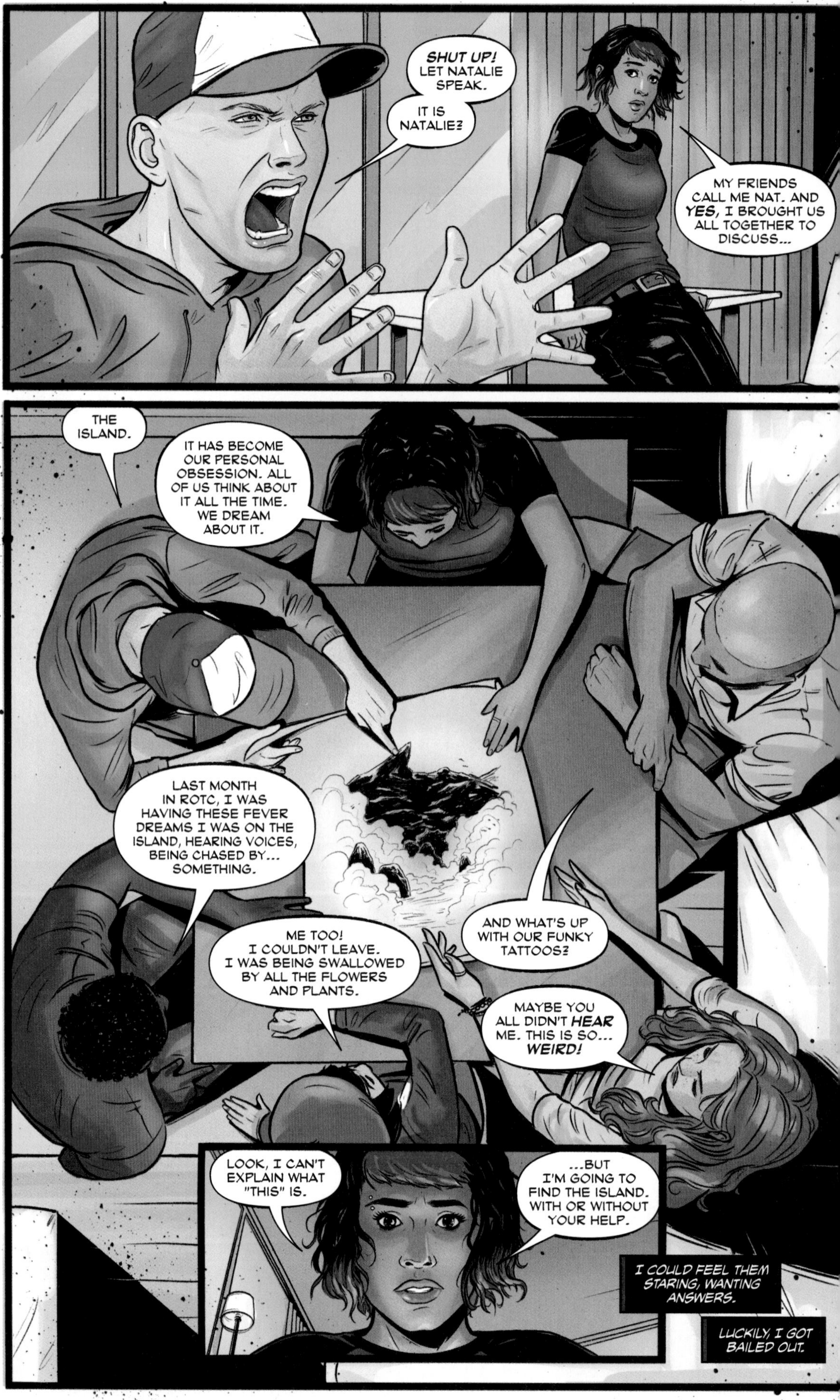
SHUT UP! LET NATALIE SPEAK.
IT IS NATALIE?
MY FRIENDS CALL ME NAT. AND YES, I BROUGHT US ALL TOGETHER TO DISCUSS...
THE ISLAND.
IT HAS BECOME OUR PERSONAL OBSESSION. ALL OF US THINK ABOUT IT ALL THE TIME. WE DREAM ABOUT IT.
LAST MONTH IN ROTC, I WAS HAVING THESE FEVER DREAMS I WAS ON THE ISLAND, HEARING VOICES, BEING CHASED BY... SOMETHING.
ME TOO! I COULDN'T LEAVE. I WAS BEING SWALLOWED BY ALL THE FLOWERS AND PLANTS.
AND WHAT'S UP WITH OUR FUNKY TATTOOS?
MAYBE YOU ALL DIDN'T HEAR ME. THIS IS SO... WEIRD!
LOOK, I CAN'T EXPLAIN WHAT "THIS" IS.
...BUT I'M GOING TO FIND THE ISLAND. WITH OR WITHOUT YOUR HELP.
I COULD FEEL THEM STARING, WANTING ANSWERS.
LUCKILY, I GOT BAILED OUT.

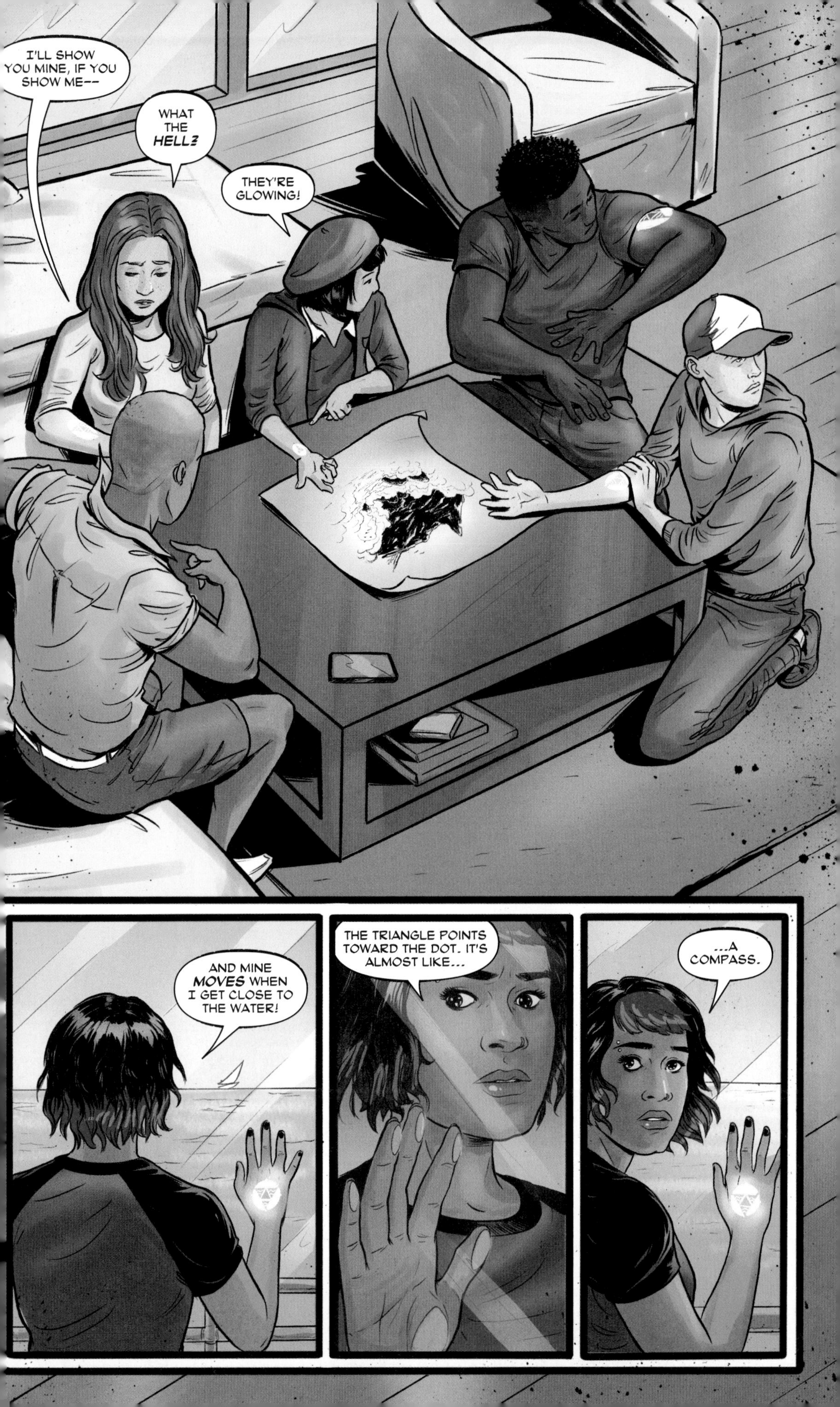
I'LL SHOW YOU MINE, IF YOU SHOW ME--
WHAT THE *HELL?*
THEY'RE GLOWING!
AND MINE *MOVES* WHEN I GET CLOSE TO THE WATER!
THE TRIANGLE POINTS TOWARD THE DOT. IT'S ALMOST LIKE...
...A COMPASS.

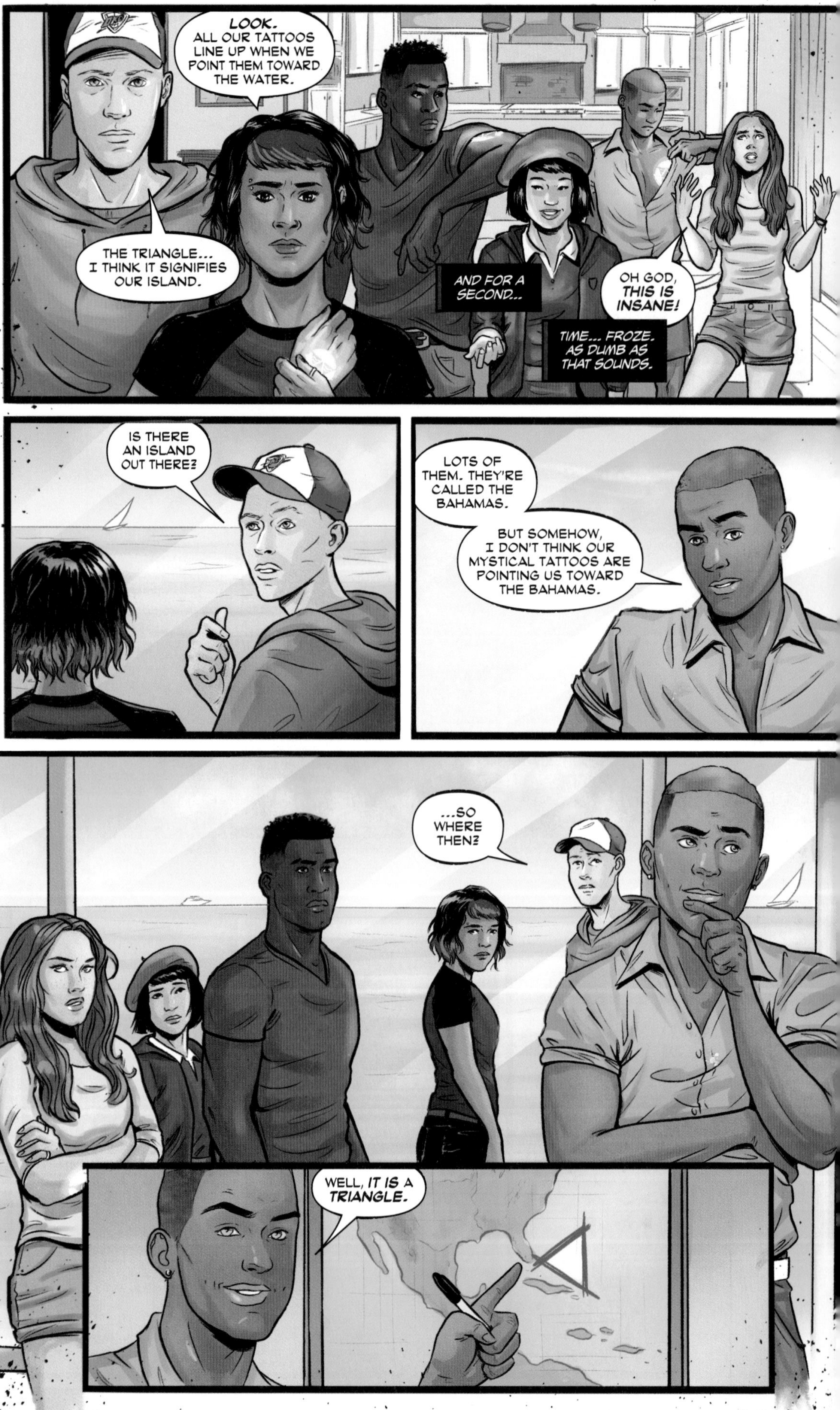
LOOK. ALL OUR TATTOOS LINE UP WHEN WE POINT THEM TOWARD THE WATER.
THE TRIANGLE... I THINK IT SIGNIFIES OUR ISLAND.
AND FOR A SECOND...
TIME... FROZE. AS DUMB AS THAT SOUNDS.
OH GOD, THIS IS INSANE!
IS THERE AN ISLAND OUT THERE?
LOTS OF THEM. THEY'RE CALLED THE BAHAMAS.
BUT SOMEHOW, I DON'T THINK OUR MYSTICAL TATTOOS ARE POINTING US TOWARD THE BAHAMAS.
...SO WHERE THEN?
WELL, IT IS A TRIANGLE.

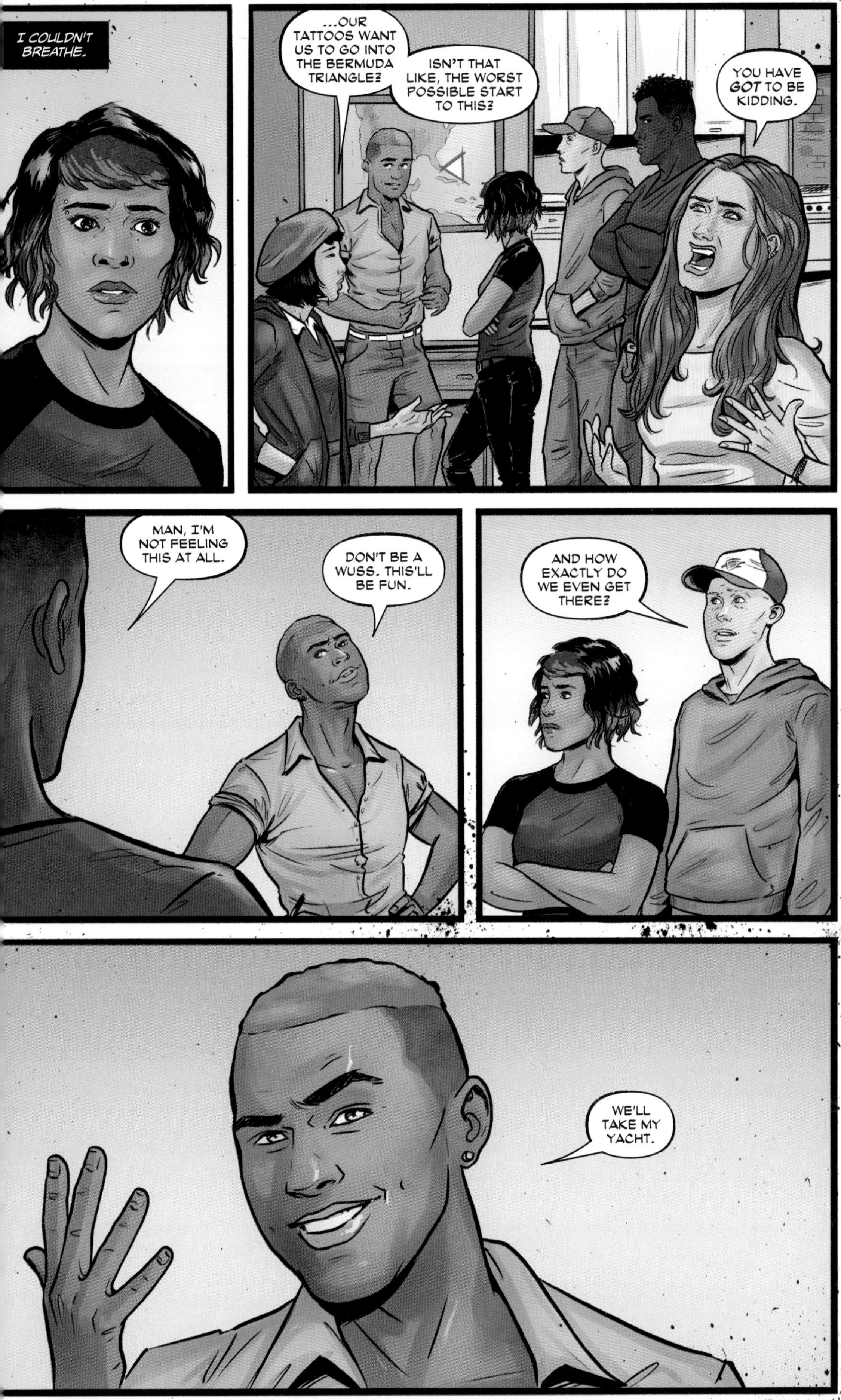
I COULDN'T BREATHE.
...OUR TATTOOS WANT US TO GO INTO THE BERMUDA TRIANGLE?
ISN'T THAT LIKE, THE WORST POSSIBLE START TO THIS?
YOU HAVE GOT TO BE KIDDING.
MAN, I'M NOT FEELING THIS AT ALL.
DON'T BE A WUSS. THIS'LL BE FUN.
AND HOW EXACTLY DO WE EVEN GET THERE?
WE'LL TAKE MY YACHT.

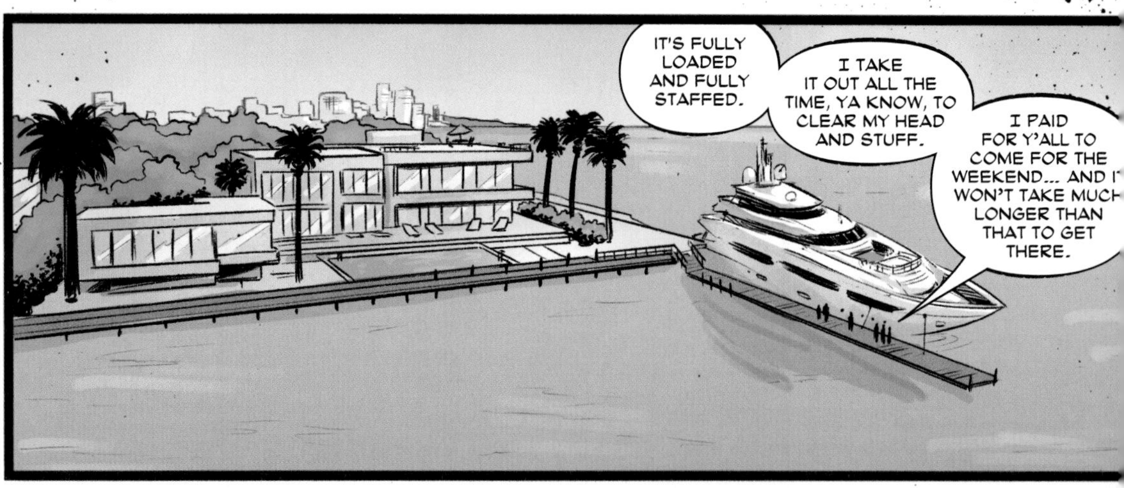
IT'S FULLY LOADED AND FULLY STAFFED.
I TAKE IT OUT ALL THE TIME, YA KNOW, TO CLEAR MY HEAD AND STUFF.
I PAID FOR Y'ALL TO COME FOR THE WEEKEND... AND IT WON'T TAKE MUCH LONGER THAN THAT TO GET THERE.

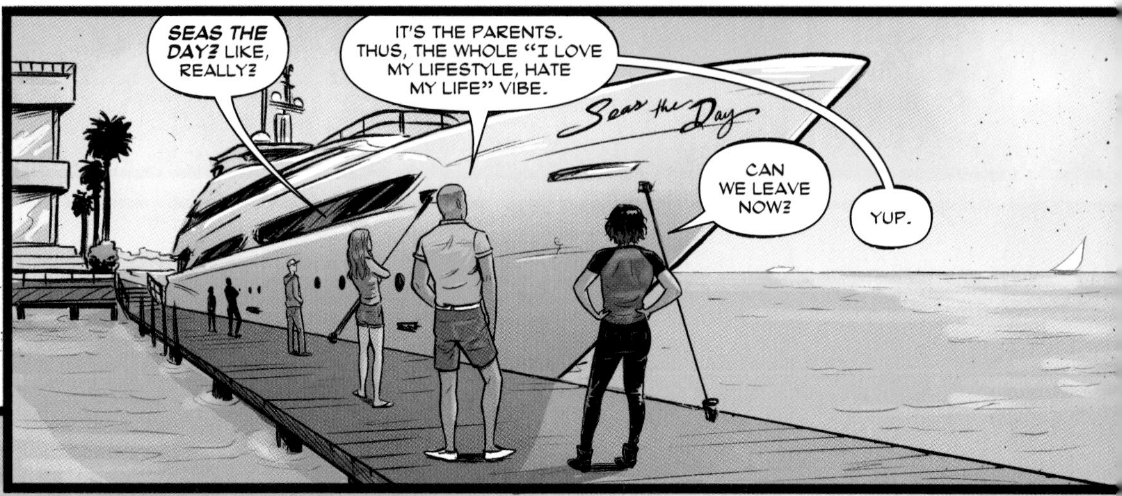
SEAS THE DAY? LIKE, REALLY?
IT'S THE PARENTS. THUS, THE WHOLE "I LOVE MY LIFESTYLE, HATE MY LIFE" VIBE.
Seas the Day
CAN WE LEAVE NOW?
YUP.

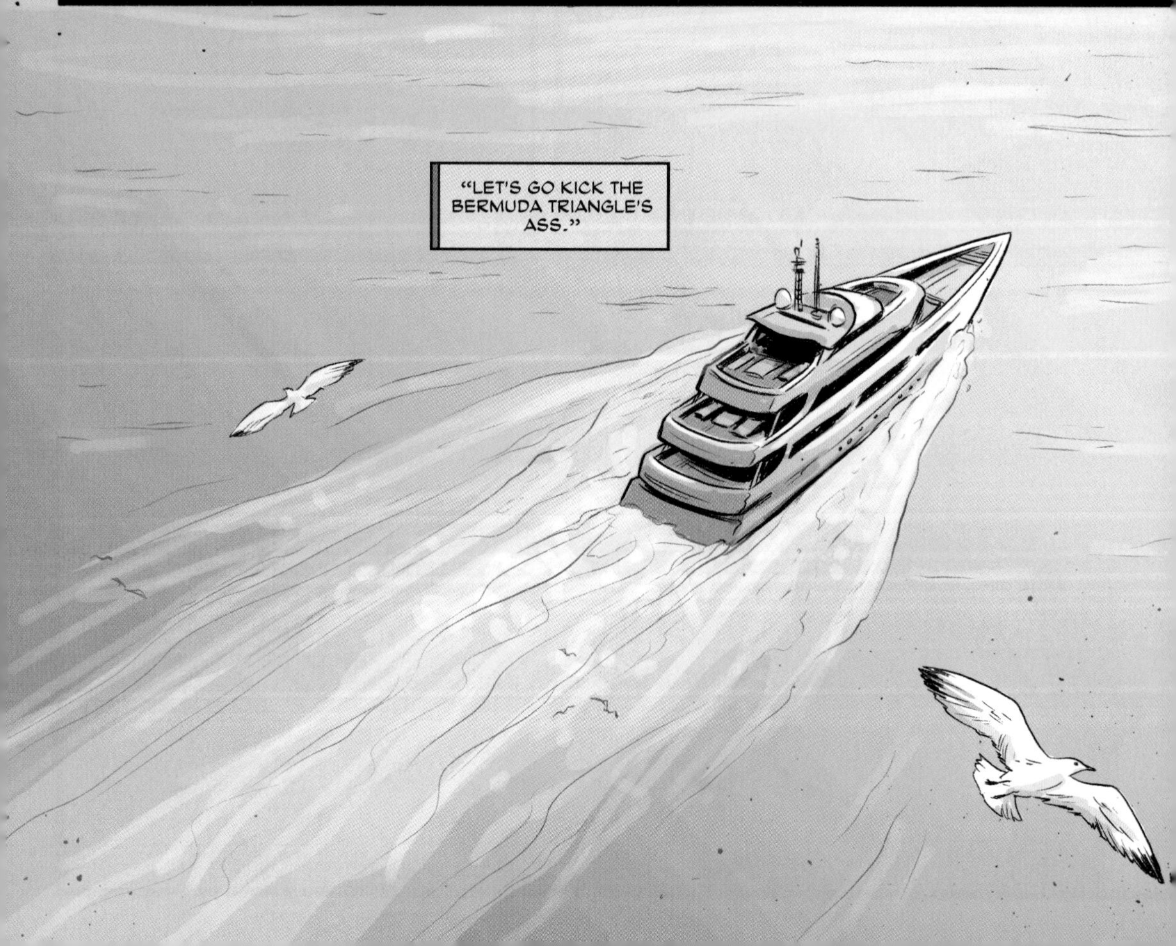
"LET'S GO KICK THE BERMUDA TRIANGLE'S ASS."

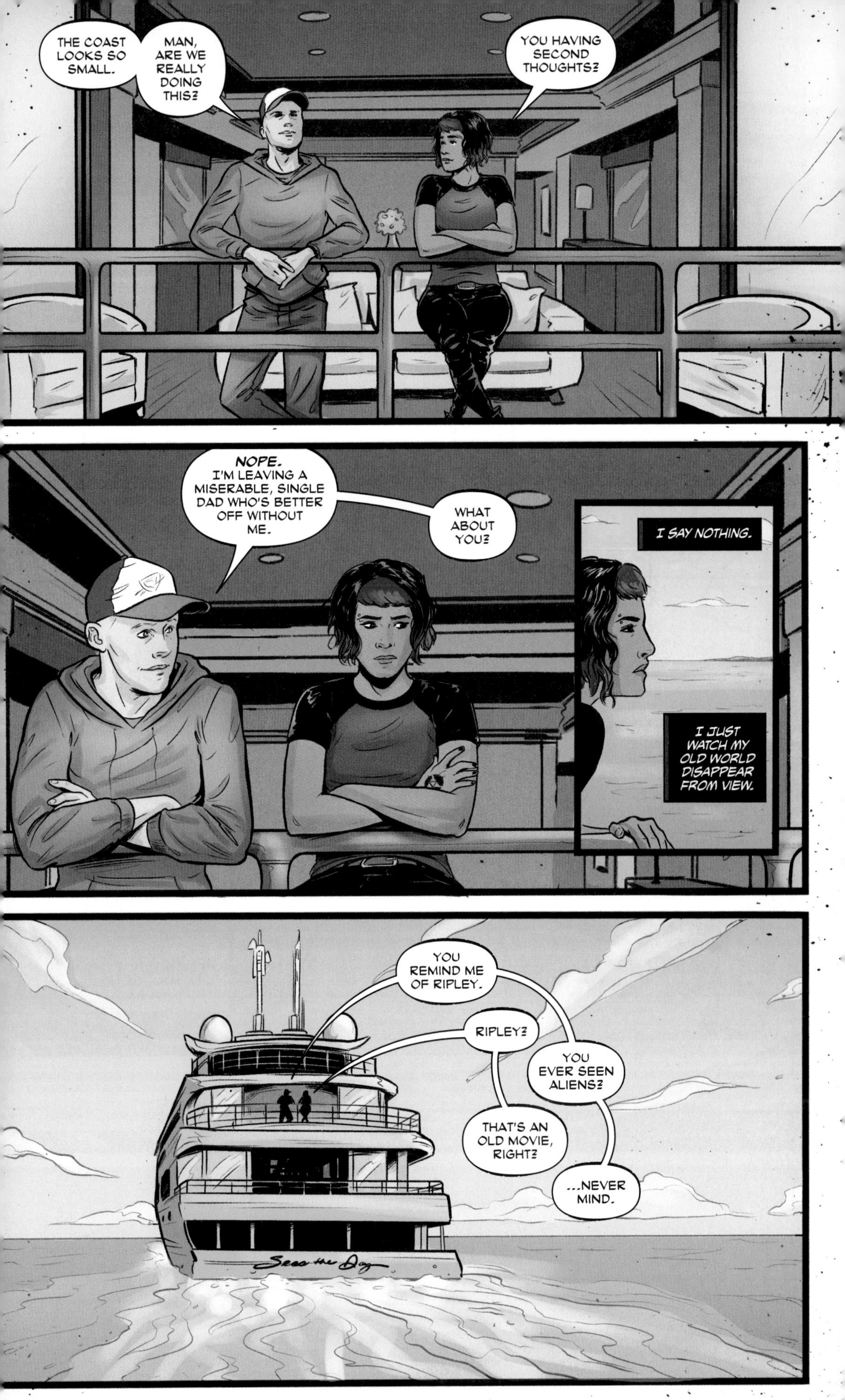
THE COAST LOOKS SO SMALL.
MAN, ARE WE REALLY DOING THIS?
YOU HAVING SECOND THOUGHTS?
NOPE. I'M LEAVING A MISERABLE, SINGLE DAD WHO'S BETTER OFF WITHOUT ME.
WHAT ABOUT YOU?
I SAY NOTHING.
I JUST WATCH MY OLD WORLD DISAPPEAR FROM VIEW.
YOU REMIND ME OF RIPLEY.
RIPLEY?
YOU EVER SEEN ALIENS?
THAT'S AN OLD MOVIE, RIGHT?
...NEVER MIND.

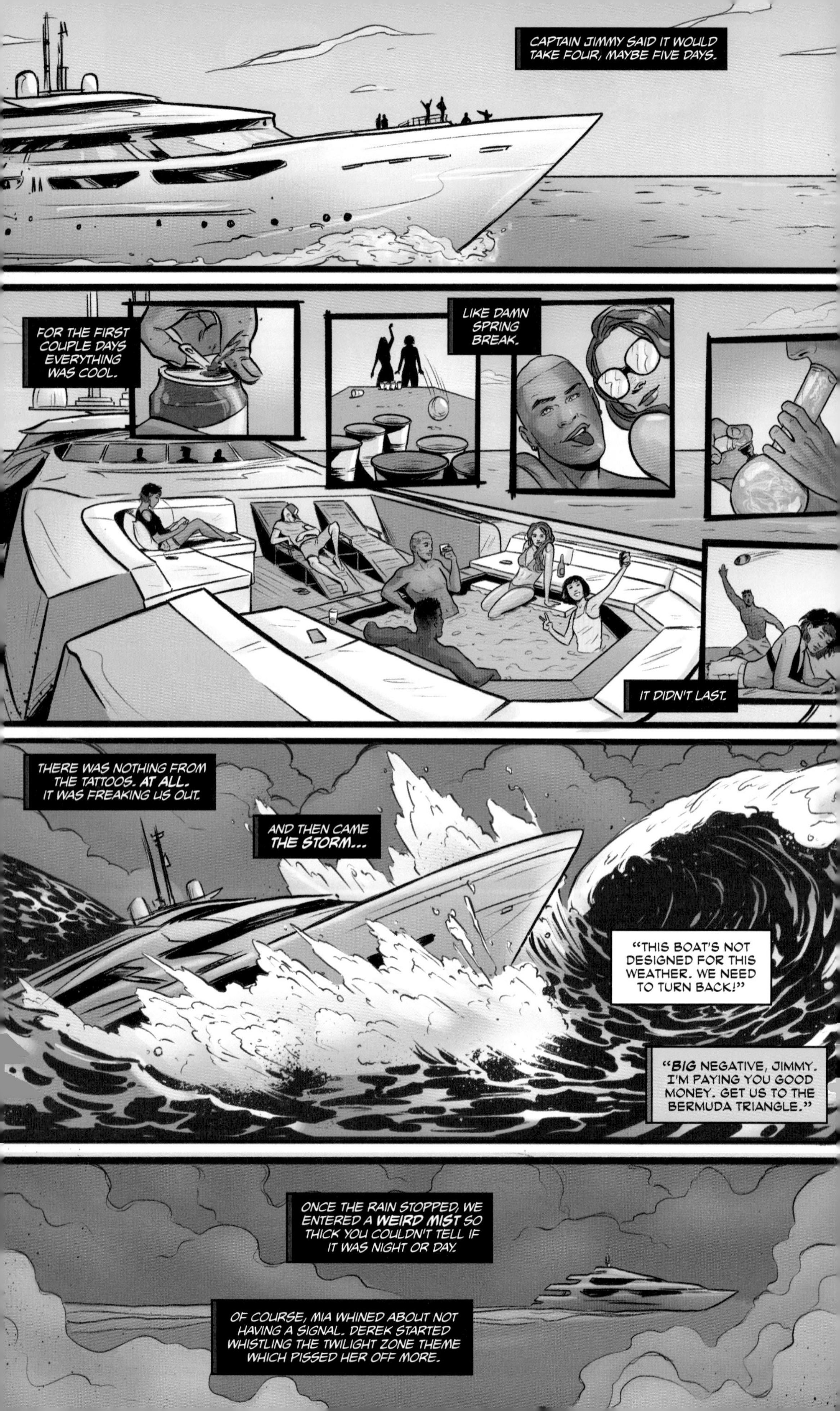
CAPTAIN JIMMY SAID IT WOULD TAKE FOUR, MAYBE FIVE DAYS.
FOR THE FIRST COUPLE DAYS EVERYTHING WAS COOL.
LIKE DAMN SPRING BREAK.
IT DIDN'T LAST.
THERE WAS NOTHING FROM THE TATTOOS. AT ALL. IT WAS FREAKING US OUT.
AND THEN CAME THE STORM...
"THIS BOAT'S NOT DESIGNED FOR THIS WEATHER. WE NEED TO TURN BACK!"
"BIG NEGATIVE, JIMMY. I'M PAYING YOU GOOD MONEY. GET US TO THE BERMUDA TRIANGLE."
ONCE THE RAIN STOPPED, WE ENTERED A WEIRD MIST SO THICK YOU COULDN'T TELL IF IT WAS NIGHT OR DAY.
OF COURSE, MIA WHINED ABOUT NOT HAVING A SIGNAL. DEREK STARTED WHISTLING THE TWILIGHT ZONE THEME WHICH PISSED HER OFF MORE.

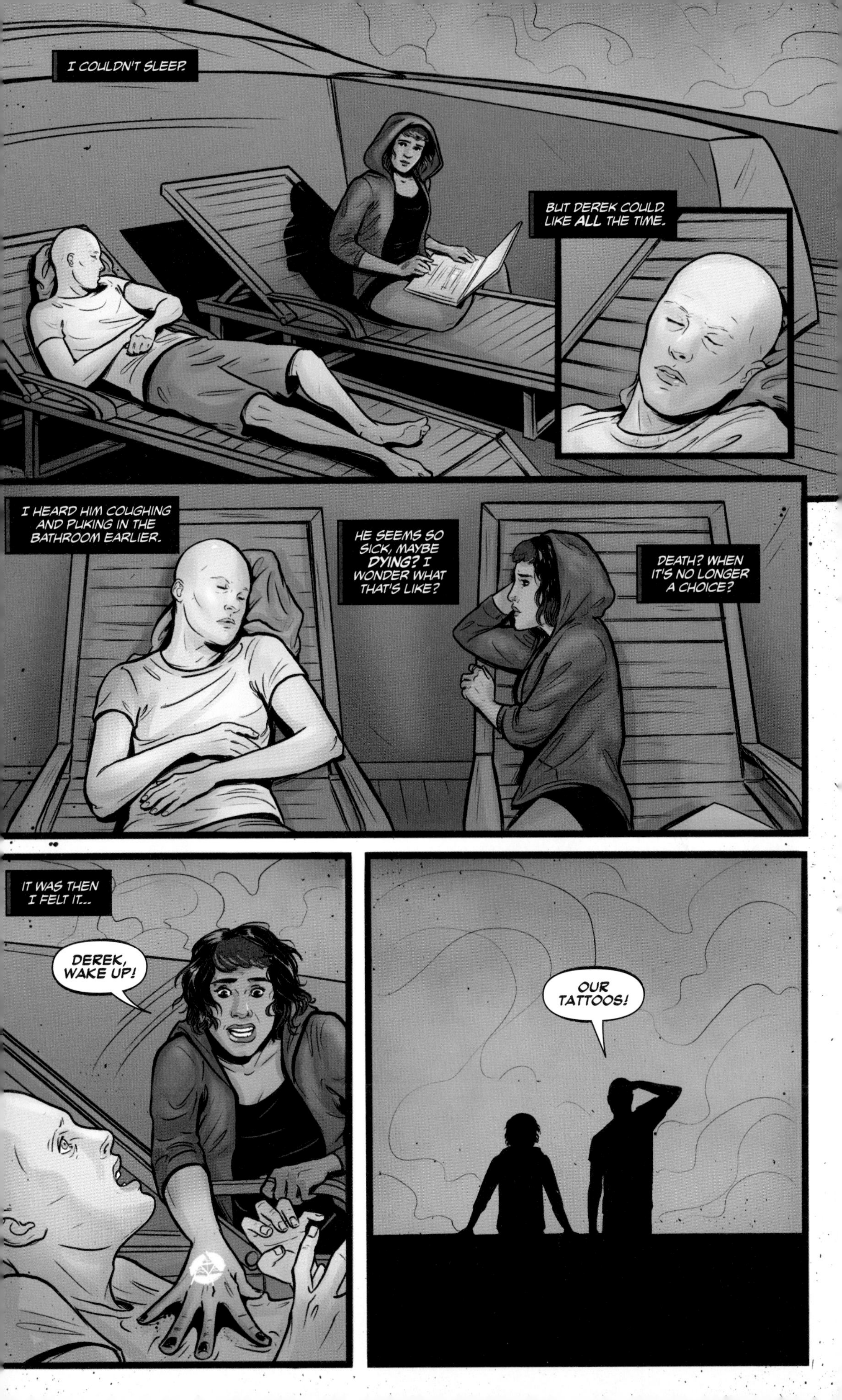
I COULDN'T SLEEP.
BUT DEREK COULD. LIKE ALL THE TIME.
I HEARD HIM COUGHING AND PUKING IN THE BATHROOM EARLIER.
HE SEEMS SO SICK, MAYBE DYING? I WONDER WHAT THAT'S LIKE?
DEATH? WHEN IT'S NO LONGER A CHOICE?
IT WAS THEN I FELT IT...
DEREK, WAKE UP!
OUR TATTOOS!

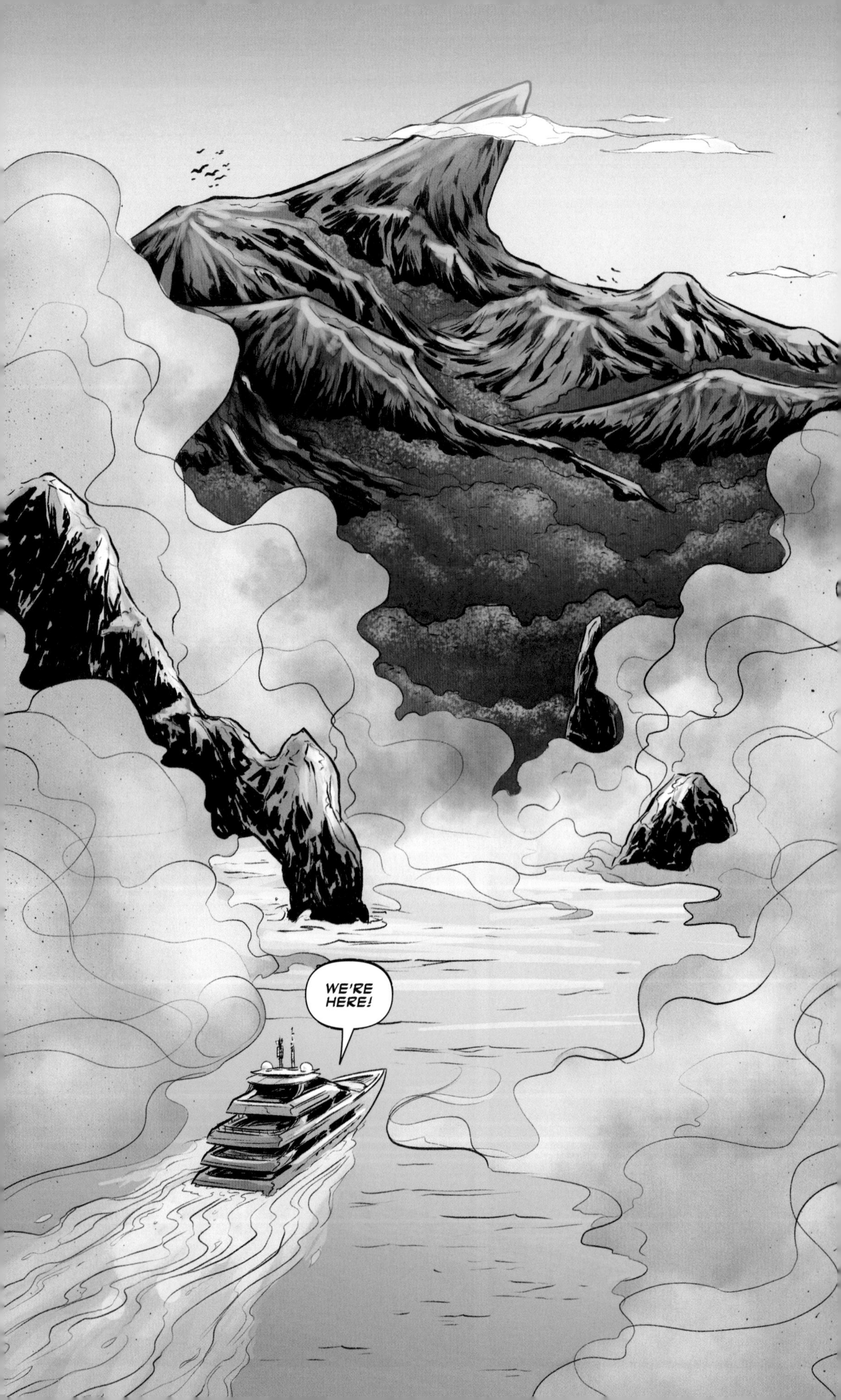
WE'RE HERE!

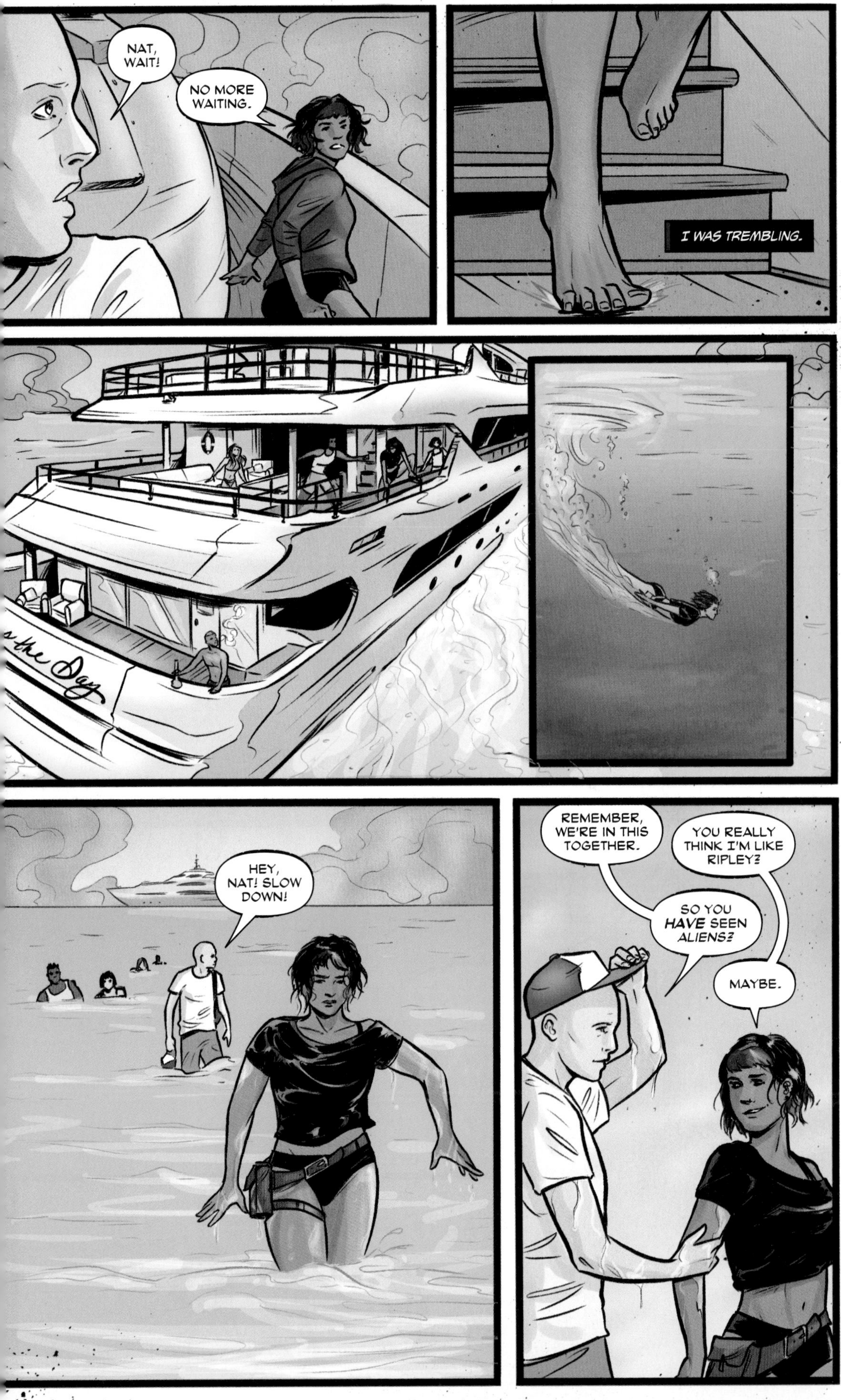

NAT, WAIT!
NO MORE WAITING.
I WAS TREMBLING.
HEY, NAT! SLOW DOWN!
REMEMBER, WE'RE IN THIS TOGETHER.
YOU REALLY THINK I'M LIKE RIPLEY?
SO YOU **HAVE** SEEN ALIENS?
MAYBE.

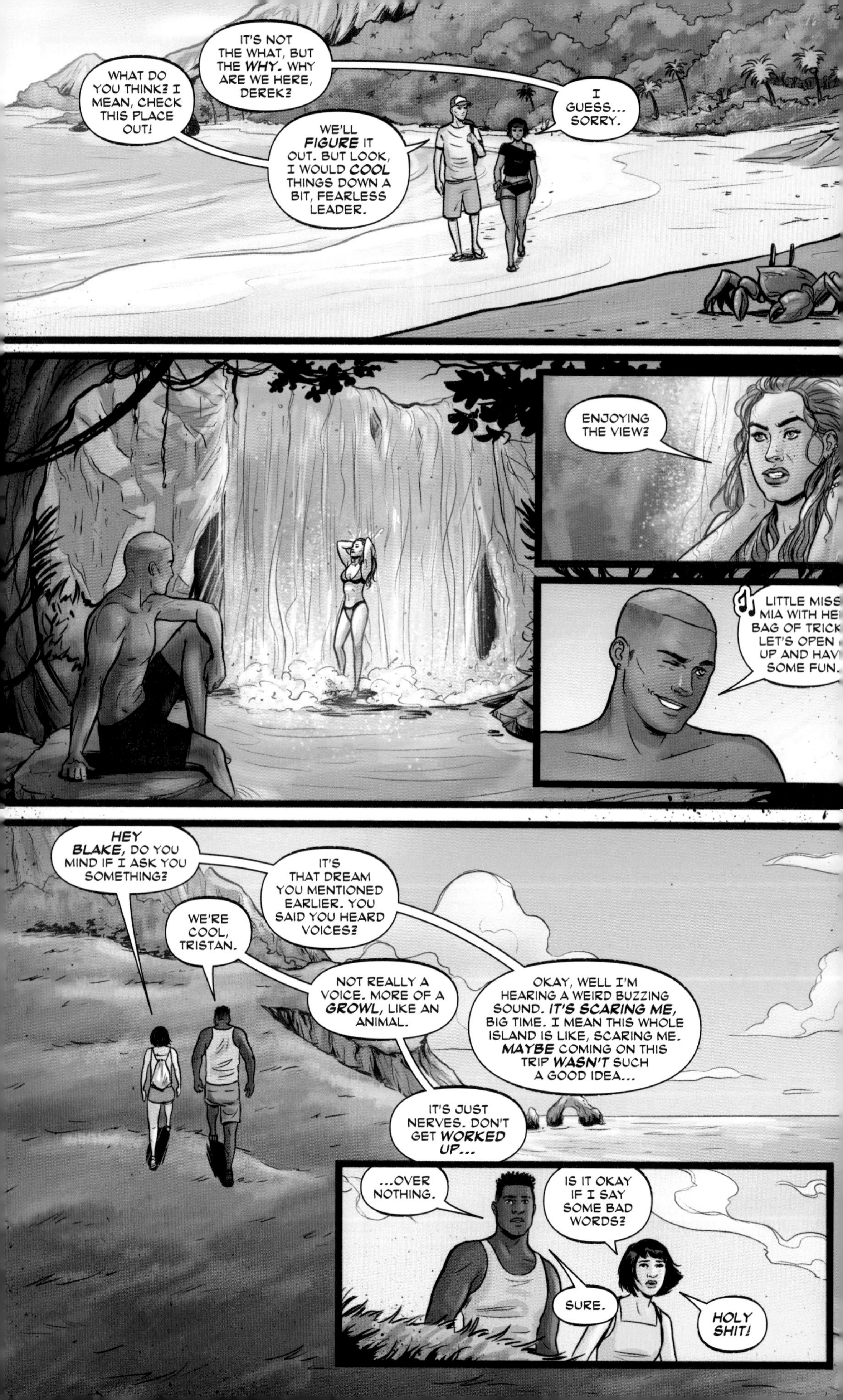
WHAT DO YOU THINK? I MEAN, CHECK THIS PLACE OUT!
IT'S NOT THE WHAT, BUT THE WHY. WHY ARE WE HERE, DEREK?
I GUESS... SORRY.
WE'LL FIGURE IT OUT. BUT LOOK, I WOULD COOL THINGS DOWN A BIT, FEARLESS LEADER.
ENJOYING THE VIEW?
LITTLE MISS MIA WITH HE BAG OF TRICK LET'S OPEN UP AND HAV SOME FUN.
HEY BLAKE, DO YOU MIND IF I ASK YOU SOMETHING?
WE'RE COOL, TRISTAN.
IT'S THAT DREAM YOU MENTIONED EARLIER. YOU SAID YOU HEARD VOICES?
NOT REALLY A VOICE. MORE OF A GROWL, LIKE AN ANIMAL.
OKAY, WELL I'M HEARING A WEIRD BUZZING SOUND. IT'S SCARING ME, BIG TIME. I MEAN THIS WHOLE ISLAND IS LIKE, SCARING ME. MAYBE COMING ON THIS TRIP WASN'T SUCH A GOOD IDEA...
IT'S JUST NERVES. DON'T GET WORKED UP...
...OVER NOTHING.
IS IT OKAY IF I SAY SOME BAD WORDS?
SURE.
HOLY SHIT!

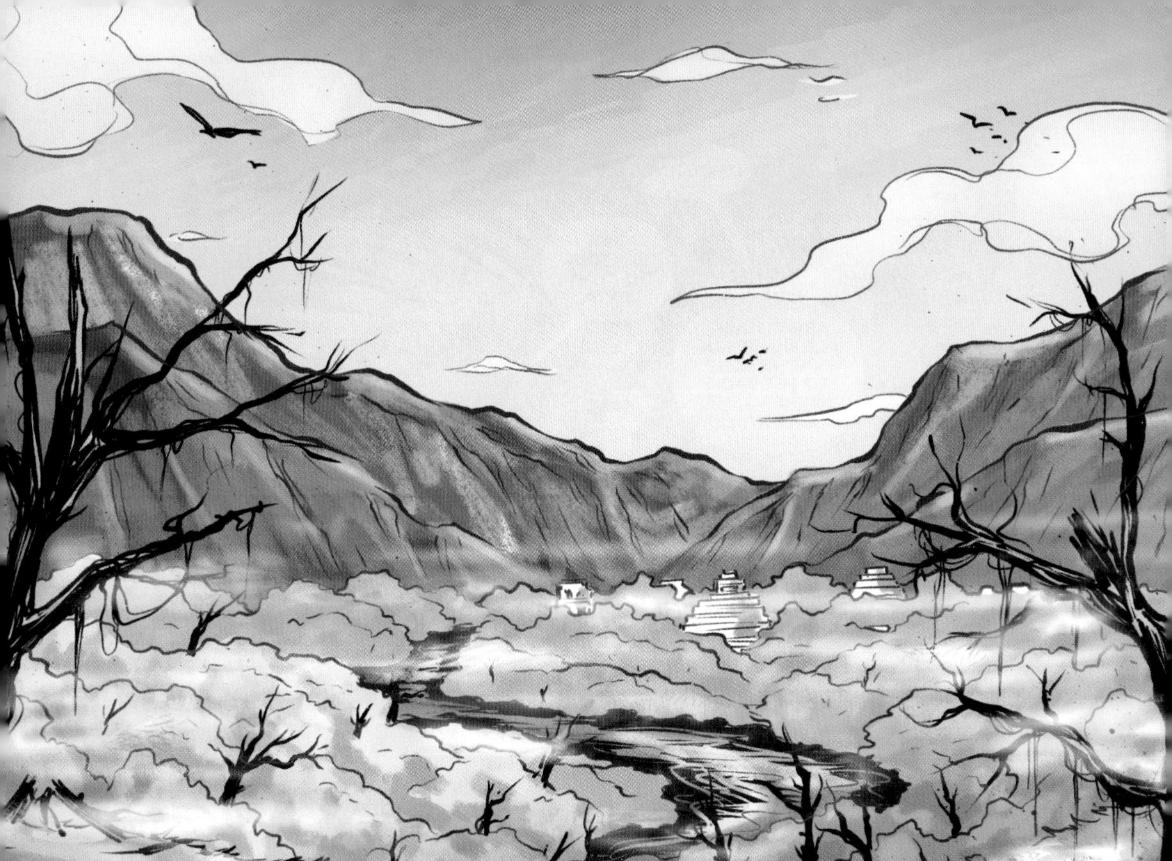

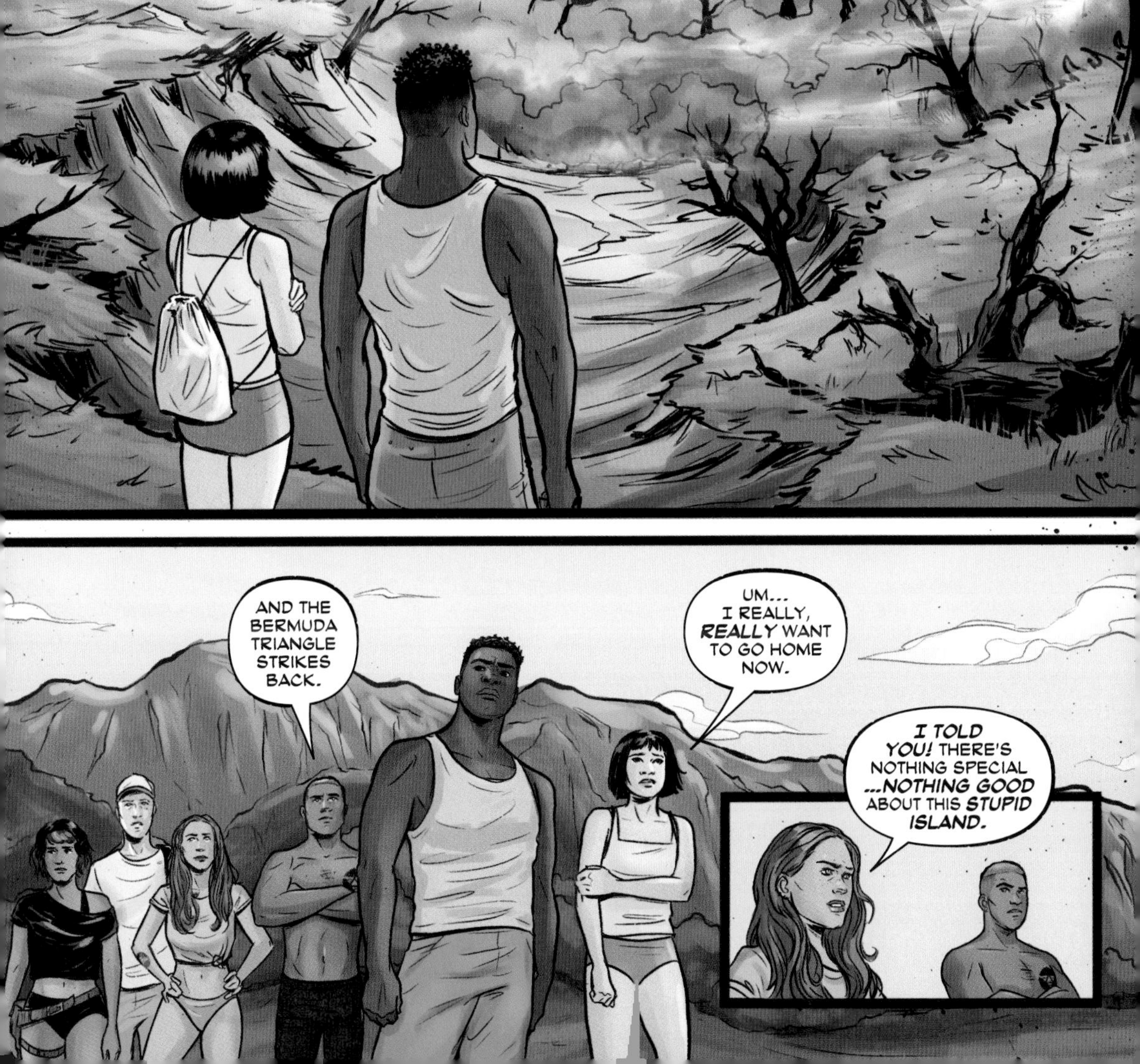
AND THE BERMUDA TRIANGLE STRIKES BACK.
UM... I REALLY, REALLY WANT TO GO HOME NOW.
I TOLD YOU! THERE'S NOTHING SPECIAL ...NOTHING GOOD ABOUT THIS STUPID ISLAND.

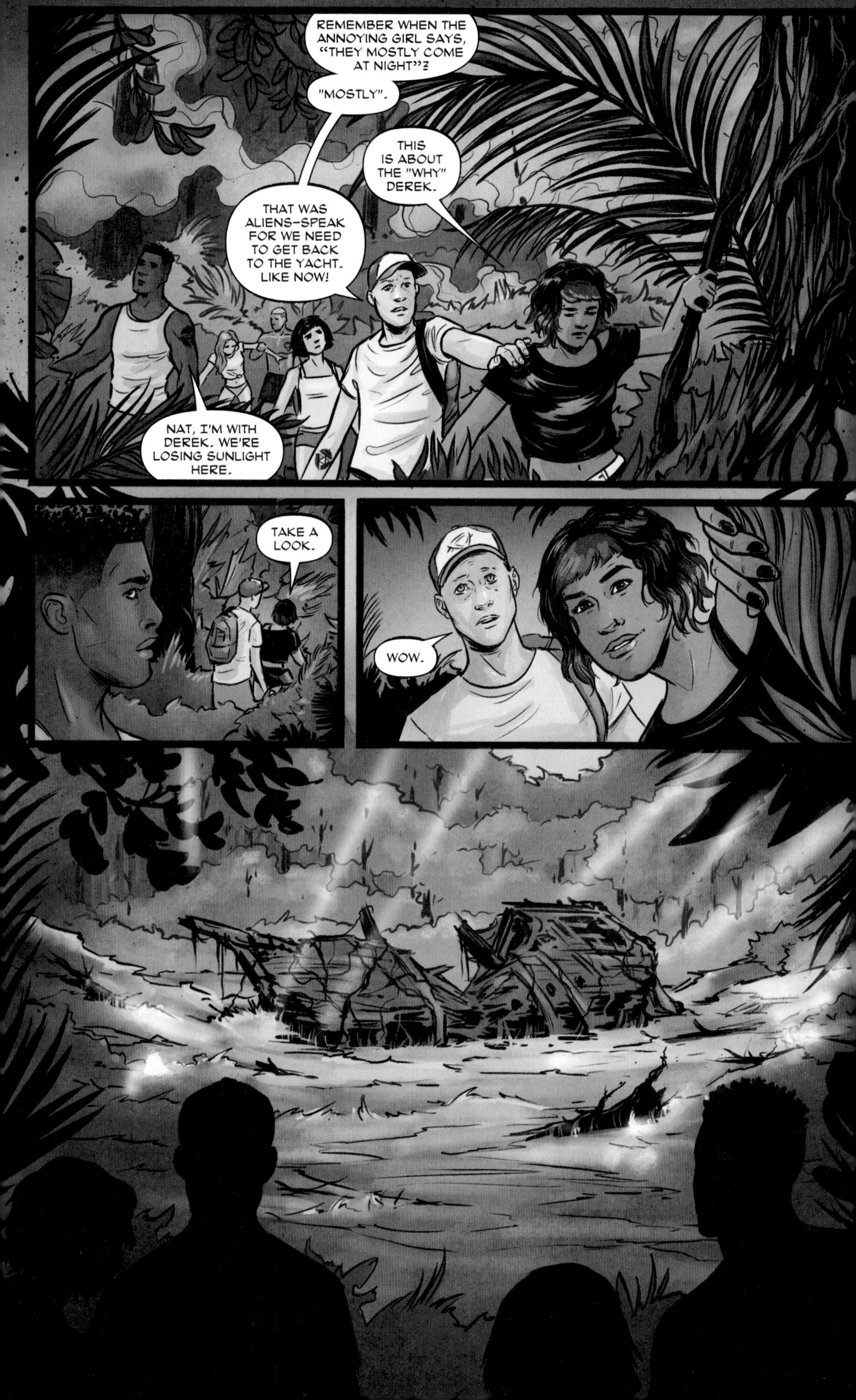

REMEMBER WHEN THE ANNOYING GIRL SAYS, "THEY MOSTLY COME AT NIGHT"?
"MOSTLY".
THAT WAS ALIENS-SPEAK FOR WE NEED TO GET BACK TO THE YACHT. LIKE NOW!
THIS IS ABOUT THE "WHY" DEREK.
NAT, I'M WITH DEREK. WE'RE LOSING SUNLIGHT HERE.
TAKE A LOOK.
WOW.

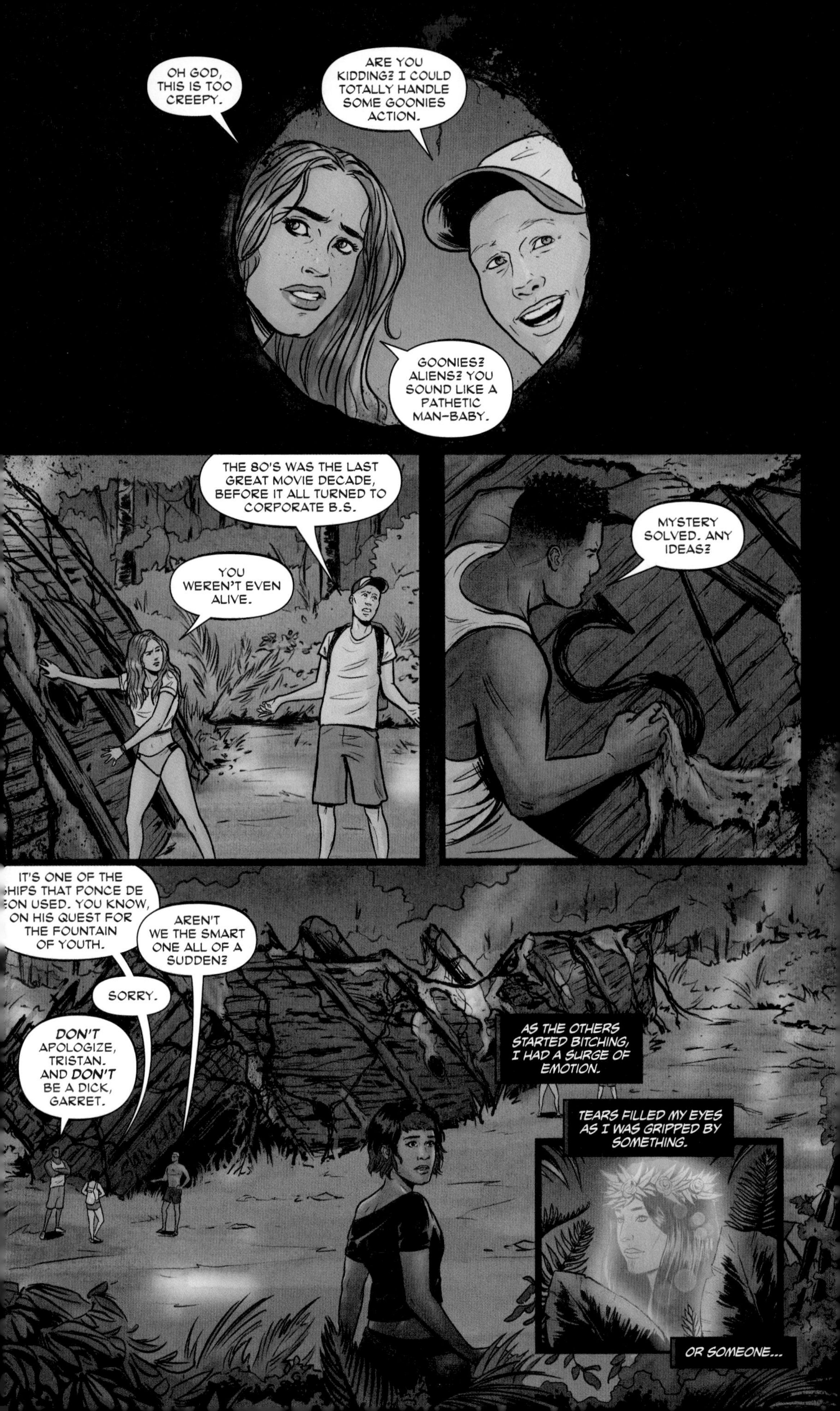

OH GOD, THIS IS TOO CREEPY.
ARE YOU KIDDING? I COULD TOTALLY HANDLE SOME GOONIES ACTION.
GOONIES? ALIENS? YOU SOUND LIKE A PATHETIC MAN-BABY.
THE 80'S WAS THE LAST GREAT MOVIE DECADE, BEFORE IT ALL TURNED TO CORPORATE B.S.
YOU WEREN'T EVEN ALIVE.
MYSTERY SOLVED. ANY IDEAS?
IT'S ONE OF THE SHIPS THAT PONCE DE LEON USED. YOU KNOW, ON HIS QUEST FOR THE FOUNTAIN OF YOUTH.
AREN'T WE THE SMART ONE ALL OF A SUDDEN?
SORRY.
DON'T APOLOGIZE, TRISTAN. AND DON'T BE A DICK, GARRET.
AS THE OTHERS STARTED BITCHING, I HAD A SURGE OF EMOTION.
TEARS FILLED MY EYES AS I WAS GRIPPED BY SOMETHING.
OR SOMEONE...

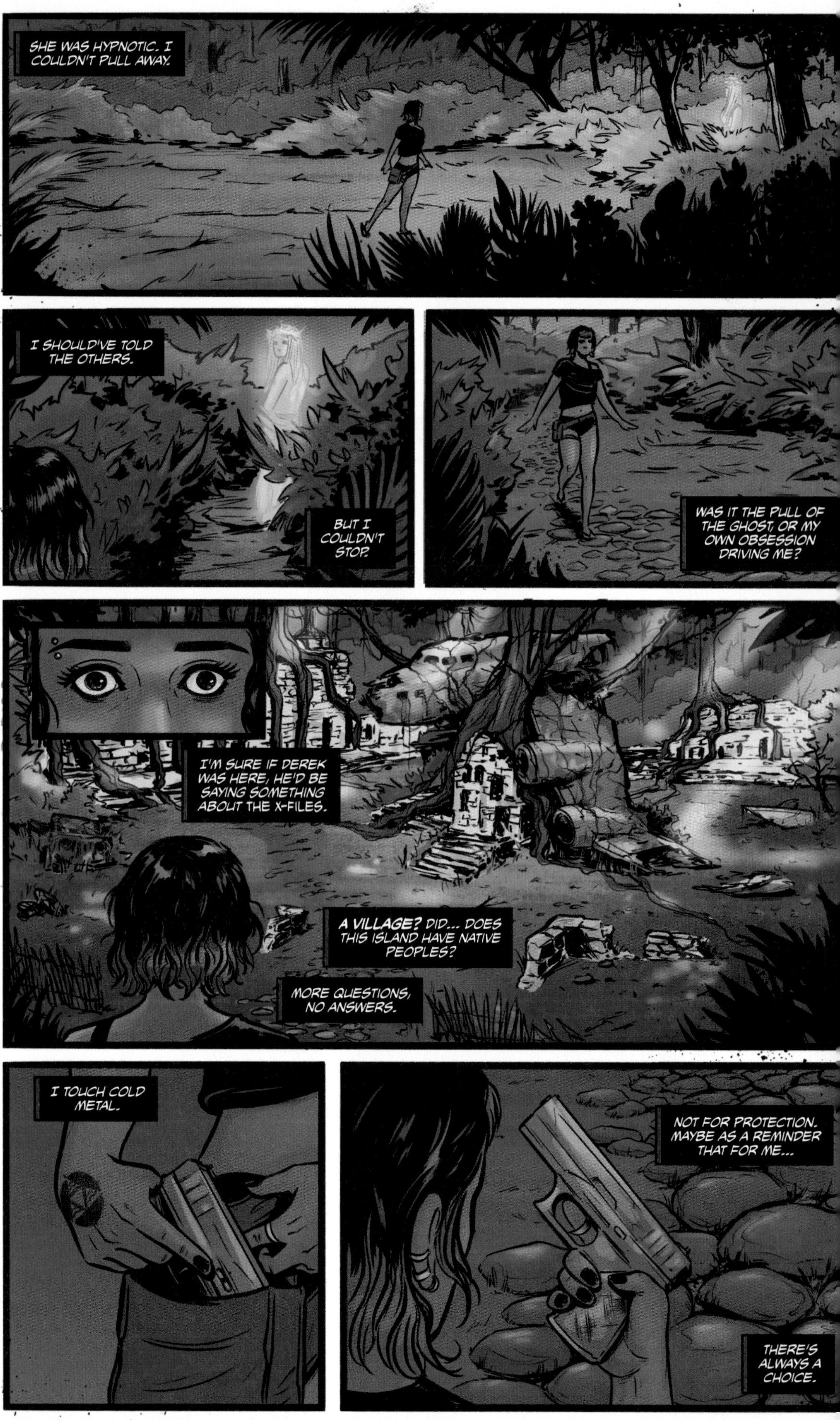
SHE WAS HYPNOTIC. I COULDN'T PULL AWAY.
I SHOULD'VE TOLD THE OTHERS.
BUT I COULDN'T STOP.
WAS IT THE PULL OF THE GHOST, OR MY OWN OBSESSION DRIVING ME?
I'M SURE IF DEREK WAS HERE, HE'D BE SAYING SOMETHING ABOUT THE X-FILES.
A VILLAGE? DID... DOES THIS ISLAND HAVE NATIVE PEOPLES?
MORE QUESTIONS, NO ANSWERS.
I TOUCH COLD METAL.
NOT FOR PROTECTION. MAYBE AS A REMINDER THAT FOR ME...
THERE'S ALWAYS A CHOICE.

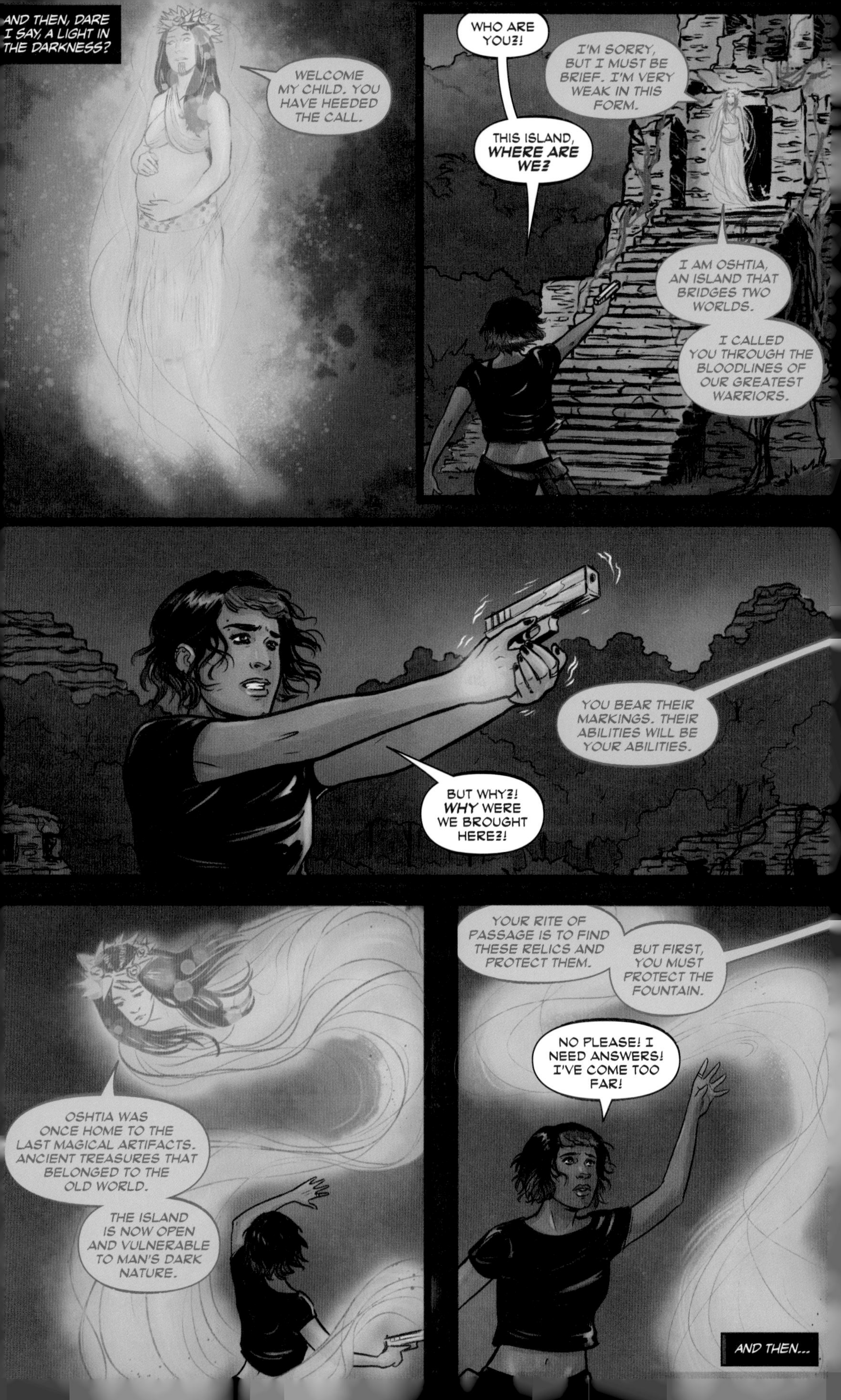
AND THEN, DARE I SAY, A LIGHT IN THE DARKNESS?
WELCOME MY CHILD. YOU HAVE HEEDED THE CALL.
WHO ARE YOU?!
THIS ISLAND, WHERE ARE WE?
I'M SORRY, BUT I MUST BE BRIEF. I'M VERY WEAK IN THIS FORM.
I AM OSHTIA, AN ISLAND THAT BRIDGES TWO WORLDS.
I CALLED YOU THROUGH THE BLOODLINES OF OUR GREATEST WARRIORS.
YOU BEAR THEIR MARKINGS. THEIR ABILITIES WILL BE YOUR ABILITIES.
BUT WHY?! WHY WERE WE BROUGHT HERE?!
OSHTIA WAS ONCE HOME TO THE LAST MAGICAL ARTIFACTS. ANCIENT TREASURES THAT BELONGED TO THE OLD WORLD.
THE ISLAND IS NOW OPEN AND VULNERABLE TO MAN'S DARK NATURE.
YOUR RITE OF PASSAGE IS TO FIND THESE RELICS AND PROTECT THEM.
BUT FIRST, YOU MUST PROTECT THE FOUNTAIN.
NO PLEASE! I NEED ANSWERS! I'VE COME TOO FAR!
AND THEN...

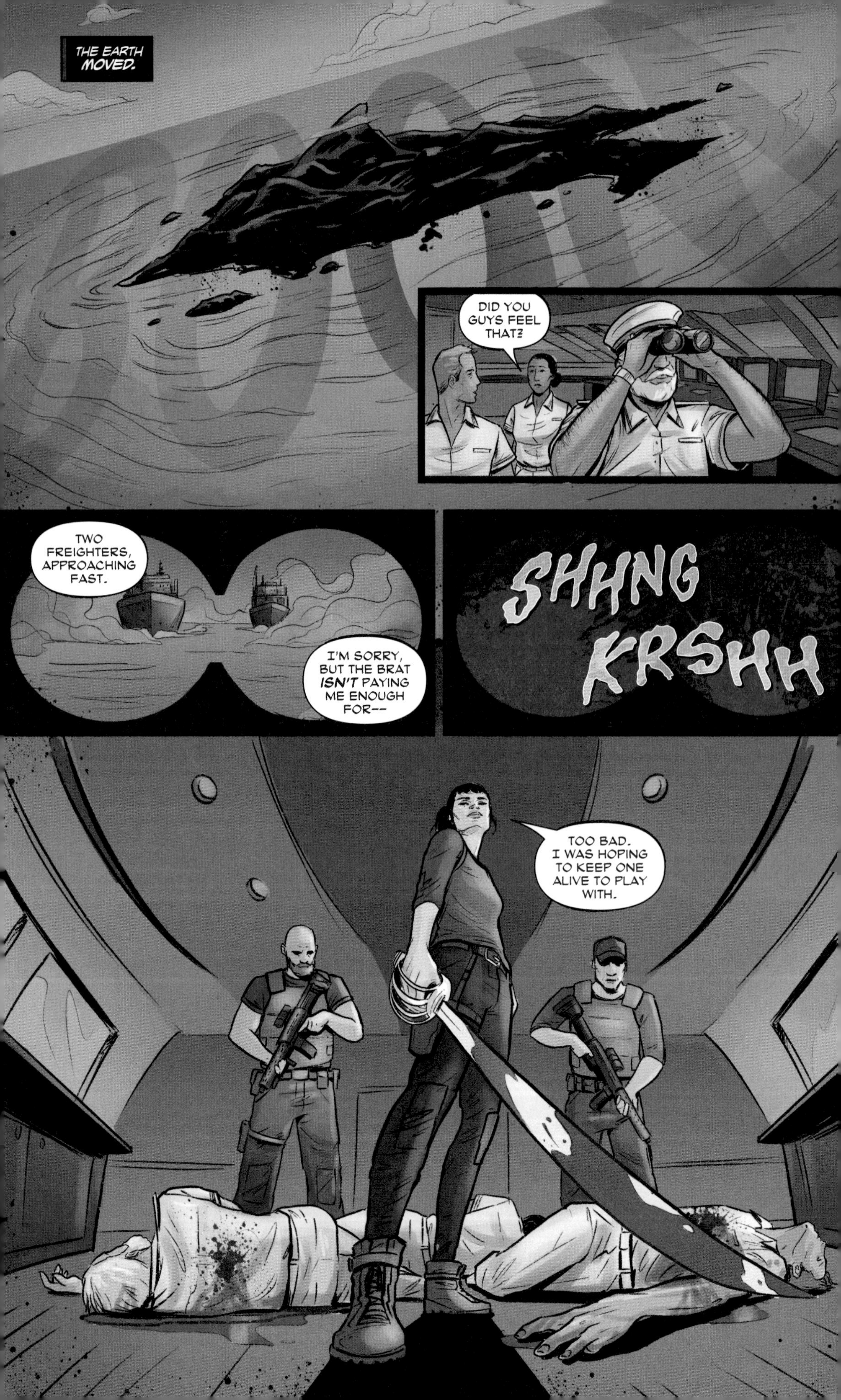

THE EARTH MOVED.
DID YOU GUYS FEEL THAT?
TWO FREIGHTERS, APPROACHING FAST.
I'M SORRY, BUT THE BRAT ISN'T PAYING ME ENOUGH FOR--
SHHNG
KRSHH
TOO BAD. I WAS HOPING TO KEEP ONE ALIVE TO PLAY WITH.

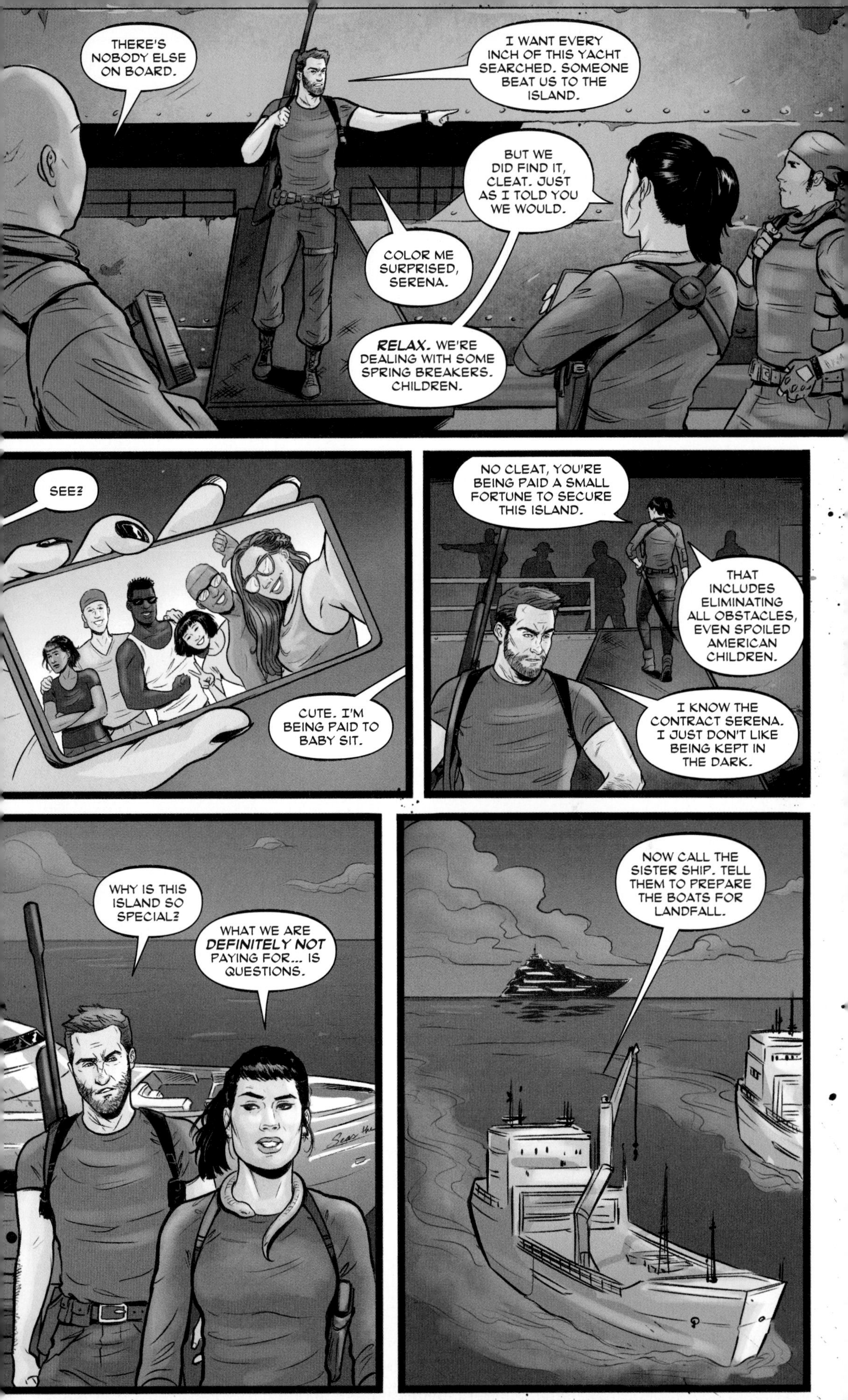
THERE'S NOBODY ELSE ON BOARD.
I WANT EVERY INCH OF THIS YACHT SEARCHED. SOMEONE BEAT US TO THE ISLAND.
BUT WE DID FIND IT, CLEAT. JUST AS I TOLD YOU WE WOULD.
COLOR ME SURPRISED, SERENA.
RELAX. WE'RE DEALING WITH SOME SPRING BREAKERS. CHILDREN.
SEE?
CUTE. I'M BEING PAID TO BABY SIT.
NO CLEAT, YOU'RE BEING PAID A SMALL FORTUNE TO SECURE THIS ISLAND.
THAT INCLUDES ELIMINATING ALL OBSTACLES, EVEN SPOILED AMERICAN CHILDREN.
I KNOW THE CONTRACT SERENA. I JUST DON'T LIKE BEING KEPT IN THE DARK.
WHY IS THIS ISLAND SO SPECIAL?
WHAT WE ARE DEFINITELY NOT PAYING FOR... IS QUESTIONS.
NOW CALL THE SISTER SHIP. TELL THEM TO PREPARE THE BOATS FOR LANDFALL.

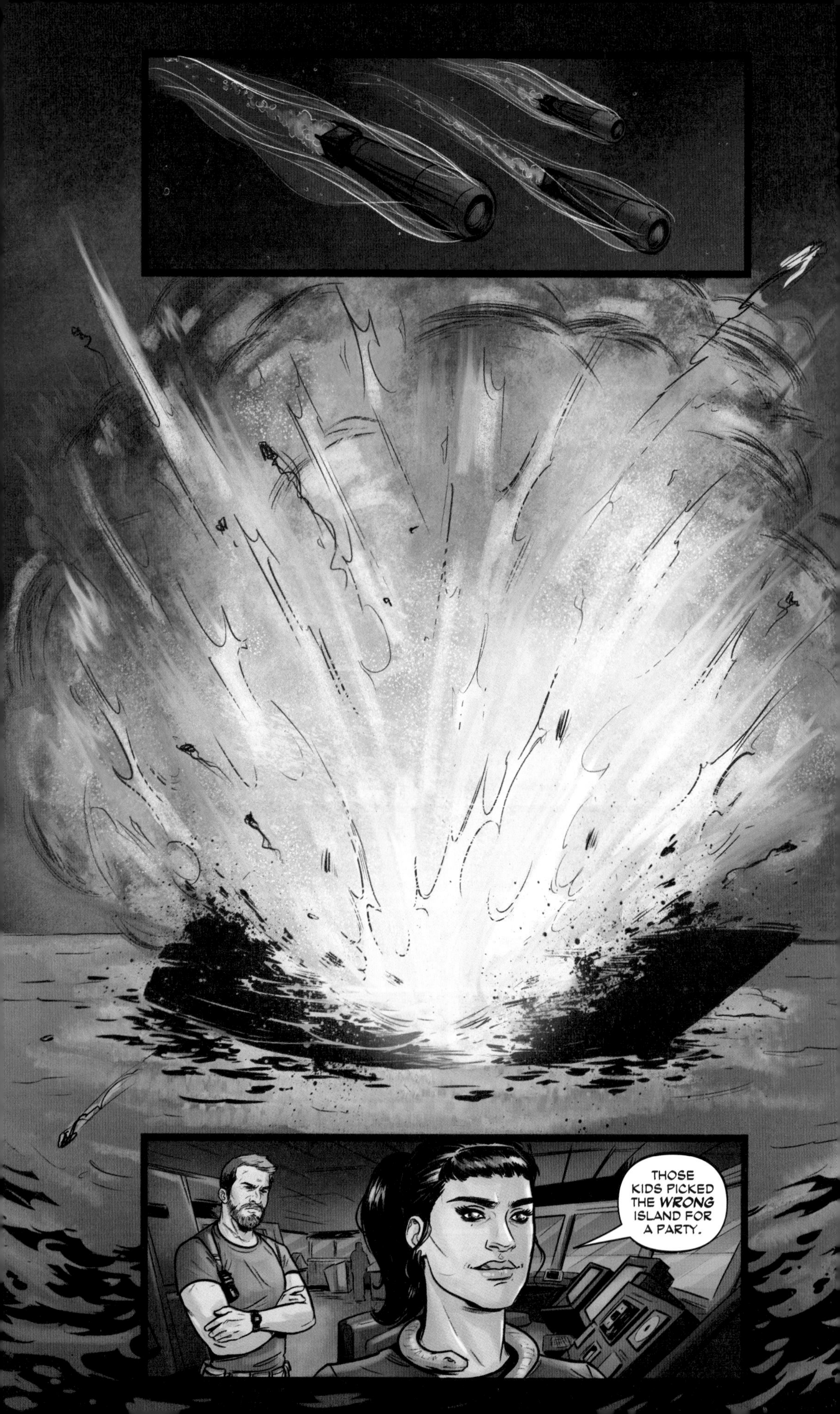
THOSE KIDS PICKED THE *WRONG* ISLAND FOR A PARTY.

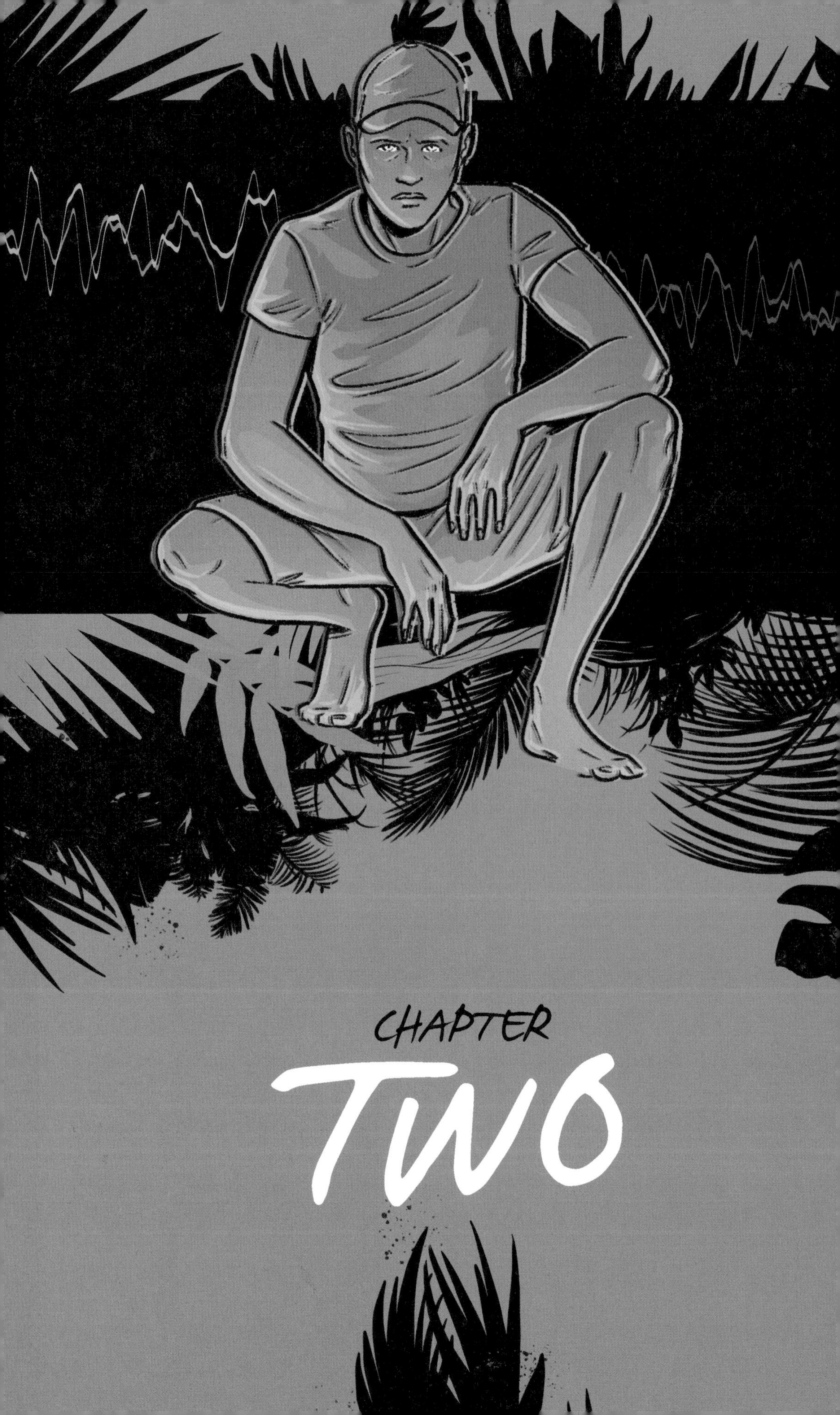
CHAPTER
TWO

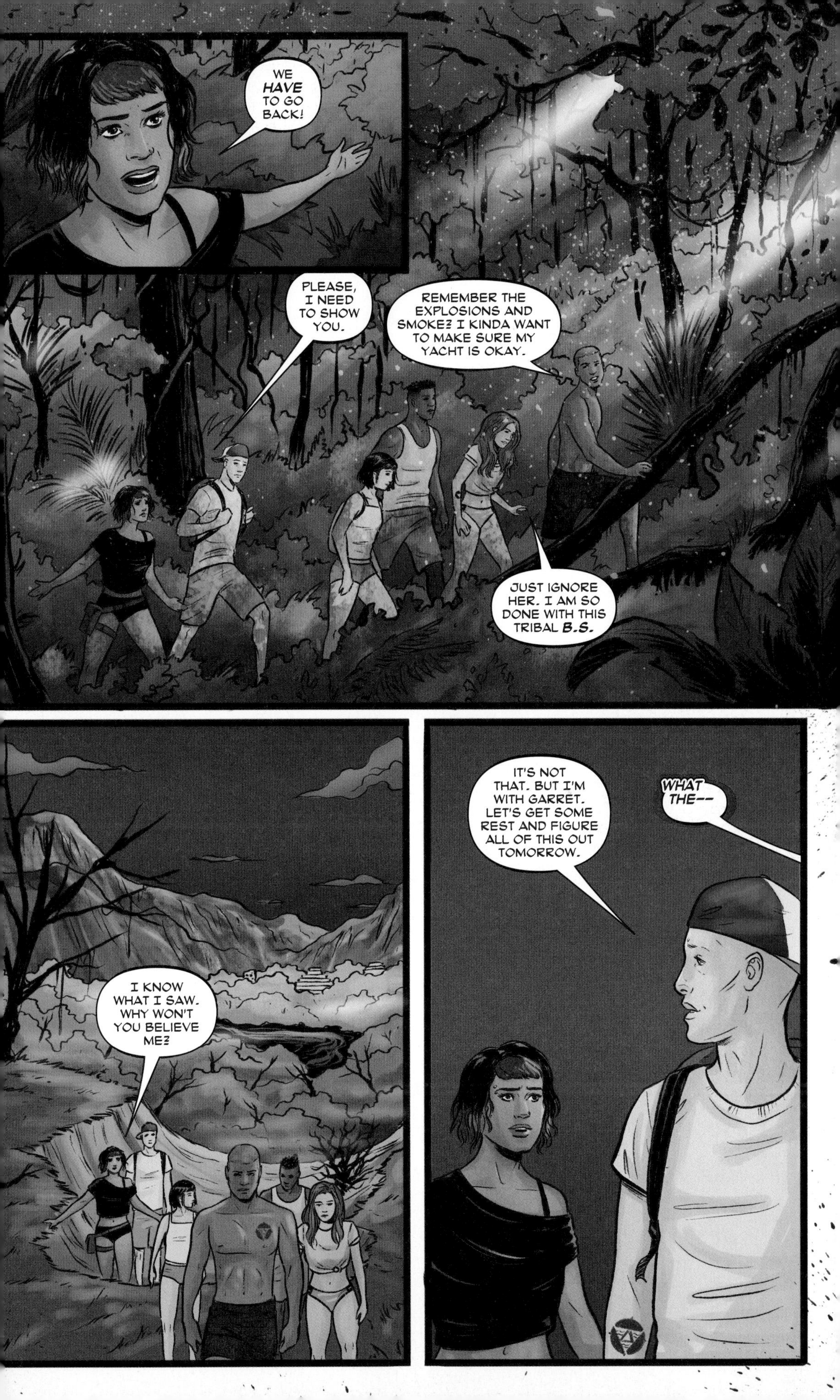
WE *HAVE* TO GO BACK!
PLEASE, I NEED TO SHOW YOU.
REMEMBER THE EXPLOSIONS AND SMOKE? I KINDA WANT TO MAKE SURE MY YACHT IS OKAY.
JUST IGNORE HER. I AM SO DONE WITH THIS TRIBAL *B.S.*
I KNOW WHAT I SAW. WHY WON'T YOU BELIEVE ME?
IT'S NOT THAT. BUT I'M WITH GARRET. LET'S GET SOME REST AND FIGURE ALL OF THIS OUT TOMORROW.
WHAT THE--

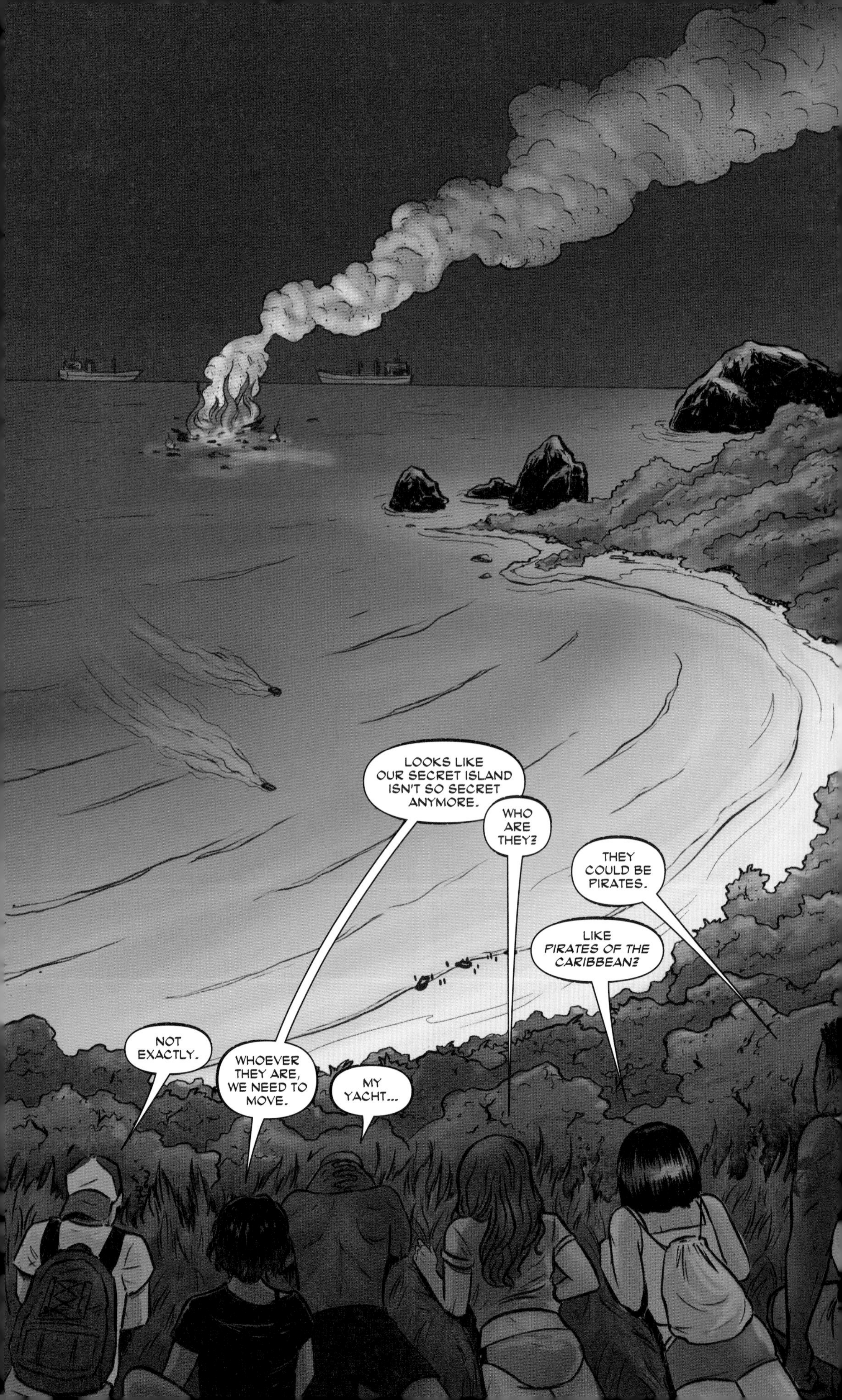
LOOKS LIKE OUR SECRET ISLAND ISN'T SO SECRET ANYMORE.
WHO ARE THEY?
THEY COULD BE PIRATES.
LIKE *PIRATES OF THE CARIBBEAN*?
NOT EXACTLY.
WHOEVER THEY ARE, WE NEED TO MOVE.
MY YACHT...

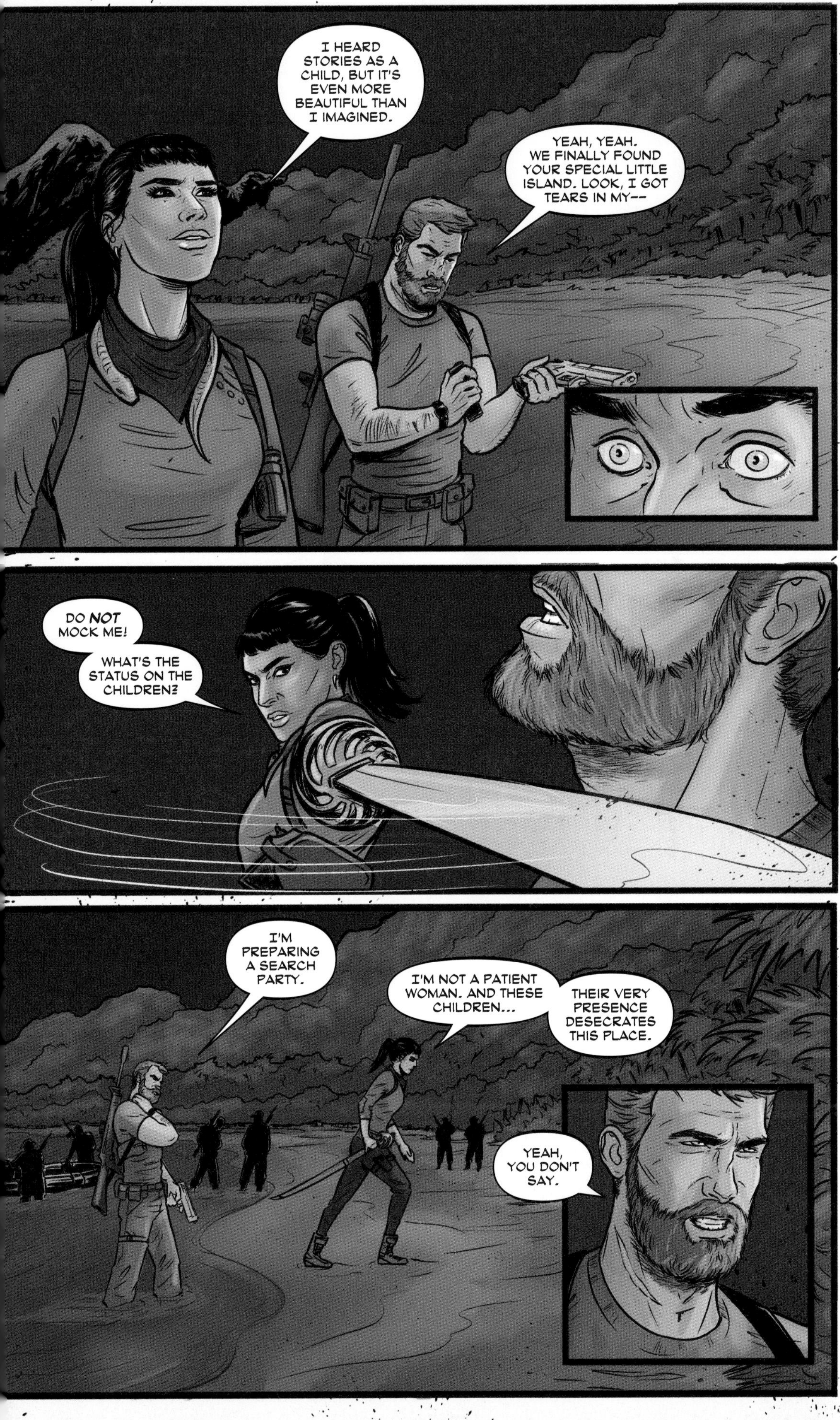
I HEARD STORIES AS A CHILD, BUT IT'S EVEN MORE BEAUTIFUL THAN I IMAGINED.
YEAH, YEAH. WE FINALLY FOUND YOUR SPECIAL LITTLE ISLAND. LOOK, I GOT TEARS IN MY--
DO NOT MOCK ME!
WHAT'S THE STATUS ON THE CHILDREN?
I'M PREPARING A SEARCH PARTY.
I'M NOT A PATIENT WOMAN. AND THESE CHILDREN...
THEIR VERY PRESENCE DESECRATES THIS PLACE.
YEAH, YOU DON'T SAY.

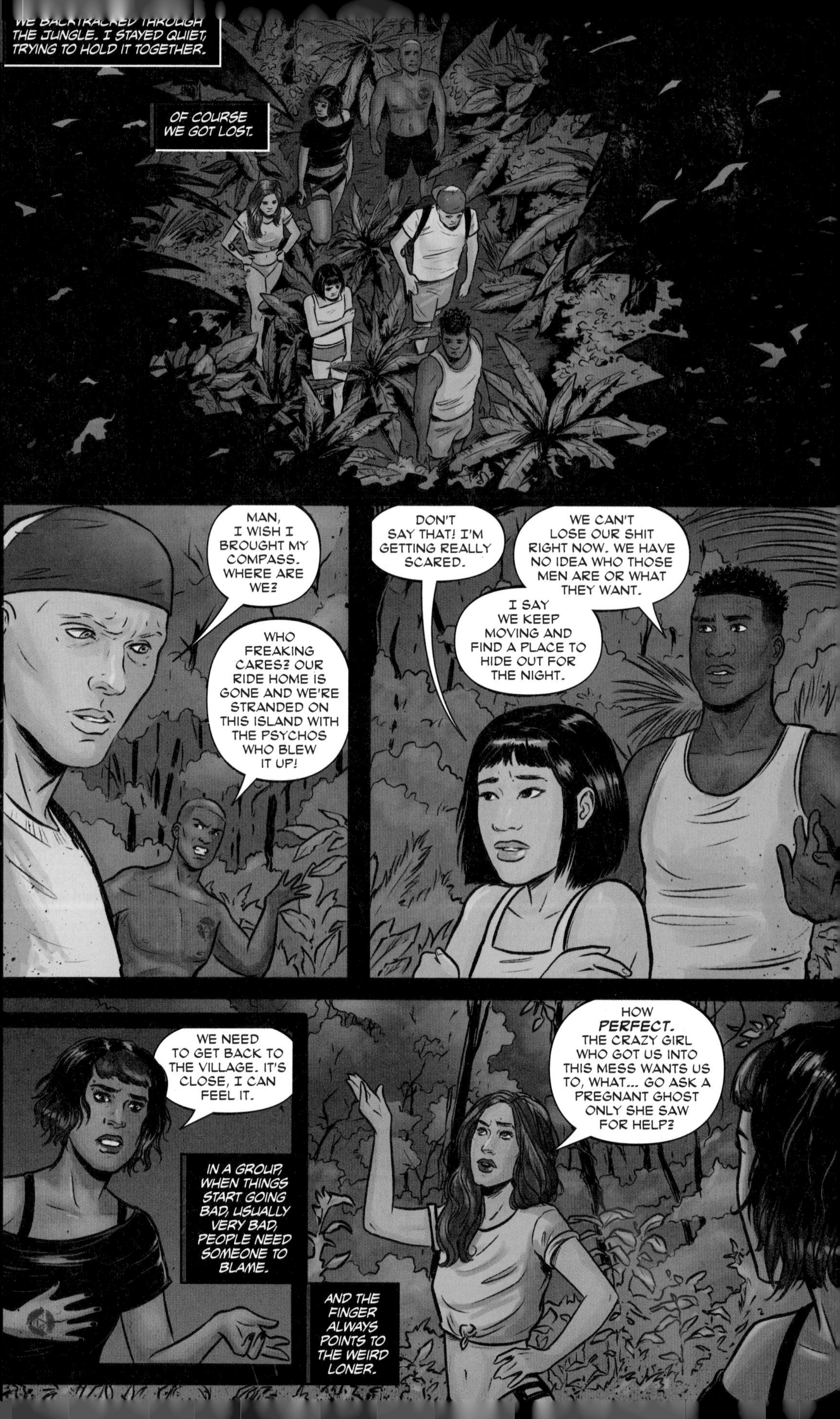
WE BACKTRACKED THROUGH THE JUNGLE. I STAYED QUIET, TRYING TO HOLD IT TOGETHER.
OF COURSE WE GOT LOST.
MAN, I WISH I BROUGHT MY COMPASS. WHERE ARE WE?
WHO FREAKING CARES? OUR RIDE HOME IS GONE AND WE'RE STRANDED ON THIS ISLAND WITH THE PSYCHOS WHO BLEW IT UP!
DON'T SAY THAT! I'M GETTING REALLY SCARED.
WE CAN'T LOSE OUR SHIT RIGHT NOW. WE HAVE NO IDEA WHO THOSE MEN ARE OR WHAT THEY WANT.
I SAY WE KEEP MOVING AND FIND A PLACE TO HIDE OUT FOR THE NIGHT.
WE NEED TO GET BACK TO THE VILLAGE. IT'S CLOSE, I CAN FEEL IT.
IN A GROUP, WHEN THINGS START GOING BAD, USUALLY VERY BAD, PEOPLE NEED SOMEONE TO BLAME.
HOW PERFECT. THE CRAZY GIRL WHO GOT US INTO THIS MESS WANTS US TO, WHAT... GO ASK A PREGNANT GHOST ONLY SHE SAW FOR HELP?
AND THE FINGER ALWAYS POINTS TO THE WEIRD LONER.

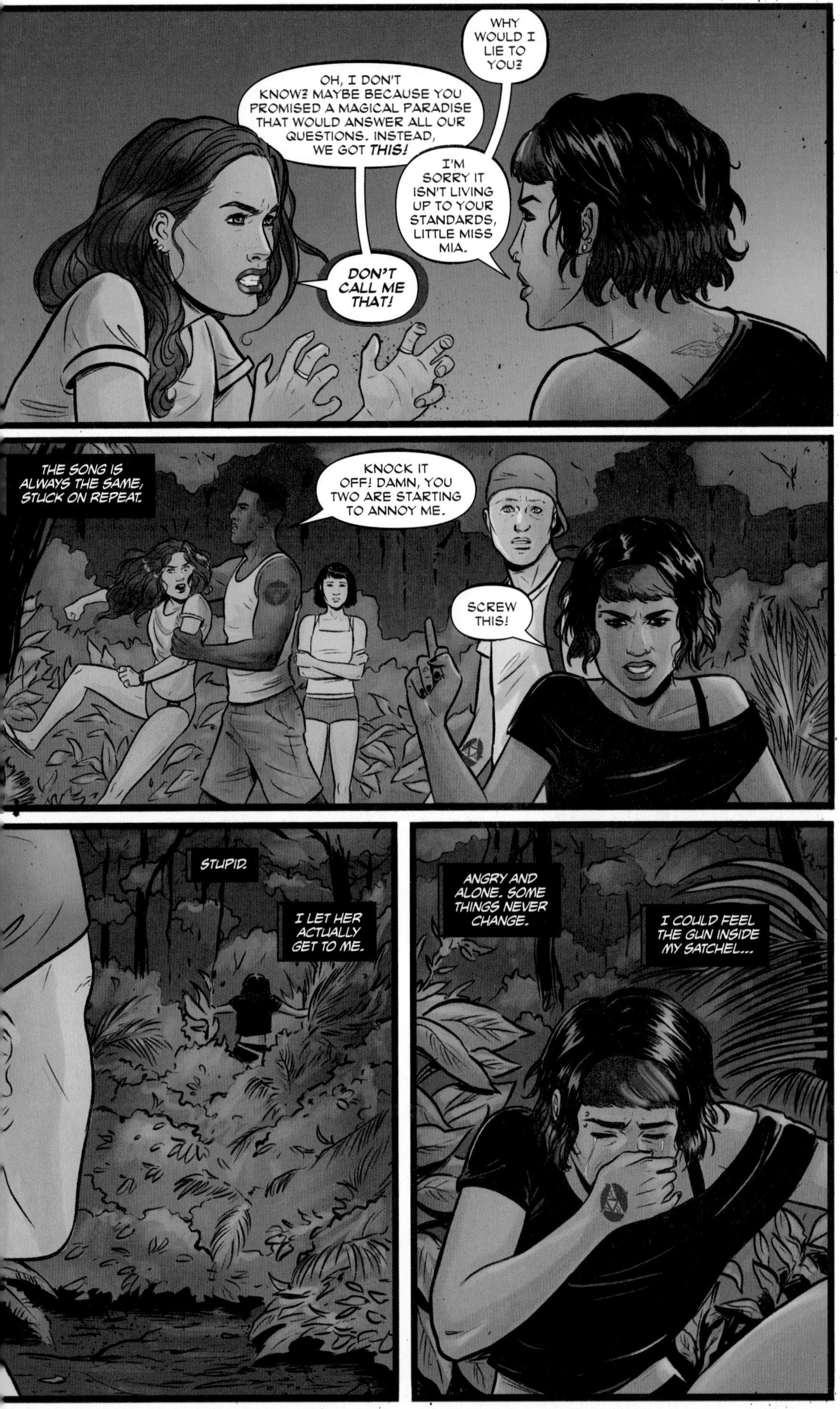
OH, I DON'T KNOW? MAYBE BECAUSE YOU PROMISED A MAGICAL PARADISE THAT WOULD ANSWER ALL OUR QUESTIONS. INSTEAD, WE GOT THIS!
WHY WOULD I LIE TO YOU?
I'M SORRY IT ISN'T LIVING UP TO YOUR STANDARDS, LITTLE MISS MIA.
DON'T CALL ME THAT!
THE SONG IS ALWAYS THE SAME, STUCK ON REPEAT.
KNOCK IT OFF! DAMN, YOU TWO ARE STARTING TO ANNOY ME.
SCREW THIS!
STUPID.
I LET HER ACTUALLY GET TO ME.
ANGRY AND ALONE. SOME THINGS NEVER CHANGE.
I COULD FEEL THE GUN INSIDE MY SATCHEL...

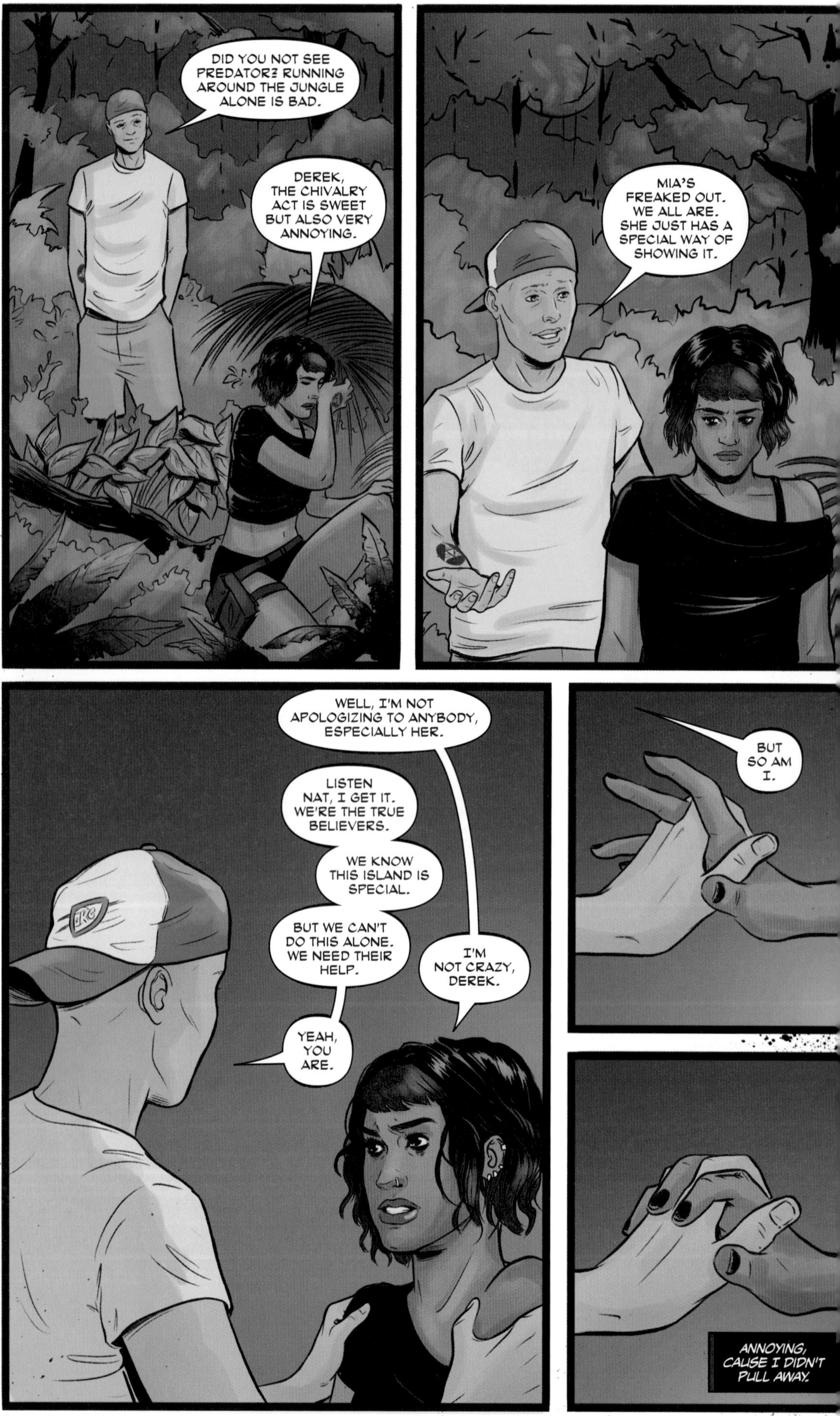
DID YOU NOT SEE PREDATOR? RUNNING AROUND THE JUNGLE ALONE IS BAD.
DEREK, THE CHIVALRY ACT IS SWEET BUT ALSO VERY ANNOYING.
MIA'S FREAKED OUT. WE ALL ARE. SHE JUST HAS A SPECIAL WAY OF SHOWING IT.
WELL, I'M NOT APOLOGIZING TO ANYBODY, ESPECIALLY HER.
LISTEN NAT, I GET IT. WE'RE THE TRUE BELIEVERS.
WE KNOW THIS ISLAND IS SPECIAL.
BUT WE CAN'T DO THIS ALONE. WE NEED THEIR HELP.
I'M NOT CRAZY, DEREK.
YEAH, YOU ARE.
BUT SO AM I.
ANNOYING, CAUSE I DIDN'T PULL AWAY.

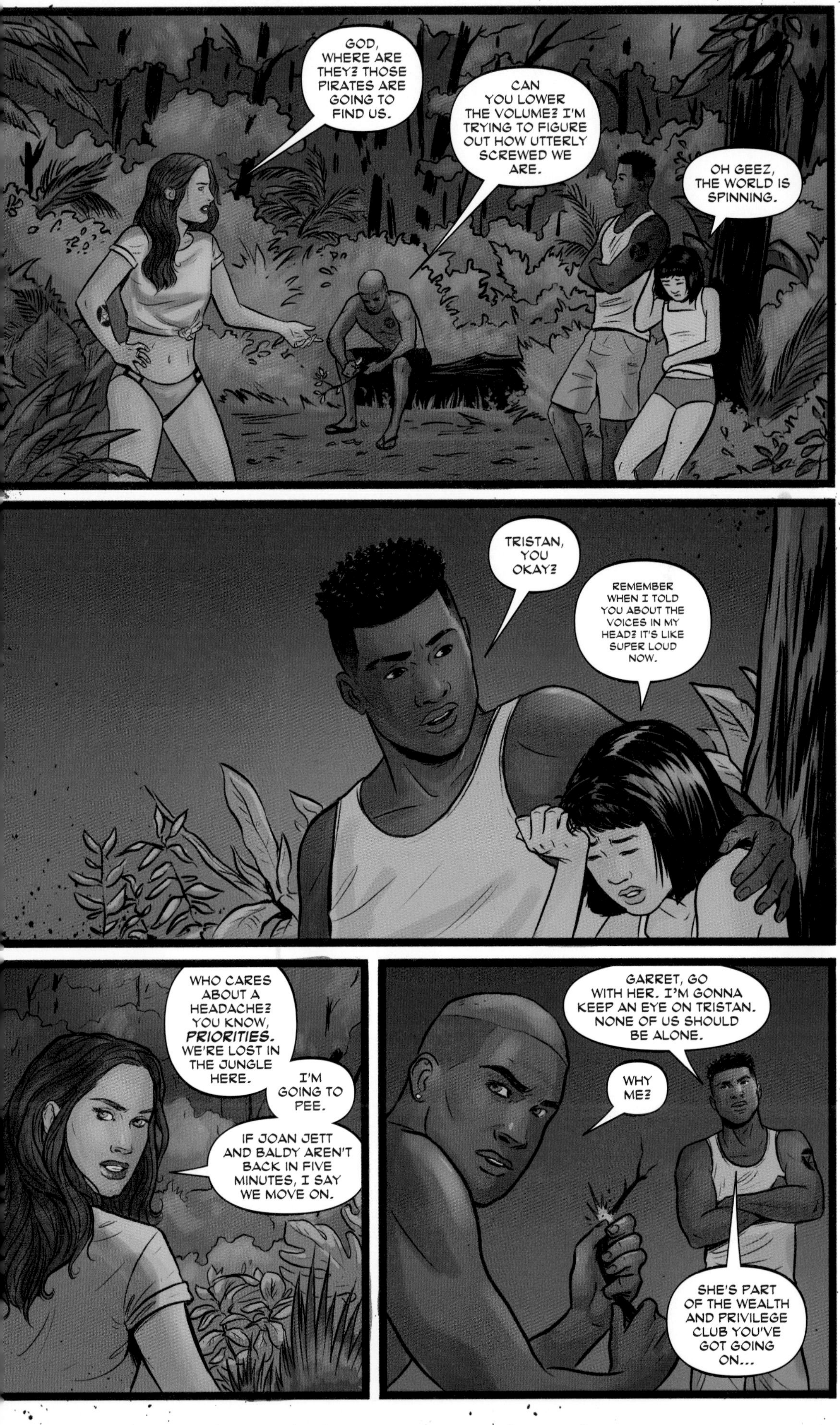

GOD, WHERE ARE THEY? THOSE PIRATES ARE GOING TO FIND US.
CAN YOU LOWER THE VOLUME? I'M TRYING TO FIGURE OUT HOW UTTERLY SCREWED WE ARE.
OH GEEZ, THE WORLD IS SPINNING.
TRISTAN, YOU OKAY?
REMEMBER WHEN I TOLD YOU ABOUT THE VOICES IN MY HEAD? IT'S LIKE SUPER LOUD NOW.
WHO CARES ABOUT A HEADACHE? YOU KNOW, PRIORITIES. WE'RE LOST IN THE JUNGLE HERE.
I'M GOING TO PEE.
IF JOAN JETT AND BALDY AREN'T BACK IN FIVE MINUTES, I SAY WE MOVE ON.
GARRET, GO WITH HER. I'M GONNA KEEP AN EYE ON TRISTAN. NONE OF US SHOULD BE ALONE.
WHY ME?
SHE'S PART OF THE WEALTH AND PRIVILEGE CLUB YOU'VE GOT GOING ON...

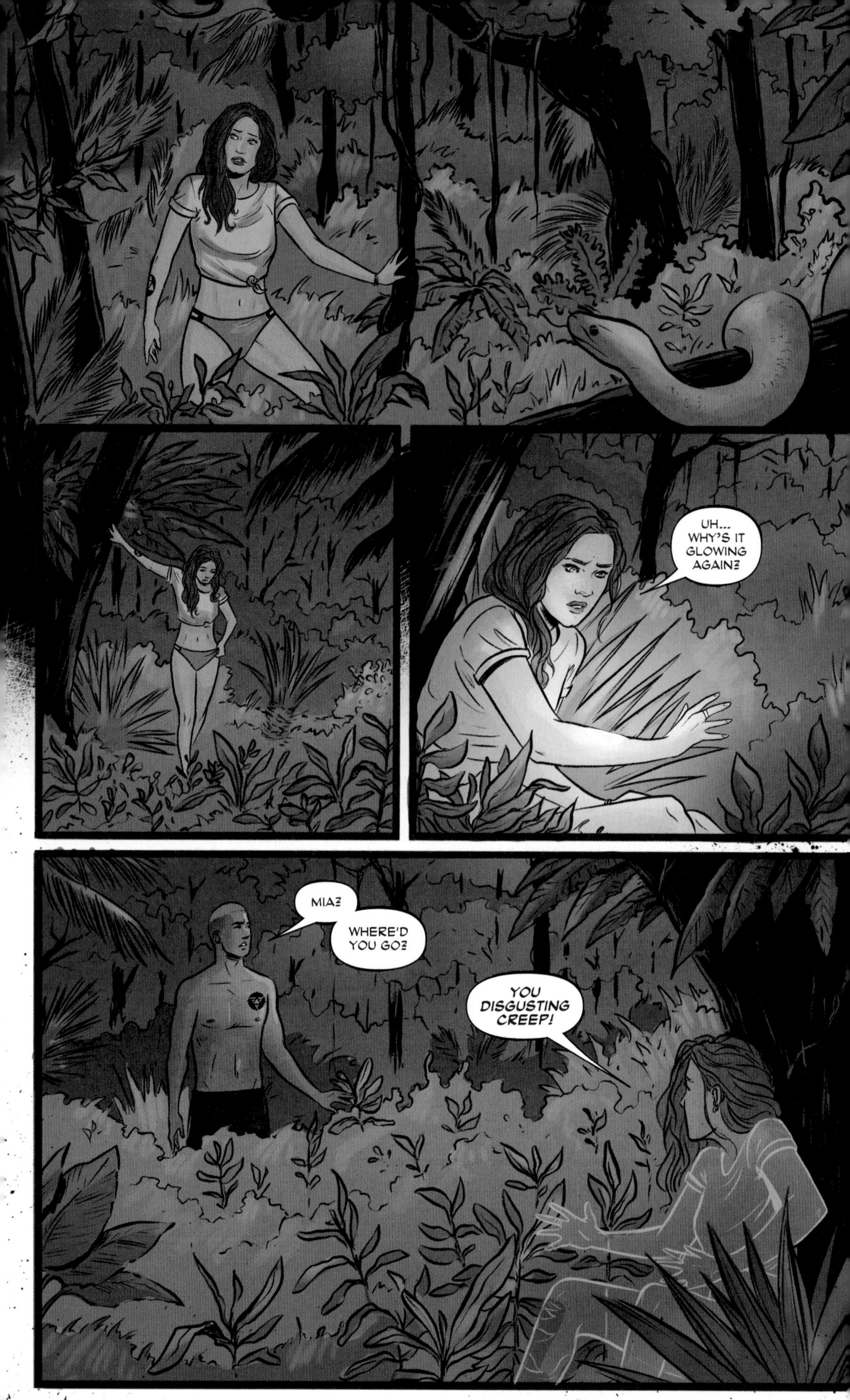
UH... WHY'S IT GLOWING AGAIN?
MIA?
WHERE'D YOU GO?
YOU DISGUSTING CREEP!

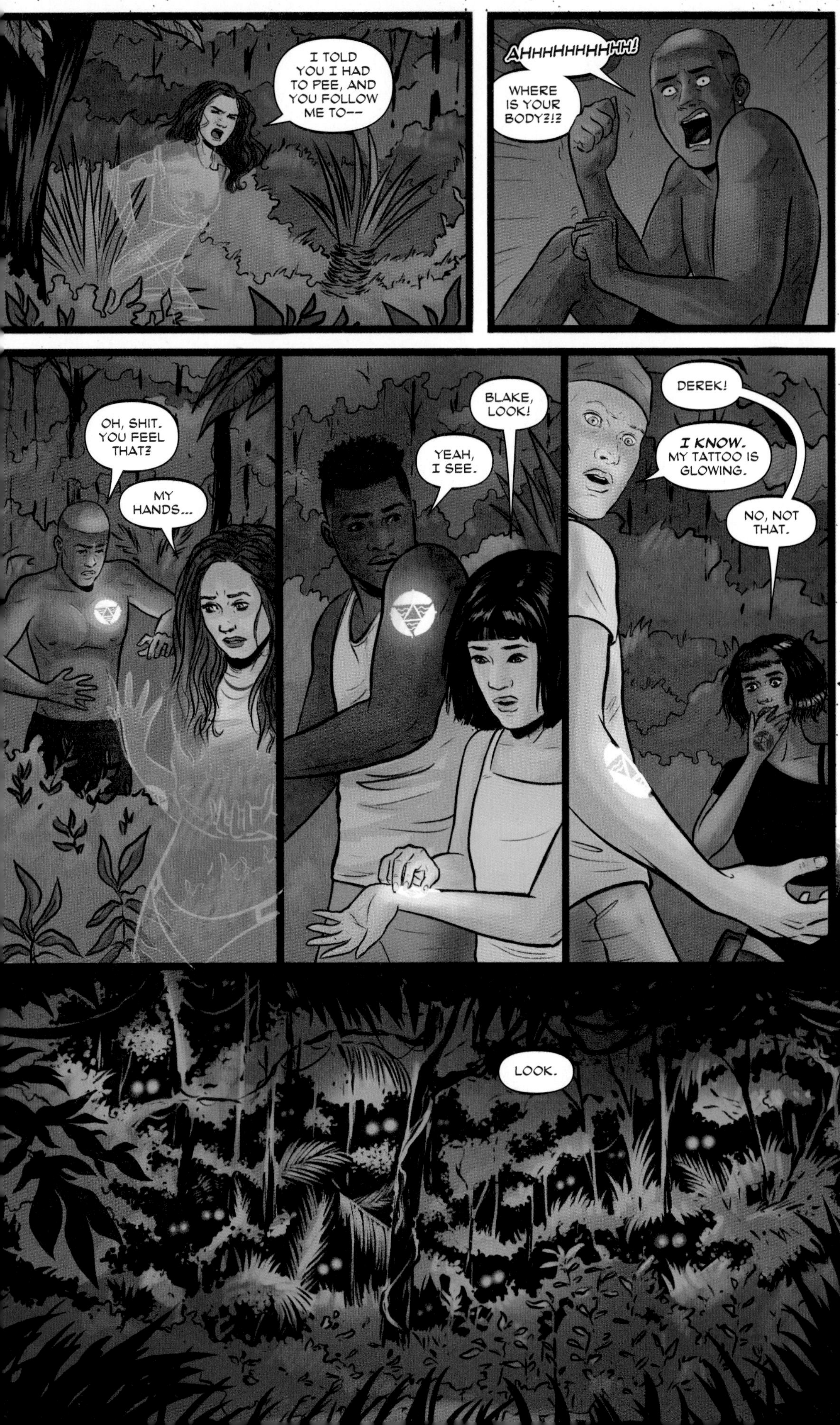
I TOLD YOU I HAD TO PEE, AND YOU FOLLOW ME TO--
AHHHHHHHHHH!
WHERE IS YOUR BODY?!?
OH, SHIT. YOU FEEL THAT?
MY HANDS...
BLAKE, LOOK!
YEAH, I SEE.
DEREK!
I KNOW. MY TATTOO IS GLOWING.
NO, NOT THAT.
LOOK.

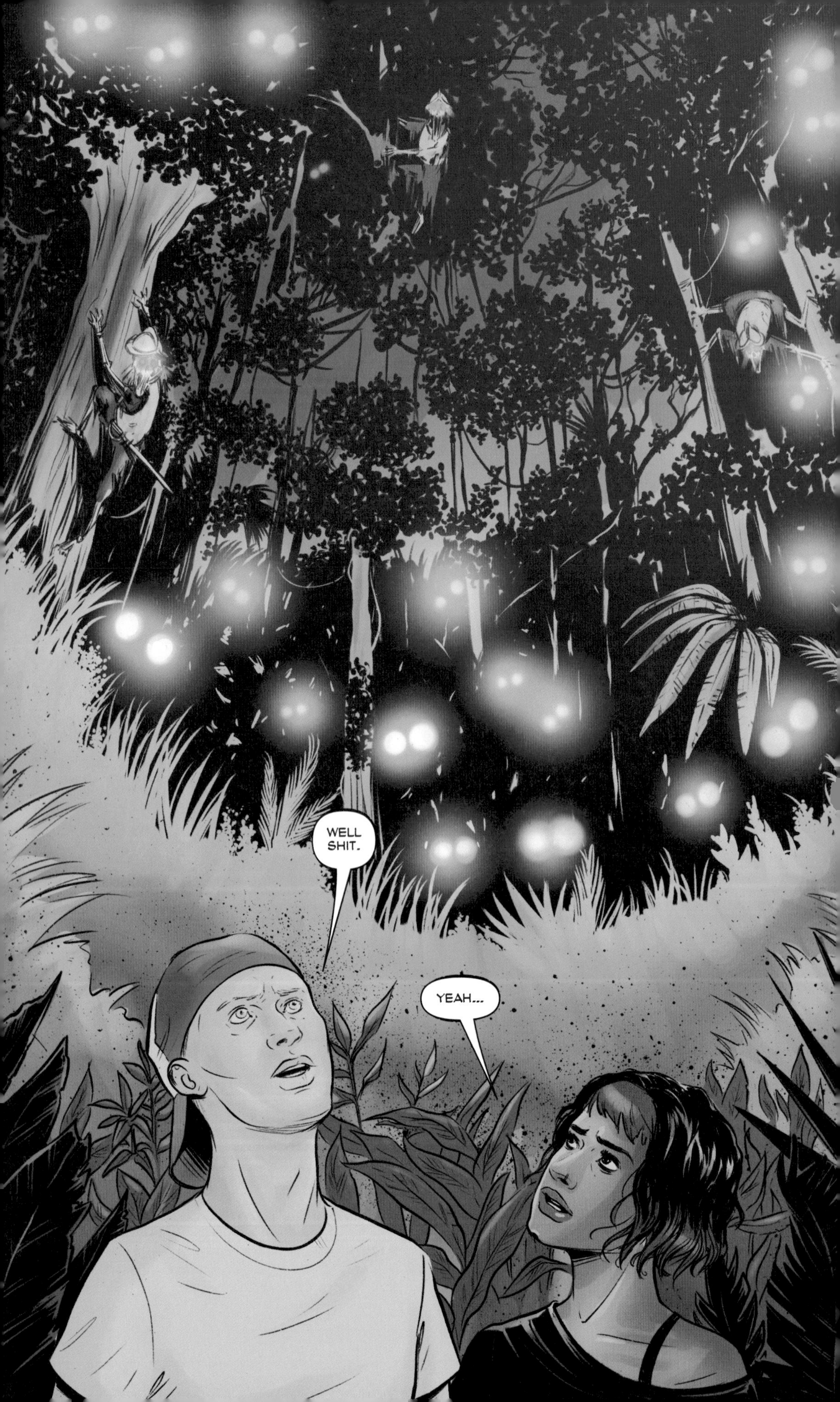
WELL SHIT.
YEAH...

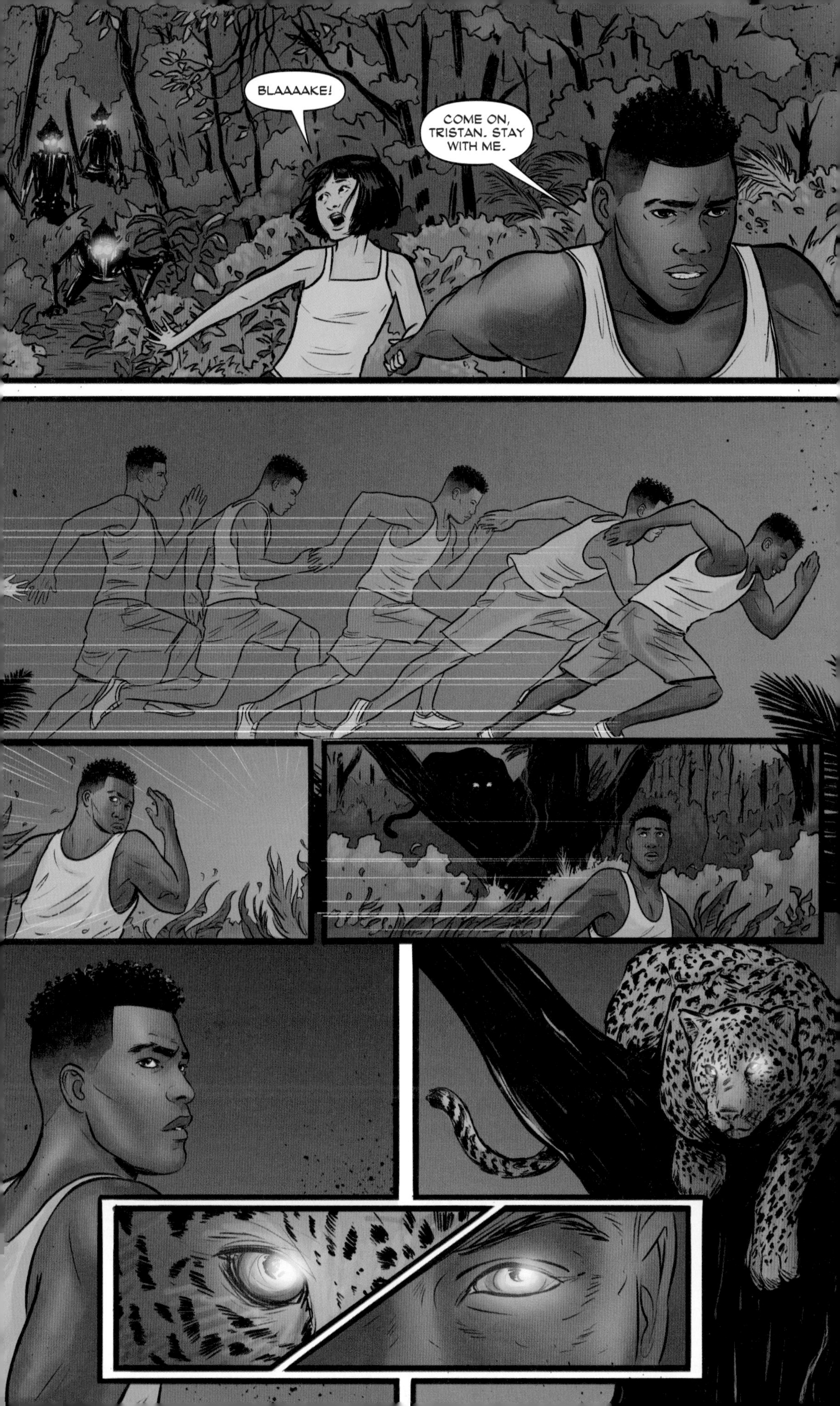
BLAAAAKE!
COME ON, TRISTAN. STAY WITH ME.

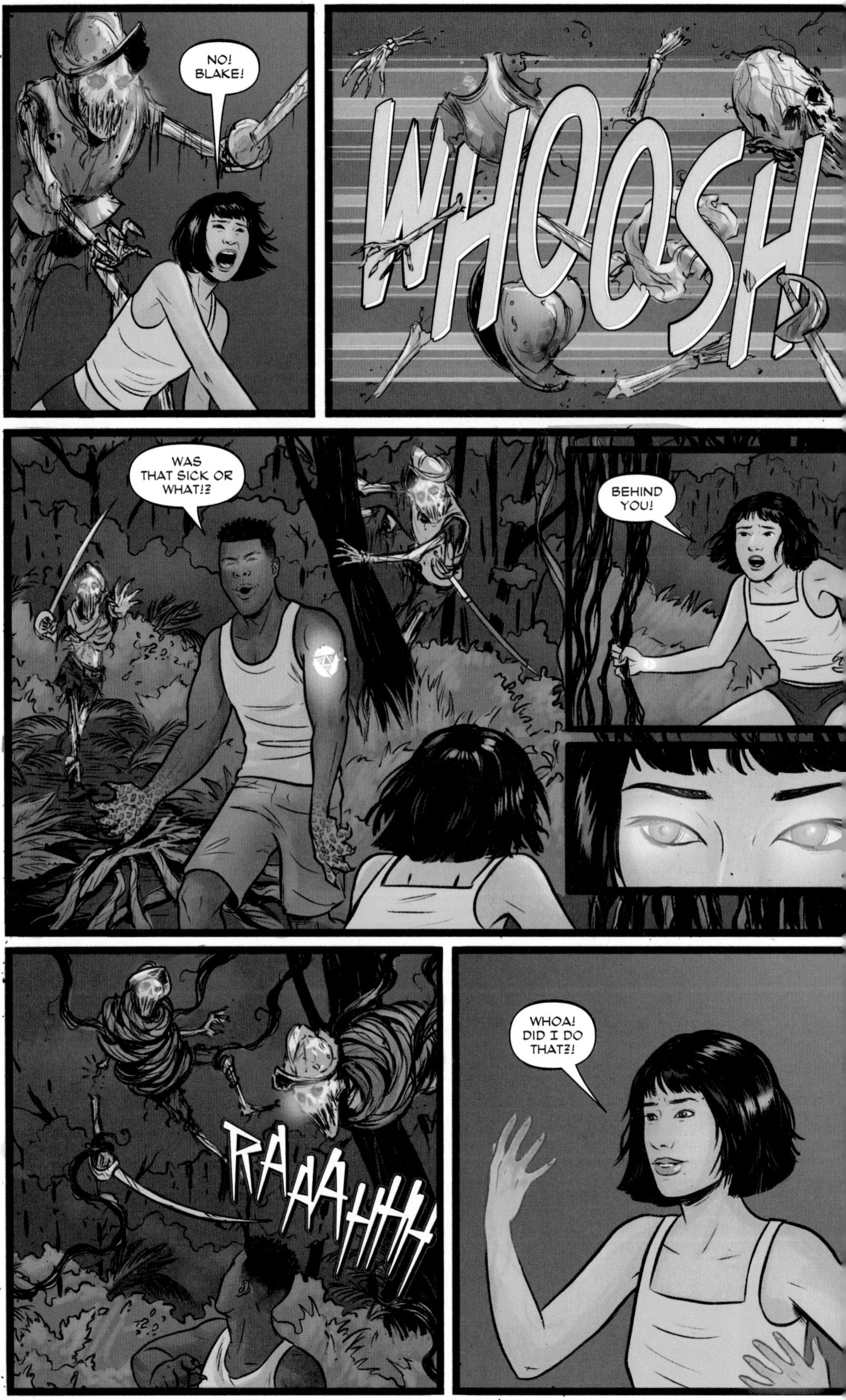
NO! BLAKE!
WHOOSH
WAS THAT SICK OR WHAT!?
BEHIND YOU!
RAAAHHH
WHOA! DID I DO THAT?!

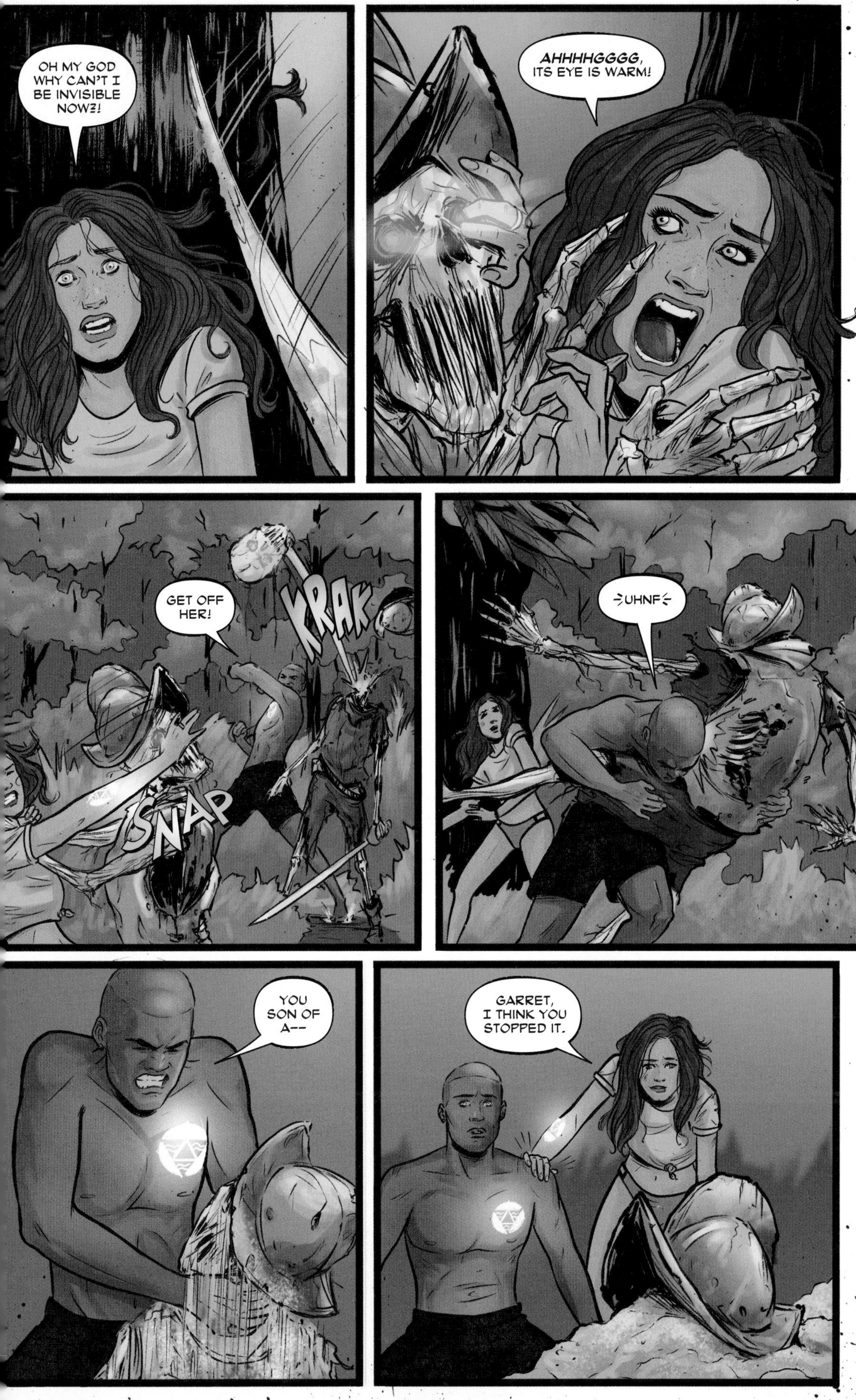
OH MY GOD WHY CAN'T I BE INVISIBLE NOW?!
AHHHHGGGG, ITS EYE IS WARM!
GET OFF HER!
KRAK
SNAP
UHNF
YOU SON OF A--
GARRET, I THINK YOU STOPPED IT.

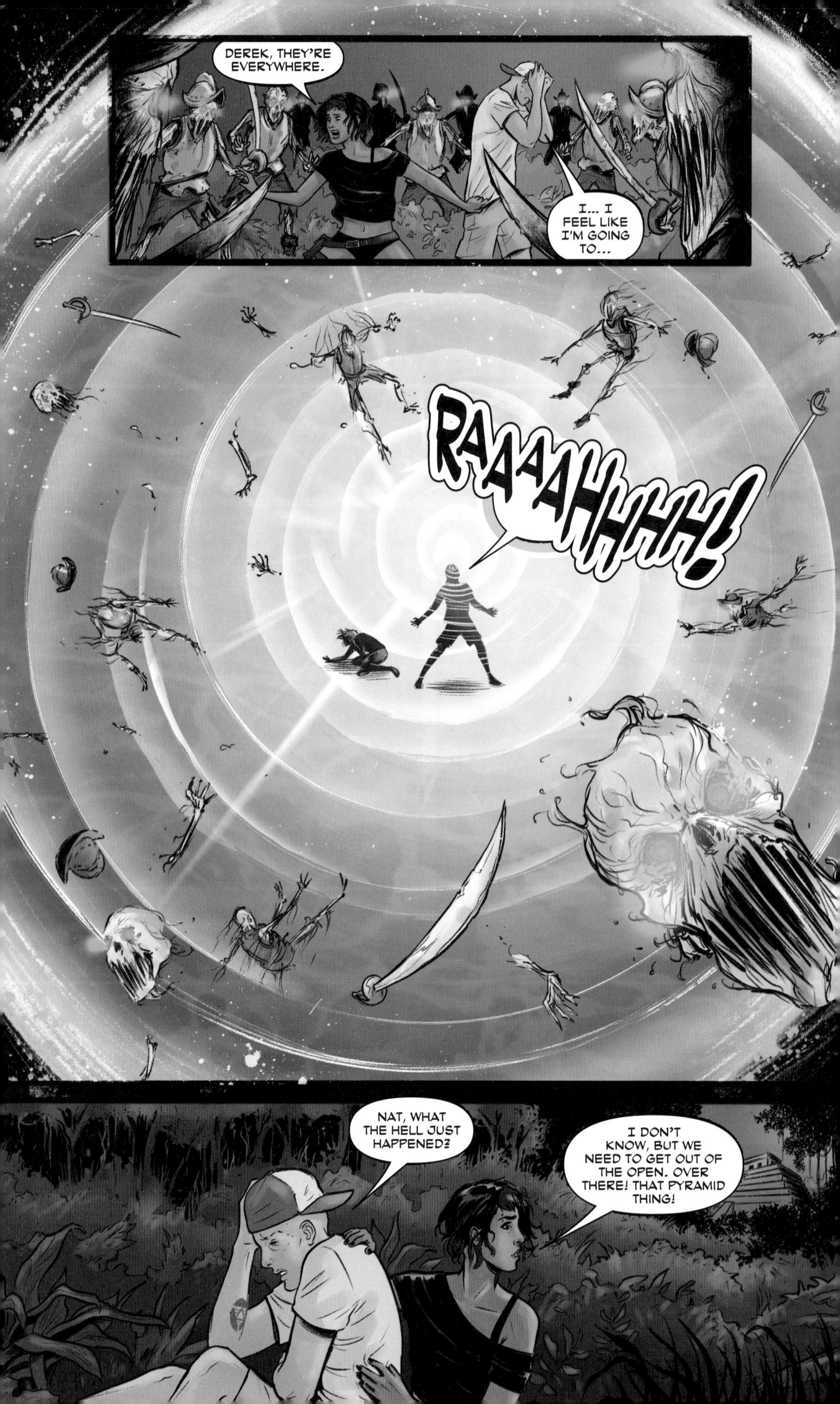
DEREK, THEY'RE EVERYWHERE.
I... I FEEL LIKE I'M GOING TO...
RAAAAHHHHH!
NAT, WHAT THE HELL JUST HAPPENED?
I DON'T KNOW, BUT WE NEED TO GET OUT OF THE OPEN. OVER THERE! THAT PYRAMID THING!

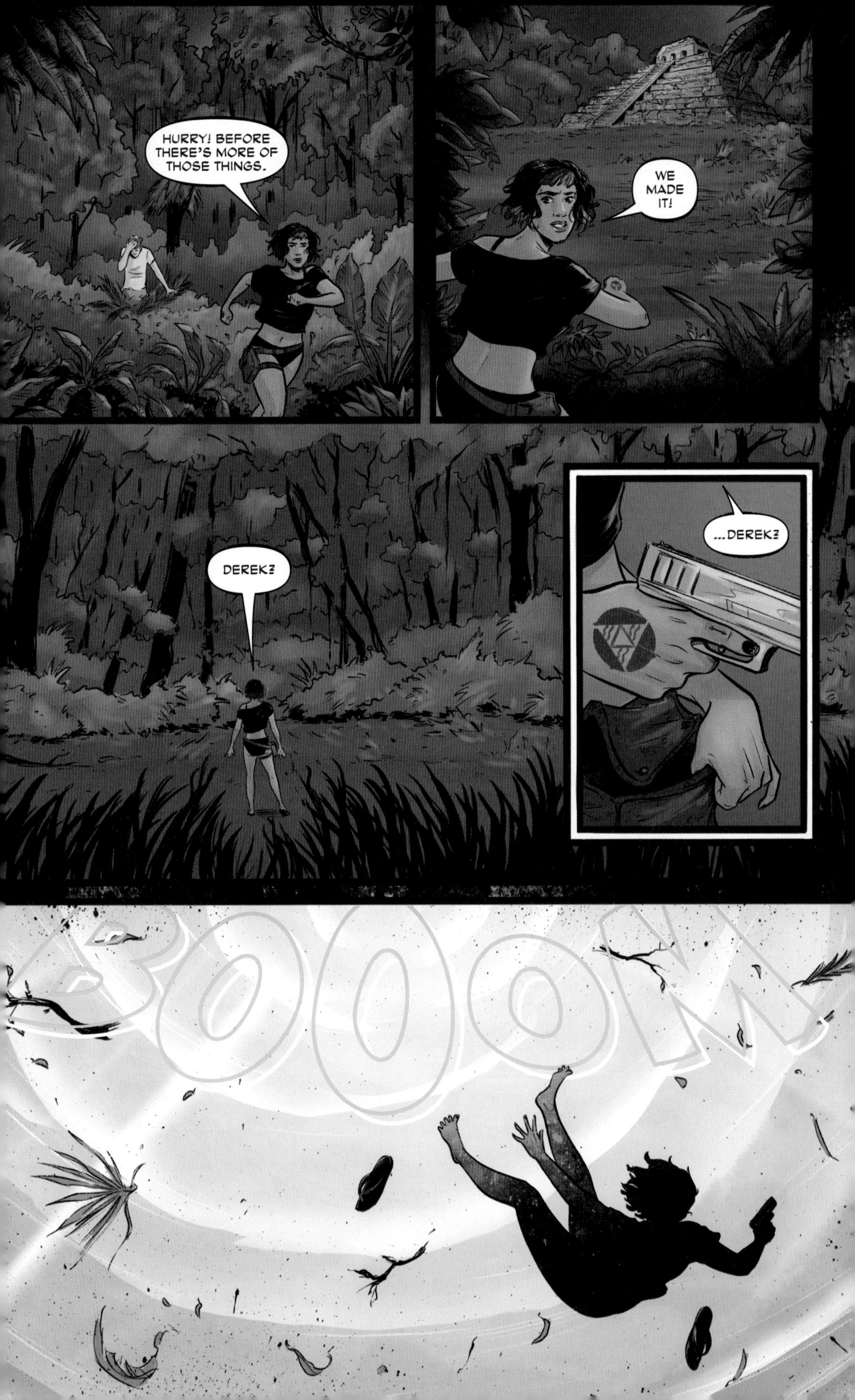
HURRY! BEFORE THERE'S MORE OF THOSE THINGS.
WE MADE IT!
DEREK?
...DEREK?
BOOOM

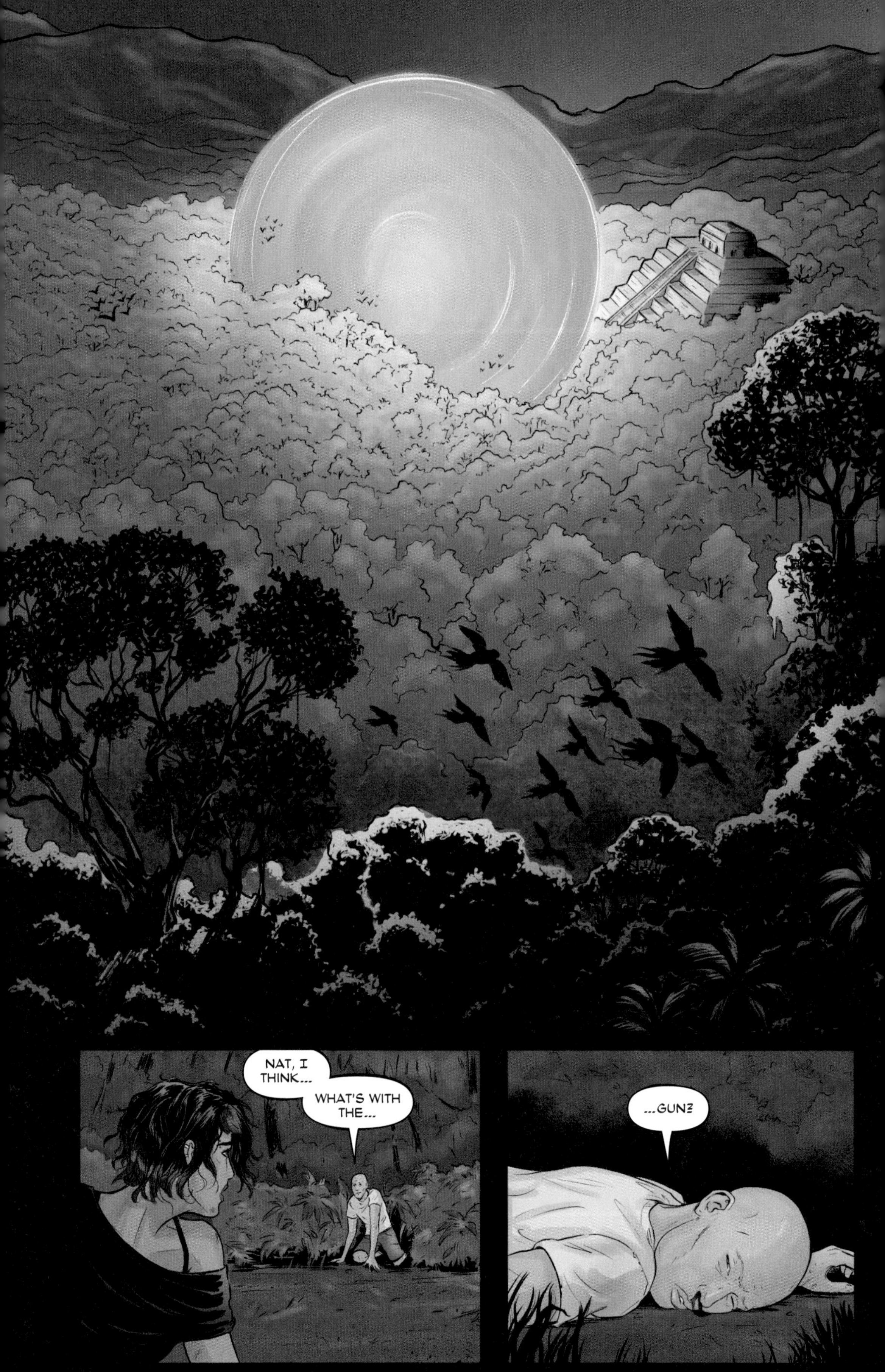
NAT, I THINK...
WHAT'S WITH THE...
...GUN?

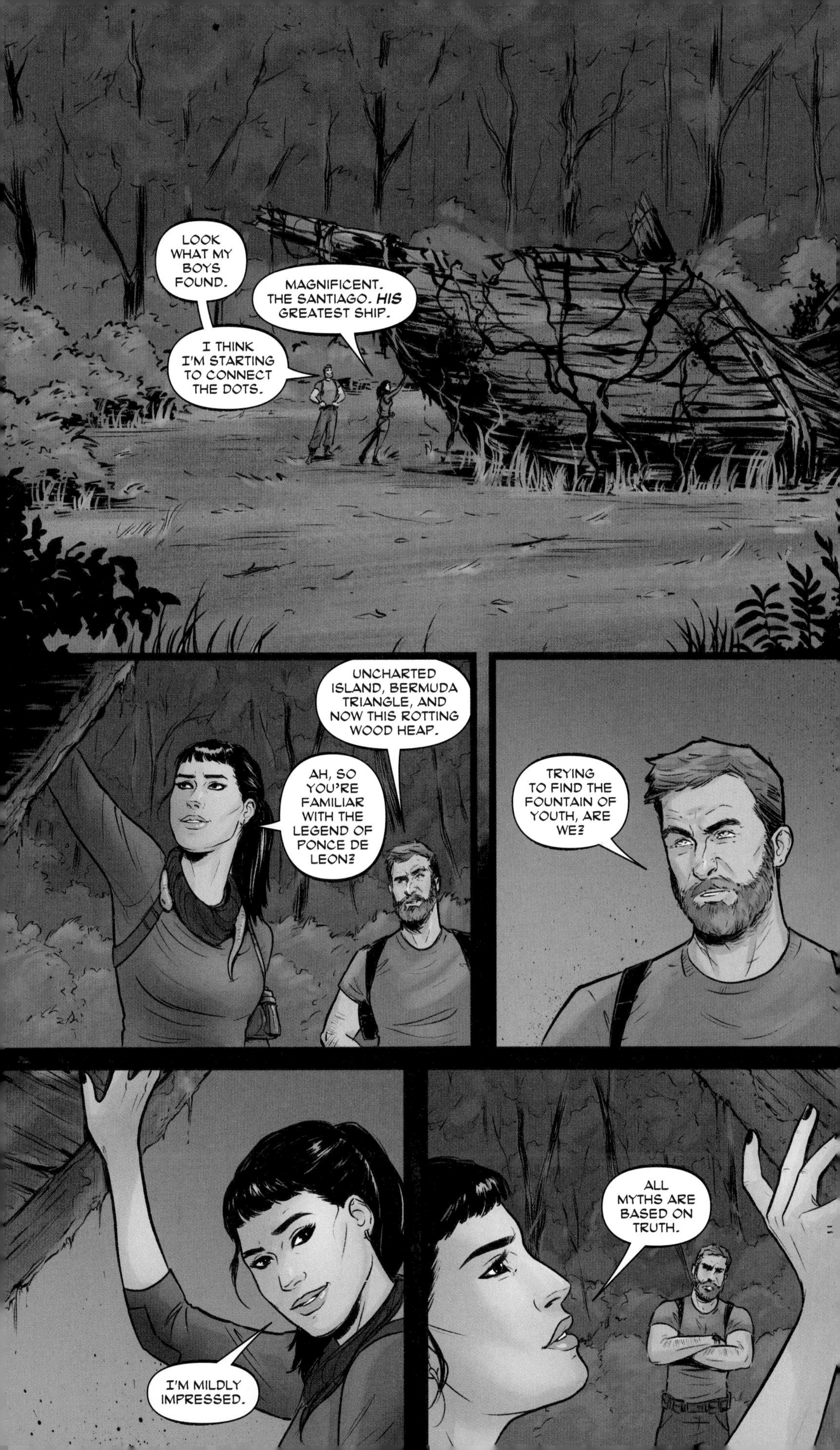
LOOK WHAT MY BOYS FOUND.
MAGNIFICENT. THE SANTIAGO. HIS GREATEST SHIP.
I THINK I'M STARTING TO CONNECT THE DOTS.
UNCHARTED ISLAND, BERMUDA TRIANGLE, AND NOW THIS ROTTING WOOD HEAP.
AH, SO YOU'RE FAMILIAR WITH THE LEGEND OF PONCE DE LEON?
TRYING TO FIND THE FOUNTAIN OF YOUTH, ARE WE?
I'M MILDLY IMPRESSED.
ALL MYTHS ARE BASED ON TRUTH.

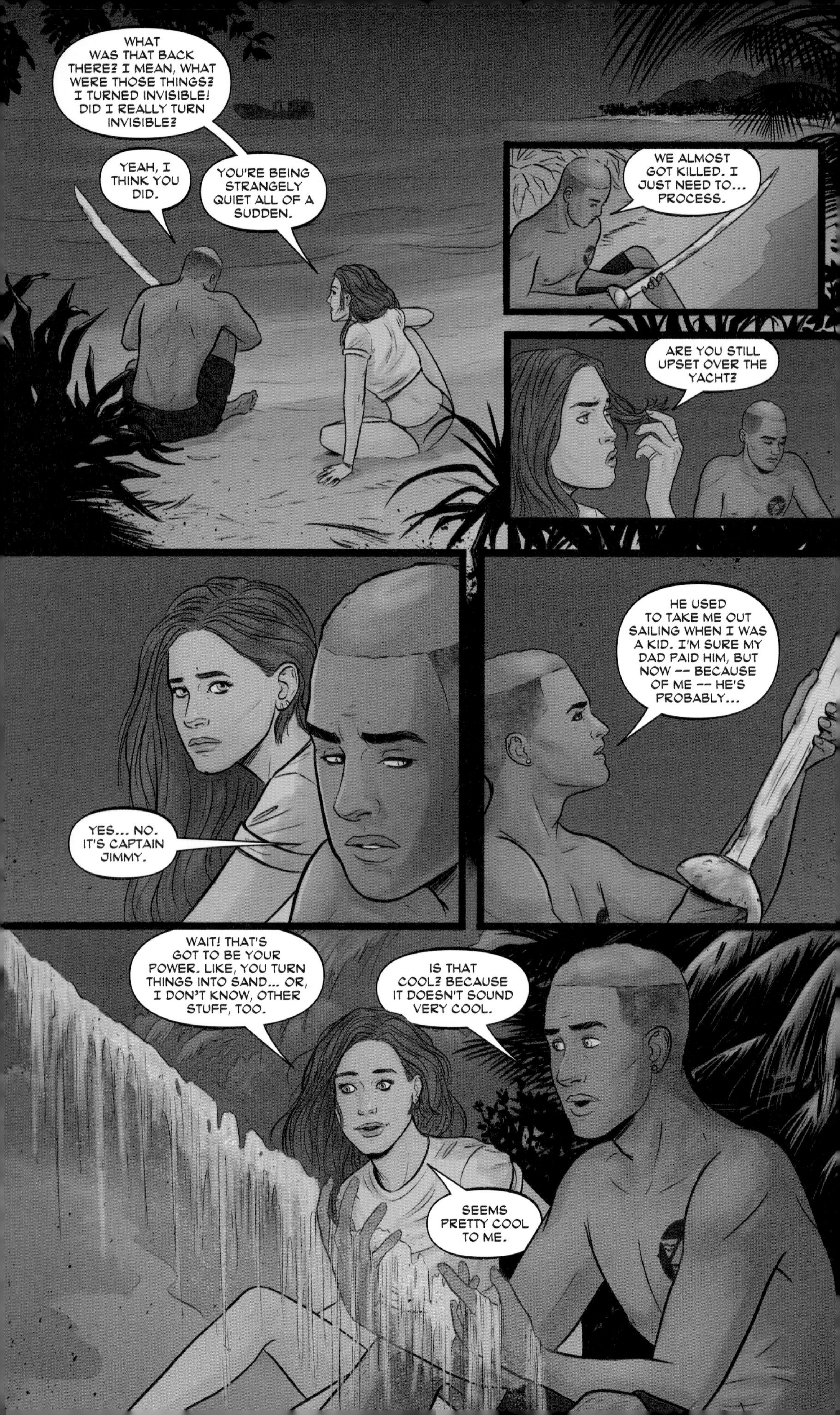
WHAT WAS THAT BACK THERE? I MEAN, WHAT WERE THOSE THINGS? I TURNED INVISIBLE! DID I REALLY TURN INVISIBLE?
YEAH, I THINK YOU DID.
YOU'RE BEING STRANGELY QUIET ALL OF A SUDDEN.
WE ALMOST GOT KILLED. I JUST NEED TO... PROCESS.
ARE YOU STILL UPSET OVER THE YACHT?
YES... NO. IT'S CAPTAIN JIMMY.
HE USED TO TAKE ME OUT SAILING WHEN I WAS A KID. I'M SURE MY DAD PAID HIM, BUT NOW -- BECAUSE OF ME -- HE'S PROBABLY...
WAIT! THAT'S GOT TO BE YOUR POWER. LIKE, YOU TURN THINGS INTO SAND... OR, I DON'T KNOW, OTHER STUFF, TOO.
IS THAT COOL? BECAUSE IT DOESN'T SOUND VERY COOL.
SEEMS PRETTY COOL TO ME.

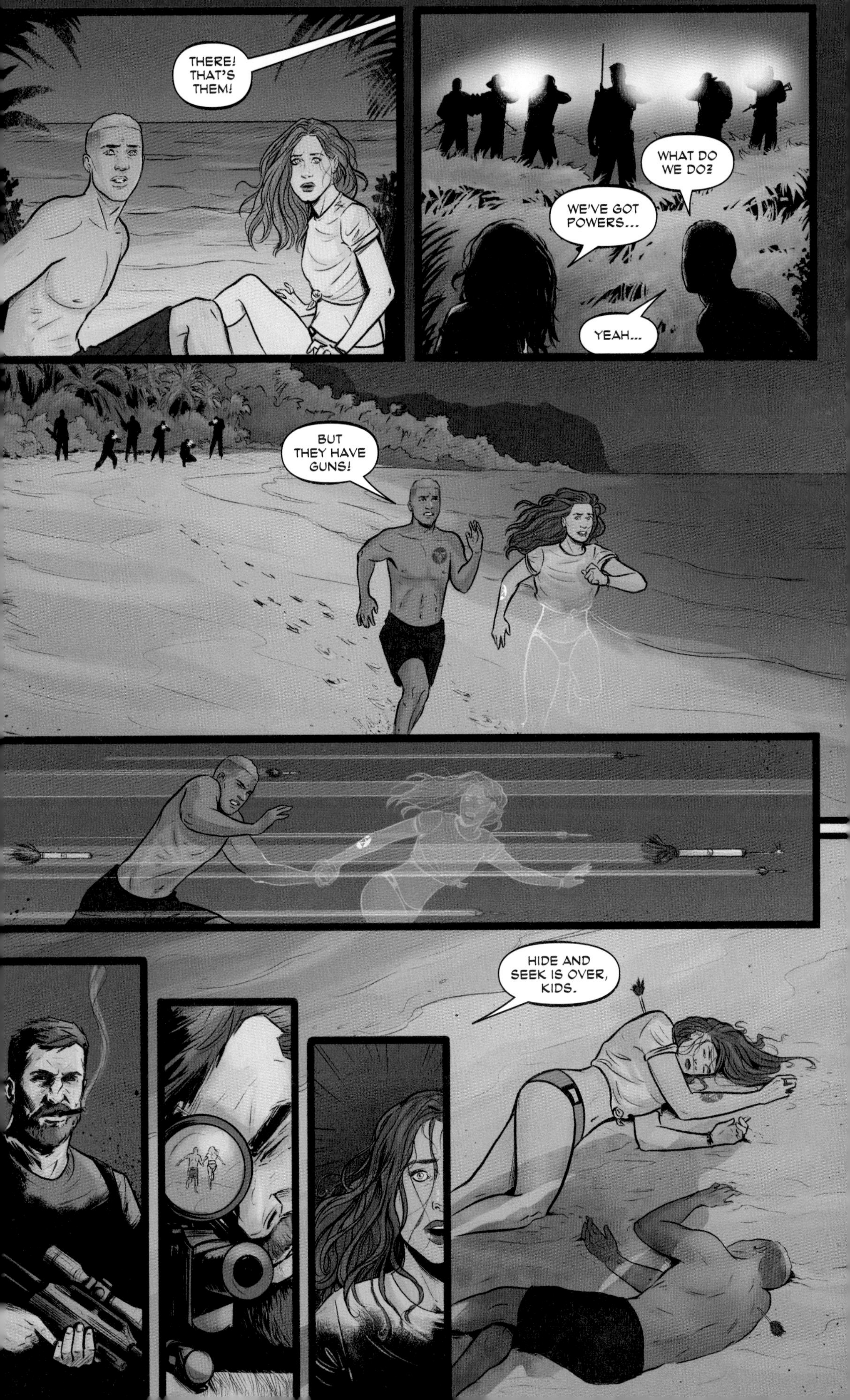
THERE! THAT'S THEM!
WHAT DO WE DO?
WE'VE GOT POWERS...
YEAH...
BUT THEY HAVE GUNS!
HIDE AND SEEK IS OVER, KIDS.

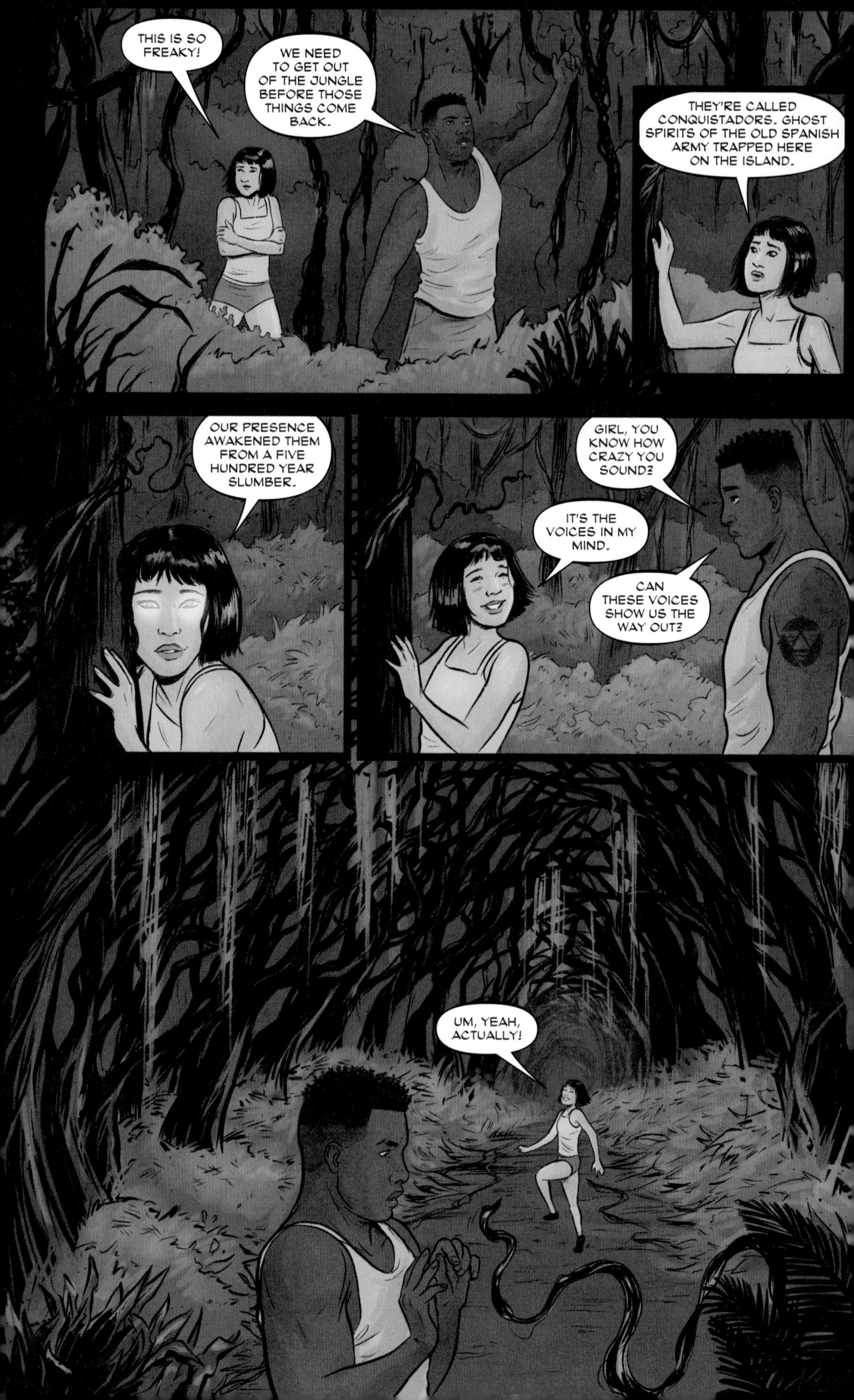

THIS IS SO FREAKY!
WE NEED TO GET OUT OF THE JUNGLE BEFORE THOSE THINGS COME BACK.
THEY'RE CALLED CONQUISTADORS. GHOST SPIRITS OF THE OLD SPANISH ARMY TRAPPED HERE ON THE ISLAND.
OUR PRESENCE AWAKENED THEM FROM A FIVE HUNDRED YEAR SLUMBER.
GIRL, YOU KNOW HOW CRAZY YOU SOUND?
IT'S THE VOICES IN MY MIND.
CAN THESE VOICES SHOW US THE WAY OUT?
UM, YEAH, ACTUALLY!

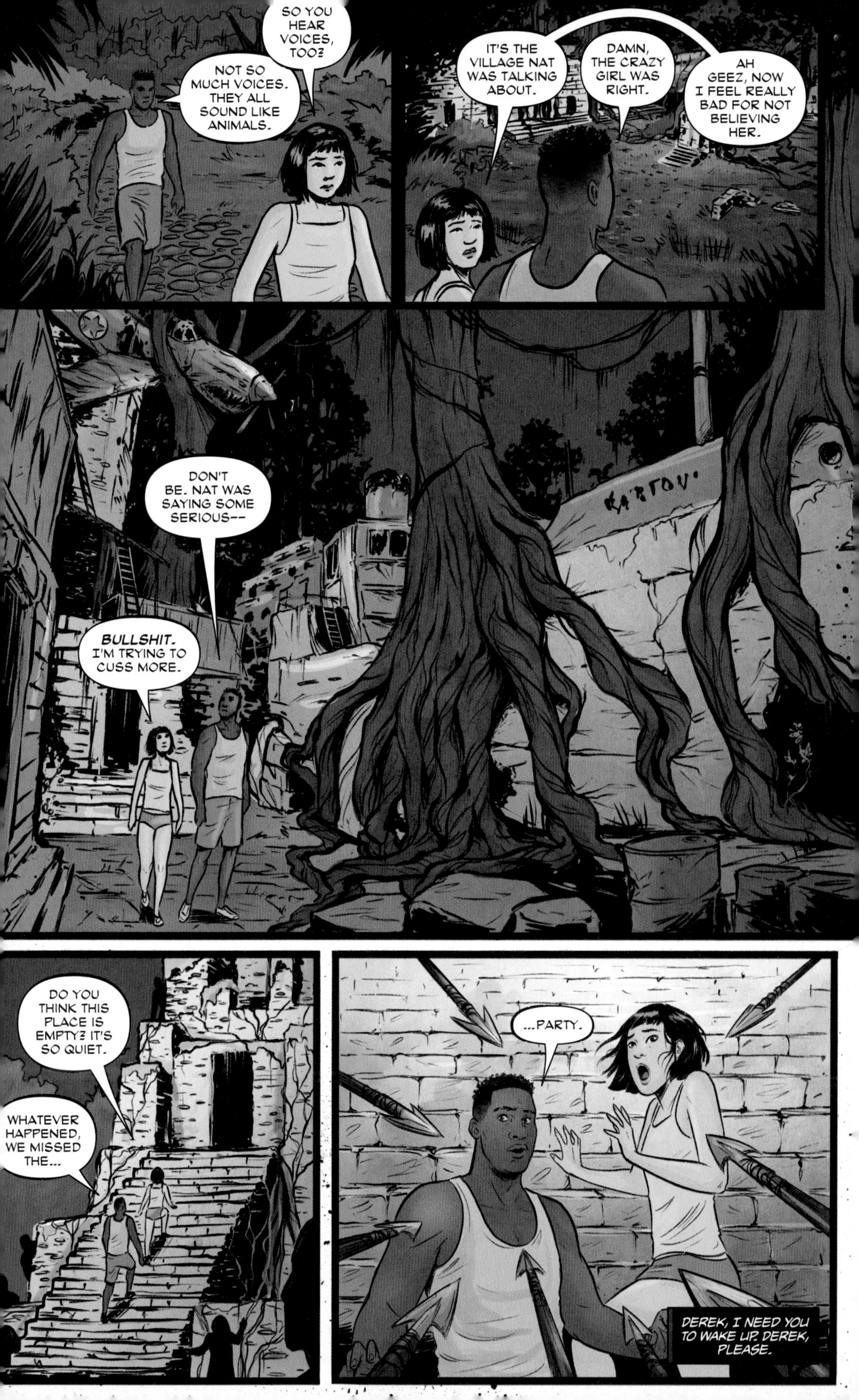
SO YOU HEAR VOICES, TOO?
NOT SO MUCH VOICES. THEY ALL SOUND LIKE ANIMALS.
IT'S THE VILLAGE NAT WAS TALKING ABOUT.
DAMN, THE CRAZY GIRL WAS RIGHT.
AH GEEZ, NOW I FEEL REALLY BAD FOR NOT BELIEVING HER.
DON'T BE. NAT WAS SAYING SOME SERIOUS--
BULLSHIT. I'M TRYING TO CUSS MORE.
DO YOU THINK THIS PLACE IS EMPTY? IT'S SO QUIET.
WHATEVER HAPPENED, WE MISSED THE...
...PARTY.
DEREK, I NEED YOU TO WAKE UP. DEREK, PLEASE.

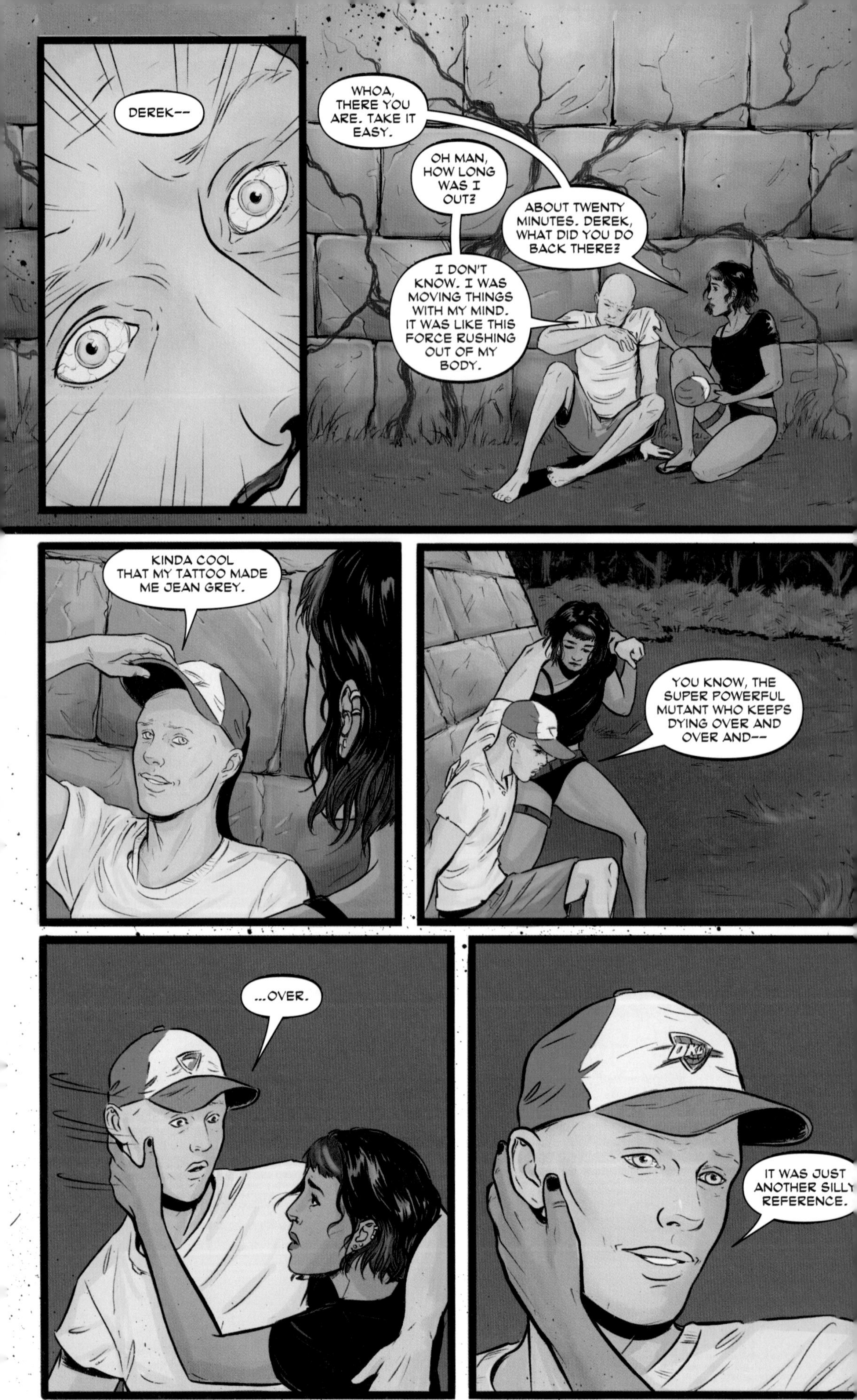
DEREK--
WHOA, THERE YOU ARE. TAKE IT EASY.
OH MAN, HOW LONG WAS I OUT?
ABOUT TWENTY MINUTES. DEREK, WHAT DID YOU DO BACK THERE?
I DON'T KNOW. I WAS MOVING THINGS WITH MY MIND. IT WAS LIKE THIS FORCE RUSHING OUT OF MY BODY.
KINDA COOL THAT MY TATTOO MADE ME JEAN GREY.
YOU KNOW, THE SUPER POWERFUL MUTANT WHO KEEPS DYING OVER AND OVER AND--
...OVER.
IT WAS JUST ANOTHER SILLY REFERENCE.

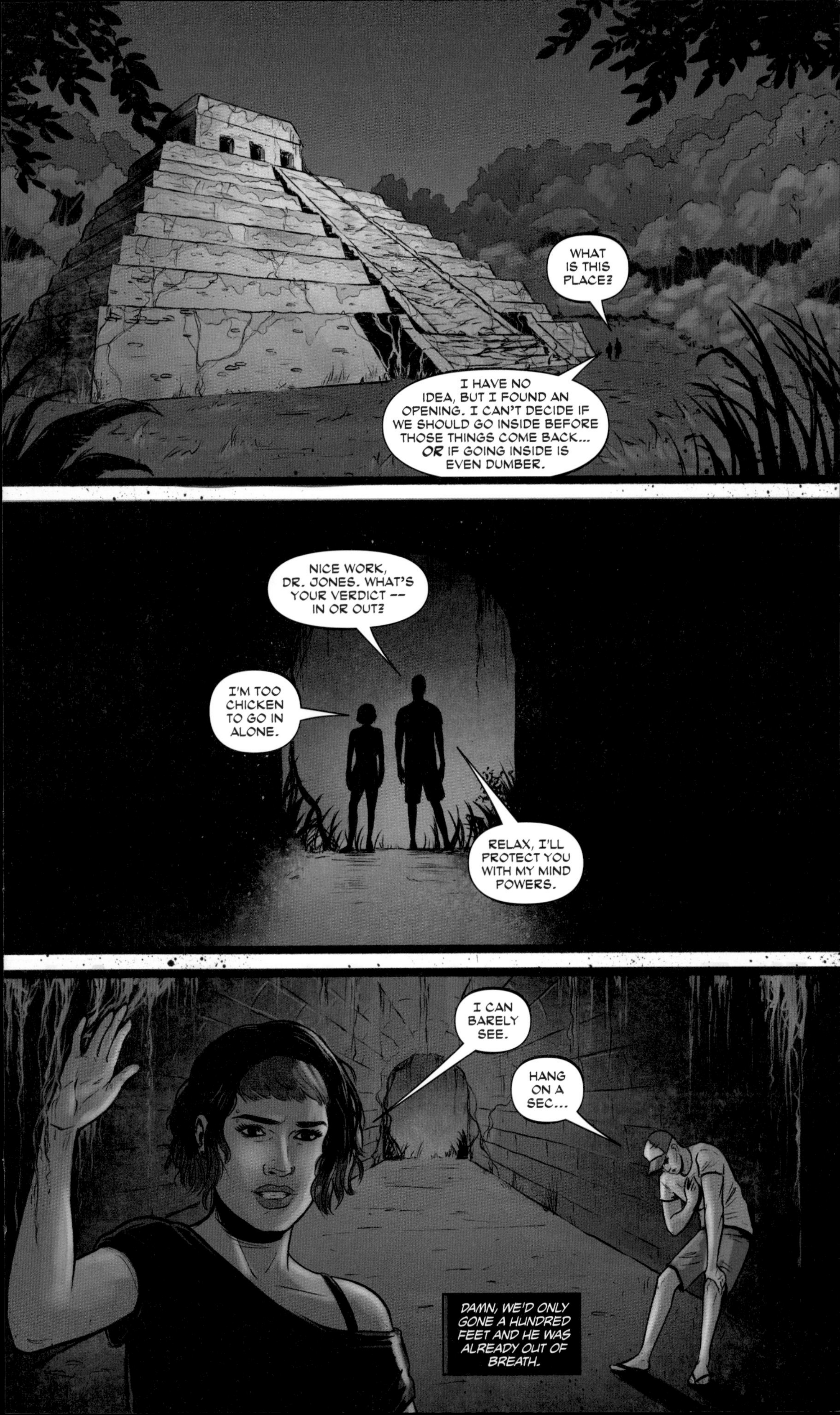
WHAT IS THIS PLACE?
I HAVE NO IDEA, BUT I FOUND AN OPENING. I CAN'T DECIDE IF WE SHOULD GO INSIDE BEFORE THOSE THINGS COME BACK... OR IF GOING INSIDE IS EVEN DUMBER.
NICE WORK, DR. JONES. WHAT'S YOUR VERDICT -- IN OR OUT?
I'M TOO CHICKEN TO GO IN ALONE.
RELAX, I'LL PROTECT YOU WITH MY MIND POWERS.
I CAN BARELY SEE.
HANG ON A SEC...
DAMN, WE'D ONLY GONE A HUNDRED FEET AND HE WAS ALREADY OUT OF BREATH.

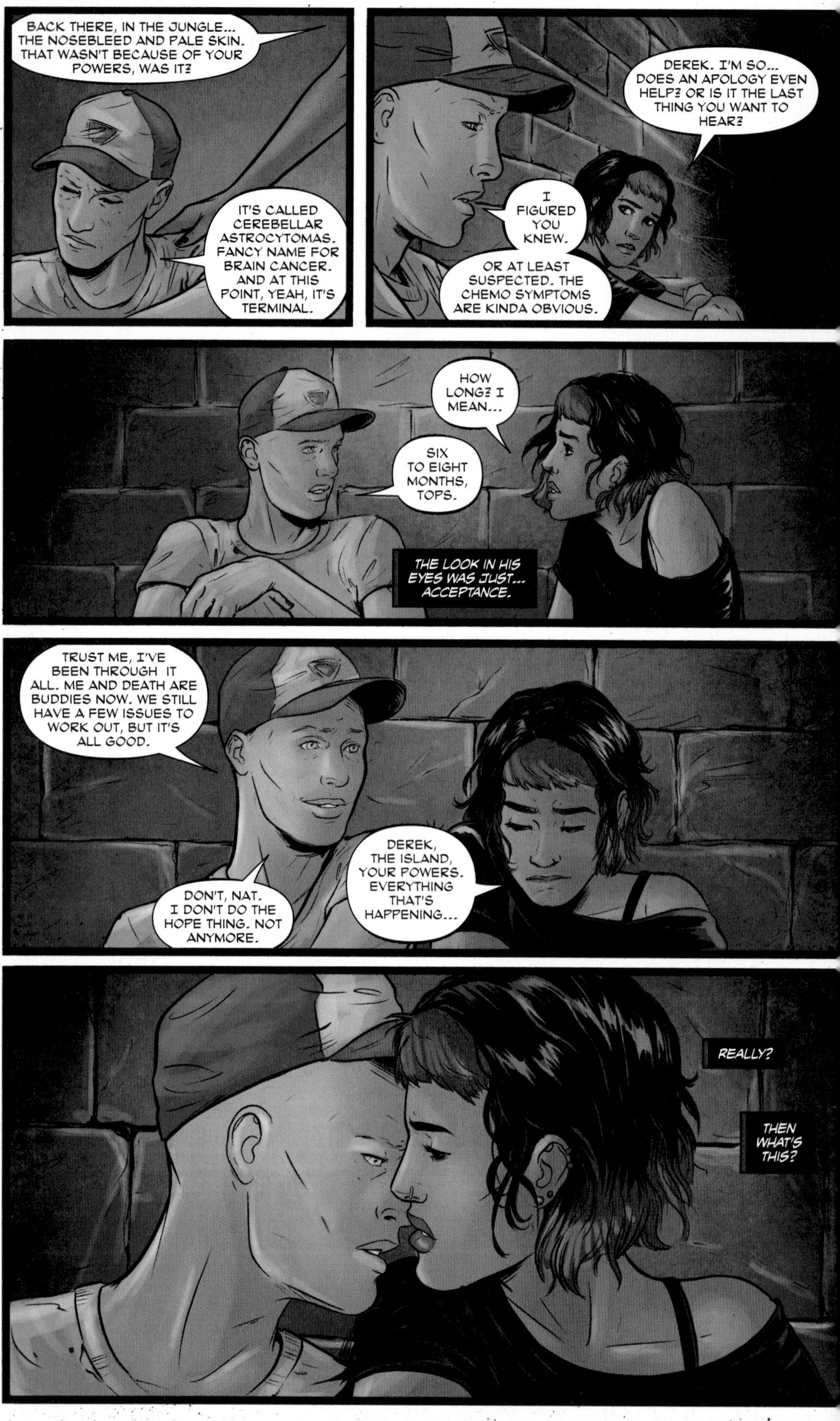
BACK THERE, IN THE JUNGLE... THE NOSEBLEED AND PALE SKIN. THAT WASN'T BECAUSE OF YOUR POWERS, WAS IT?
IT'S CALLED CEREBELLAR ASTROCYTOMAS. FANCY NAME FOR BRAIN CANCER. AND AT THIS POINT, YEAH, IT'S TERMINAL.
DEREK. I'M SO... DOES AN APOLOGY EVEN HELP? OR IS IT THE LAST THING YOU WANT TO HEAR?
I FIGURED YOU KNEW.
OR AT LEAST SUSPECTED. THE CHEMO SYMPTOMS ARE KINDA OBVIOUS.
HOW LONG? I MEAN...
SIX TO EIGHT MONTHS, TOPS.
THE LOOK IN HIS EYES WAS JUST... ACCEPTANCE.
TRUST ME, I'VE BEEN THROUGH IT ALL. ME AND DEATH ARE BUDDIES NOW. WE STILL HAVE A FEW ISSUES TO WORK OUT, BUT IT'S ALL GOOD.
DEREK, THE ISLAND, YOUR POWERS. EVERYTHING THAT'S HAPPENING...
DON'T, NAT. I DON'T DO THE HOPE THING. NOT ANYMORE.
REALLY?
THEN WHAT'S THIS?

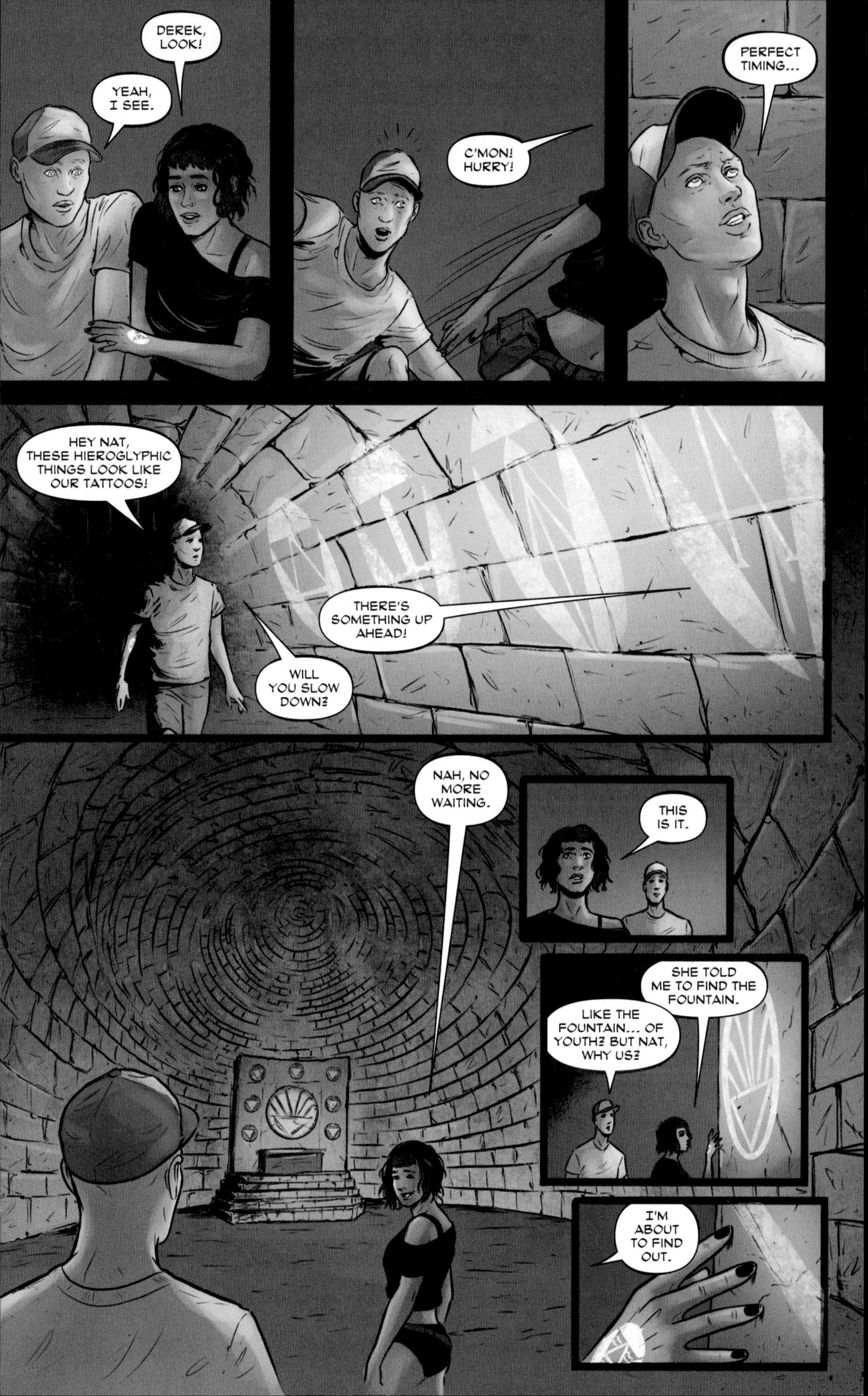
DEREK, LOOK!
YEAH, I SEE.
C'MON! HURRY!
PERFECT TIMING...
HEY NAT, THESE HIEROGLYPHIC THINGS LOOK LIKE OUR TATTOOS!
THERE'S SOMETHING UP AHEAD!
WILL YOU SLOW DOWN?
NAH, NO MORE WAITING.
THIS IS IT.
SHE TOLD ME TO FIND THE FOUNTAIN.
LIKE THE FOUNTAIN... OF YOUTH? BUT NAT, WHY US?
I'M ABOUT TO FIND OUT.

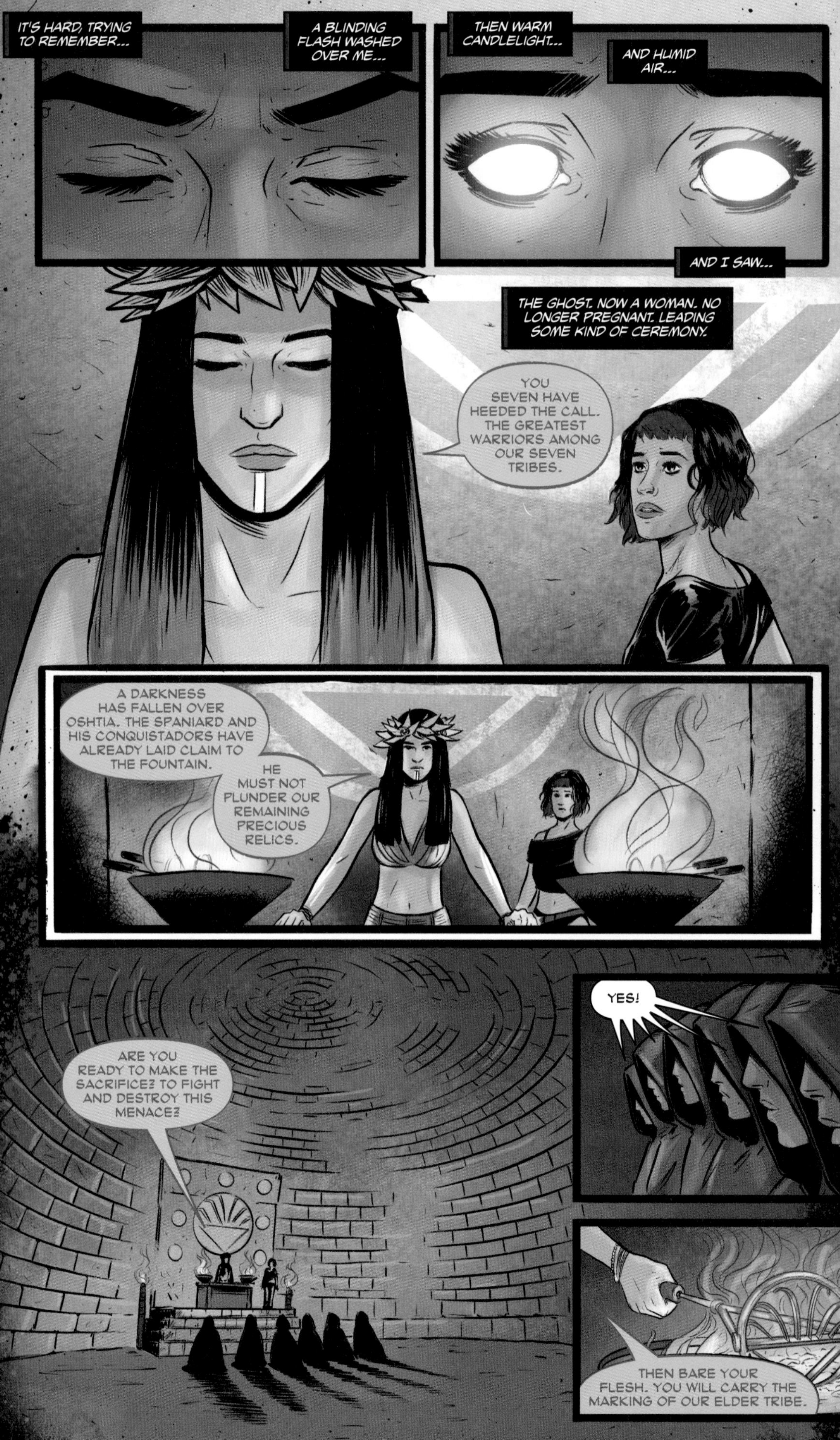

IT'S HARD, TRYING TO REMEMBER...
A BLINDING FLASH WASHED OVER ME...
THEN WARM CANDLELIGHT...
AND HUMID AIR...
AND I SAW...
THE GHOST. NOW A WOMAN. NO LONGER PREGNANT. LEADING SOME KIND OF CEREMONY.
YOU SEVEN HAVE HEEDED THE CALL. THE GREATEST WARRIORS AMONG OUR SEVEN TRIBES.
A DARKNESS HAS FALLEN OVER OSHTIA. THE SPANIARD AND HIS CONQUISTADORS HAVE ALREADY LAID CLAIM TO THE FOUNTAIN.
HE MUST NOT PLUNDER OUR REMAINING PRECIOUS RELICS.
ARE YOU READY TO MAKE THE SACRIFICE? TO FIGHT AND DESTROY THIS MENACE?
YES!
THEN BARE YOUR FLESH. YOU WILL CARRY THE MARKING OF OUR ELDER TRIBE.

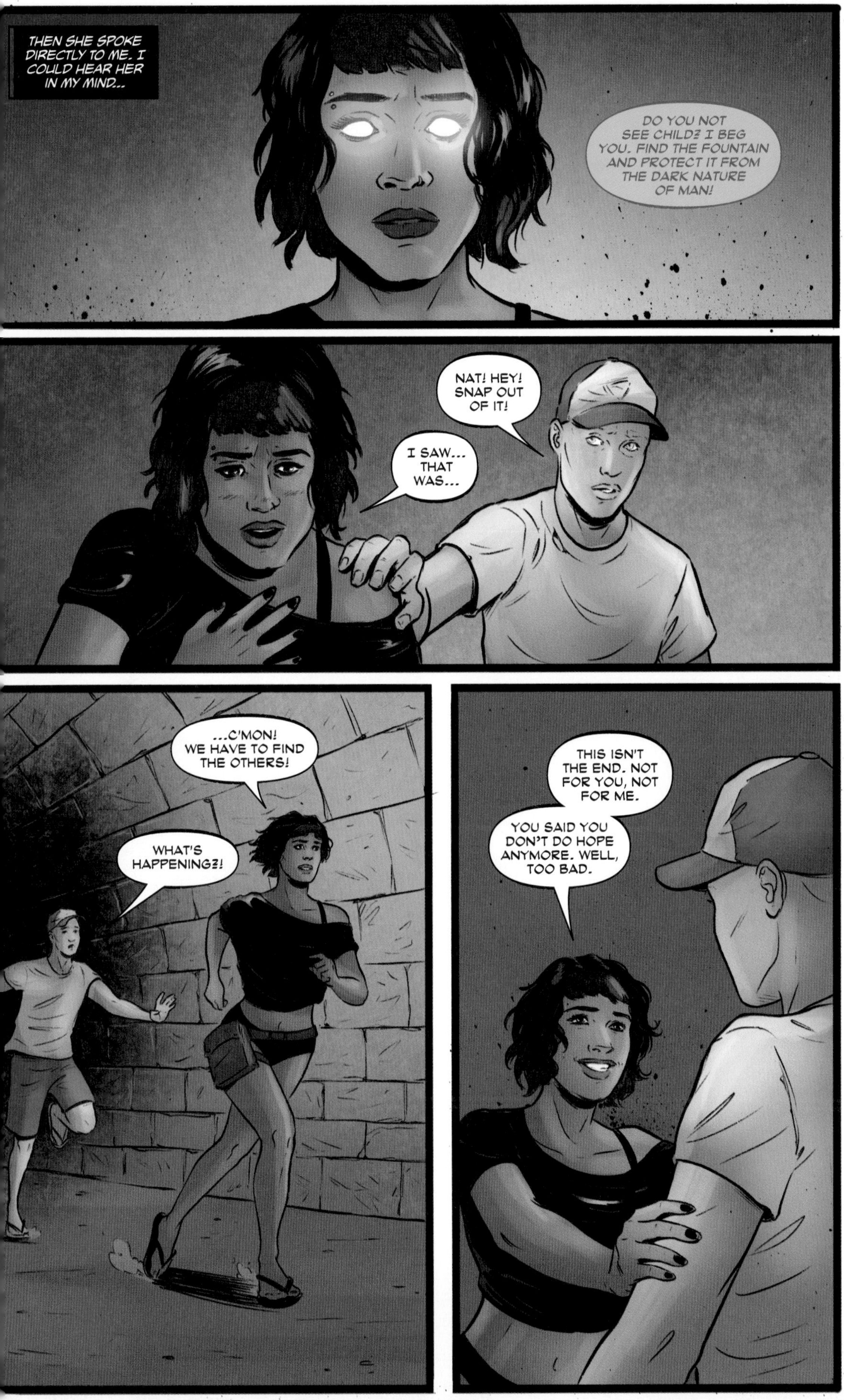

THEN SHE SPOKE DIRECTLY TO ME. I COULD HEAR HER IN MY MIND...
DO YOU NOT SEE CHILD? I BEG YOU. FIND THE FOUNTAIN AND PROTECT IT FROM THE DARK NATURE OF MAN!
NAT! HEY! SNAP OUT OF IT!
I SAW... THAT WAS...
...C'MON! WE HAVE TO FIND THE OTHERS!
WHAT'S HAPPENING?!
THIS ISN'T THE END. NOT FOR YOU, NOT FOR ME.
YOU SAID YOU DON'T DO HOPE ANYMORE. WELL, TOO BAD.

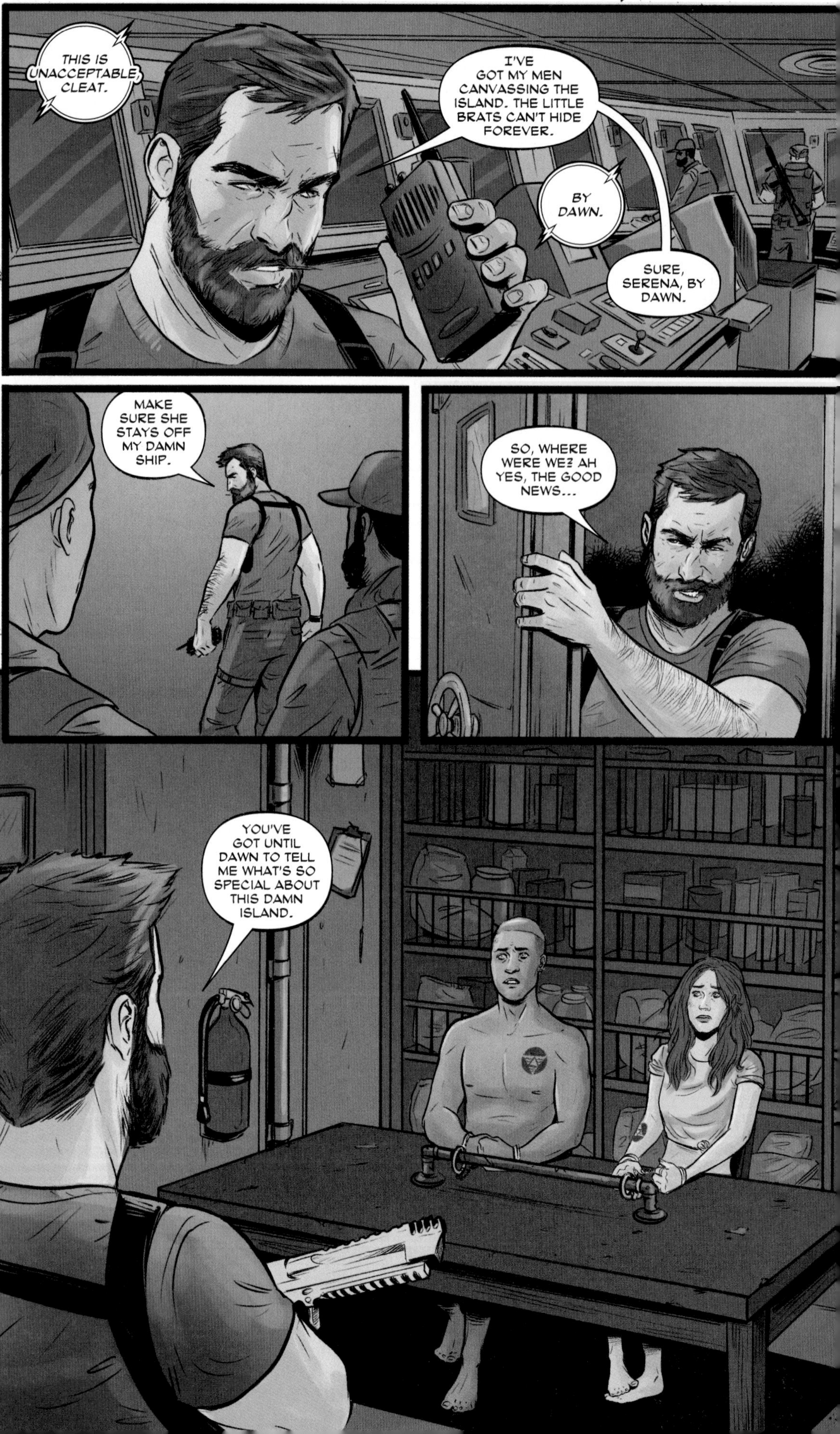
THIS IS UNACCEPTABLE, CLEAT.
I'VE GOT MY MEN CANVASSING THE ISLAND. THE LITTLE BRATS CAN'T HIDE FOREVER.
BY DAWN.
SURE, SERENA, BY DAWN.
MAKE SURE SHE STAYS OFF MY DAMN SHIP.
SO, WHERE WERE WE? AH YES, THE GOOD NEWS...
YOU'VE GOT UNTIL DAWN TO TELL ME WHAT'S SO SPECIAL ABOUT THIS DAMN ISLAND.

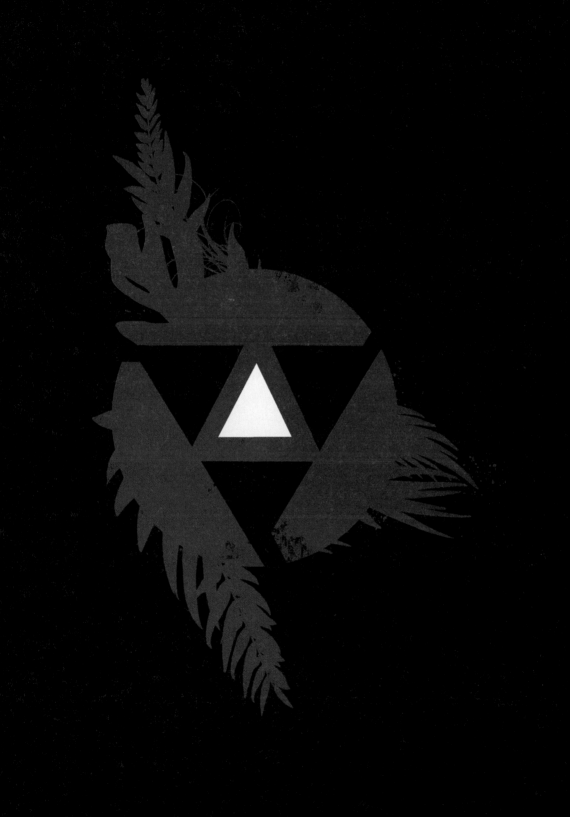

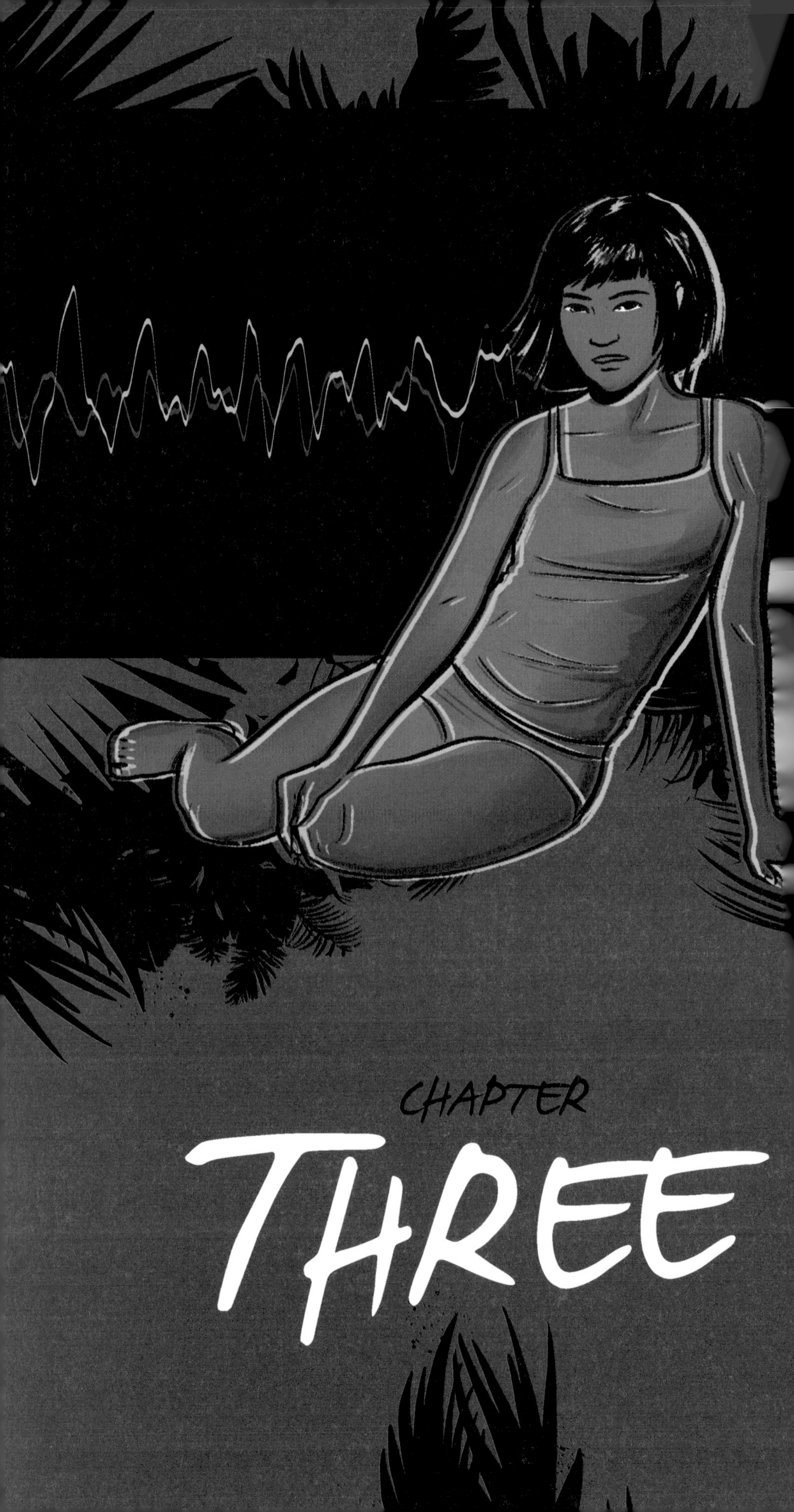
CHAPTER
THREE

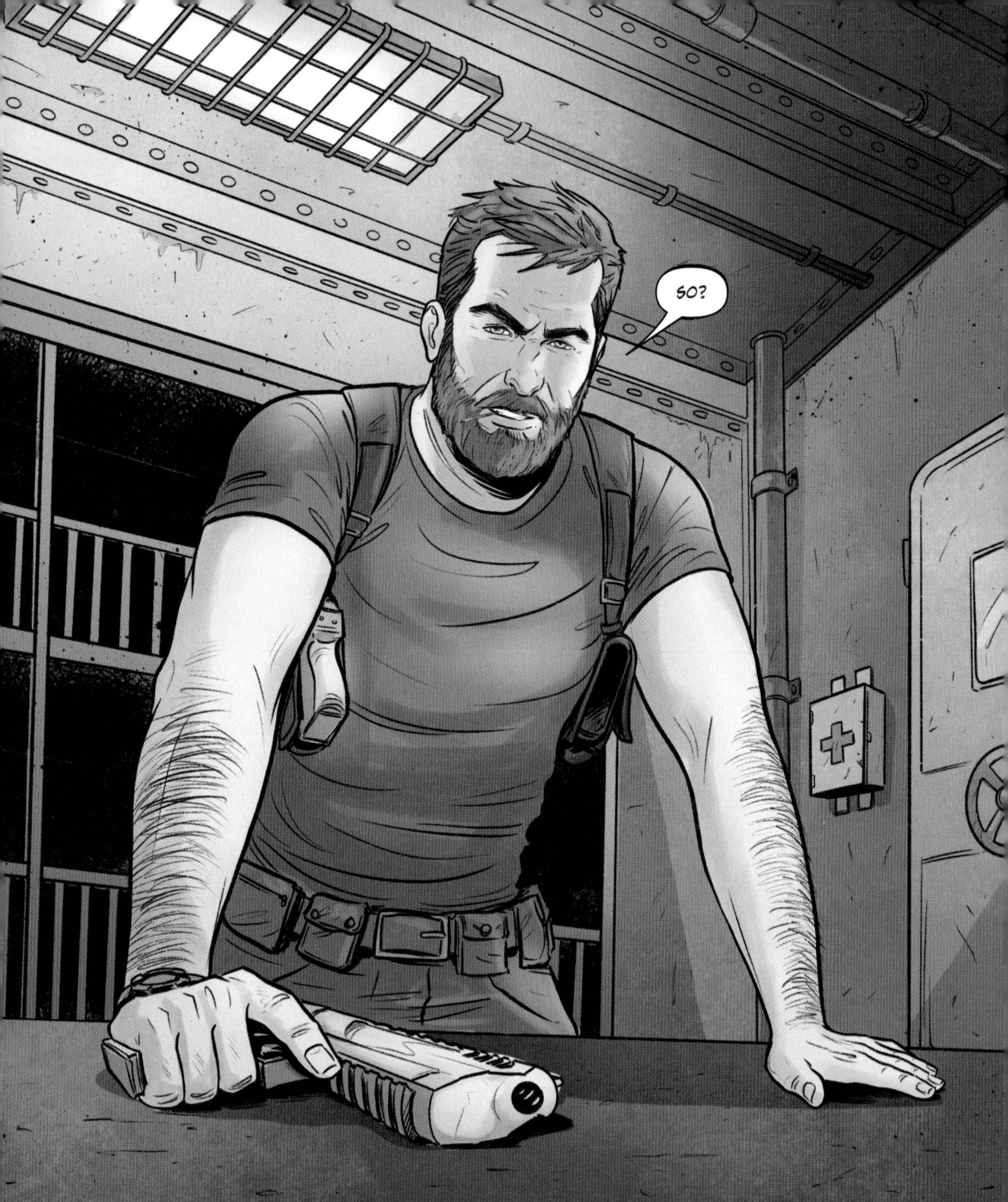
SO?

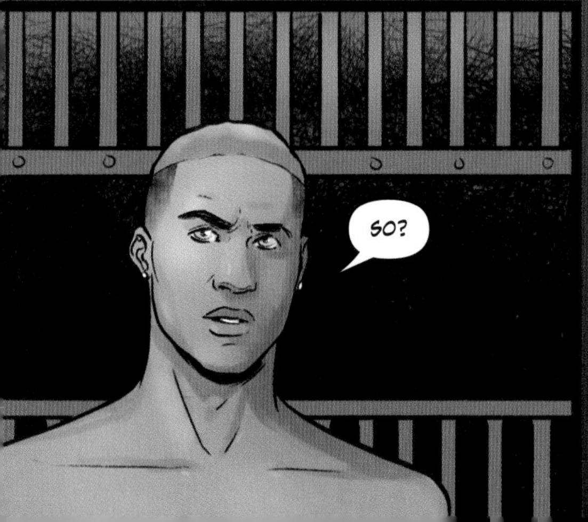
SO?

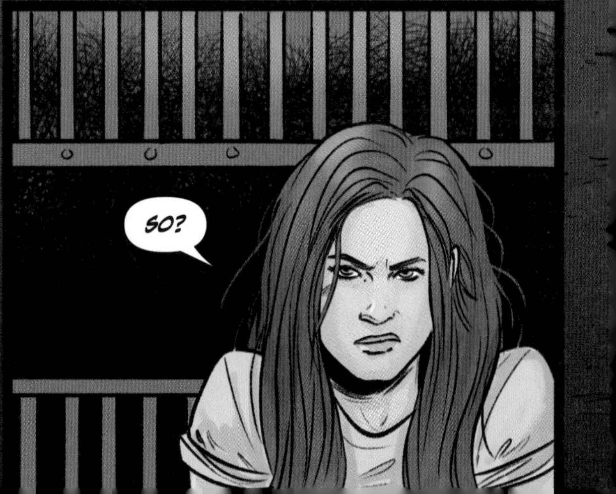
SO?

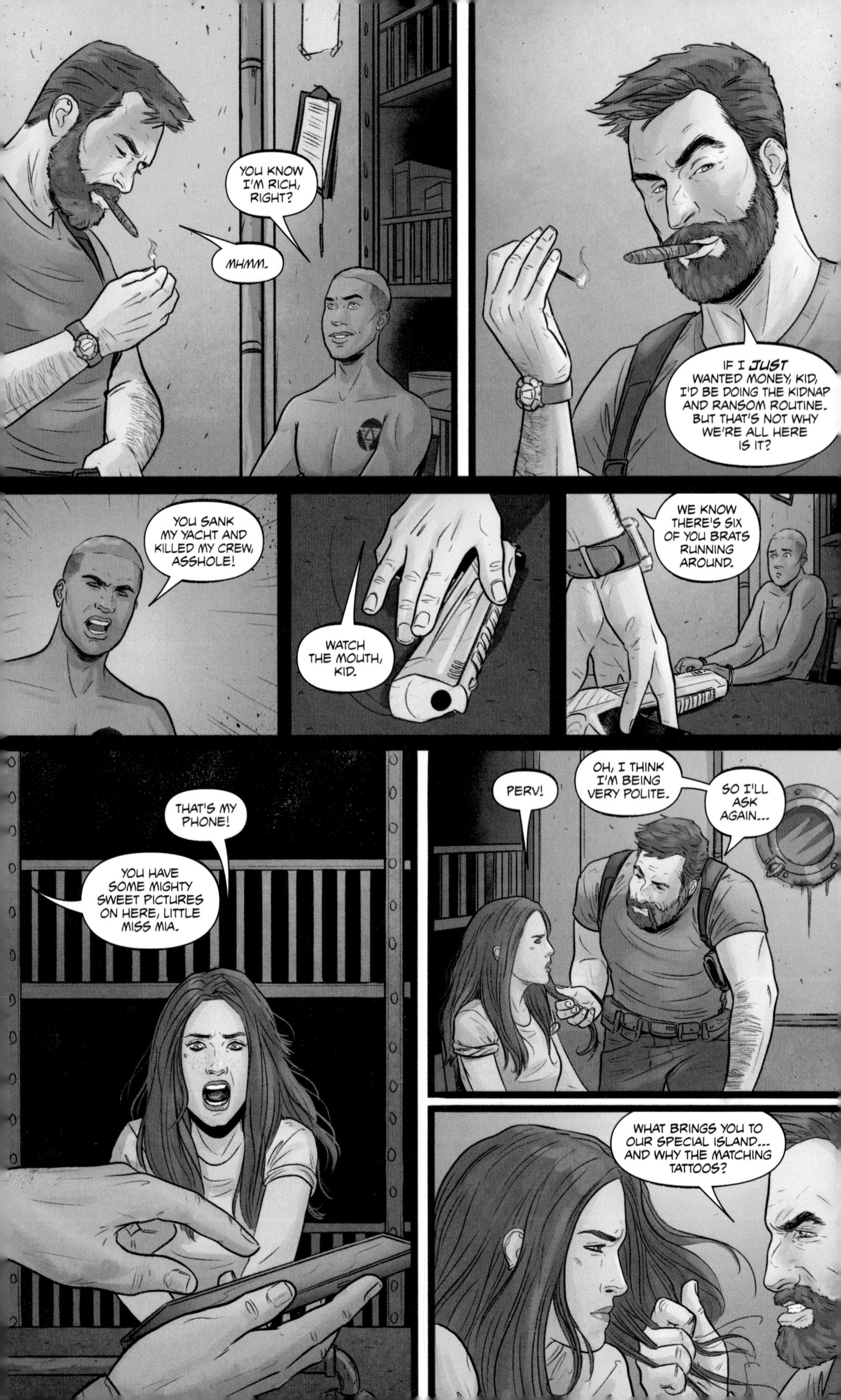
YOU KNOW I'M RICH, RIGHT?
MHMM.
IF I JUST WANTED MONEY, KID, I'D BE DOING THE KIDNAP AND RANSOM ROUTINE. BUT THAT'S NOT WHY WE'RE ALL HERE IS IT?
YOU SANK MY YACHT AND KILLED MY CREW, ASSHOLE!
WATCH THE MOUTH, KID.
WE KNOW THERE'S SIX OF YOU BRATS RUNNING AROUND.
THAT'S MY PHONE!
YOU HAVE SOME MIGHTY SWEET PICTURES ON HERE, LITTLE MISS MIA.
PERV!
OH, I THINK I'M BEING VERY POLITE.
SO I'LL ASK AGAIN...
WHAT BRINGS YOU TO OUR SPECIAL ISLAND... AND WHY THE MATCHING TATTOOS?

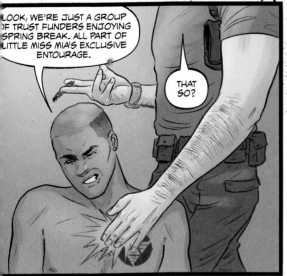

LOOK, WE'RE JUST A GROUP OF TRUST FUNDERS ENJOYING SPRING BREAK. ALL PART OF LITTLE MISS MIA'S EXCLUSIVE ENTOURAGE.

THAT SO?

AND THESE STUPID TATTOOS ARE A RESULT OF A DRUNKEN NIGHT TOGETHER.

YOU WISH...

WHICH BRINGS US BACK TO... SO?

SO TALK LIKE AN ADULT.

MAGICAL ISLANDS ARE FOR KIDS. IT'S NONSENSE AND YOU--

FUNNY, I NEVER SAID A WORD ABOUT MAGIC.

I FORGOT HOW MUCH I HATE AMERICANS...*AND* TEENAGERS.

SERENA IS NOT ON THE FREIGHTER. SHE LEFT A FEW HOURS AGO. ALONE.

GOOD, THAT BUYS US SOME MORE TIME.

CLEAT, YOU DON'T ACTUALLY BELIEVE THOSE KIDS?

CAN'T SAY I'M NOT... *CURIOUS.*

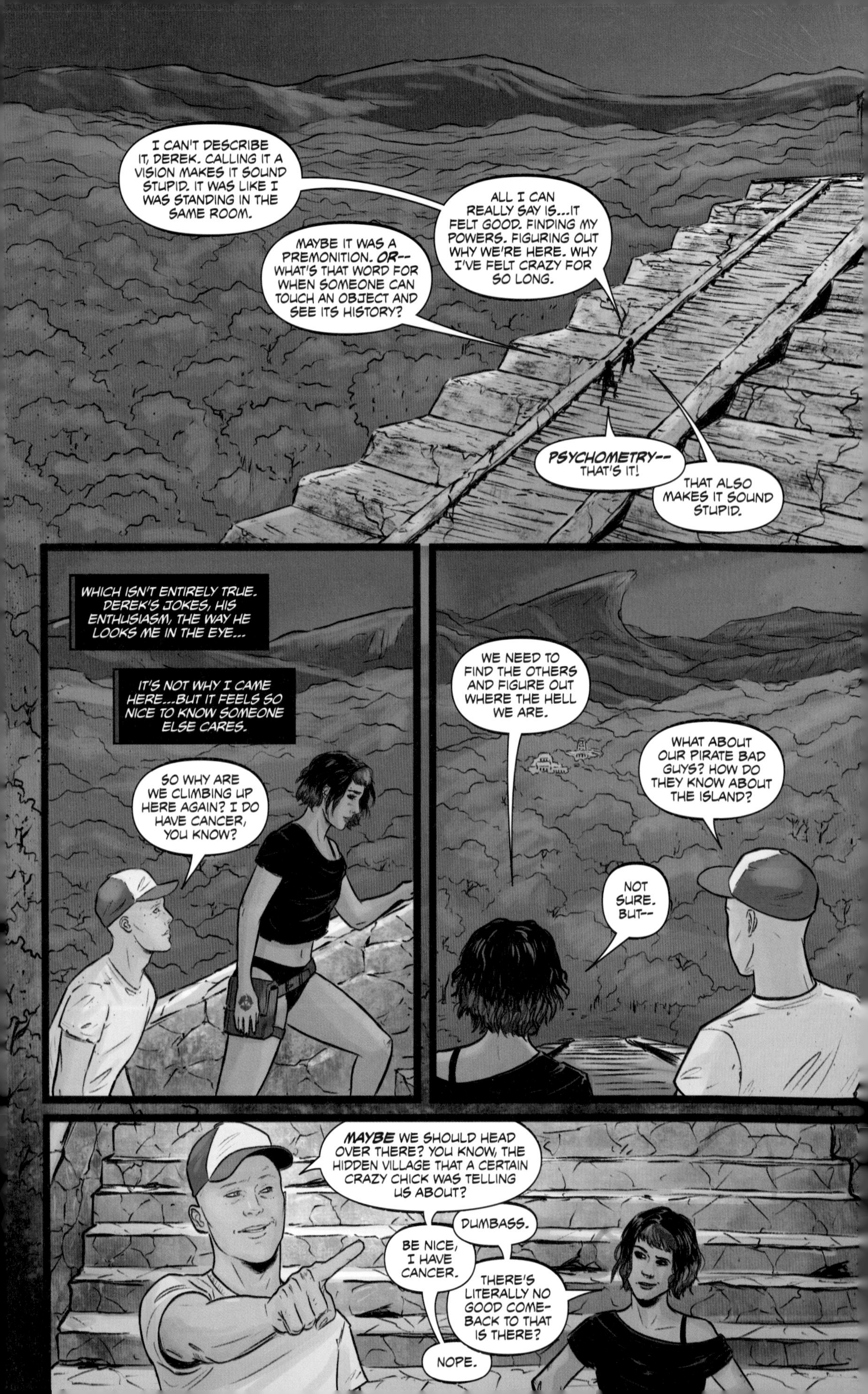
I CAN'T DESCRIBE IT, DEREK. CALLING IT A VISION MAKES IT SOUND STUPID. IT WAS LIKE I WAS STANDING IN THE SAME ROOM.
ALL I CAN REALLY SAY IS...IT FELT GOOD. FINDING MY POWERS. FIGURING OUT WHY WE'RE HERE. WHY I'VE FELT CRAZY FOR SO LONG.
MAYBE IT WAS A PREMONITION. *OR--* WHAT'S THAT WORD FOR WHEN SOMEONE CAN TOUCH AN OBJECT AND SEE ITS HISTORY?
PSYCHOMETRY-- THAT'S IT!
THAT ALSO MAKES IT SOUND STUPID.
WHICH ISN'T ENTIRELY TRUE. DEREK'S JOKES, HIS ENTHUSIASM, THE WAY HE LOOKS ME IN THE EYE...
IT'S NOT WHY I CAME HERE...BUT IT FEELS SO NICE TO KNOW SOMEONE ELSE CARES.
SO WHY ARE WE CLIMBING UP HERE AGAIN? I DO HAVE CANCER, YOU KNOW?
WE NEED TO FIND THE OTHERS AND FIGURE OUT WHERE THE HELL WE ARE.
WHAT ABOUT OUR PIRATE BAD GUYS? HOW DO THEY KNOW ABOUT THE ISLAND?
NOT SURE. BUT--
MAYBE WE SHOULD HEAD OVER THERE? YOU KNOW, THE HIDDEN VILLAGE THAT A CERTAIN CRAZY CHICK WAS TELLING US ABOUT?
DUMBASS.
BE NICE, I HAVE CANCER.
THERE'S LITERALLY NO GOOD COME-BACK TO THAT IS THERE?
NOPE.

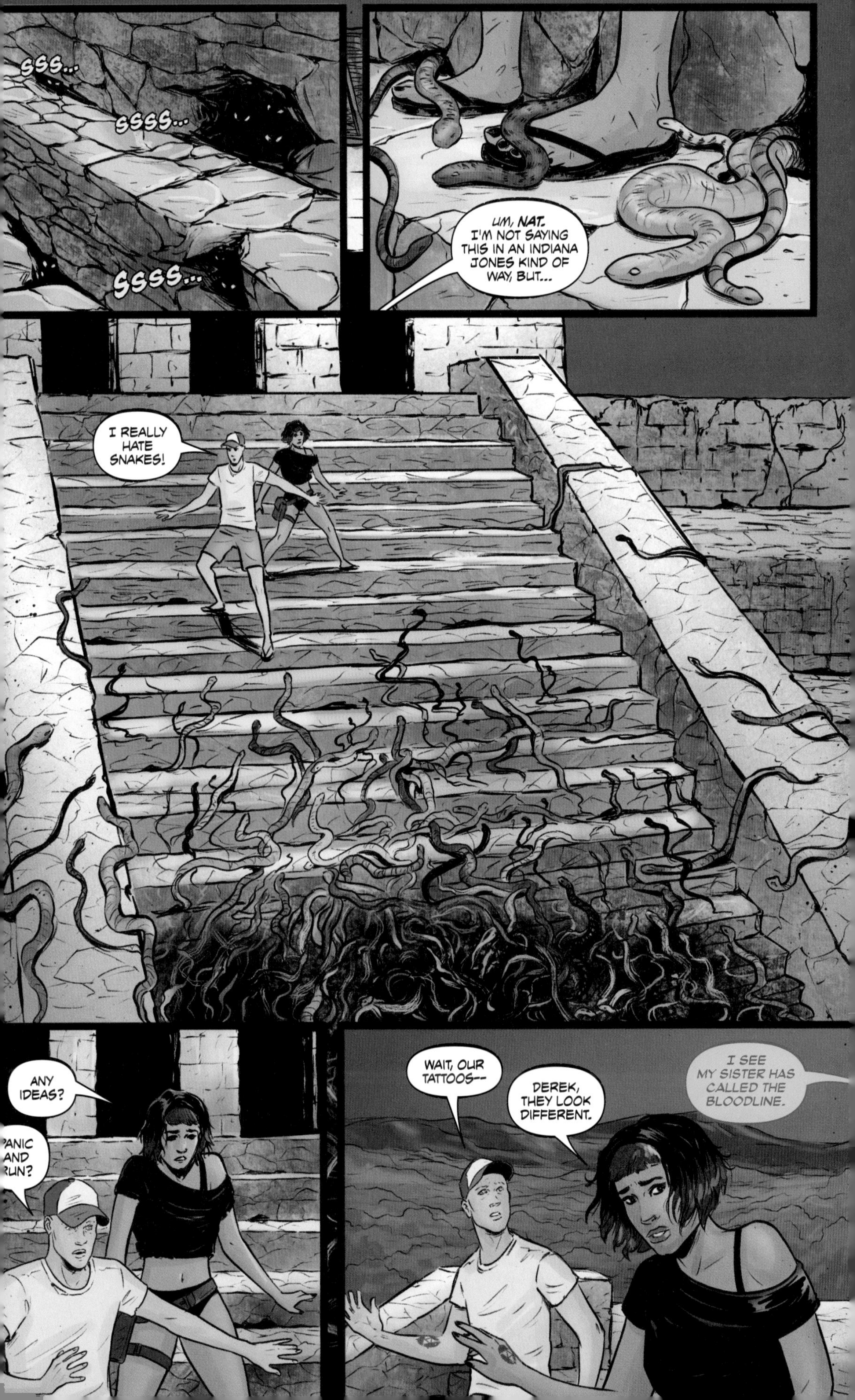
SSS...
SSSS...
SSSS...
UM, NAT. I'M NOT SAYING THIS IN AN INDIANA JONES KIND OF WAY, BUT...
I REALLY HATE SNAKES!
ANY IDEAS?
PANIC AND RUN?
WAIT, OUR TATTOOS--
DEREK, THEY LOOK DIFFERENT.
I SEE MY SISTER HAS CALLED THE BLOODLINE.

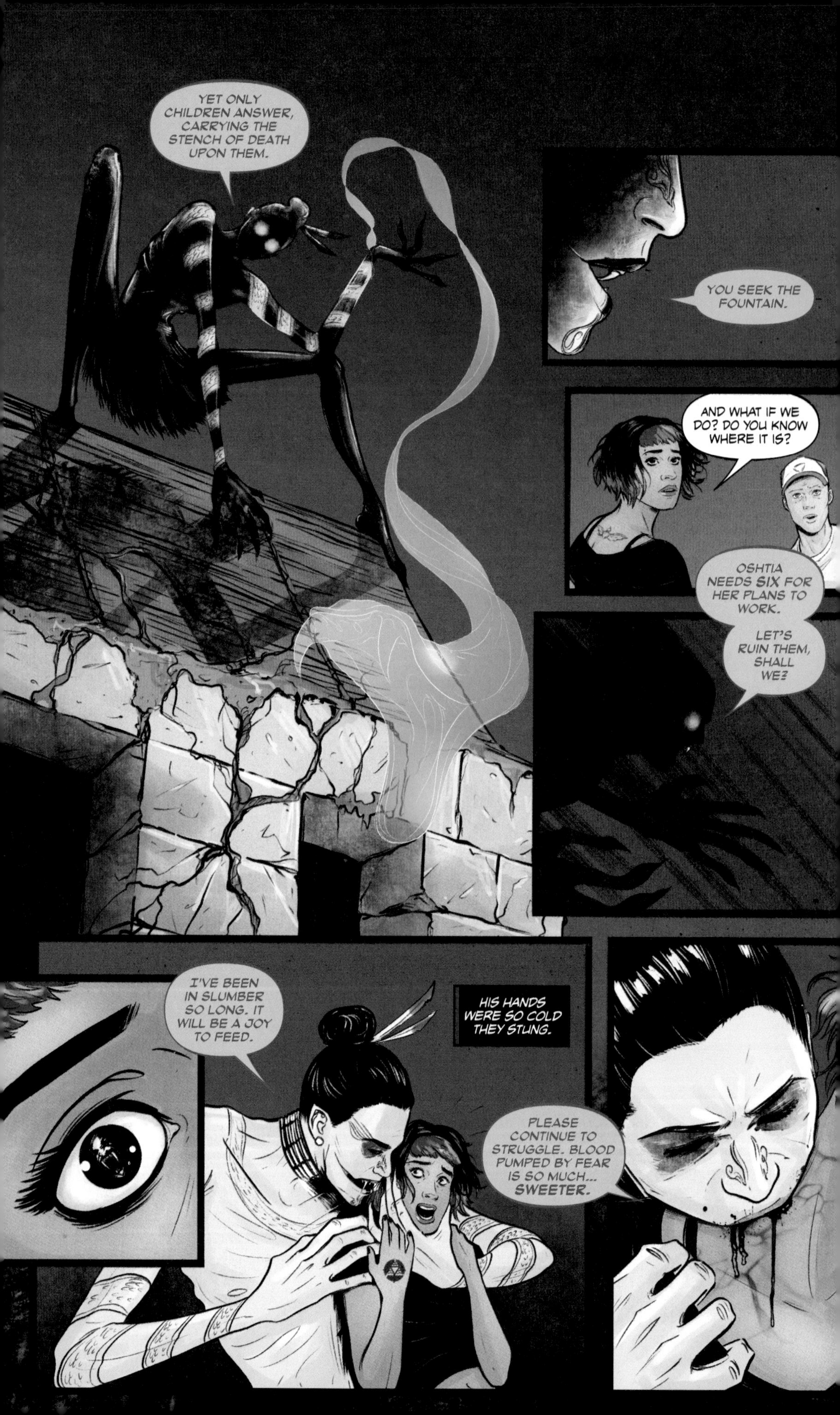
YET ONLY CHILDREN ANSWER, CARRYING THE STENCH OF DEATH UPON THEM.
YOU SEEK THE FOUNTAIN.
AND WHAT IF WE DO? DO YOU KNOW WHERE IT IS?
OSHTIA NEEDS SIX FOR HER PLANS TO WORK.
LET'S RUIN THEM, SHALL WE?
I'VE BEEN IN SLUMBER SO LONG. IT WILL BE A JOY TO FEED.
HIS HANDS WERE SO COLD THEY STUNG.
PLEASE CONTINUE TO STRUGGLE. BLOOD PUMPED BY FEAR IS SO MUCH... SWEETER.

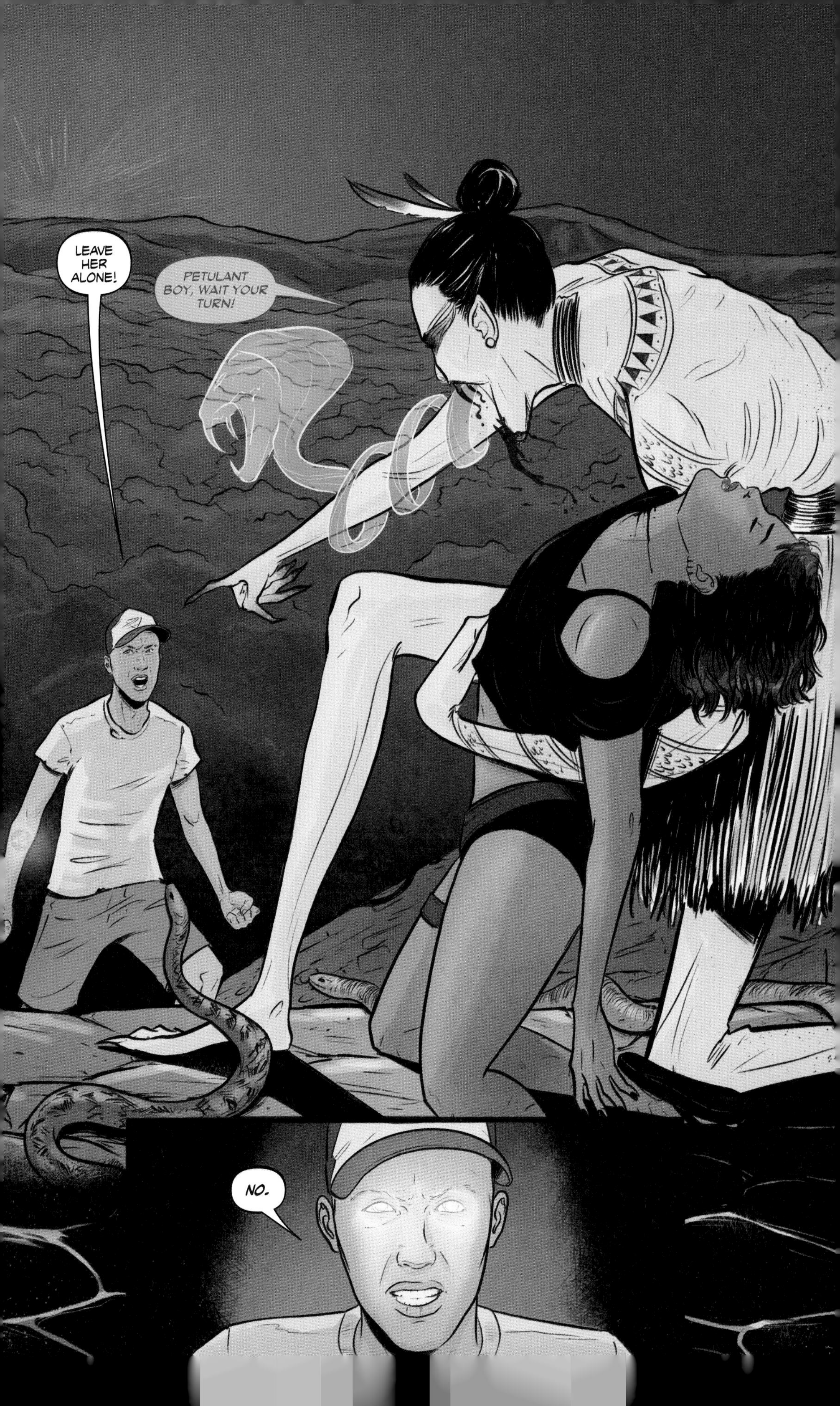
LEAVE HER ALONE!
PETULANT BOY, WAIT YOUR TURN!
NO.

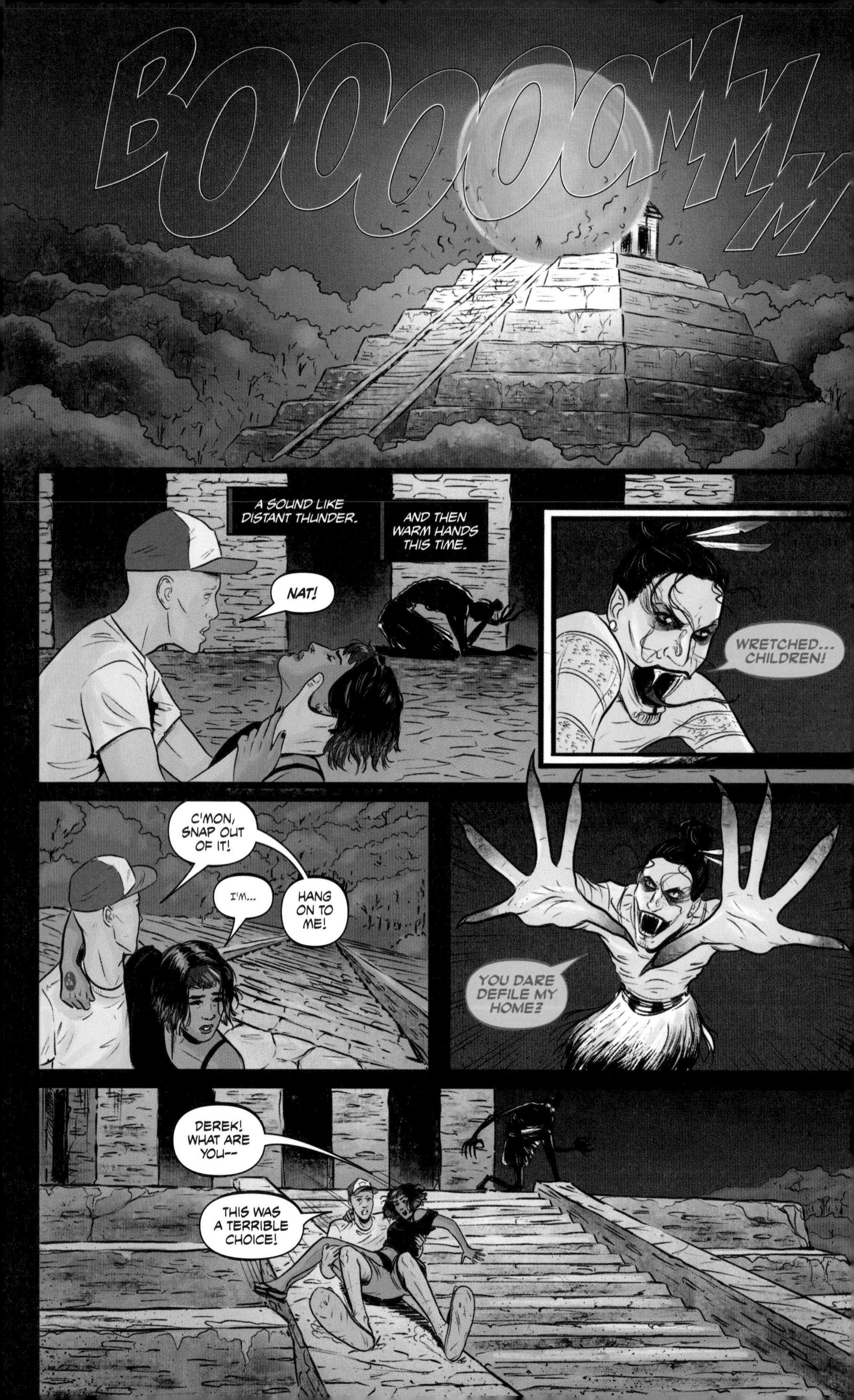
BOOOOOMMM
A SOUND LIKE DISTANT THUNDER.
AND THEN WARM HANDS THIS TIME.
NAT!
WRETCHED... CHILDREN!
C'MON, SNAP OUT OF IT!
I'M...
HANG ON TO ME!
YOU DARE DEFILE MY HOME?
DEREK! WHAT ARE YOU--
THIS WAS A TERRIBLE CHOICE!

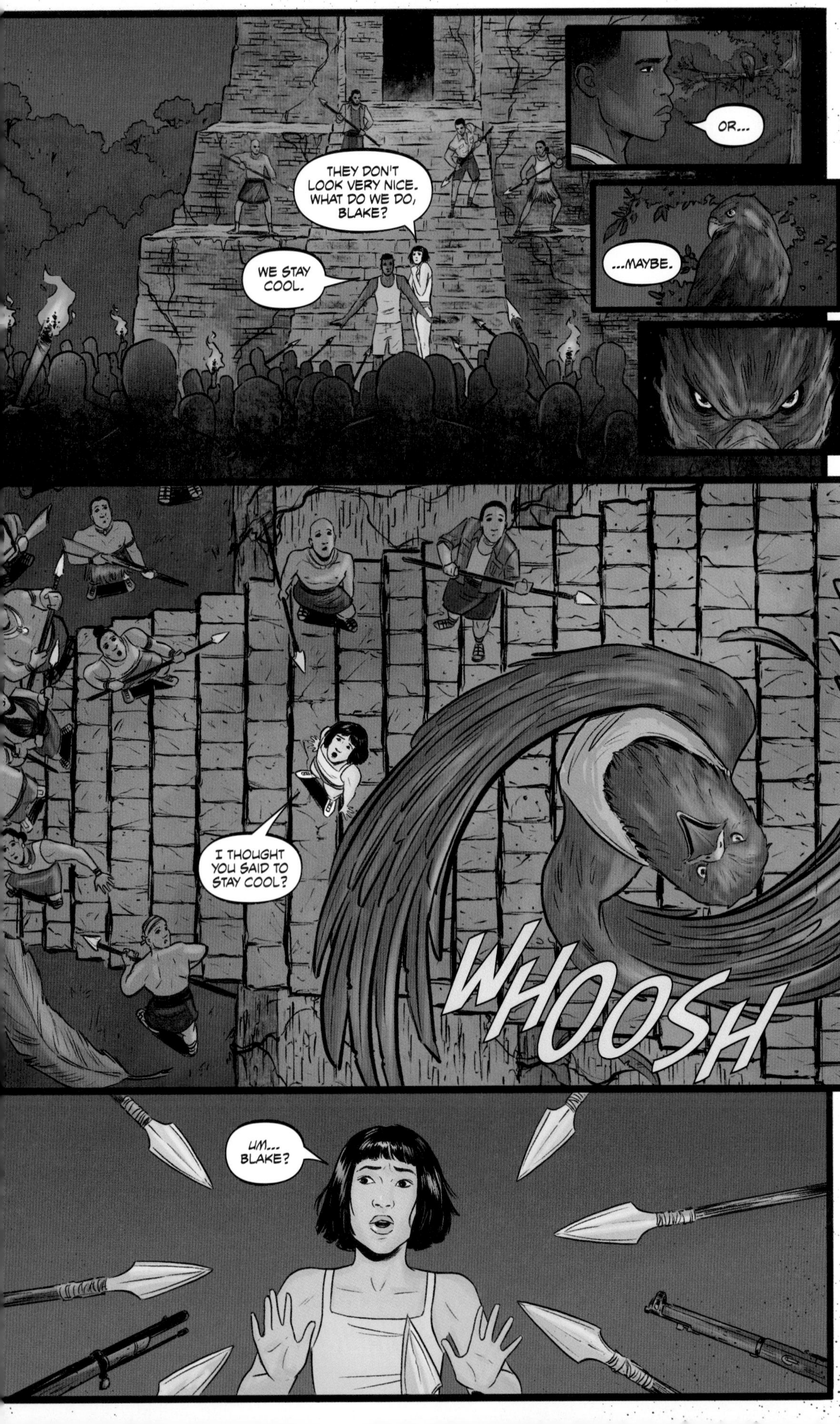
THEY DON'T LOOK VERY NICE. WHAT DO WE DO, BLAKE?
WE STAY COOL.
OR...
...MAYBE.
I THOUGHT YOU SAID TO STAY COOL?
WHOOSH
UM... BLAKE?

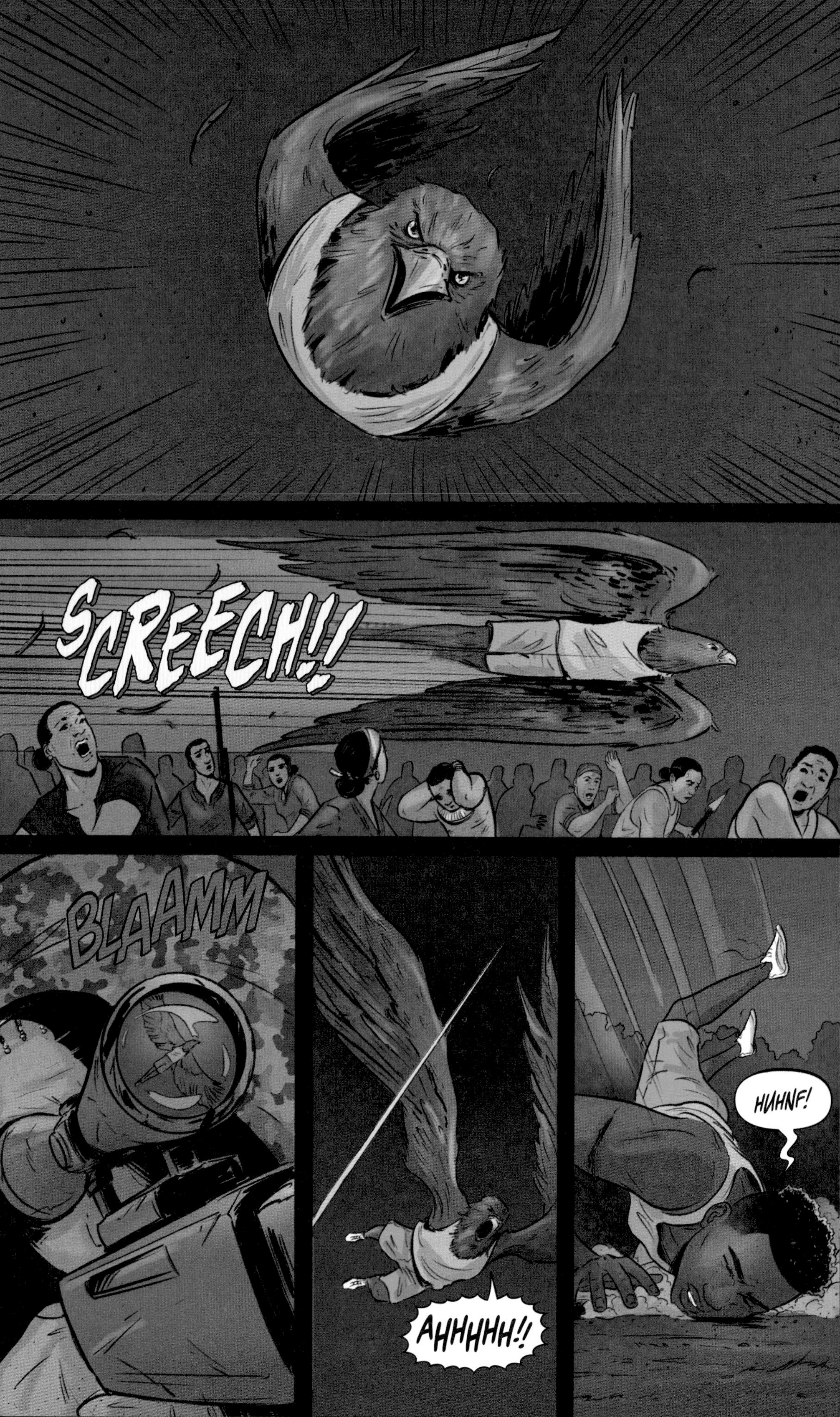
SCREECH!!
BLAAMM
AHHHHH!!
HUHNF!

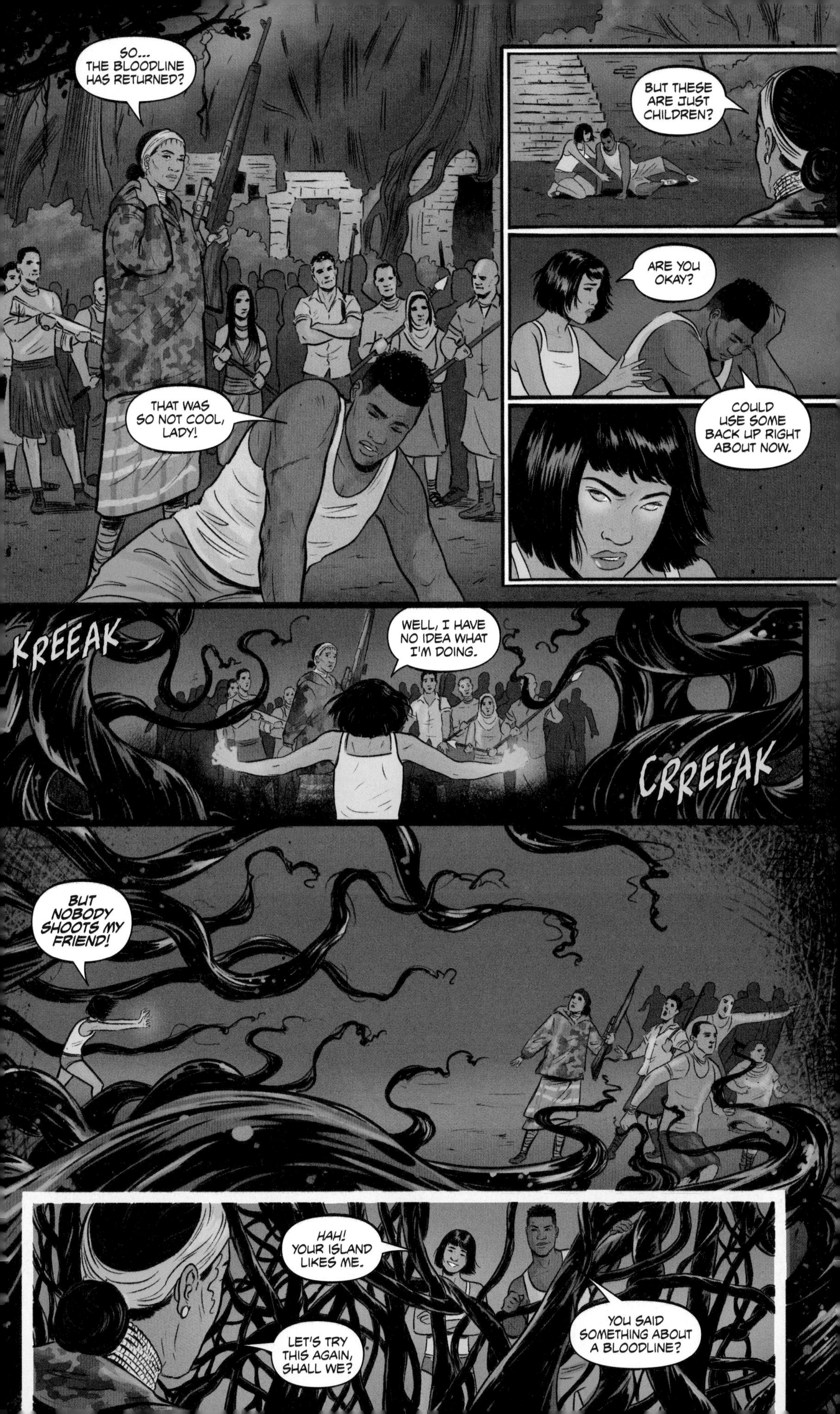
SO... THE BLOODLINE HAS RETURNED?
THAT WAS SO NOT COOL, LADY!
BUT THESE ARE JUST CHILDREN?
ARE YOU OKAY?
COULD USE SOME BACK UP RIGHT ABOUT NOW.
KREEAK
WELL, I HAVE NO IDEA WHAT I'M DOING.
CRREEAK
BUT NOBODY SHOOTS MY FRIEND!
HAH! YOUR ISLAND LIKES ME.
LET'S TRY THIS AGAIN, SHALL WE?
YOU SAID SOMETHING ABOUT A BLOODLINE?

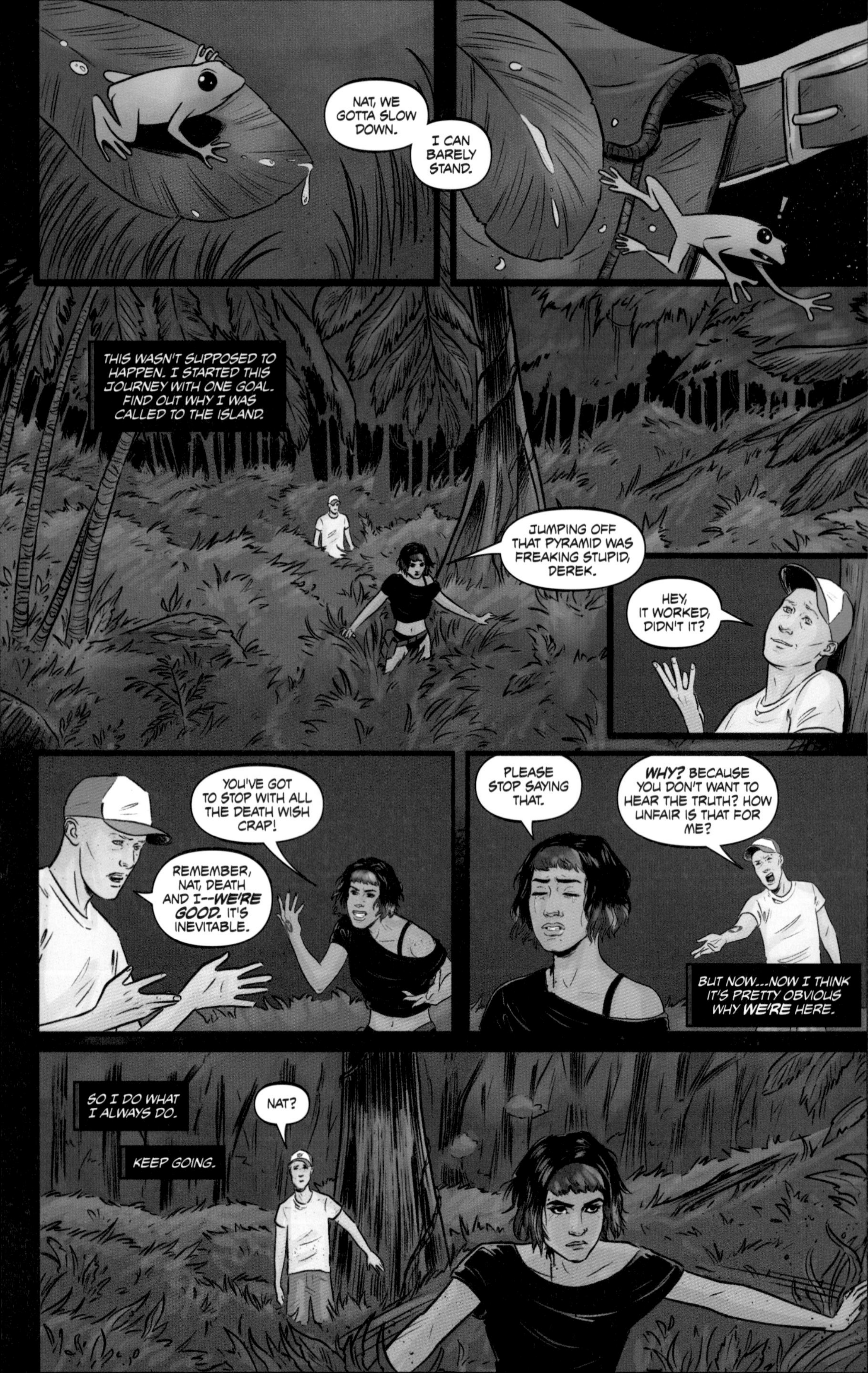
NAT, WE GOTTA SLOW DOWN.
I CAN BARELY STAND.
!
THIS WASN'T SUPPOSED TO HAPPEN. I STARTED THIS JOURNEY WITH ONE GOAL. FIND OUT WHY I WAS CALLED TO THE ISLAND.
JUMPING OFF THAT PYRAMID WAS FREAKING STUPID, DEREK.
HEY, IT WORKED, DIDN'T IT?
YOU'VE GOT TO STOP WITH ALL THE DEATH WISH CRAP!
REMEMBER, NAT, DEATH AND I--WE'RE GOOD. IT'S INEVITABLE.
PLEASE STOP SAYING THAT.
WHY? BECAUSE YOU DON'T WANT TO HEAR THE TRUTH? HOW UNFAIR IS THAT FOR ME?
BUT NOW...NOW I THINK IT'S PRETTY OBVIOUS WHY WE'RE HERE.
SO I DO WHAT I ALWAYS DO.
NAT?
KEEP GOING.

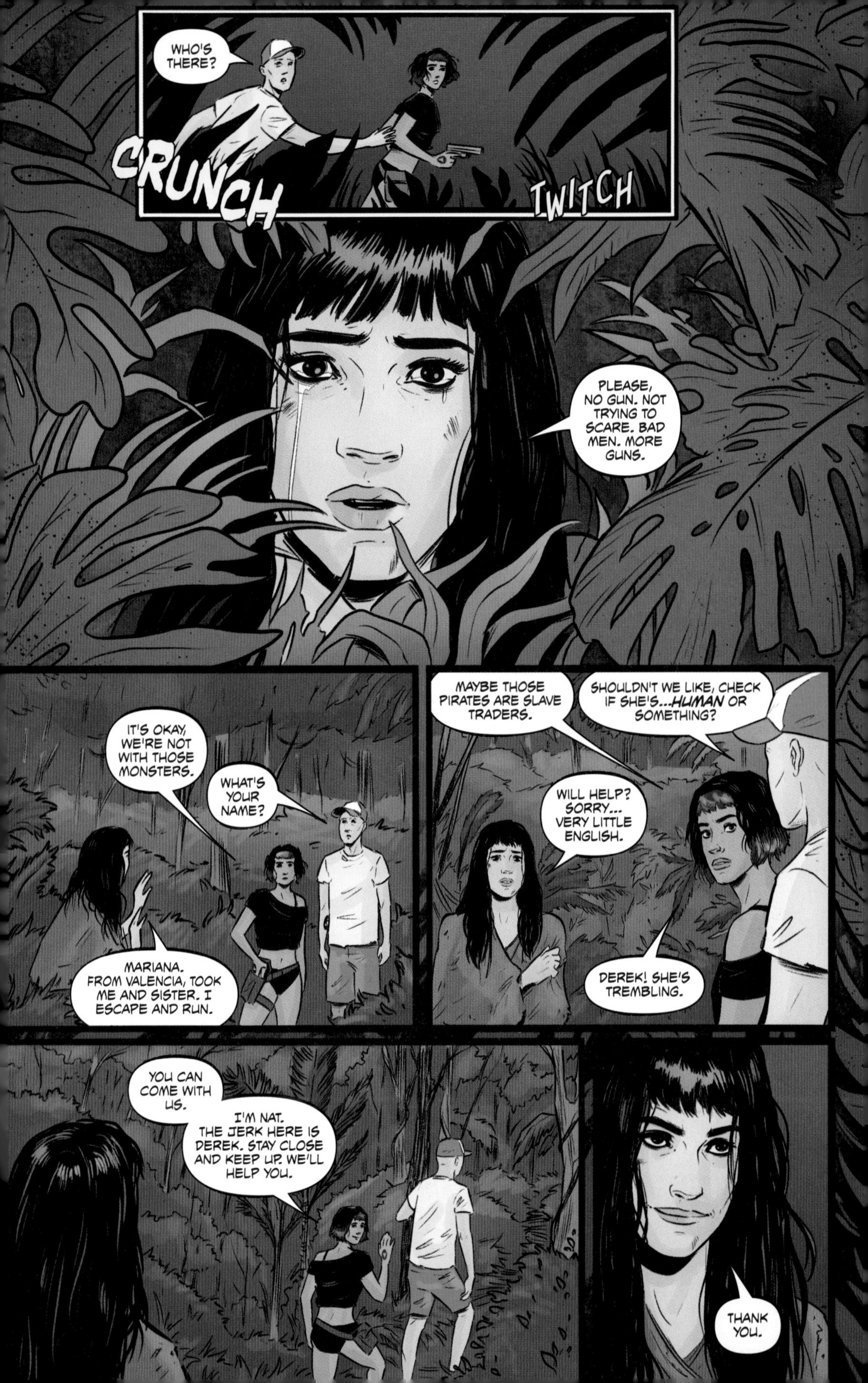
WHO'S THERE?
CRUNCH
TWITCH
PLEASE, NO GUN. NOT TRYING TO SCARE. BAD MEN. MORE GUNS.
IT'S OKAY, WE'RE NOT WITH THOSE MONSTERS.
WHAT'S YOUR NAME?
MARIANA. FROM VALENCIA, TOOK ME AND SISTER. I ESCAPE AND RUN.
MAYBE THOSE PIRATES ARE SLAVE TRADERS.
SHOULDN'T WE LIKE, CHECK IF SHE'S...*HUMAN* OR SOMETHING?
WILL HELP? SORRY... VERY LITTLE ENGLISH.
DEREK! SHE'S TREMBLING.
YOU CAN COME WITH US.
I'M NAT. THE JERK HERE IS DEREK. STAY CLOSE AND KEEP UP. WE'LL HELP YOU.
THANK YOU.

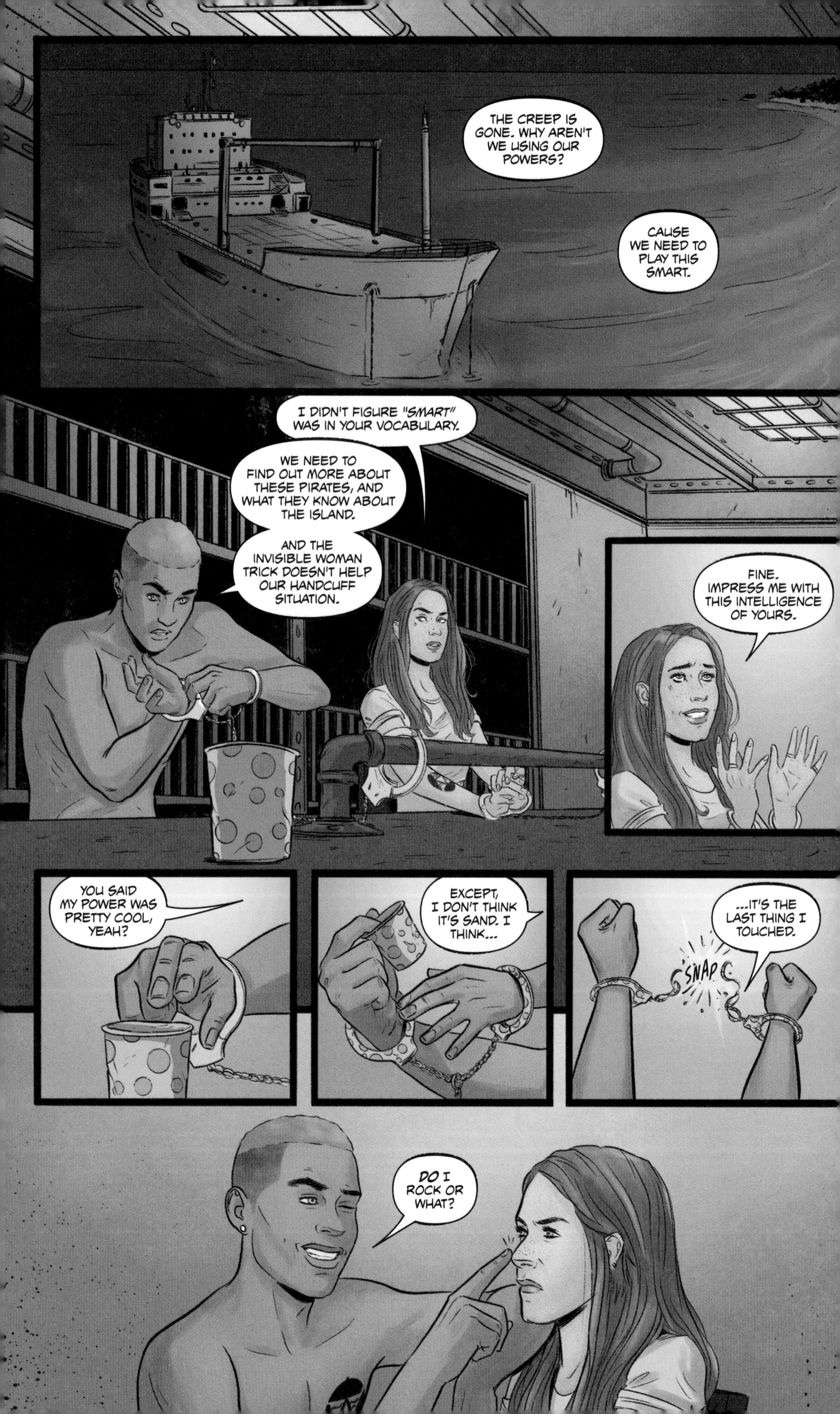

THE CREEP IS GONE. WHY AREN'T WE USING OUR POWERS?
CAUSE WE NEED TO PLAY THIS SMART.
I DIDN'T FIGURE "SMART" WAS IN YOUR VOCABULARY.
WE NEED TO FIND OUT MORE ABOUT THESE PIRATES, AND WHAT THEY KNOW ABOUT THE ISLAND.
AND THE INVISIBLE WOMAN TRICK DOESN'T HELP OUR HANDCUFF SITUATION.
FINE. IMPRESS ME WITH THIS INTELLIGENCE OF YOURS.
YOU SAID MY POWER WAS PRETTY COOL, YEAH?
EXCEPT, I DON'T THINK IT'S SAND. I THINK...
...IT'S THE LAST THING I TOUCHED.
SNAP
DO I ROCK OR WHAT?

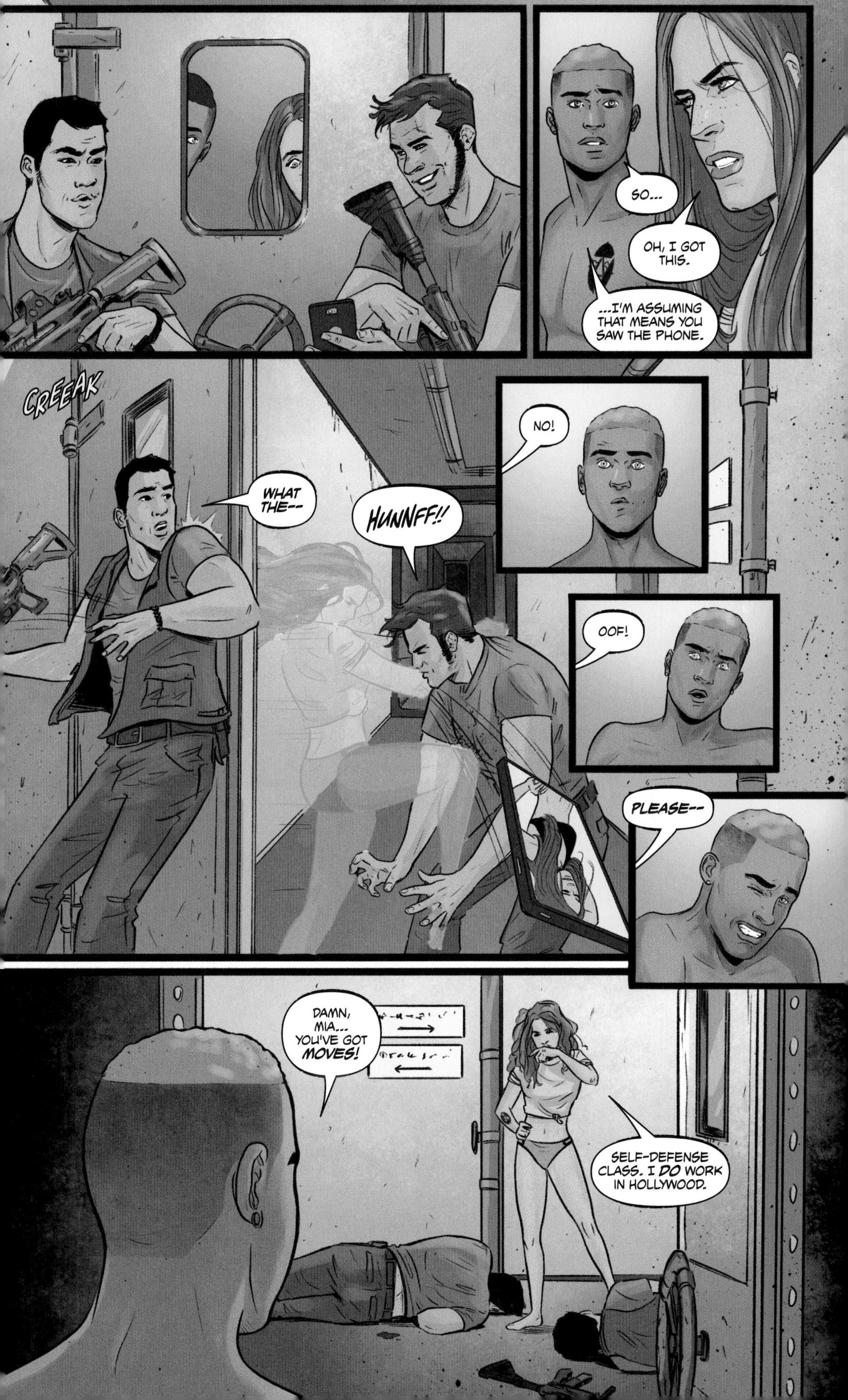
SO...
OH, I GOT THIS.
...I'M ASSUMING THAT MEANS YOU SAW THE PHONE.
CREEAK
WHAT THE--
HUNNFF!!
NO!
OOF!
PLEASE--
DAMN, MIA... YOU'VE GOT MOVES!
SELF-DEFENSE CLASS. I DO WORK IN HOLLYWOOD.

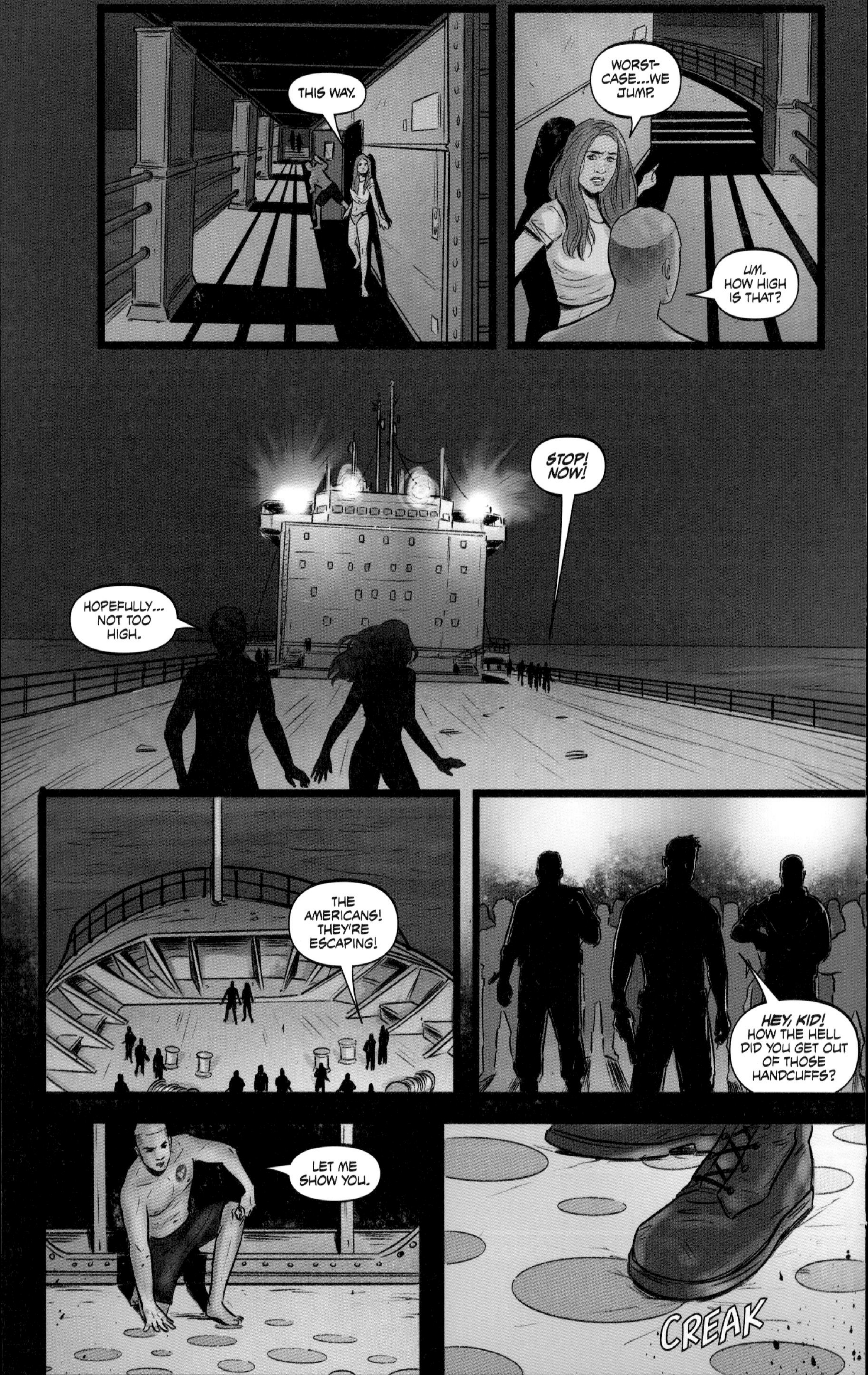
THIS WAY.
WORST-CASE...WE JUMP.
UM. HOW HIGH IS THAT?
STOP! NOW!
HOPEFULLY... NOT TOO HIGH.
THE AMERICANS! THEY'RE ESCAPING!
HEY, KID! HOW THE HELL DID YOU GET OUT OF THOSE HANDCUFFS?
LET ME SHOW YOU.
CREAK

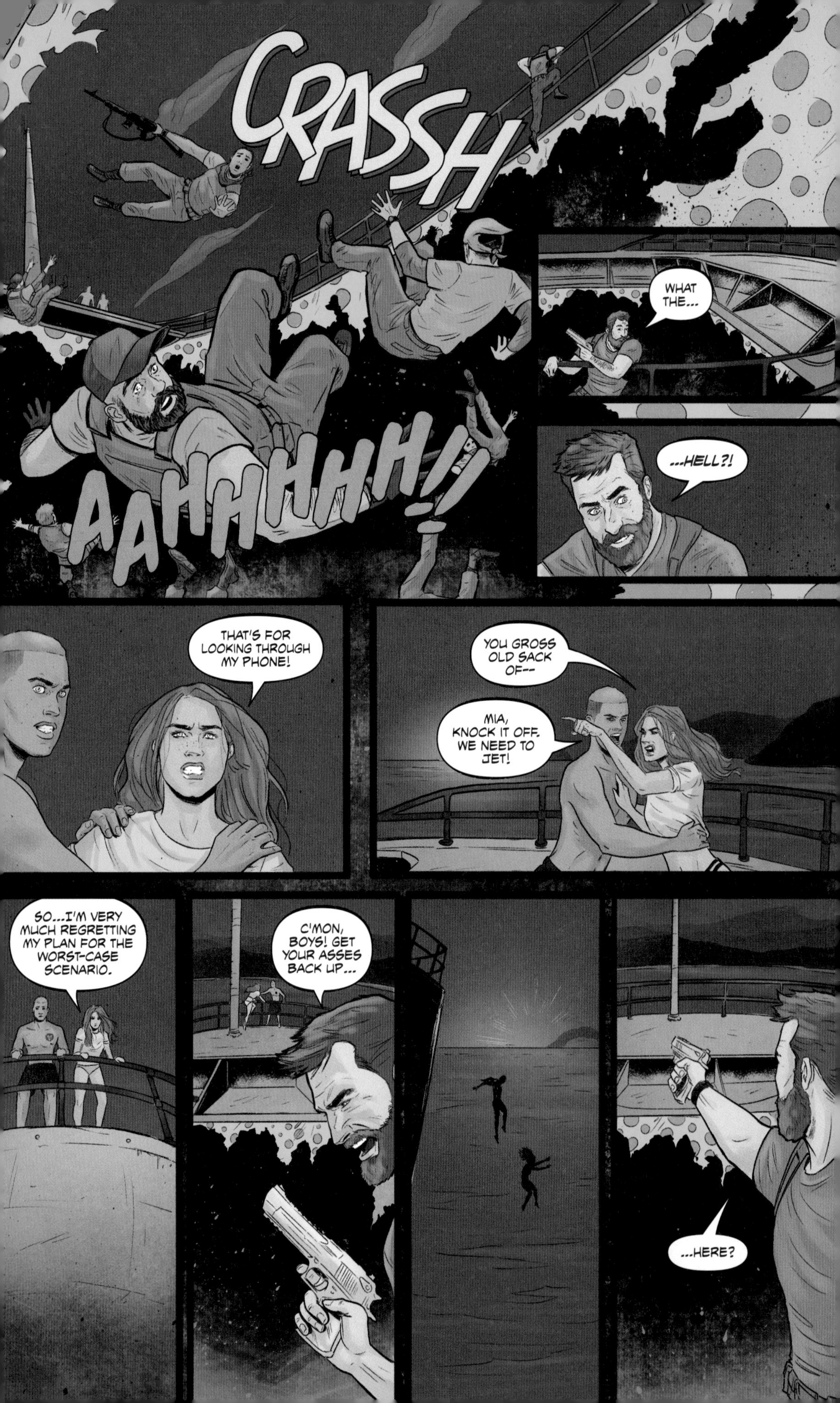
CRASSH
AAHHHHH!!
WHAT THE...
...HELL?!
THAT'S FOR LOOKING THROUGH MY PHONE!
YOU GROSS OLD SACK OF--
MIA, KNOCK IT OFF. WE NEED TO JET!
SO...I'M VERY MUCH REGRETTING MY PLAN FOR THE WORST-CASE SCENARIO.
C'MON, BOYS! GET YOUR ASSES BACK UP...
...HERE?

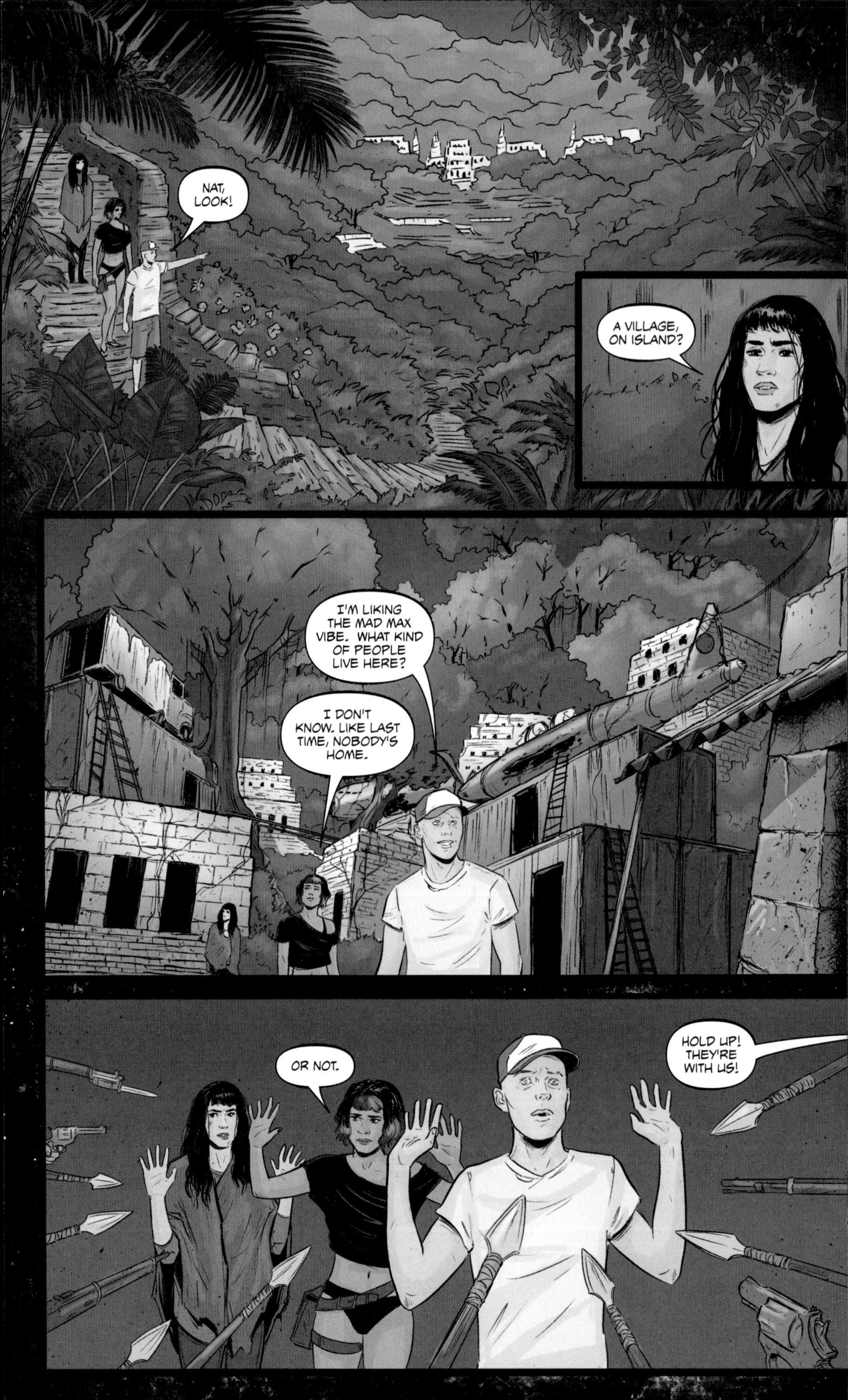
NAT, LOOK!
A VILLAGE, ON ISLAND?
I'M LIKING THE MAD MAX VIBE. WHAT KIND OF PEOPLE LIVE HERE?
I DON'T KNOW. LIKE LAST TIME, NOBODY'S HOME.
OR NOT.
HOLD UP! THEY'RE WITH US!

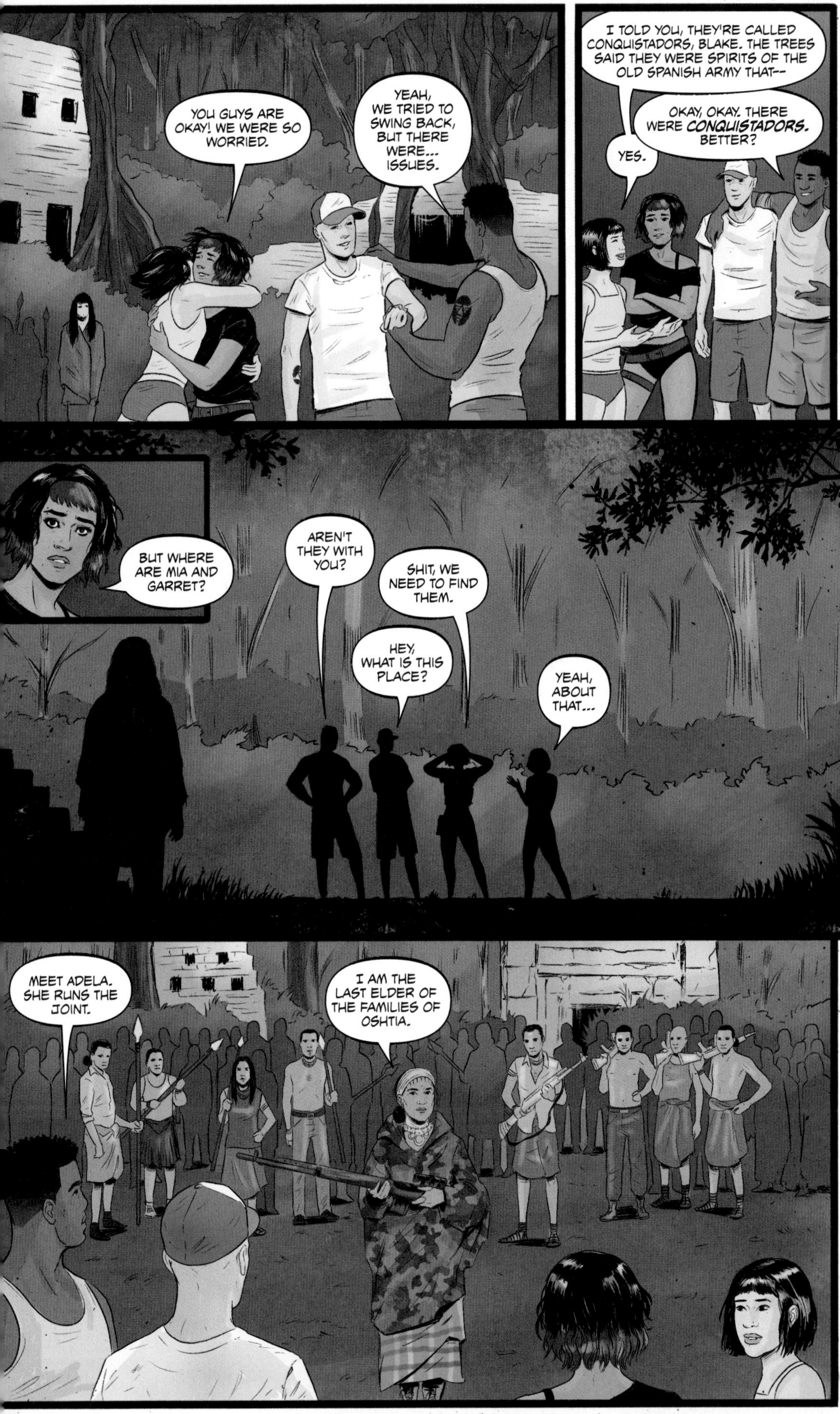
YOU GUYS ARE OKAY! WE WERE SO WORRIED.
YEAH, WE TRIED TO SWING BACK, BUT THERE WERE... ISSUES.
I TOLD YOU, THEY'RE CALLED CONQUISTADORS, BLAKE. THE TREES SAID THEY WERE SPIRITS OF THE OLD SPANISH ARMY THAT--
OKAY, OKAY. THERE WERE CONQUISTADORS. BETTER?
YES.
BUT WHERE ARE MIA AND GARRET?
AREN'T THEY WITH YOU?
SHIT, WE NEED TO FIND THEM.
HEY, WHAT IS THIS PLACE?
YEAH, ABOUT THAT...
MEET ADELA. SHE RUNS THE JOINT.
I AM THE LAST ELDER OF THE FAMILIES OF OSHTIA.

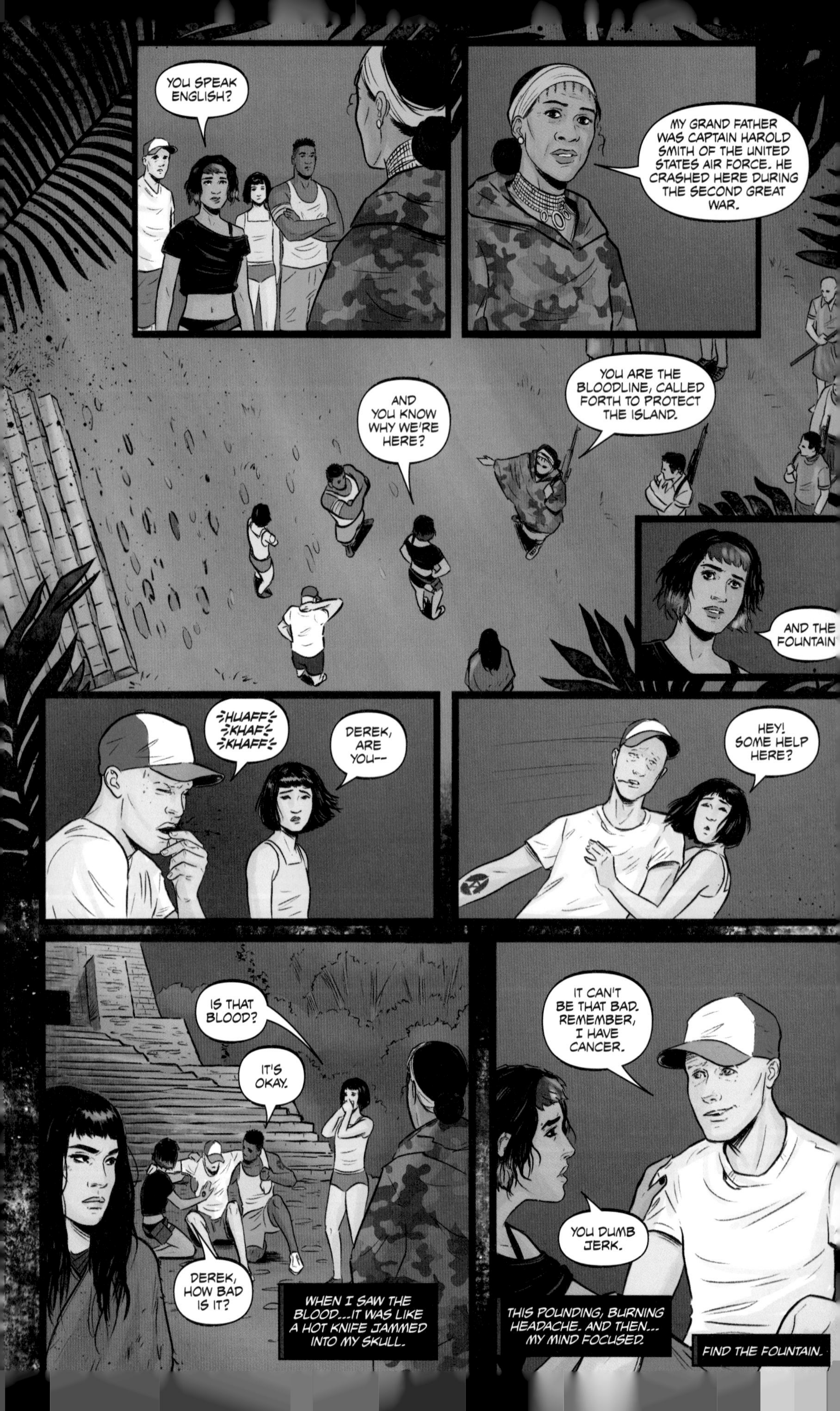
YOU SPEAK ENGLISH?
MY GRAND FATHER WAS CAPTAIN HAROLD SMITH OF THE UNITED STATES AIR FORCE. HE CRASHED HERE DURING THE SECOND GREAT WAR.
AND YOU KNOW WHY WE'RE HERE?
YOU ARE THE BLOODLINE, CALLED FORTH TO PROTECT THE ISLAND.
AND THE FOUNTAIN
HUAFF KHAF KHAFF
DEREK, ARE YOU--
HEY! SOME HELP HERE?
IS THAT BLOOD?
IT'S OKAY.
DEREK, HOW BAD IS IT?
WHEN I SAW THE BLOOD...IT WAS LIKE A HOT KNIFE JAMMED INTO MY SKULL.
IT CAN'T BE THAT BAD. REMEMBER, I HAVE CANCER.
YOU DUMB JERK.
THIS POUNDING, BURNING HEADACHE. AND THEN... MY MIND FOCUSED.
FIND THE FOUNTAIN.

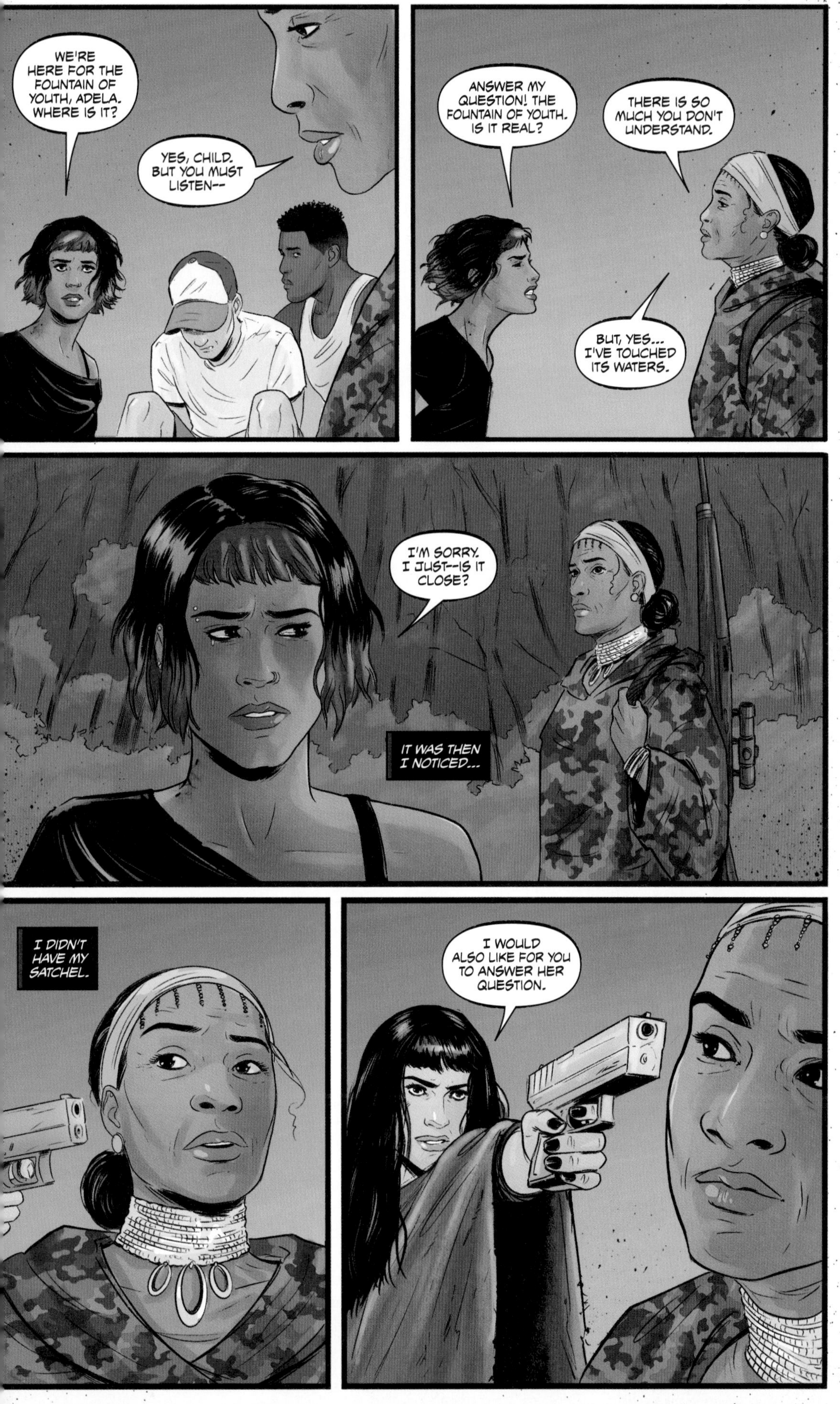
WE'RE HERE FOR THE FOUNTAIN OF YOUTH, ADELA. WHERE IS IT?
YES, CHILD. BUT YOU MUST LISTEN--
ANSWER MY QUESTION! THE FOUNTAIN OF YOUTH. IS IT REAL?
THERE IS SO MUCH YOU DON'T UNDERSTAND.
BUT, YES... I'VE TOUCHED ITS WATERS.
I'M SORRY. I JUST--IS IT CLOSE?
IT WAS THEN I NOTICED...
I DIDN'T HAVE MY SATCHEL.
I WOULD ALSO LIKE FOR YOU TO ANSWER HER QUESTION.

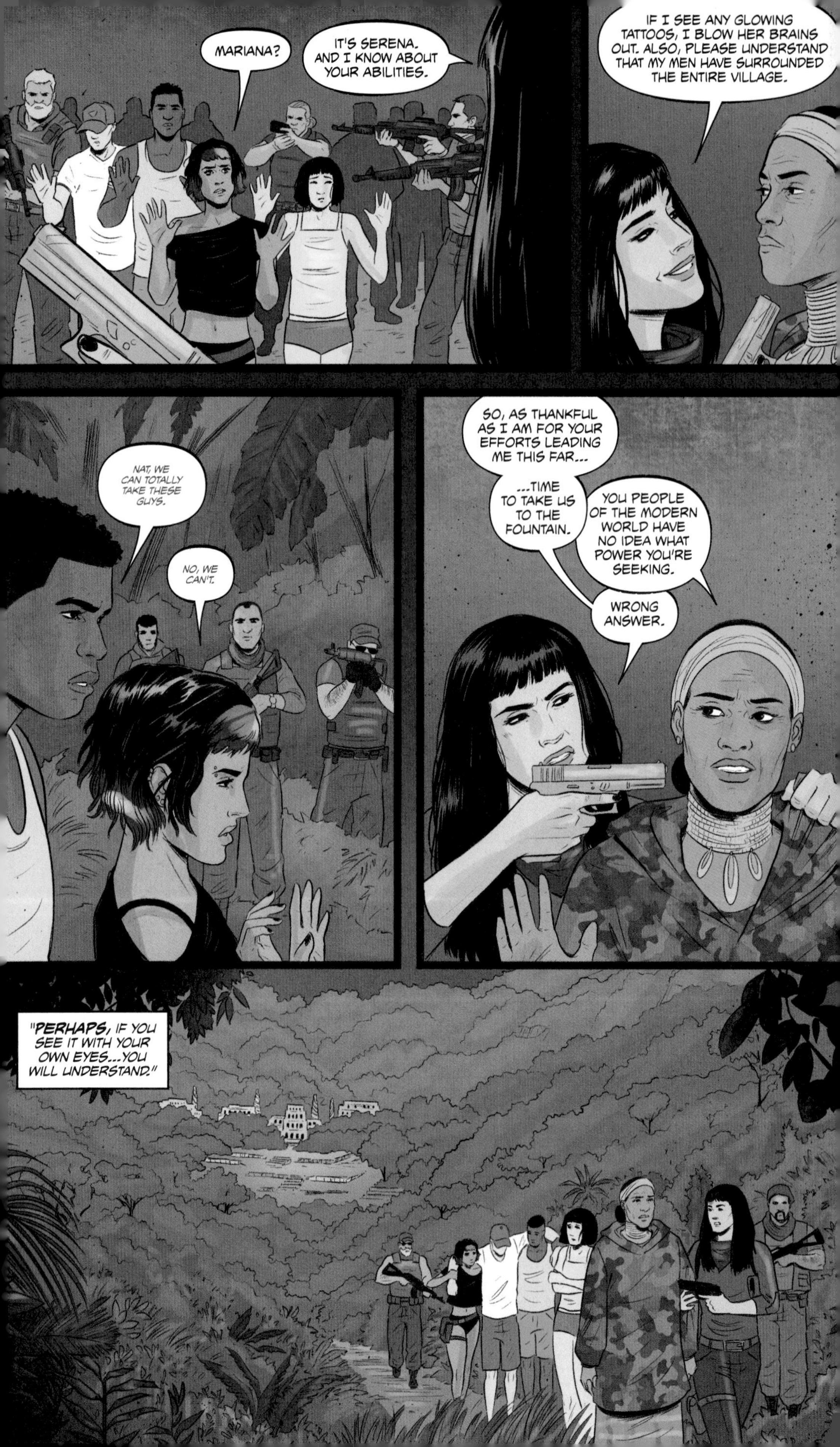
MARIANA?
IT'S SERENA. AND I KNOW ABOUT YOUR ABILITIES.
IF I SEE ANY GLOWING TATTOOS, I BLOW HER BRAINS OUT. ALSO, PLEASE UNDERSTAND THAT MY MEN HAVE SURROUNDED THE ENTIRE VILLAGE.
NAT, WE CAN TOTALLY TAKE THESE GUYS.
NO, WE CAN'T.
SO, AS THANKFUL AS I AM FOR YOUR EFFORTS LEADING ME THIS FAR...
...TIME TO TAKE US TO THE FOUNTAIN.
YOU PEOPLE OF THE MODERN WORLD HAVE NO IDEA WHAT POWER YOU'RE SEEKING.
WRONG ANSWER.
"PERHAPS, IF YOU SEE IT WITH YOUR OWN EYES...YOU WILL UNDERSTAND."

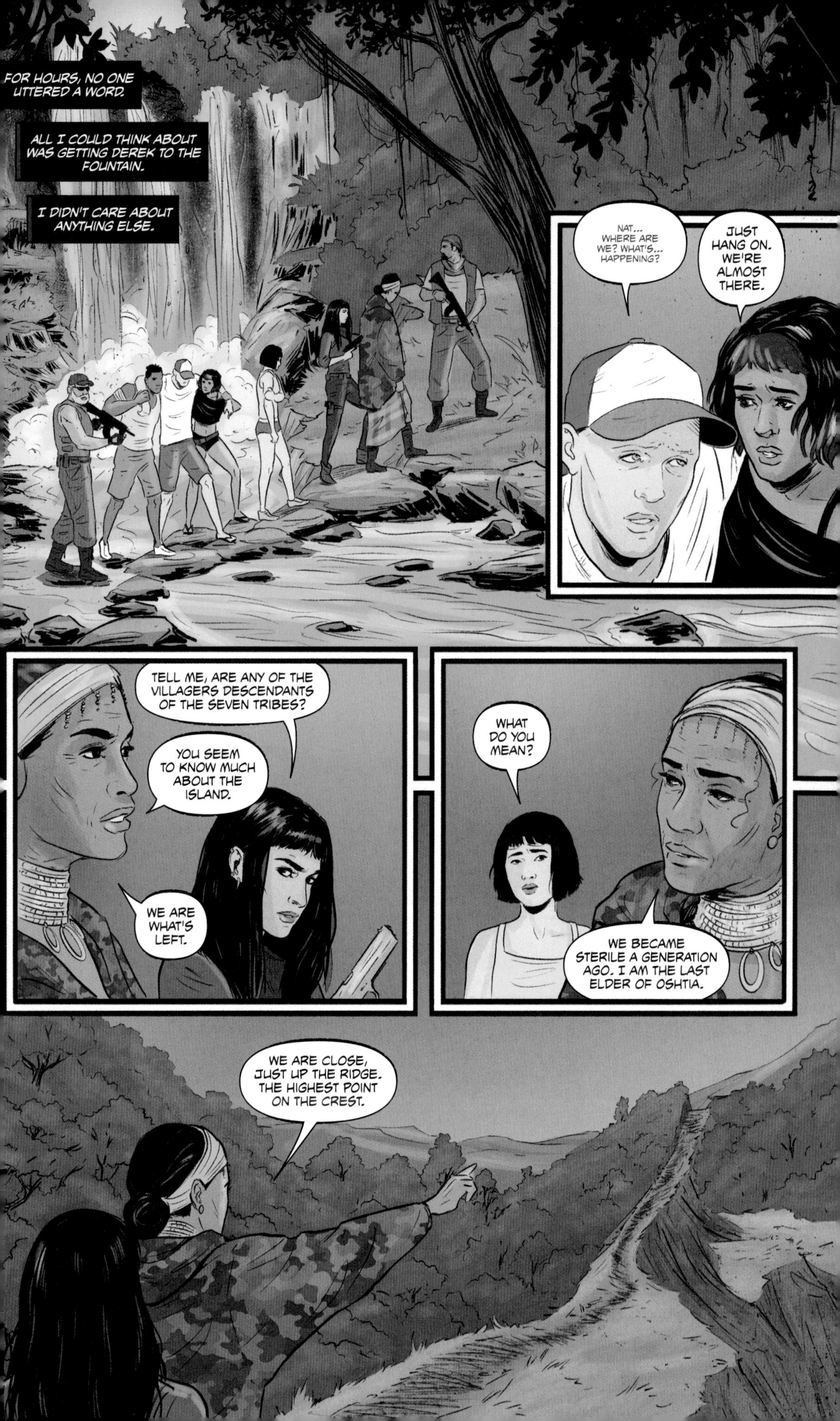

FOR HOURS, NO ONE UTTERED A WORD.
ALL I COULD THINK ABOUT WAS GETTING DEREK TO THE FOUNTAIN.
I DIDN'T CARE ABOUT ANYTHING ELSE.
NAT... WHERE ARE WE? WHAT'S... HAPPENING?
JUST HANG ON. WE'RE ALMOST THERE.
TELL ME, ARE ANY OF THE VILLAGERS DESCENDANTS OF THE SEVEN TRIBES?
YOU SEEM TO KNOW MUCH ABOUT THE ISLAND.
WE ARE WHAT'S LEFT.
WHAT DO YOU MEAN?
WE BECAME STERILE A GENERATION AGO. I AM THE LAST ELDER OF OSHTIA.
WE ARE CLOSE, JUST UP THE RIDGE. THE HIGHEST POINT ON THE CREST.

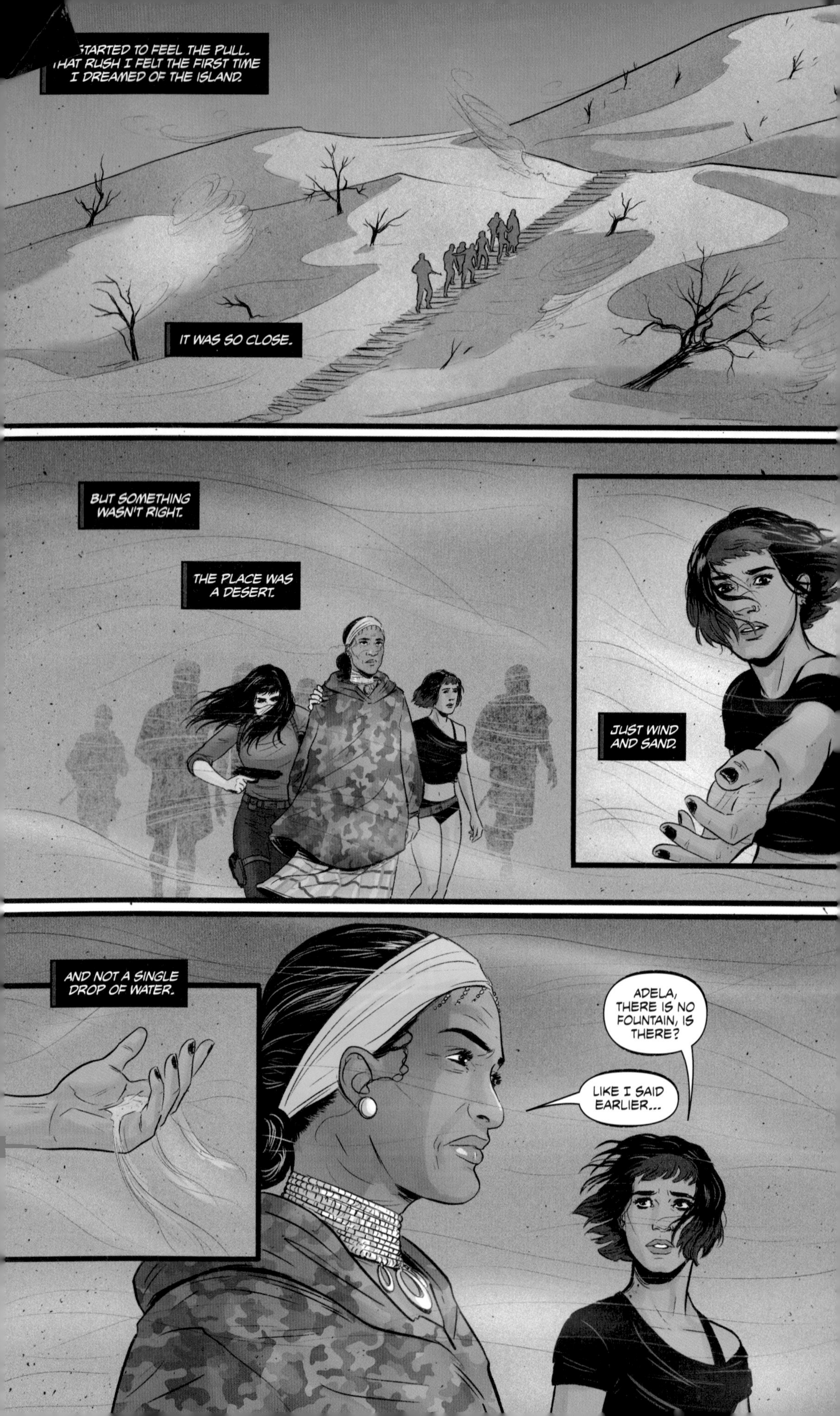

STARTED TO FEEL THE PULL. THAT RUSH I FELT THE FIRST TIME I DREAMED OF THE ISLAND.
IT WAS SO CLOSE.
BUT SOMETHING WASN'T RIGHT.
THE PLACE WAS A DESERT.
JUST WIND AND SAND.
AND NOT A SINGLE DROP OF WATER.
ADELA, THERE IS NO FOUNTAIN, IS THERE?
LIKE I SAID EARLIER...

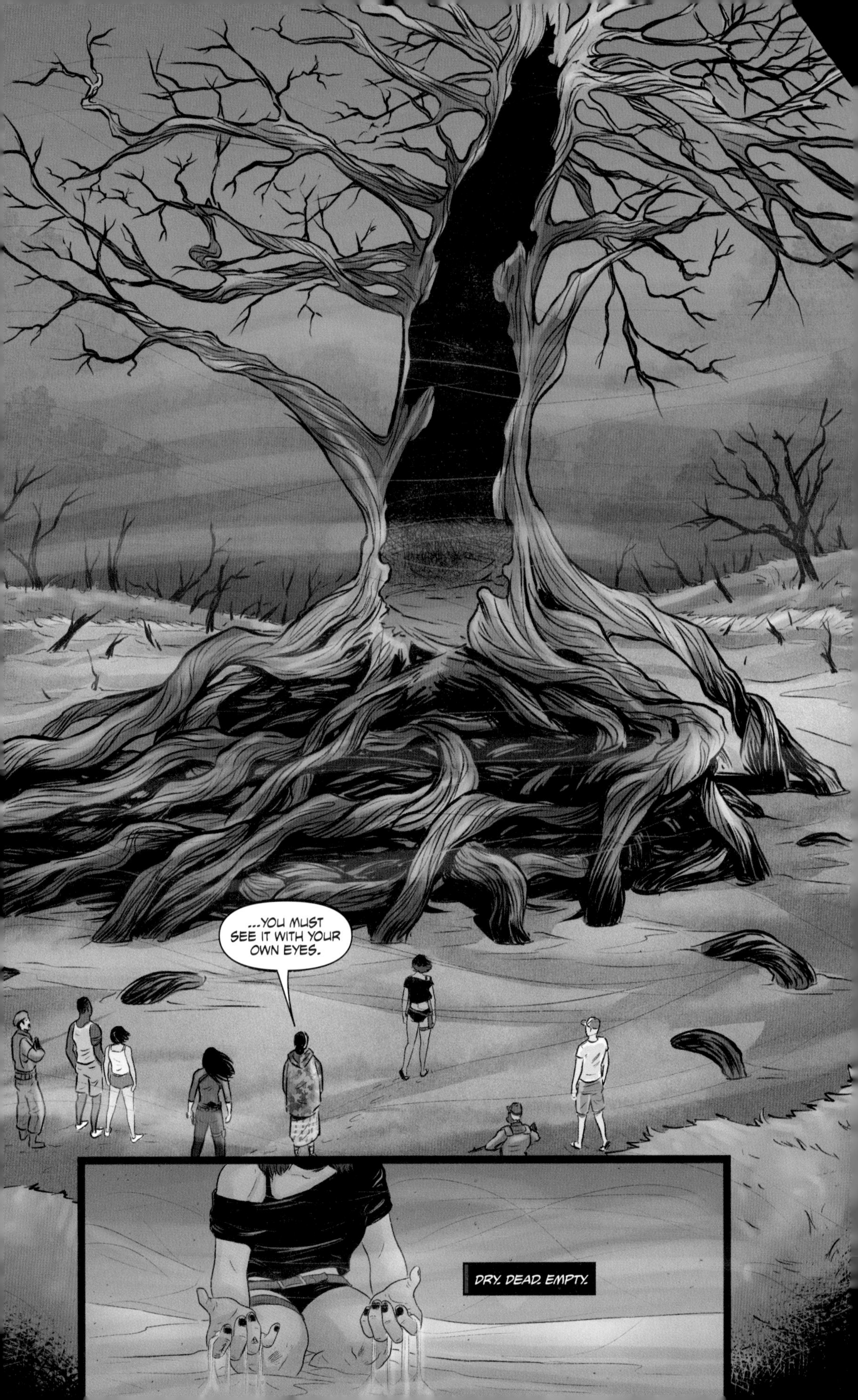
...YOU MUST SEE IT WITH YOUR OWN EYES.
DRY. DEAD. EMPTY.

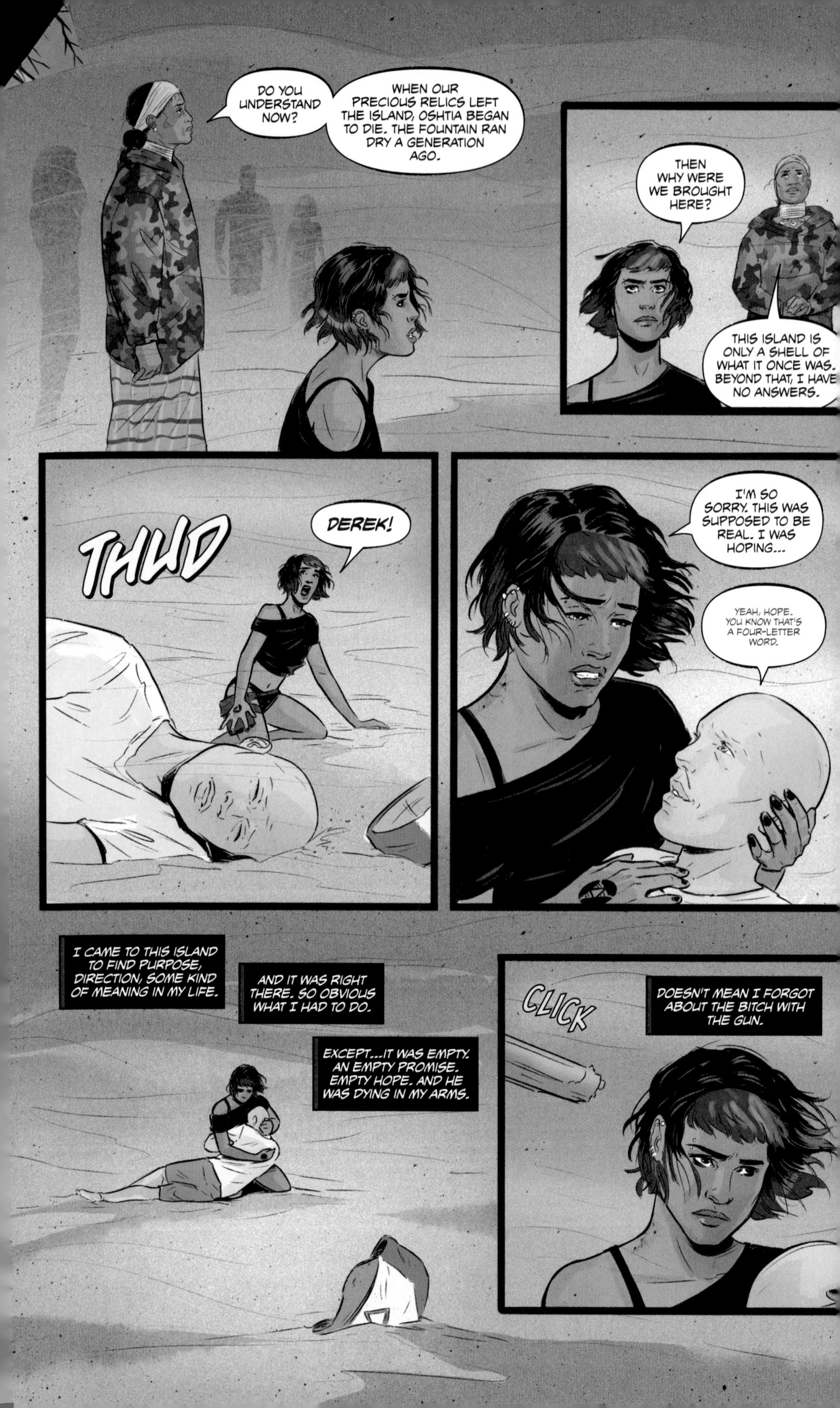

DO YOU UNDERSTAND NOW?
WHEN OUR PRECIOUS RELICS LEFT THE ISLAND, OSHTIA BEGAN TO DIE. THE FOUNTAIN RAN DRY A GENERATION AGO.
THEN WHY WERE WE BROUGHT HERE?
THIS ISLAND IS ONLY A SHELL OF WHAT IT ONCE WAS. BEYOND THAT, I HAVE NO ANSWERS.
THUD
DEREK!
I'M SO SORRY. THIS WAS SUPPOSED TO BE REAL. I WAS HOPING...
YEAH, HOPE. YOU KNOW THAT'S A FOUR-LETTER WORD.
I CAME TO THIS ISLAND TO FIND PURPOSE, DIRECTION, SOME KIND OF MEANING IN MY LIFE.
AND IT WAS RIGHT THERE. SO OBVIOUS WHAT I HAD TO DO.
EXCEPT...IT WAS EMPTY. AN EMPTY PROMISE. EMPTY HOPE. AND HE WAS DYING IN MY ARMS.
CLICK
DOESN'T MEAN I FORGOT ABOUT THE BITCH WITH THE GUN.

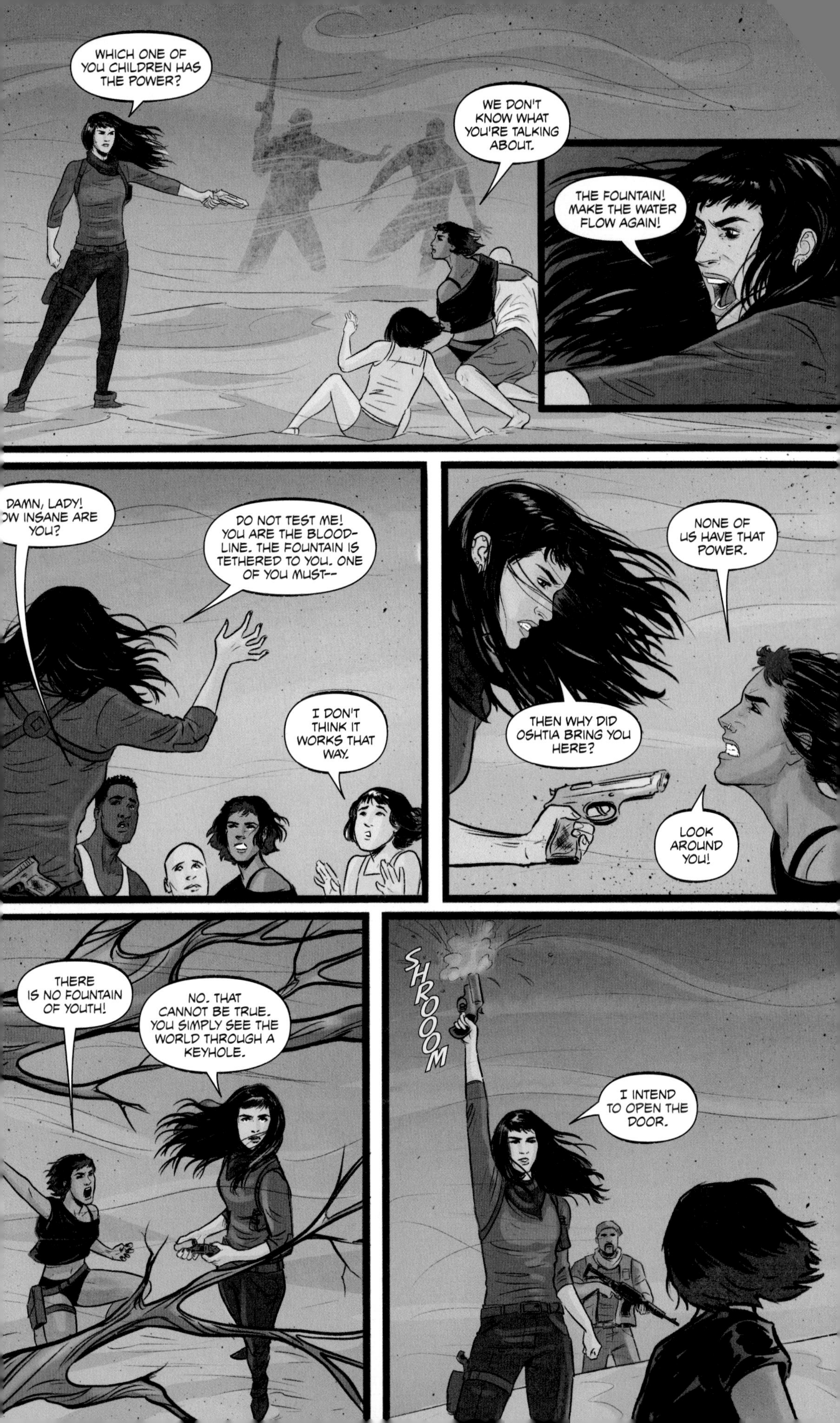
WHICH ONE OF YOU CHILDREN HAS THE POWER?
WE DON'T KNOW WHAT YOU'RE TALKING ABOUT.
THE FOUNTAIN! MAKE THE WATER FLOW AGAIN!
DAMN, LADY! OW INSANE ARE YOU?
DO NOT TEST ME! YOU ARE THE BLOOD-LINE. THE FOUNTAIN IS TETHERED TO YOU. ONE OF YOU MUST--
I DON'T THINK IT WORKS THAT WAY.
NONE OF US HAVE THAT POWER.
THEN WHY DID OSHTIA BRING YOU HERE?
LOOK AROUND YOU!
THERE IS NO FOUNTAIN OF YOUTH!
NO. THAT CANNOT BE TRUE. YOU SIMPLY SEE THE WORLD THROUGH A KEYHOLE.
SHROOOM
I INTEND TO OPEN THE DOOR.

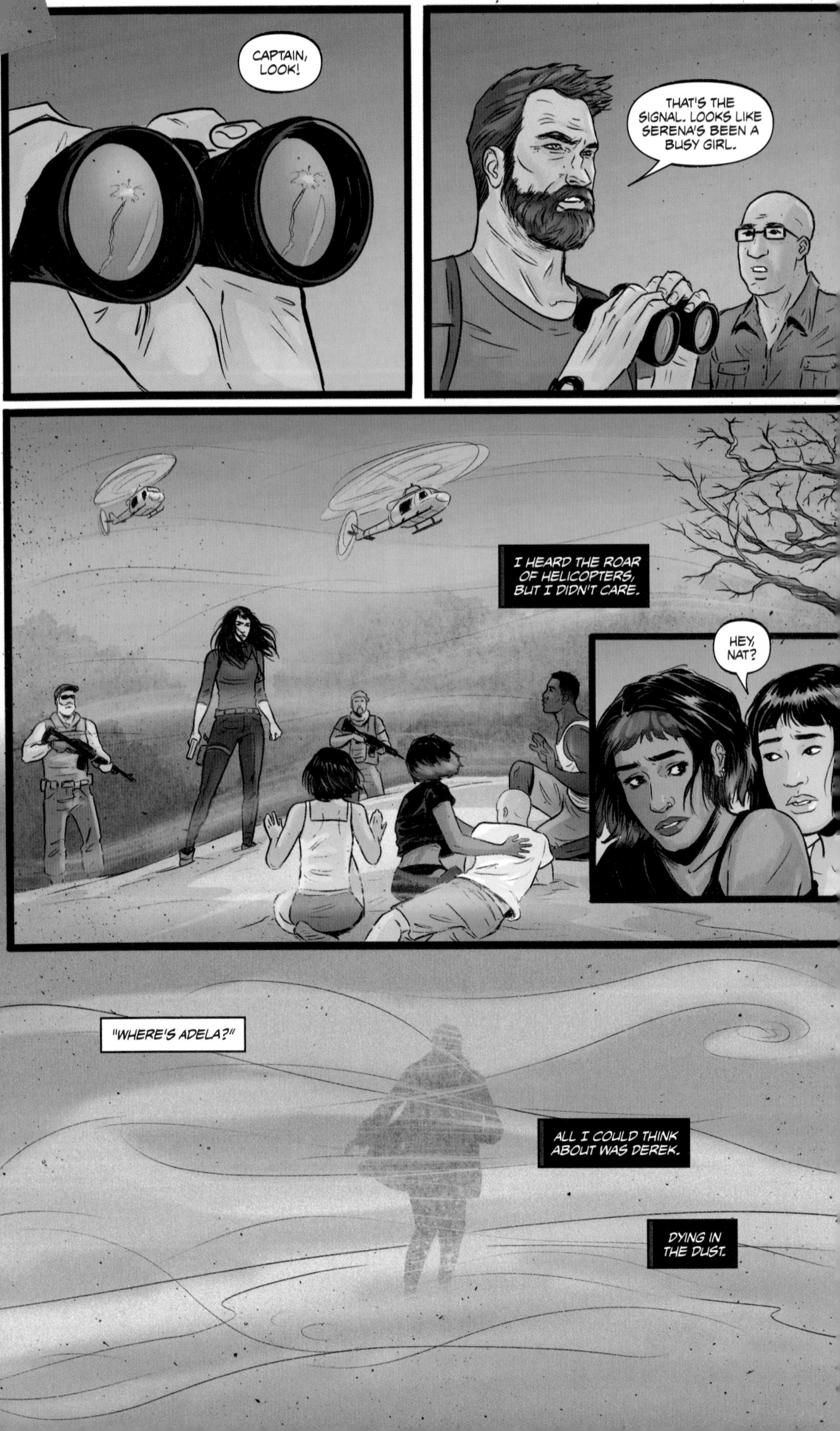
CAPTAIN, LOOK!
THAT'S THE SIGNAL. LOOKS LIKE SERENA'S BEEN A BUSY GIRL.
I HEARD THE ROAR OF HELICOPTERS, BUT I DIDN'T CARE.
HEY, NAT?
"WHERE'S ADELA?"
ALL I COULD THINK ABOUT WAS DEREK.
DYING IN THE DUST.

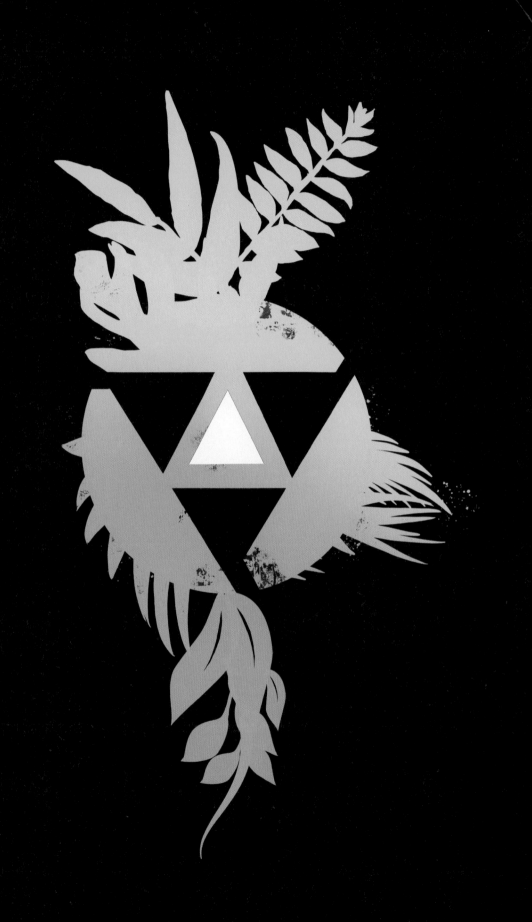

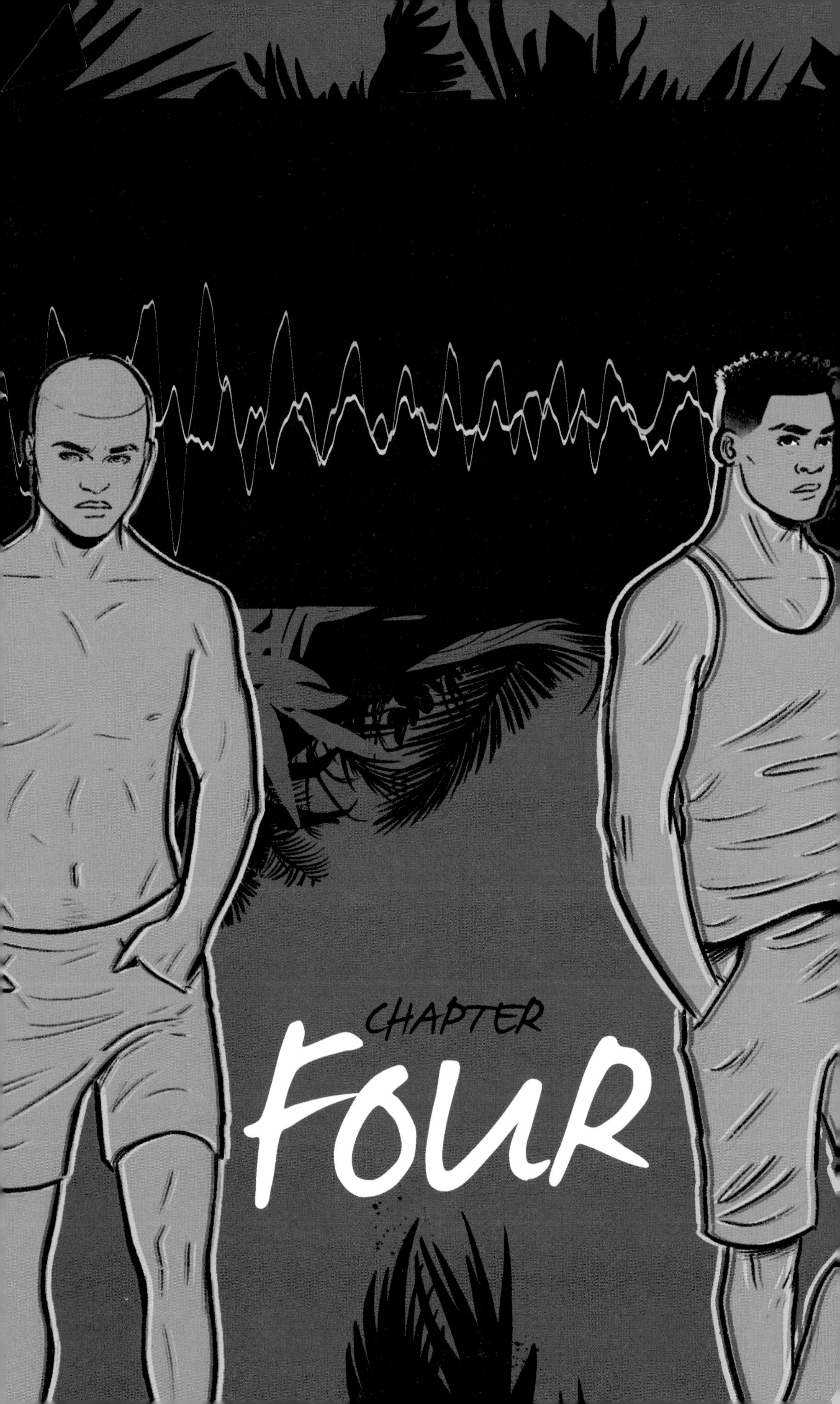
CHAPTER
FOUR

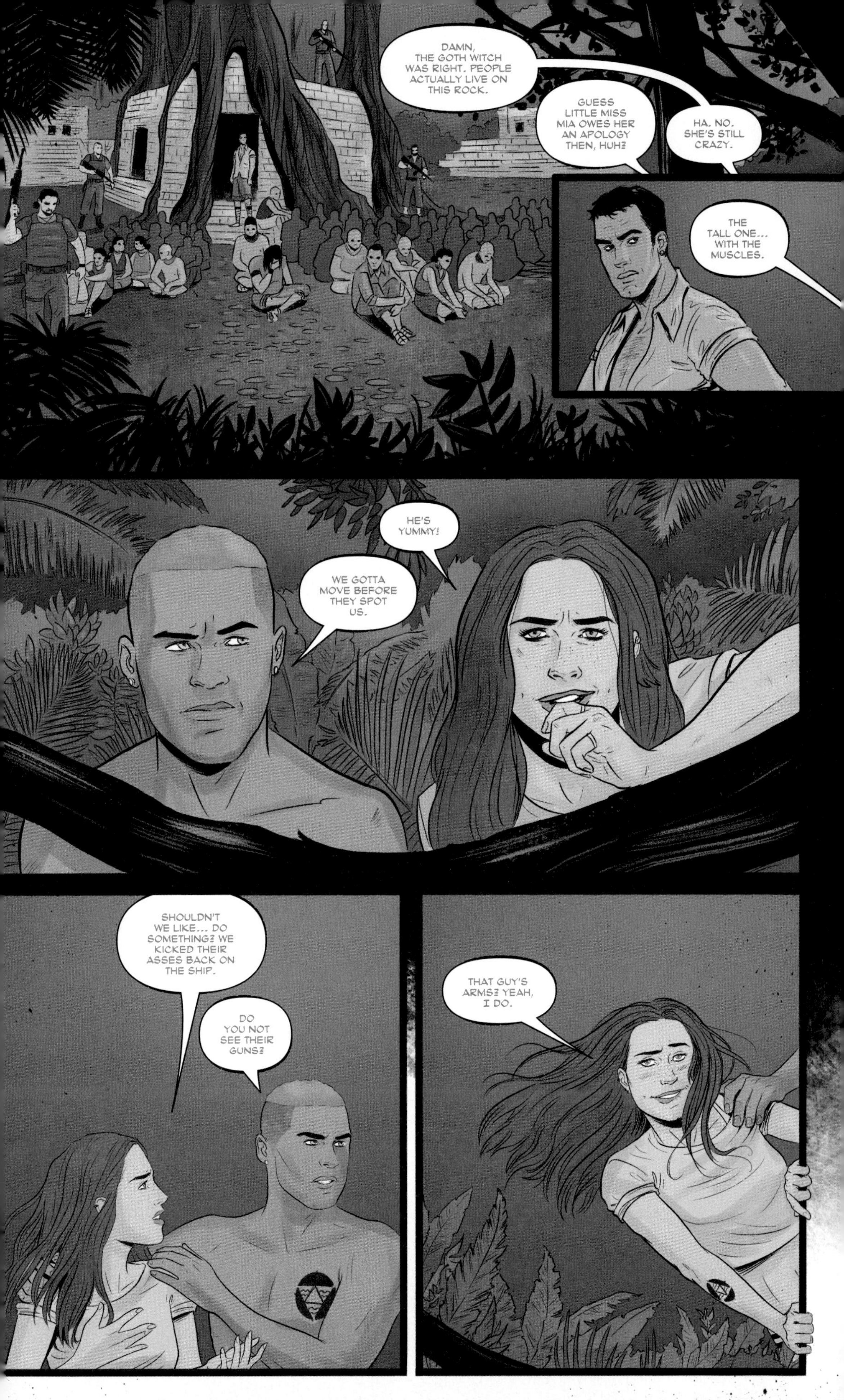
DAMN, THE GOTH WITCH WAS RIGHT. PEOPLE ACTUALLY LIVE ON THIS ROCK.
GUESS LITTLE MISS MIA OWES HER AN APOLOGY THEN, HUH?
HA. NO. SHE'S STILL CRAZY.
THE TALL ONE... WITH THE MUSCLES.
HE'S YUMMY!
WE GOTTA MOVE BEFORE THEY SPOT US.
SHOULDN'T WE LIKE... DO SOMETHING? WE KICKED THEIR ASSES BACK ON THE SHIP.
DO YOU NOT SEE THEIR GUNS?
THAT GUY'S ARMS? YEAH, I DO.

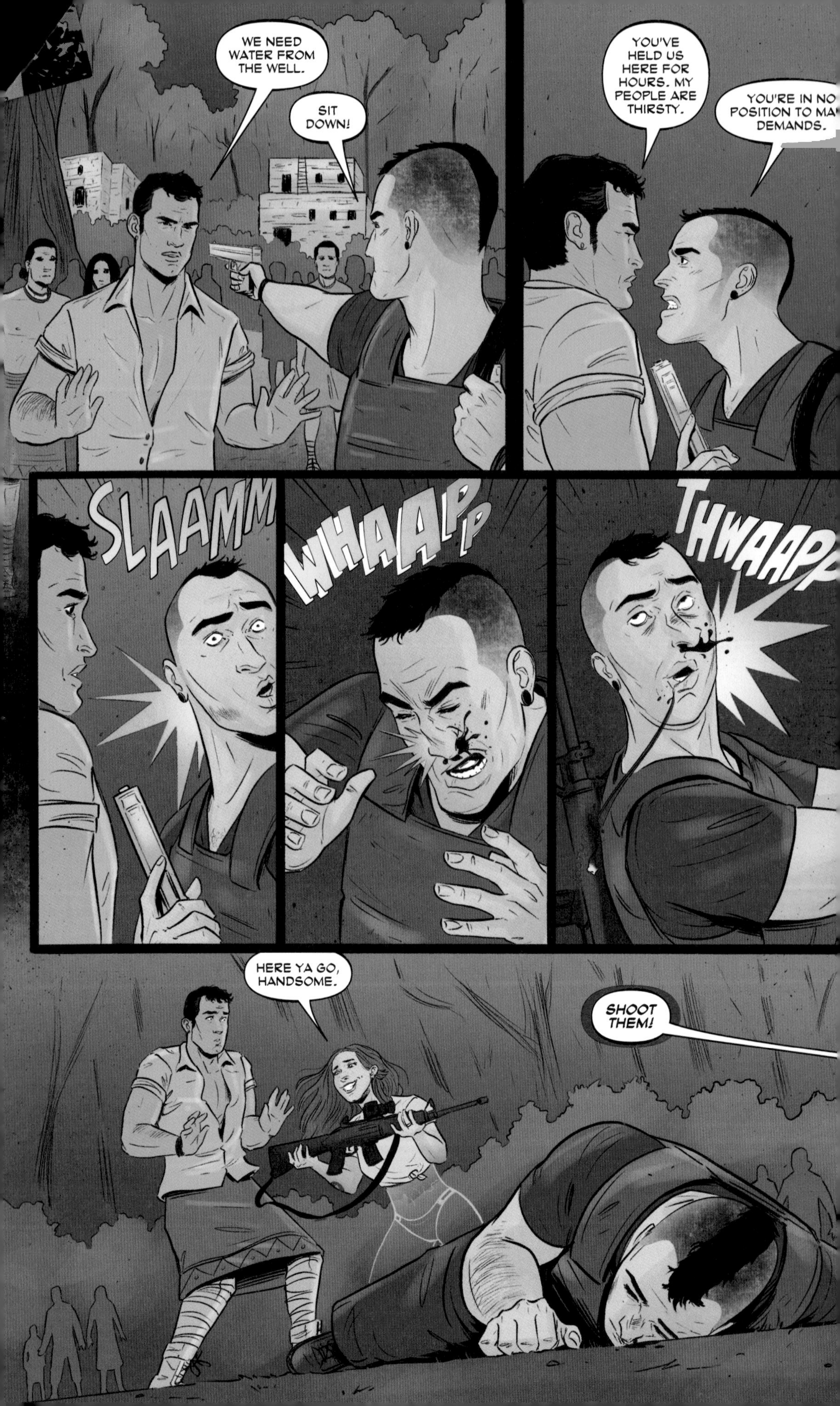
WE NEED WATER FROM THE WELL.
SIT DOWN!
YOU'VE HELD US HERE FOR HOURS. MY PEOPLE ARE THIRSTY.
YOU'RE IN NO POSITION TO MA DEMANDS.
SLAAMM
WHAALP
THWAAPP
HERE YA GO, HANDSOME.
SHOOT THEM!

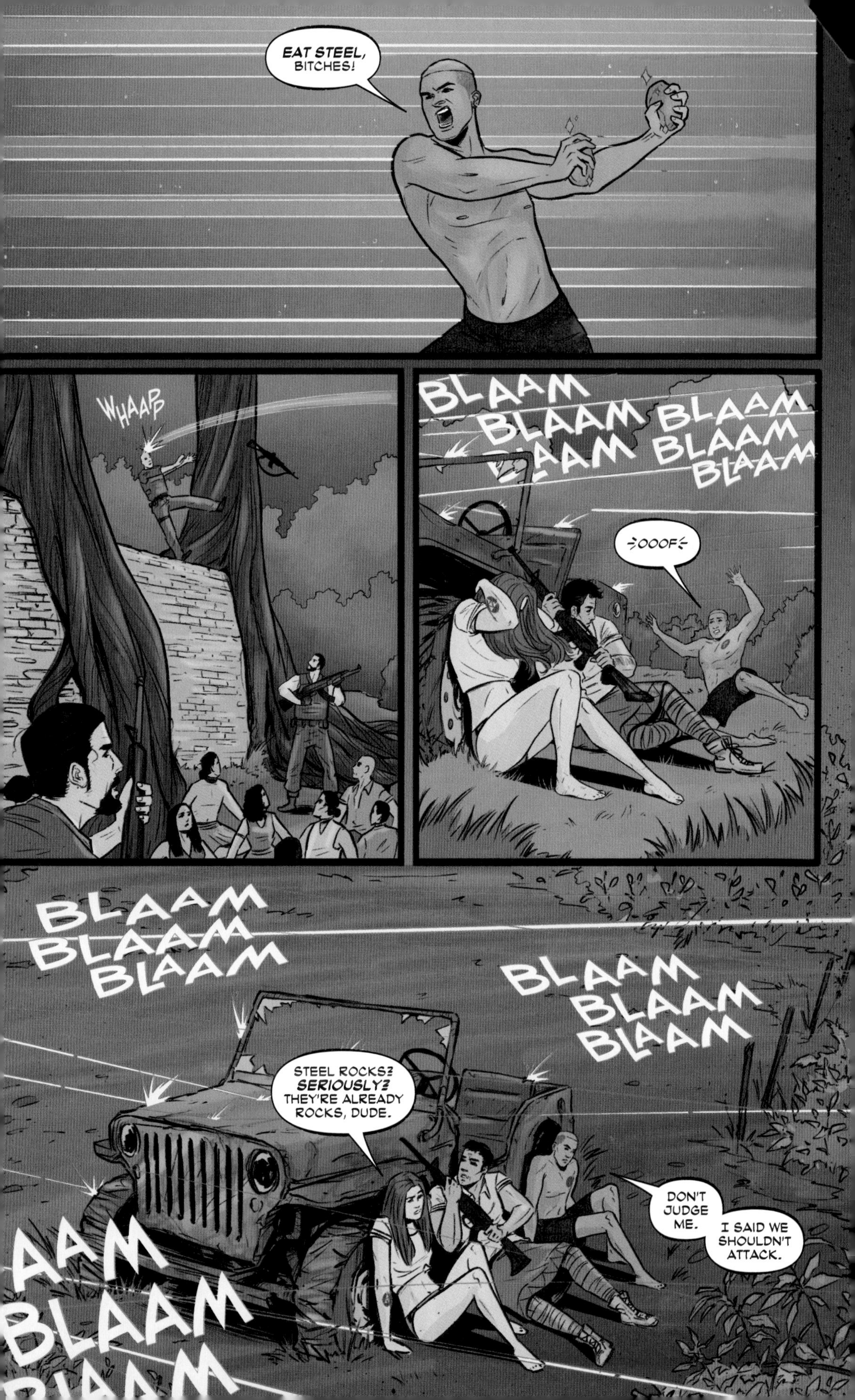
EAT STEEL, BITCHES!
WHAAPP
BLAAM BLAAM BLAAM BLAAM BLAAM BLAAM
OOOF
BLAAM BLAAM BLAAM
BLAAM BLAAM BLAAM
STEEL ROCKS? SERIOUSLY? THEY'RE ALREADY ROCKS, DUDE.
DON'T JUDGE ME.
I SAID WE SHOULDN'T ATTACK.
AAM BLAAM

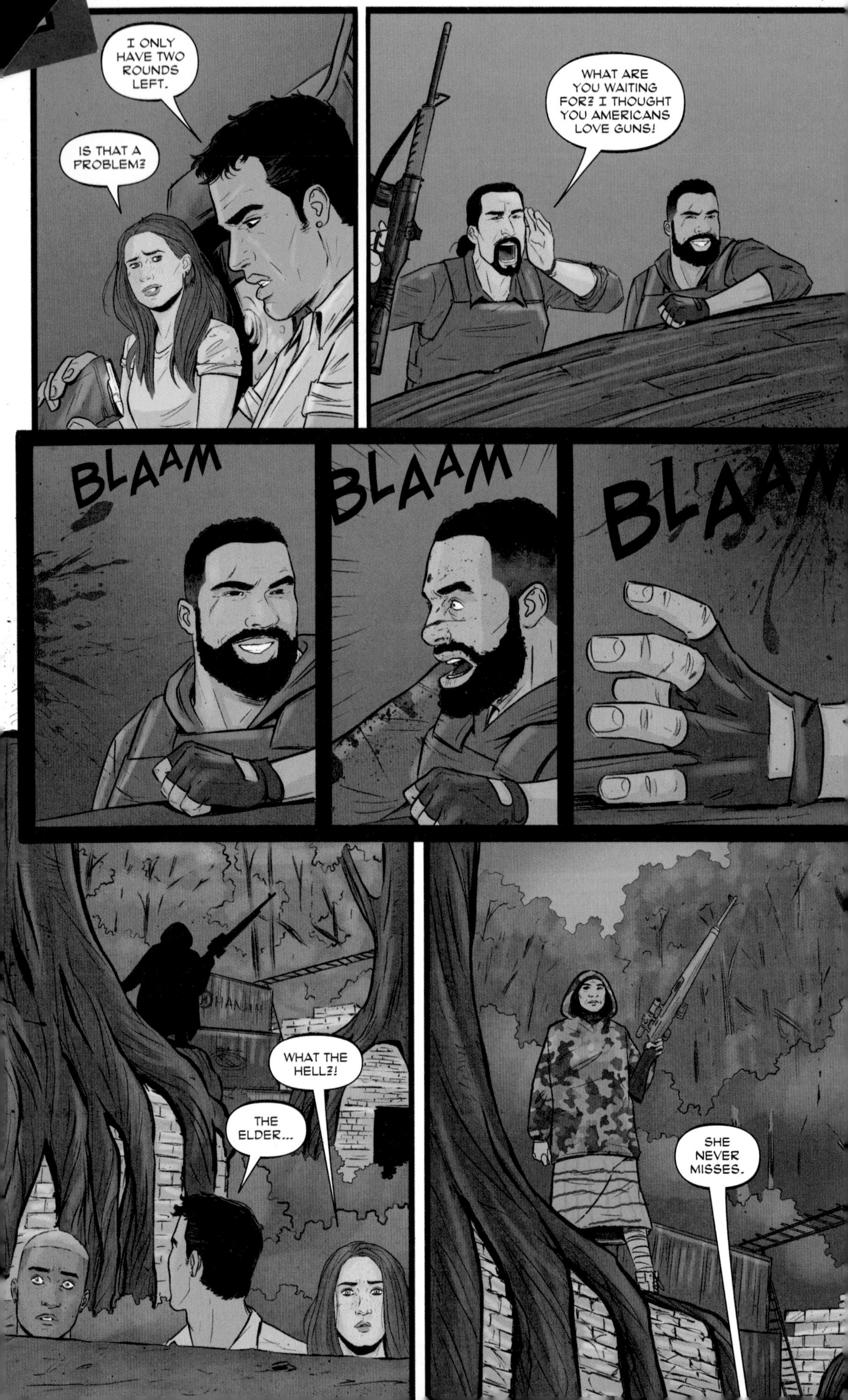
I ONLY HAVE TWO ROUNDS LEFT.
IS THAT A PROBLEM?
WHAT ARE YOU WAITING FOR? I THOUGHT YOU AMERICANS LOVE GUNS!
BLAAM
BLAAM
BLAAM
WHAT THE HELL?!
THE ELDER...
SHE NEVER MISSES.

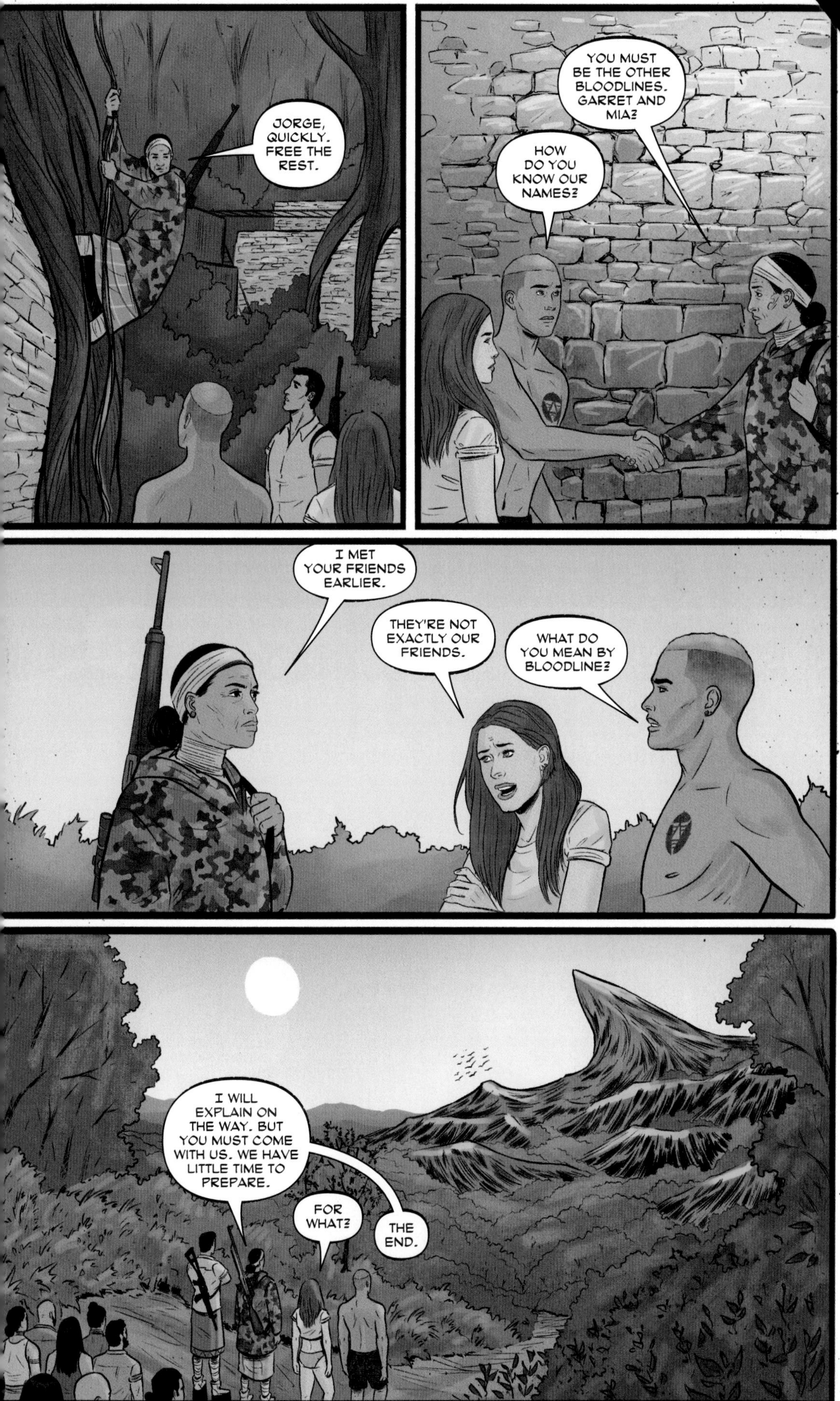
JORGE, QUICKLY. FREE THE REST.
YOU MUST BE THE OTHER BLOODLINES. GARRET AND MIA?
HOW DO YOU KNOW OUR NAMES?
I MET YOUR FRIENDS EARLIER.
THEY'RE NOT EXACTLY OUR FRIENDS.
WHAT DO YOU MEAN BY BLOODLINE?
I WILL EXPLAIN ON THE WAY. BUT YOU MUST COME WITH US. WE HAVE LITTLE TIME TO PREPARE.
FOR WHAT?
THE END.

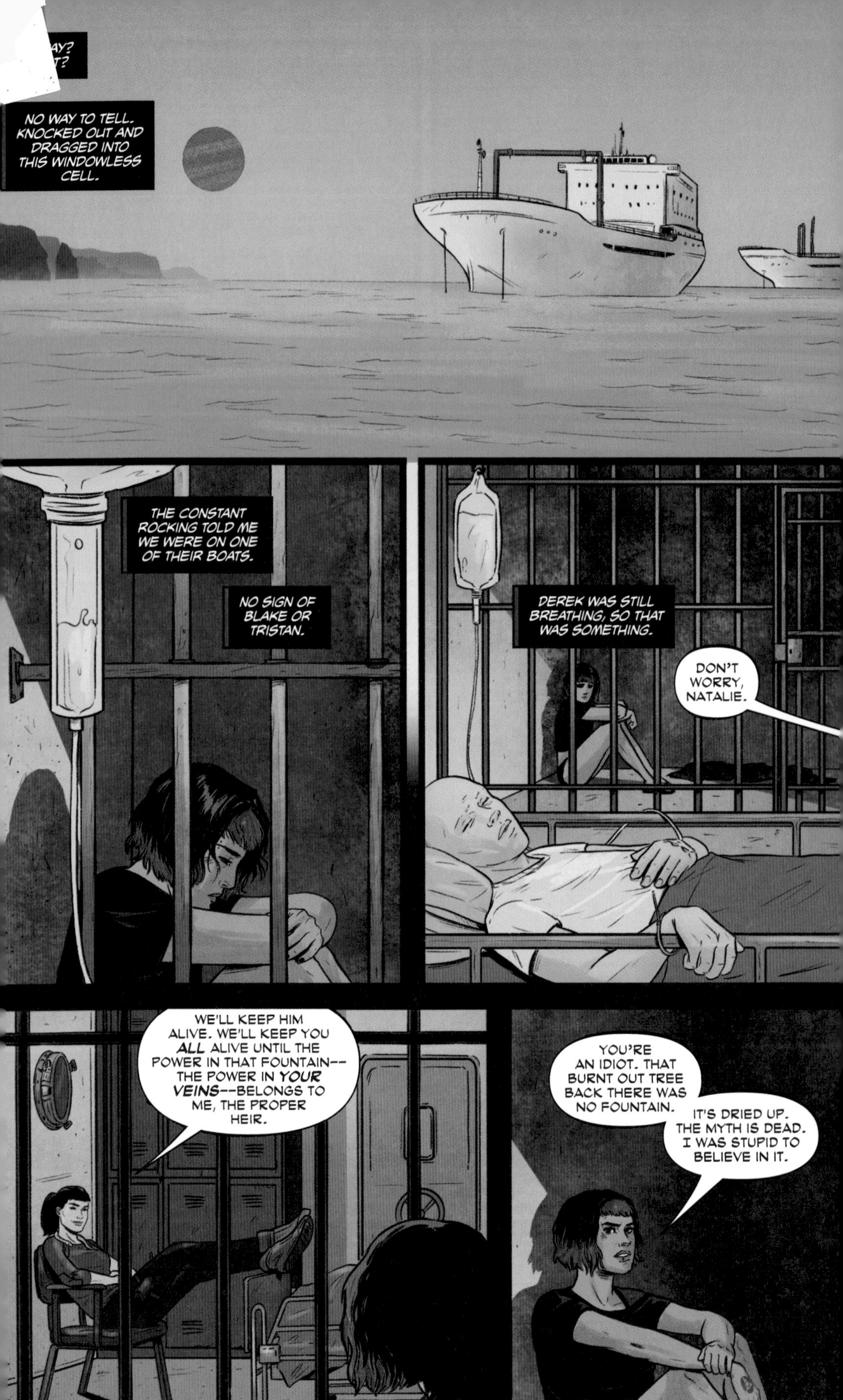
NO WAY TO TELL. KNOCKED OUT AND DRAGGED INTO THIS WINDOWLESS CELL.
THE CONSTANT ROCKING TOLD ME WE WERE ON ONE OF THEIR BOATS.
NO SIGN OF BLAKE OR TRISTAN.
DEREK WAS STILL BREATHING, SO THAT WAS SOMETHING.
DON'T WORRY, NATALIE.
WE'LL KEEP HIM ALIVE. WE'LL KEEP YOU ALL ALIVE UNTIL THE POWER IN THAT FOUNTAIN-- THE POWER IN YOUR VEINS--BELONGS TO ME, THE PROPER HEIR.
YOU'RE AN IDIOT. THAT BURNT OUT TREE BACK THERE WAS NO FOUNTAIN.
IT'S DRIED UP. THE MYTH IS DEAD. I WAS STUPID TO BELIEVE IN IT.

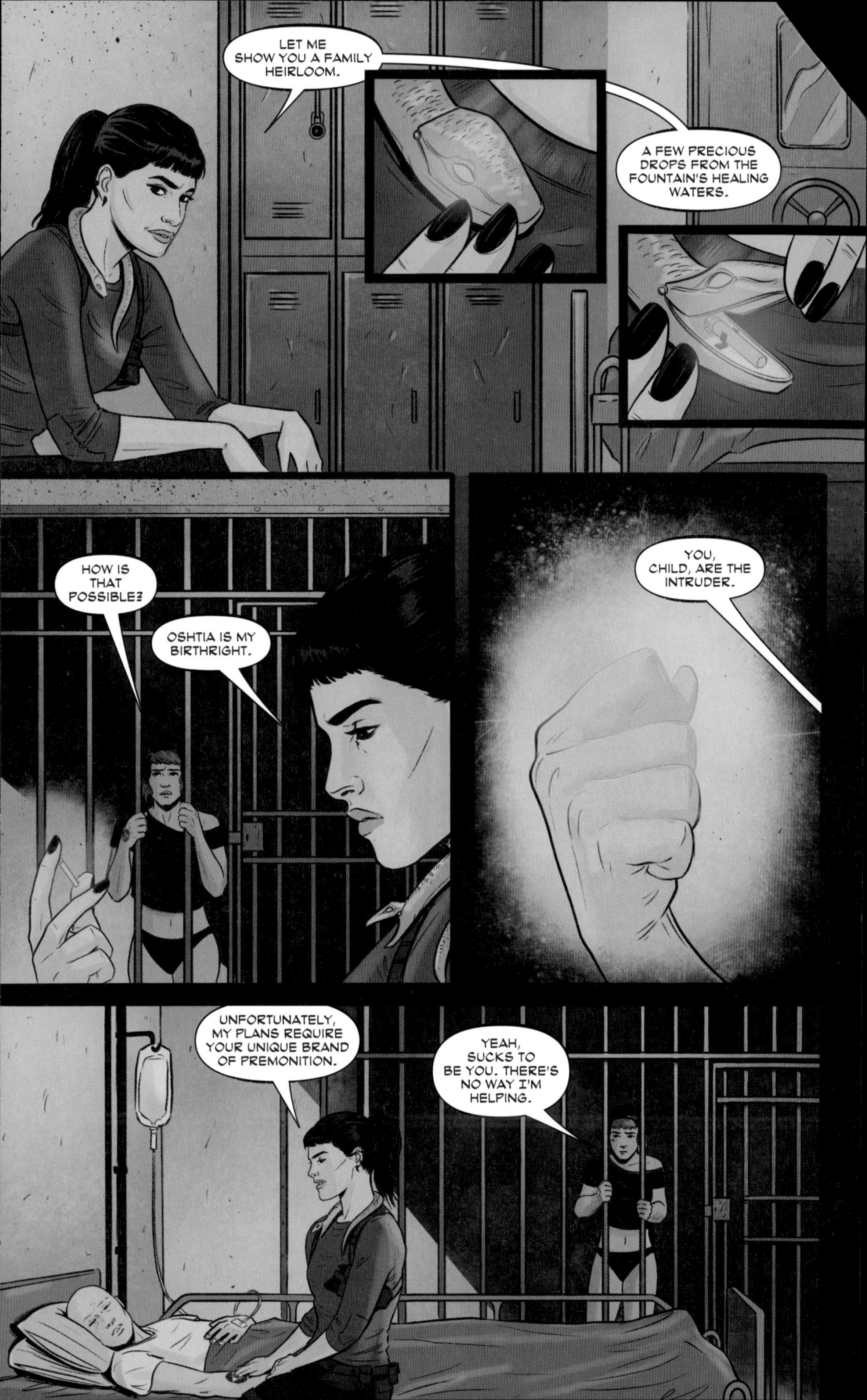
LET ME SHOW YOU A FAMILY HEIRLOOM.
A FEW PRECIOUS DROPS FROM THE FOUNTAIN'S HEALING WATERS.
HOW IS THAT POSSIBLE?
OSHTIA IS MY BIRTHRIGHT.
YOU, CHILD, ARE THE INTRUDER.
UNFORTUNATELY, MY PLANS REQUIRE YOUR UNIQUE BRAND OF PREMONITION.
YEAH, SUCKS TO BE YOU. THERE'S NO WAY I'M HELPING.

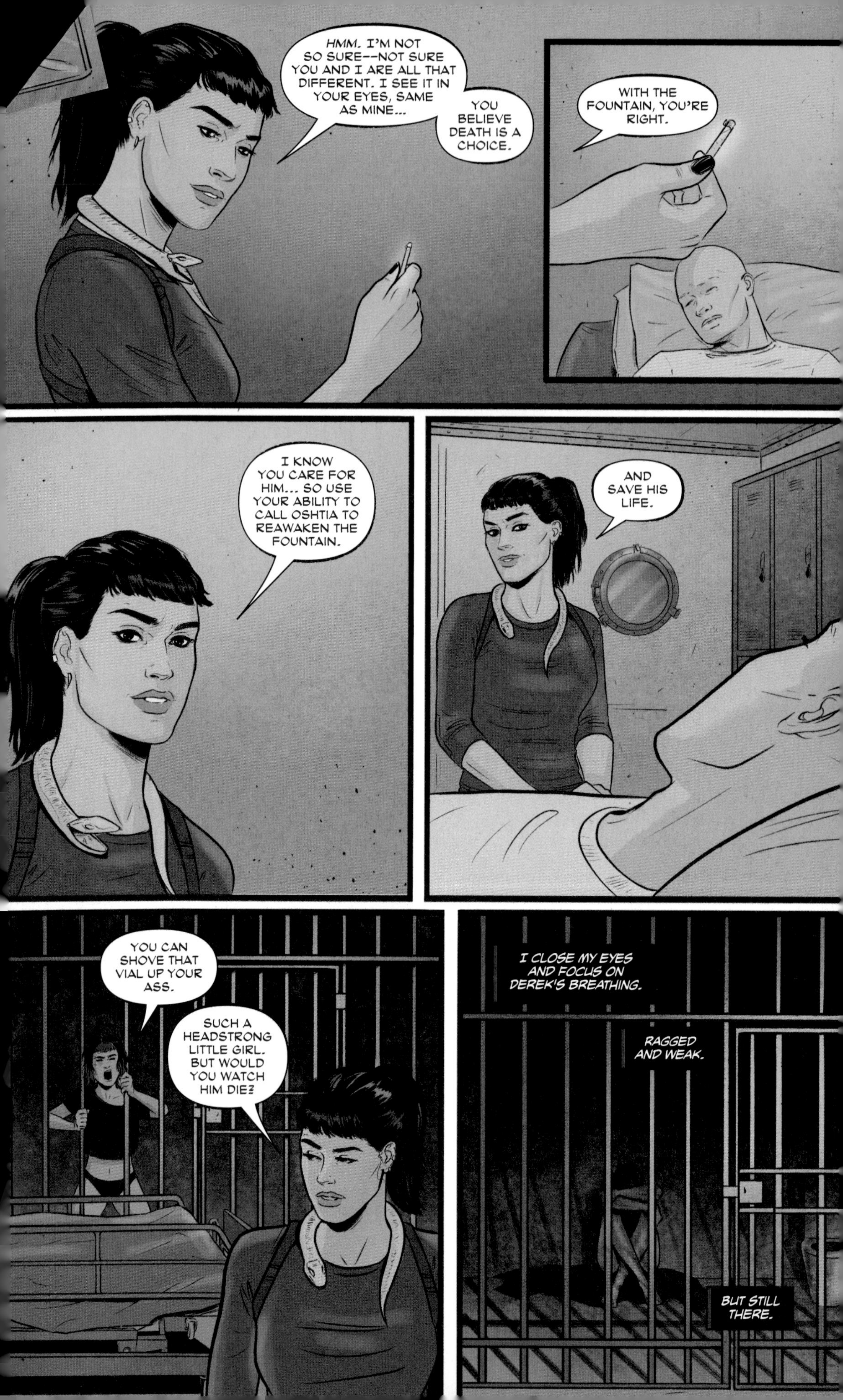
HMM. I'M NOT SO SURE--NOT SURE YOU AND I ARE ALL THAT DIFFERENT. I SEE IT IN YOUR EYES, SAME AS MINE...
YOU BELIEVE DEATH IS A CHOICE.
WITH THE FOUNTAIN, YOU'RE RIGHT.
I KNOW YOU CARE FOR HIM... SO USE YOUR ABILITY TO CALL OSHTIA TO REAWAKEN THE FOUNTAIN.
AND SAVE HIS LIFE.
YOU CAN SHOVE THAT VIAL UP YOUR ASS.
SUCH A HEADSTRONG LITTLE GIRL. BUT WOULD YOU WATCH HIM DIE?
I CLOSE MY EYES AND FOCUS ON DEREK'S BREATHING.
RAGGED AND WEAK.
BUT STILL THERE.

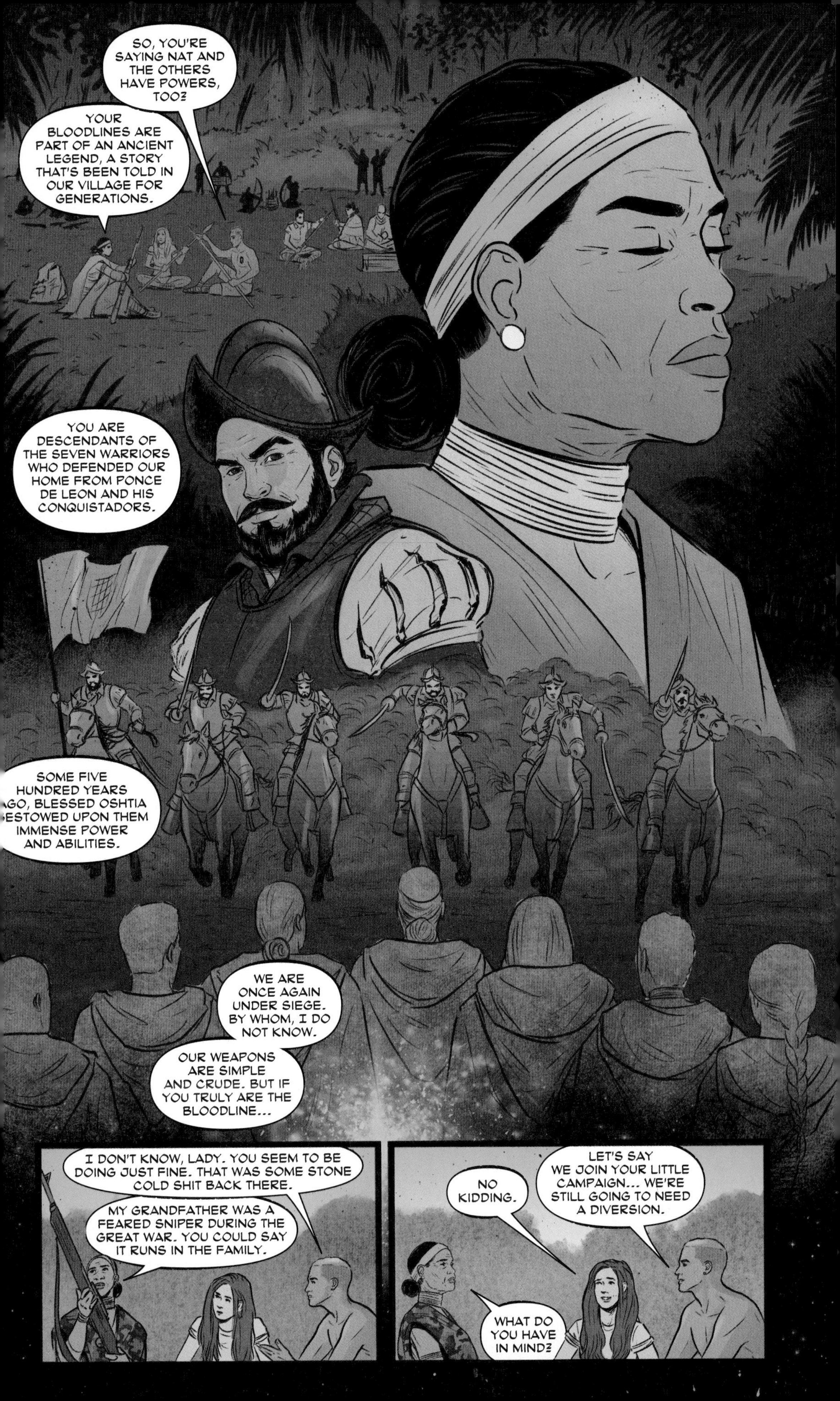

SO, YOU'RE SAYING NAT AND THE OTHERS HAVE POWERS, TOO?
YOUR BLOODLINES ARE PART OF AN ANCIENT LEGEND, A STORY THAT'S BEEN TOLD IN OUR VILLAGE FOR GENERATIONS.
YOU ARE DESCENDANTS OF THE SEVEN WARRIORS WHO DEFENDED OUR HOME FROM PONCE DE LEON AND HIS CONQUISTADORS.
SOME FIVE HUNDRED YEARS AGO, BLESSED OSHTIA BESTOWED UPON THEM IMMENSE POWER AND ABILITIES.
WE ARE ONCE AGAIN UNDER SIEGE. BY WHOM, I DO NOT KNOW.
OUR WEAPONS ARE SIMPLE AND CRUDE. BUT IF YOU TRULY ARE THE BLOODLINE...
I DON'T KNOW, LADY. YOU SEEM TO BE DOING JUST FINE. THAT WAS SOME STONE COLD SHIT BACK THERE.
MY GRANDFATHER WAS A FEARED SNIPER DURING THE GREAT WAR. YOU COULD SAY IT RUNS IN THE FAMILY.
LET'S SAY WE JOIN YOUR LITTLE CAMPAIGN... WE'RE STILL GOING TO NEED A DIVERSION.
NO KIDDING.
WHAT DO YOU HAVE IN MIND?

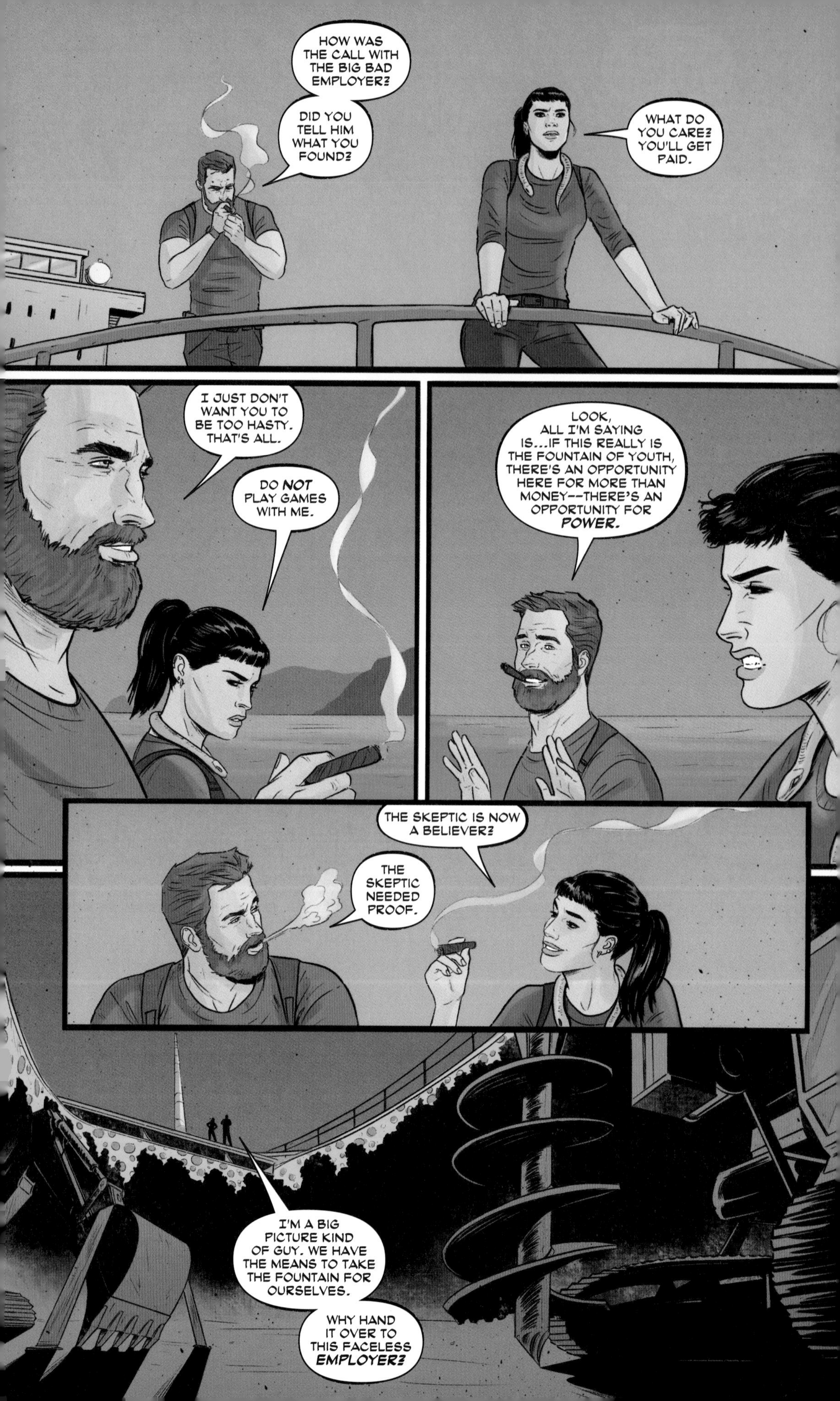
HOW WAS THE CALL WITH THE BIG BAD EMPLOYER?
DID YOU TELL HIM WHAT YOU FOUND?
WHAT DO YOU CARE? YOU'LL GET PAID.
I JUST DON'T WANT YOU TO BE TOO HASTY. THAT'S ALL.
DO NOT PLAY GAMES WITH ME.
LOOK, ALL I'M SAYING IS...IF THIS REALLY IS THE FOUNTAIN OF YOUTH, THERE'S AN OPPORTUNITY HERE FOR MORE THAN MONEY--THERE'S AN OPPORTUNITY FOR POWER.
THE SKEPTIC IS NOW A BELIEVER?
THE SKEPTIC NEEDED PROOF.
I'M A BIG PICTURE KIND OF GUY. WE HAVE THE MEANS TO TAKE THE FOUNTAIN FOR OURSELVES.
WHY HAND IT OVER TO THIS FACELESS EMPLOYER?

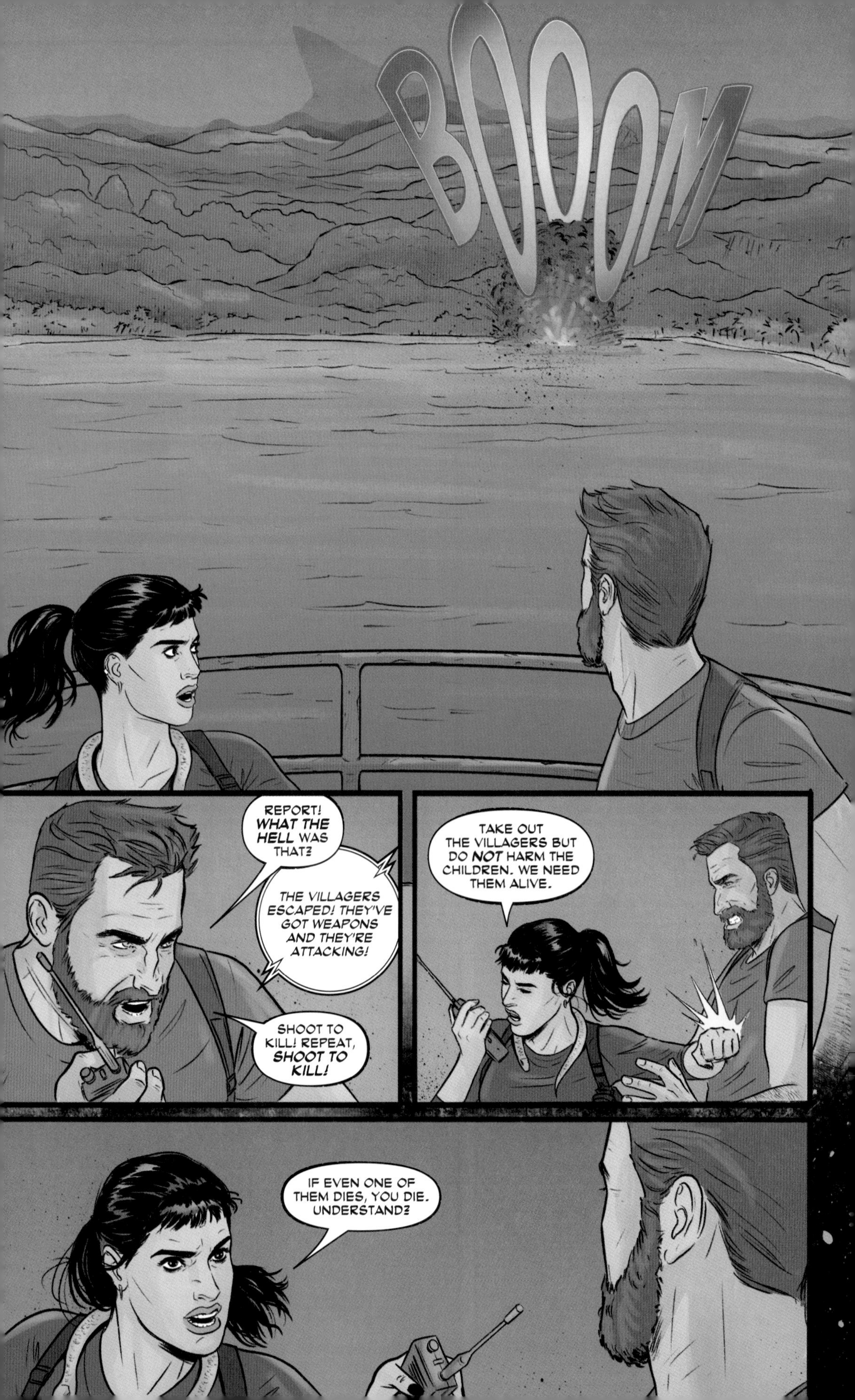
BOOOM
REPORT! WHAT THE HELL WAS THAT?
THE VILLAGERS ESCAPED! THEY'VE GOT WEAPONS AND THEY'RE ATTACKING!
SHOOT TO KILL! REPEAT, SHOOT TO KILL!
TAKE OUT THE VILLAGERS BUT DO NOT HARM THE CHILDREN. WE NEED THEM ALIVE.
IF EVEN ONE OF THEM DIES, YOU DIE. UNDERSTAND?

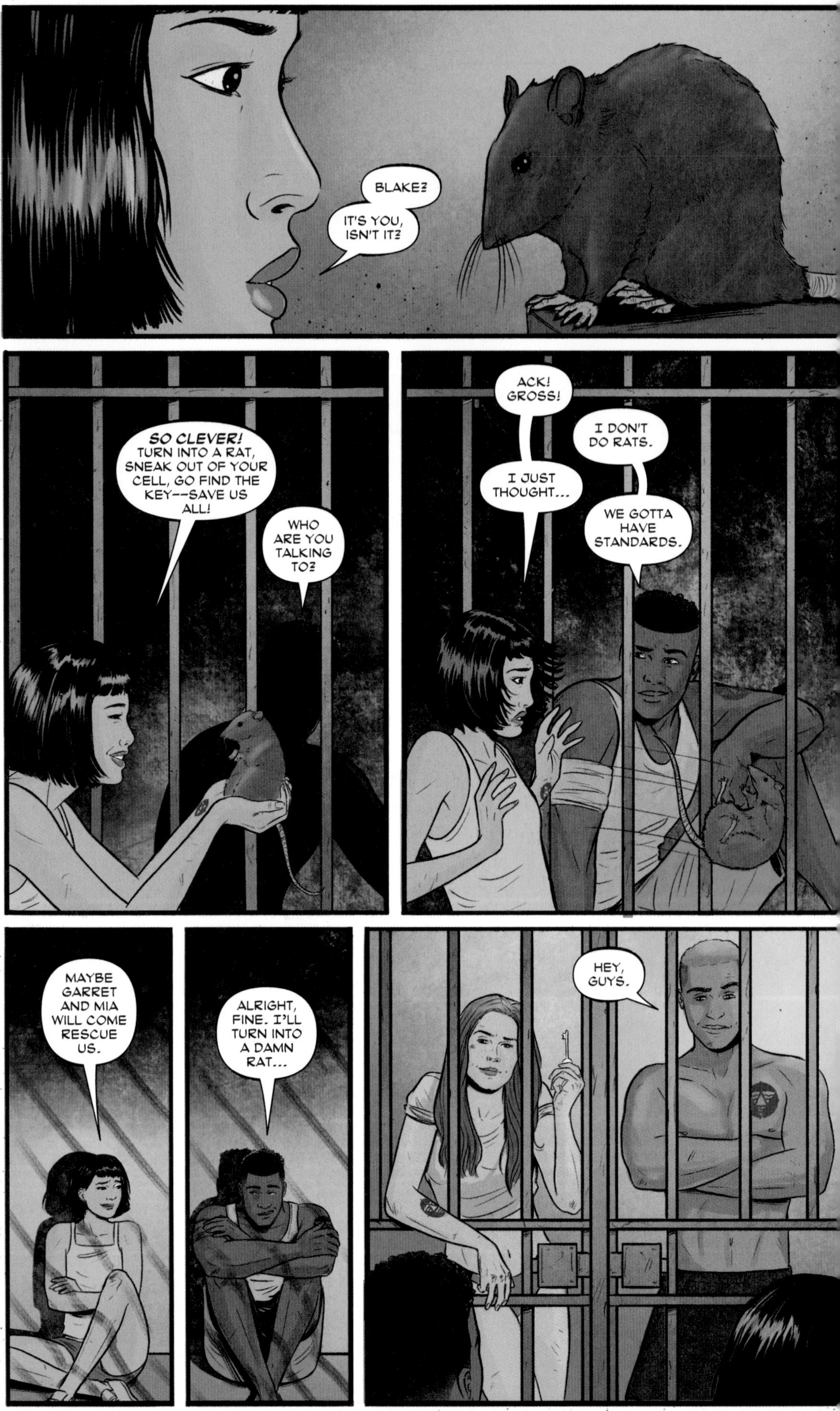
BLAKE?
IT'S YOU, ISN'T IT?
SO CLEVER! TURN INTO A RAT, SNEAK OUT OF YOUR CELL, GO FIND THE KEY--SAVE US ALL!
WHO ARE YOU TALKING TO?
ACK! GROSS!
I JUST THOUGHT...
I DON'T DO RATS.
WE GOTTA HAVE STANDARDS.
MAYBE GARRET AND MIA WILL COME RESCUE US.
ALRIGHT, FINE. I'LL TURN INTO A DAMN RAT...
HEY, GUYS.

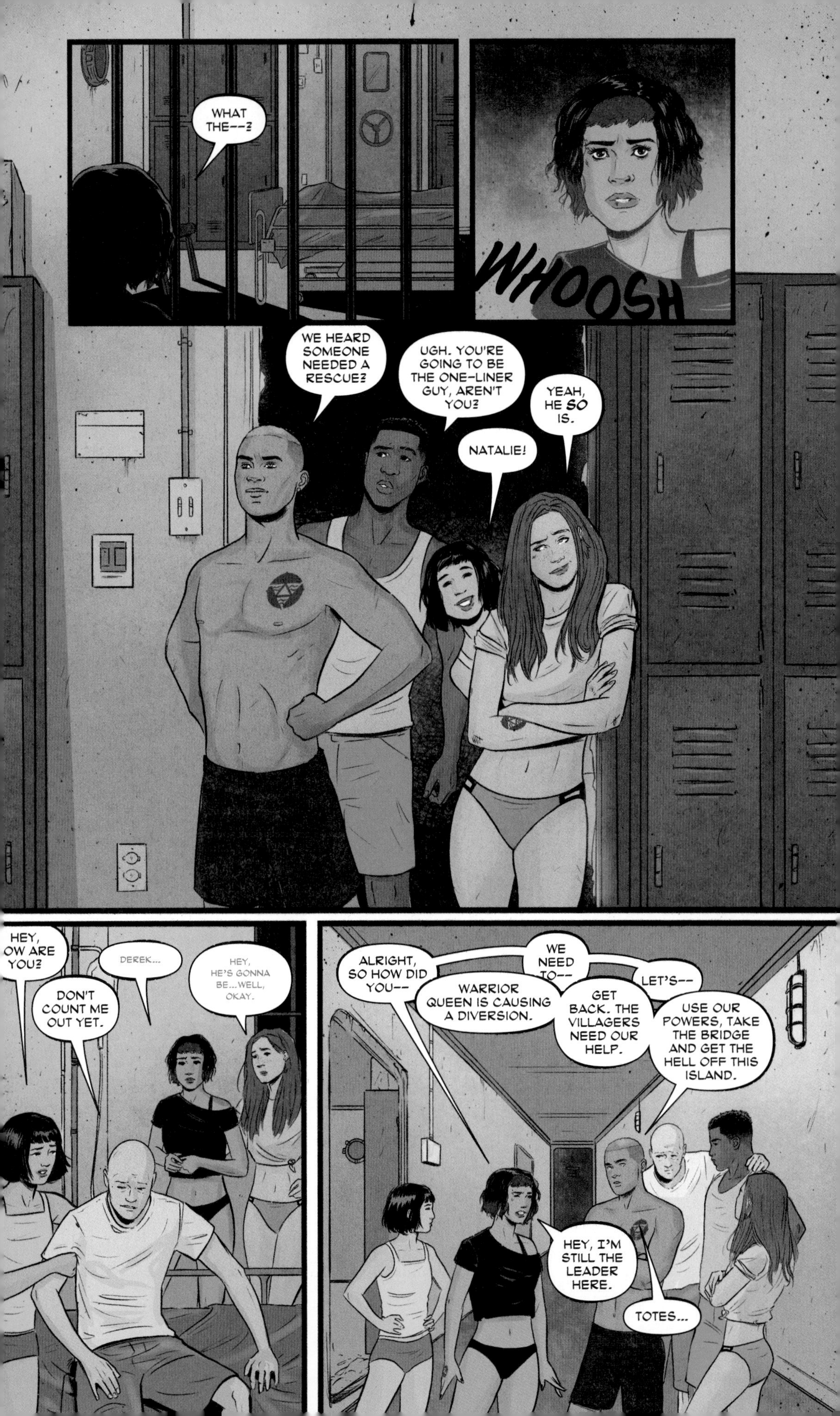
WHAT THE--?
WHOOSH
WE HEARD SOMEONE NEEDED A RESCUE?
UGH. YOU'RE GOING TO BE THE ONE-LINER GUY, AREN'T YOU?
NATALIE!
YEAH, HE SO IS.
HEY, OW ARE YOU?
DON'T COUNT ME OUT YET.
DEREK...
HEY, HE'S GONNA BE...WELL, OKAY.
ALRIGHT, SO HOW DID YOU--
WARRIOR QUEEN IS CAUSING A DIVERSION.
WE NEED TO--
GET BACK. THE VILLAGERS NEED OUR HELP.
LET'S--
USE OUR POWERS, TAKE THE BRIDGE AND GET THE HELL OFF THIS ISLAND.
HEY, I'M STILL THE LEADER HERE.
TOTES...

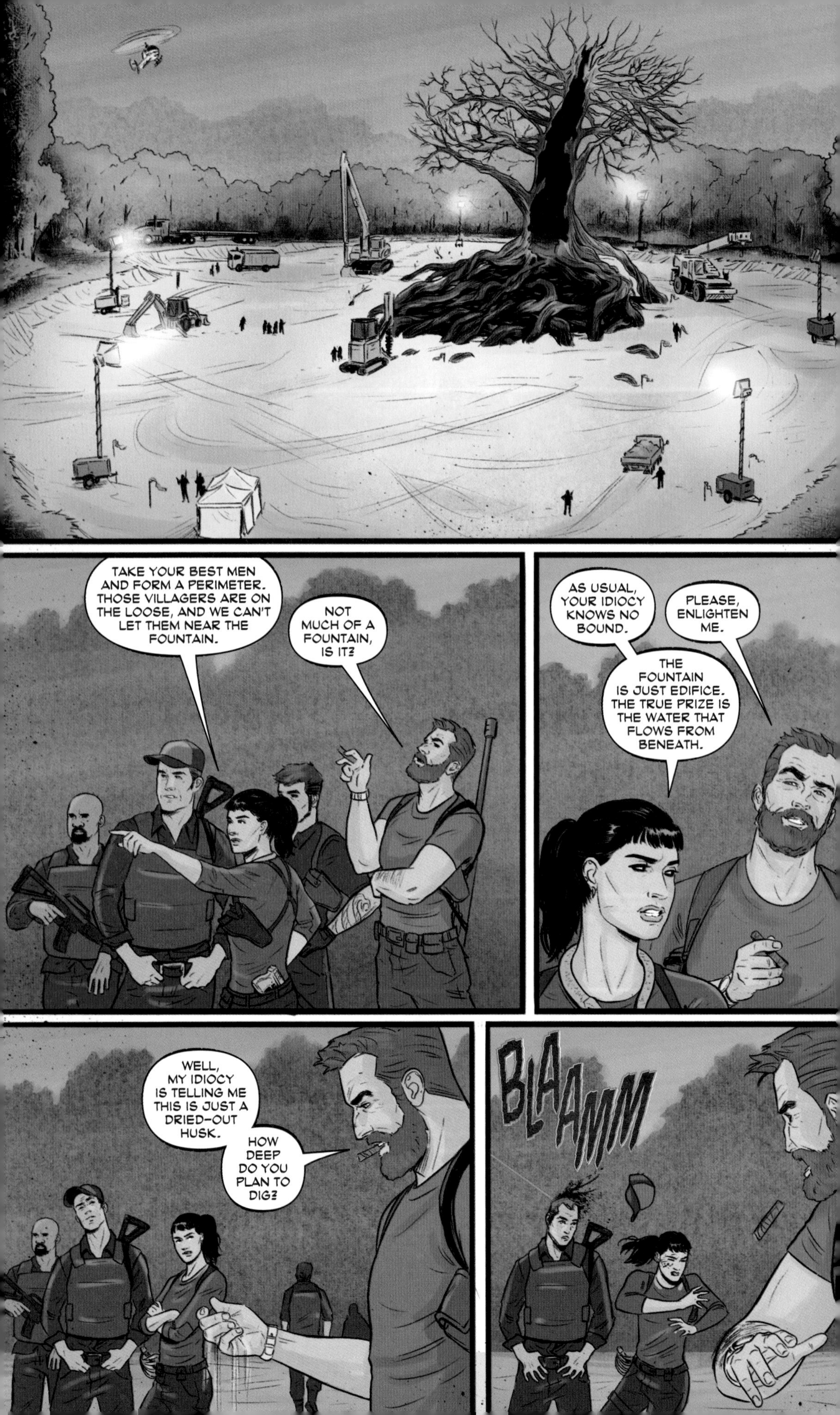
TAKE YOUR BEST MEN AND FORM A PERIMETER. THOSE VILLAGERS ARE ON THE LOOSE, AND WE CAN'T LET THEM NEAR THE FOUNTAIN.
NOT MUCH OF A FOUNTAIN, IS IT?
AS USUAL, YOUR IDIOCY KNOWS NO BOUND.
PLEASE, ENLIGHTEN ME.
THE FOUNTAIN IS JUST EDIFICE. THE TRUE PRIZE IS THE WATER THAT FLOWS FROM BENEATH.
WELL, MY IDIOCY IS TELLING ME THIS IS JUST A DRIED-OUT HUSK.
HOW DEEP DO YOU PLAN TO DIG?
BLAAMM

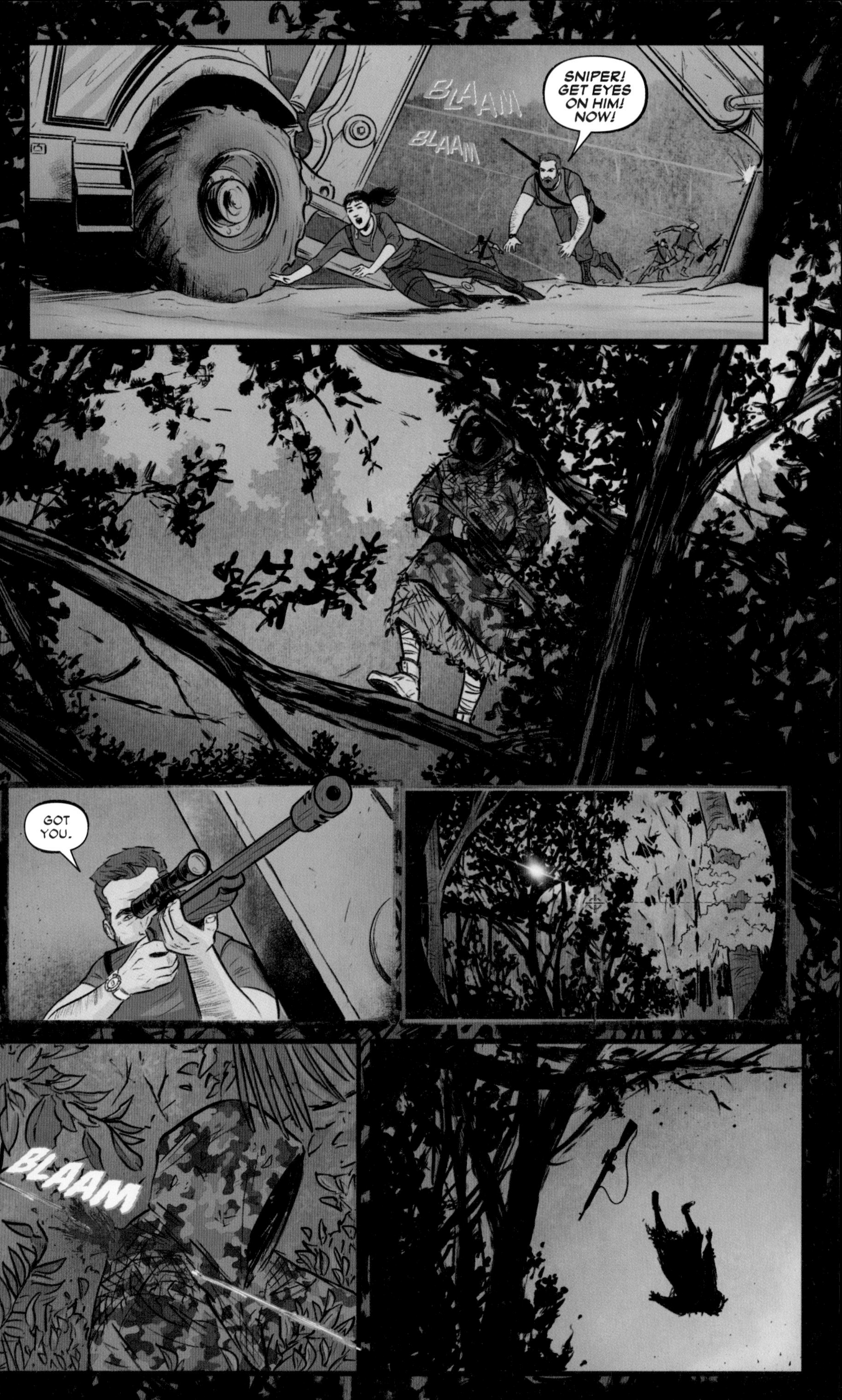
BLAAM
BLAAM
SNIPER! GET EYES ON HIM! NOW!
GOT YOU.
BLAAM

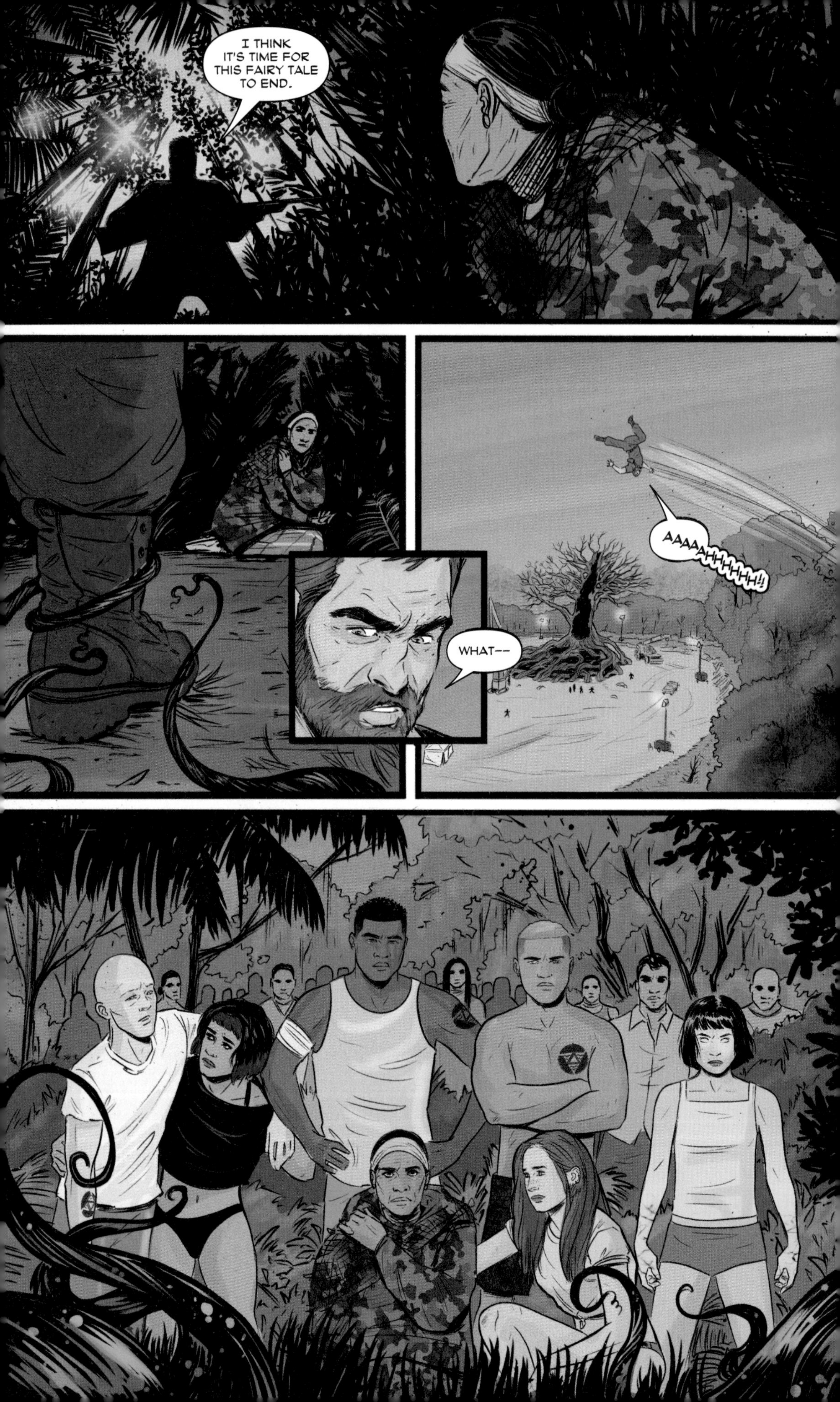
I THINK IT'S TIME FOR THIS FAIRY TALE TO END.
WHAT--
AAAAAHHHHHH!!

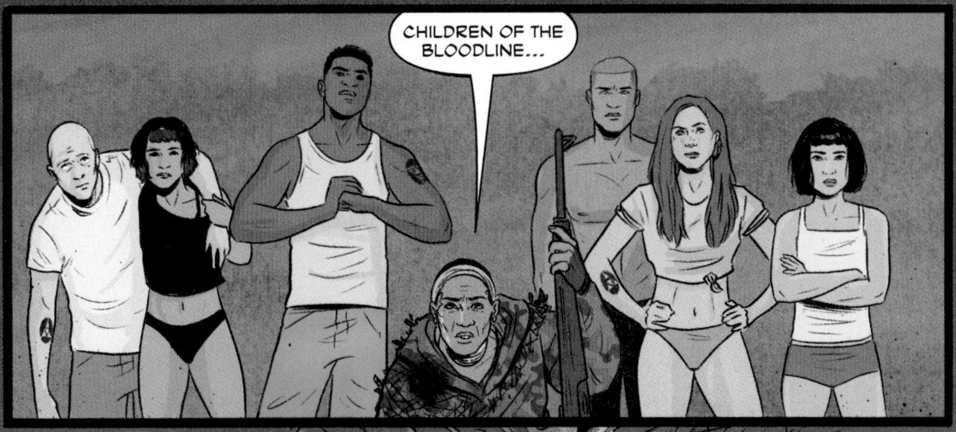
CHILDREN OF THE BLOODLINE...

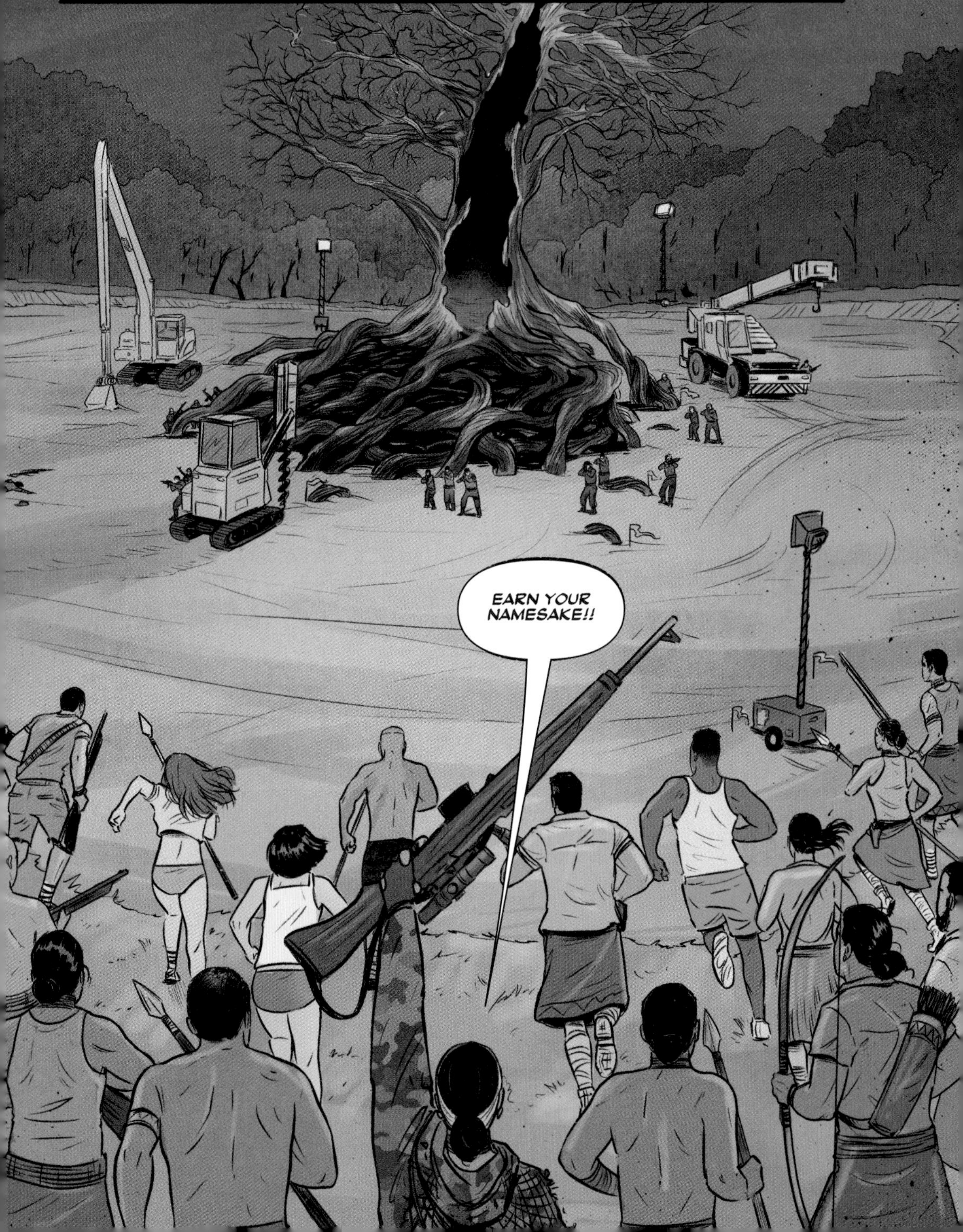
EARN YOUR NAMESAKE!!

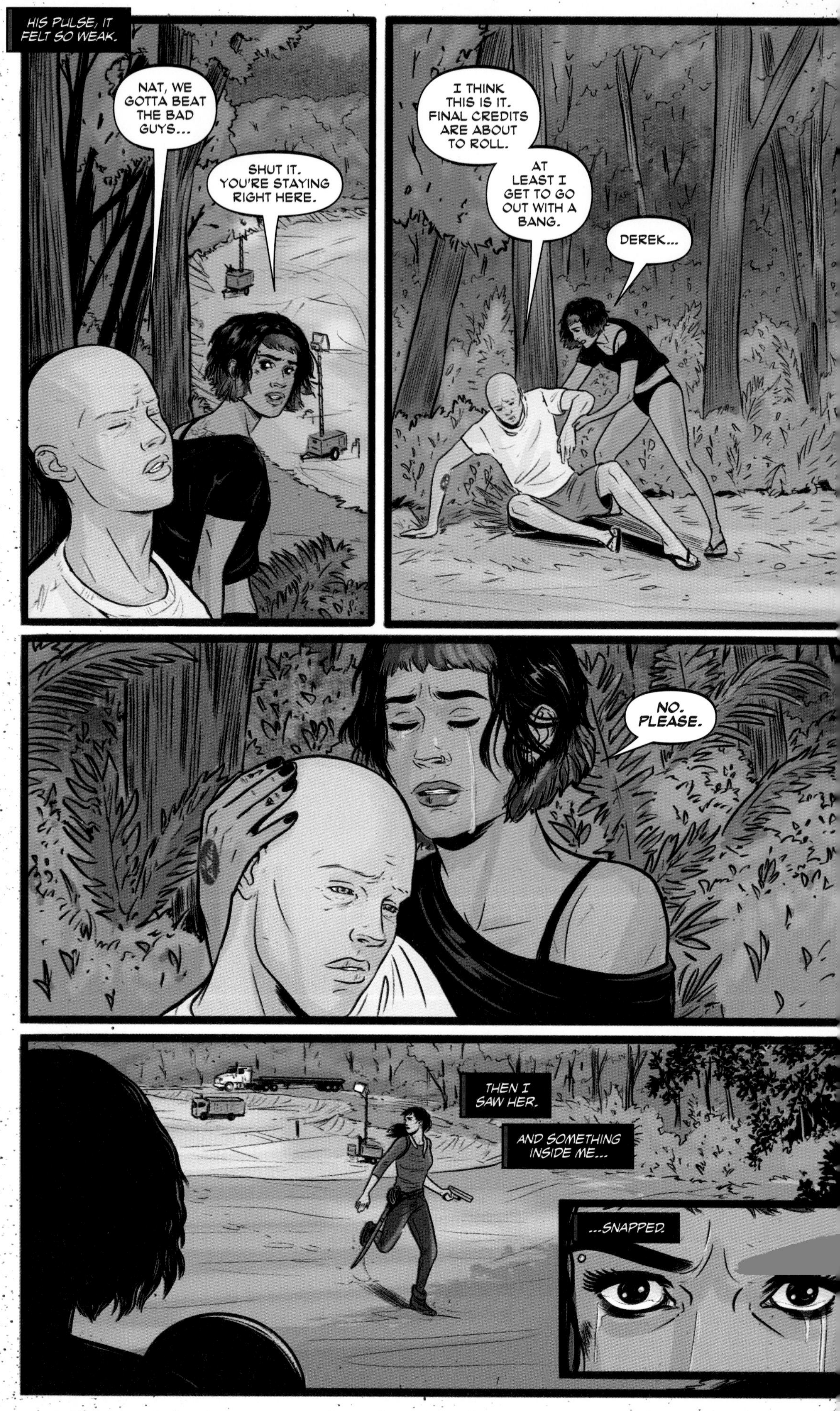
HIS PULSE, IT FELT SO WEAK.
NAT, WE GOTTA BEAT THE BAD GUYS...
SHUT IT. YOU'RE STAYING RIGHT HERE.
I THINK THIS IS IT. FINAL CREDITS ARE ABOUT TO ROLL.
AT LEAST I GET TO GO OUT WITH A BANG.
DEREK...
NO. PLEASE.
THEN I SAW HER.
AND SOMETHING INSIDE ME...
...SNAPPED.

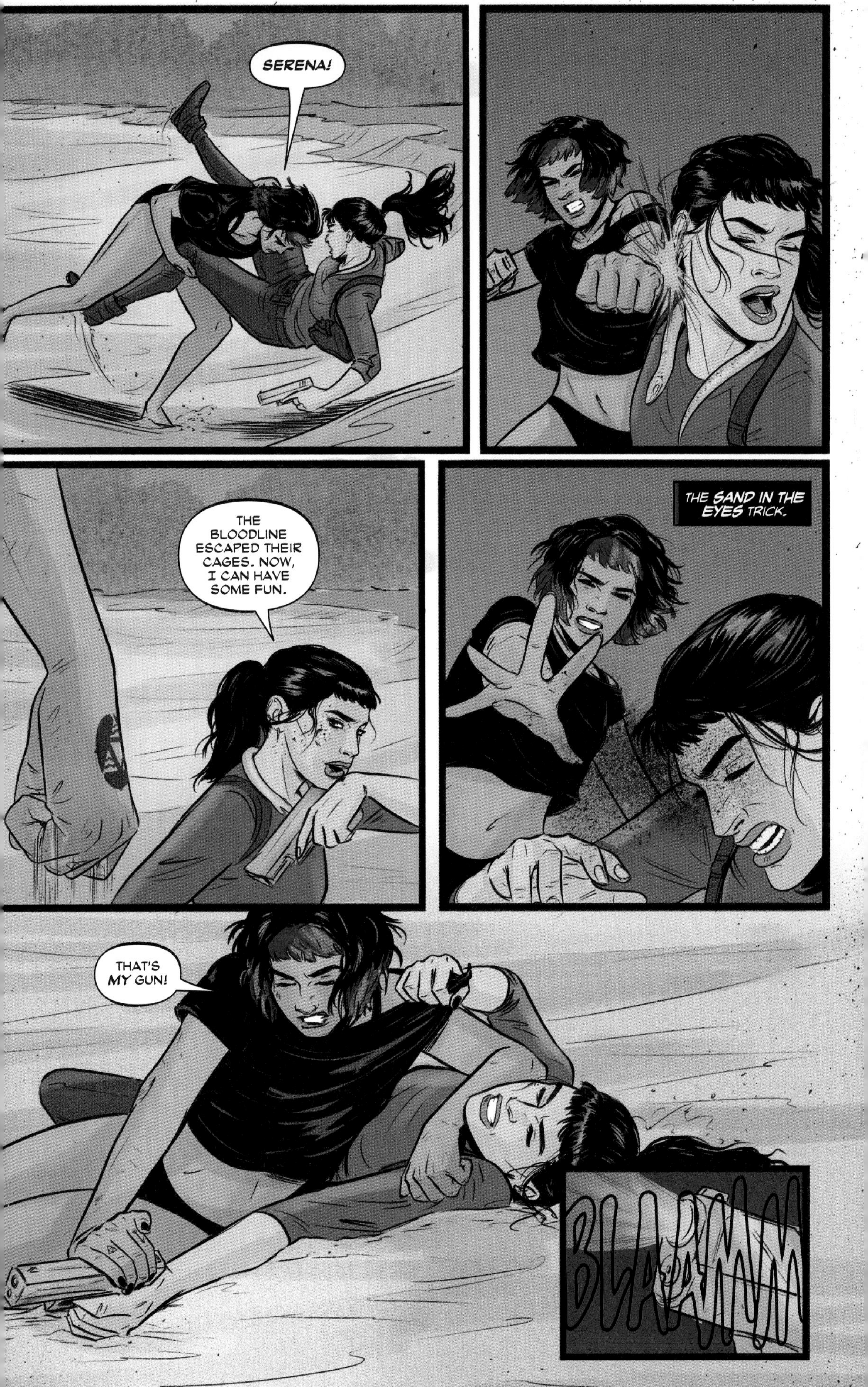
SERENA!
THE BLOODLINE ESCAPED THEIR CAGES. NOW, I CAN HAVE SOME FUN.
THE SAND IN THE EYES TRICK.
THAT'S MY GUN!
BLAAMM

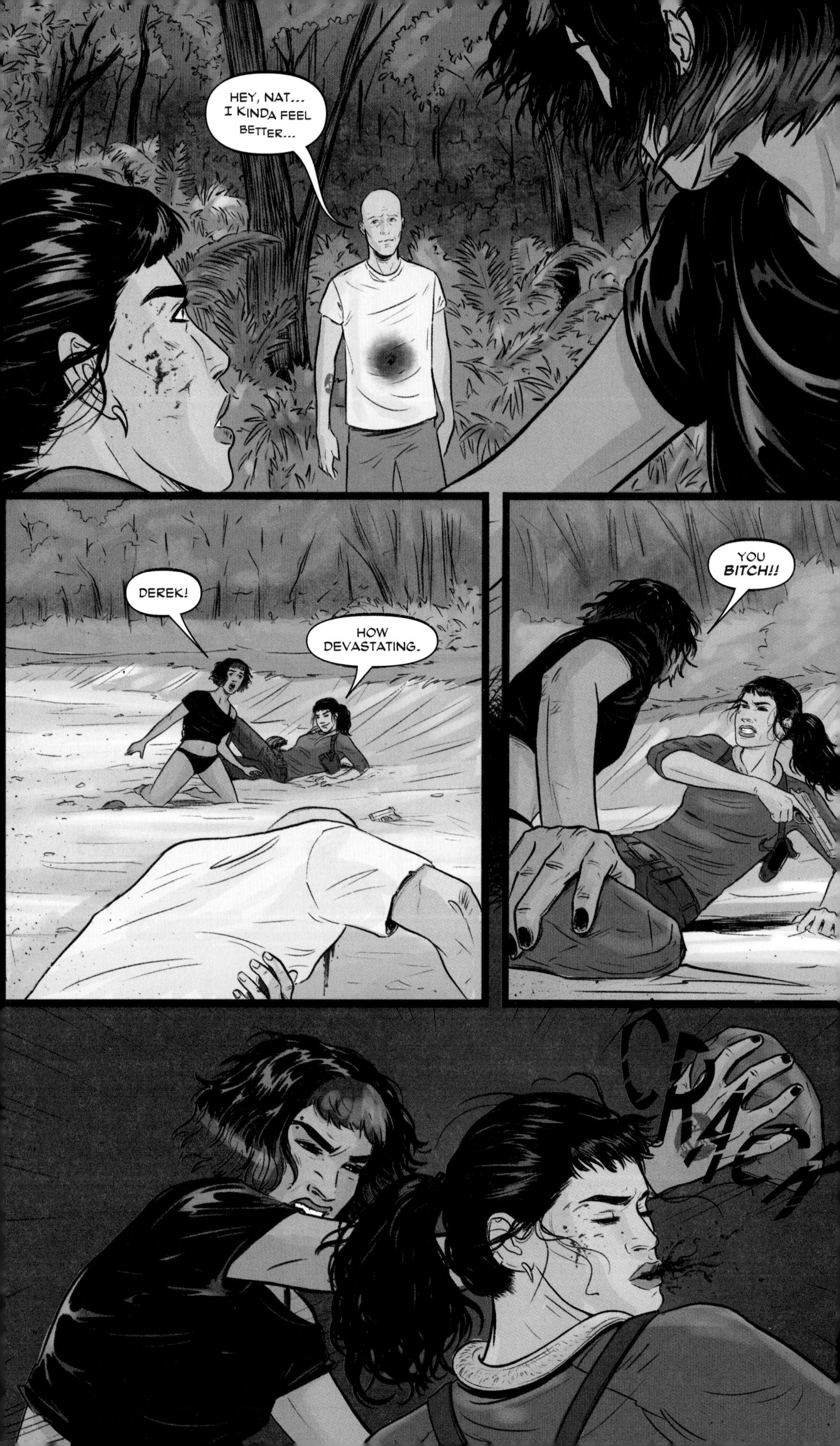
HEY, NAT... I KINDA FEEL BETTER...
DEREK!
HOW DEVASTATING.
YOU BITCH!!
CRACK

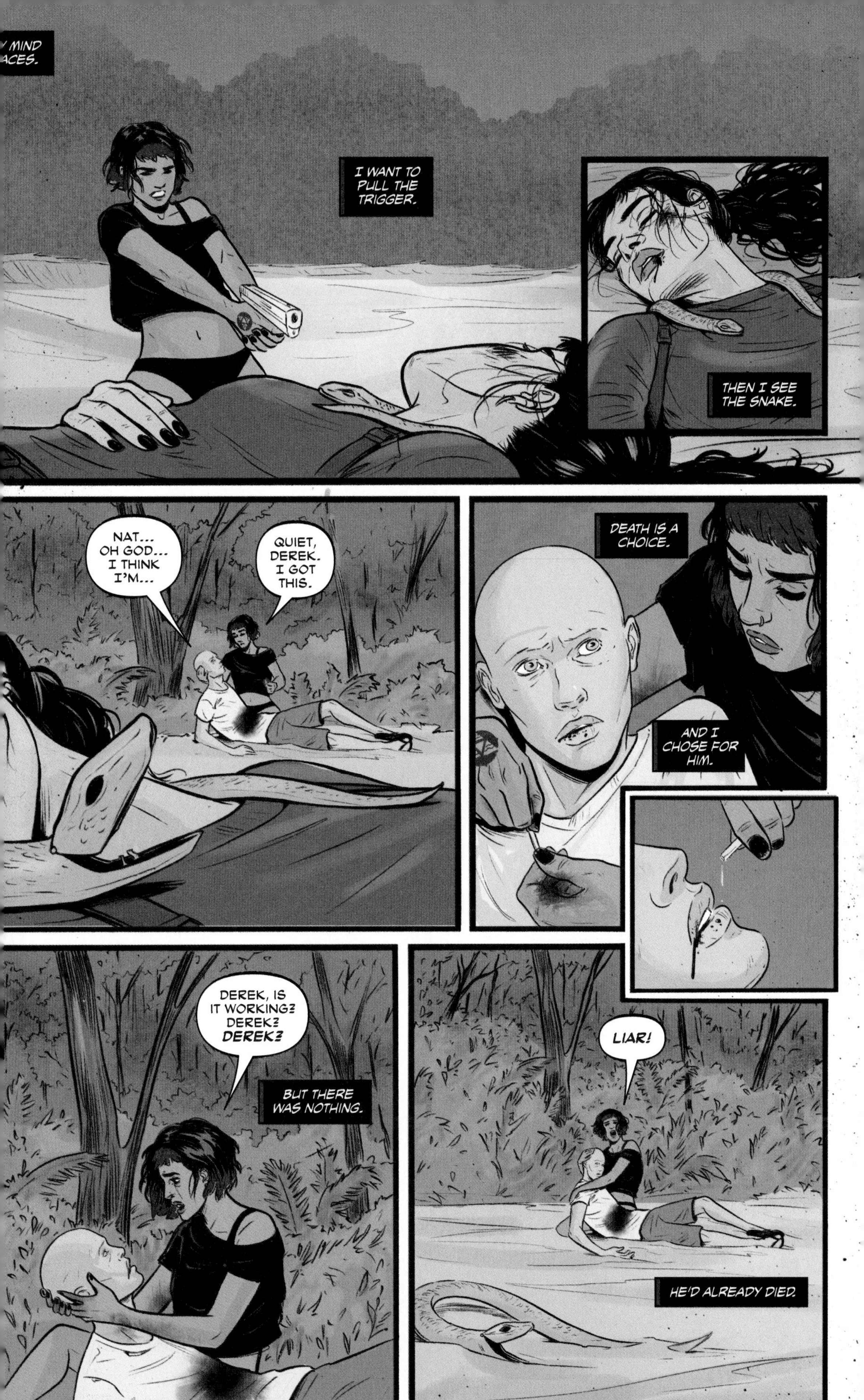
MIND
ACES.
I WANT TO PULL THE TRIGGER.
THEN I SEE THE SNAKE.
NAT... OH GOD... I THINK I'M...
QUIET, DEREK. I GOT THIS.
DEATH IS A CHOICE.
AND I CHOSE FOR HIM.
DEREK, IS IT WORKING? DEREK? DEREK?
BUT THERE WAS NOTHING.
LIAR!
HE'D ALREADY DIED.

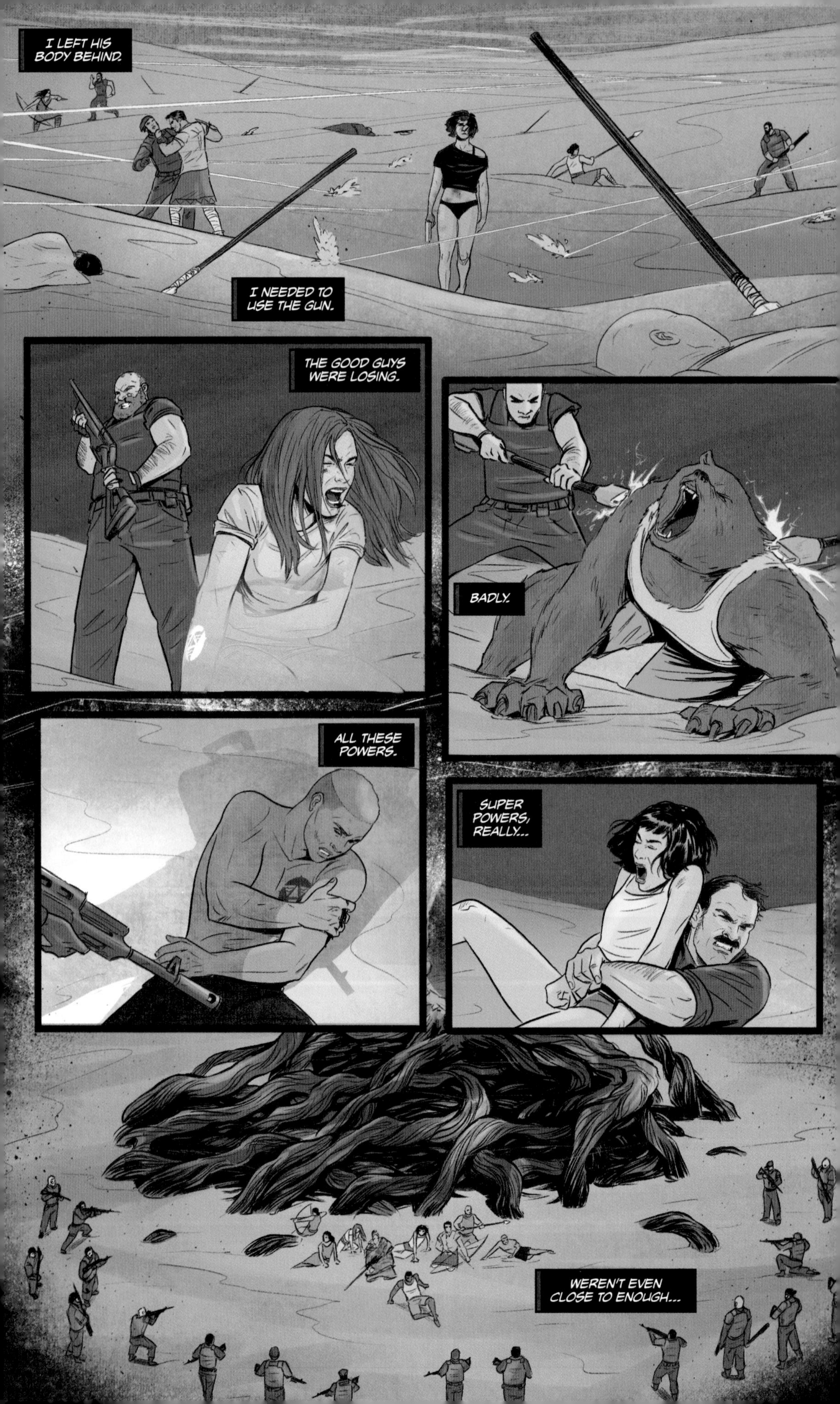
I LEFT HIS BODY BEHIND.
I NEEDED TO USE THE GUN.
THE GOOD GUYS WERE LOSING.
BADLY.
ALL THESE POWERS.
SUPER POWERS, REALLY...
WEREN'T EVEN CLOSE TO ENOUGH...

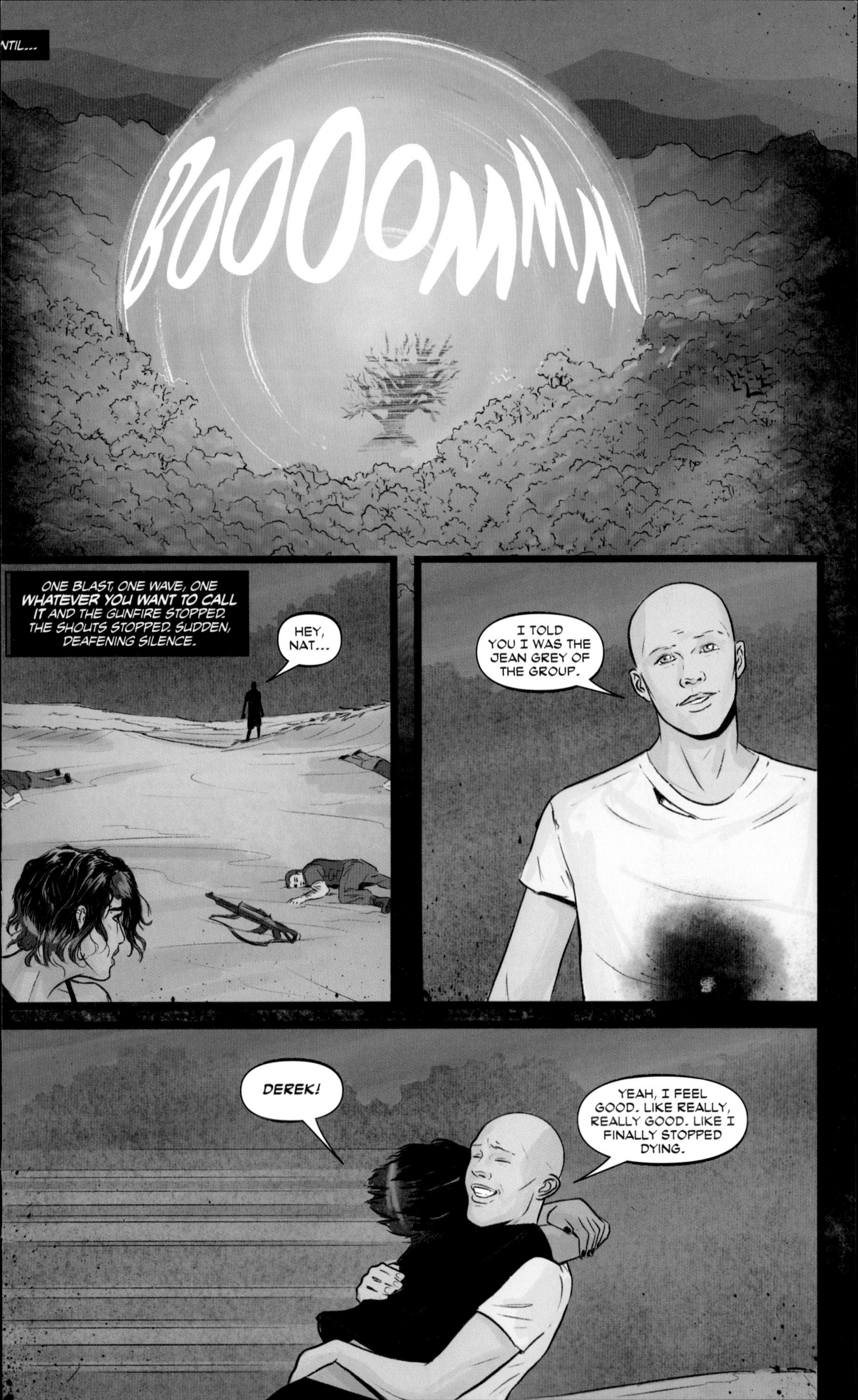
NTIL...
BOOOOMMM
ONE BLAST, ONE WAVE, ONE **WHATEVER YOU WANT TO CALL IT** AND THE GUNFIRE STOPPED. THE SHOUTS STOPPED. SUDDEN, DEAFENING SILENCE.
HEY, NAT...
I TOLD YOU I WAS THE JEAN GREY OF THE GROUP.
DEREK!
YEAH, I FEEL GOOD. LIKE REALLY, REALLY GOOD. LIKE I FINALLY STOPPED DYING.

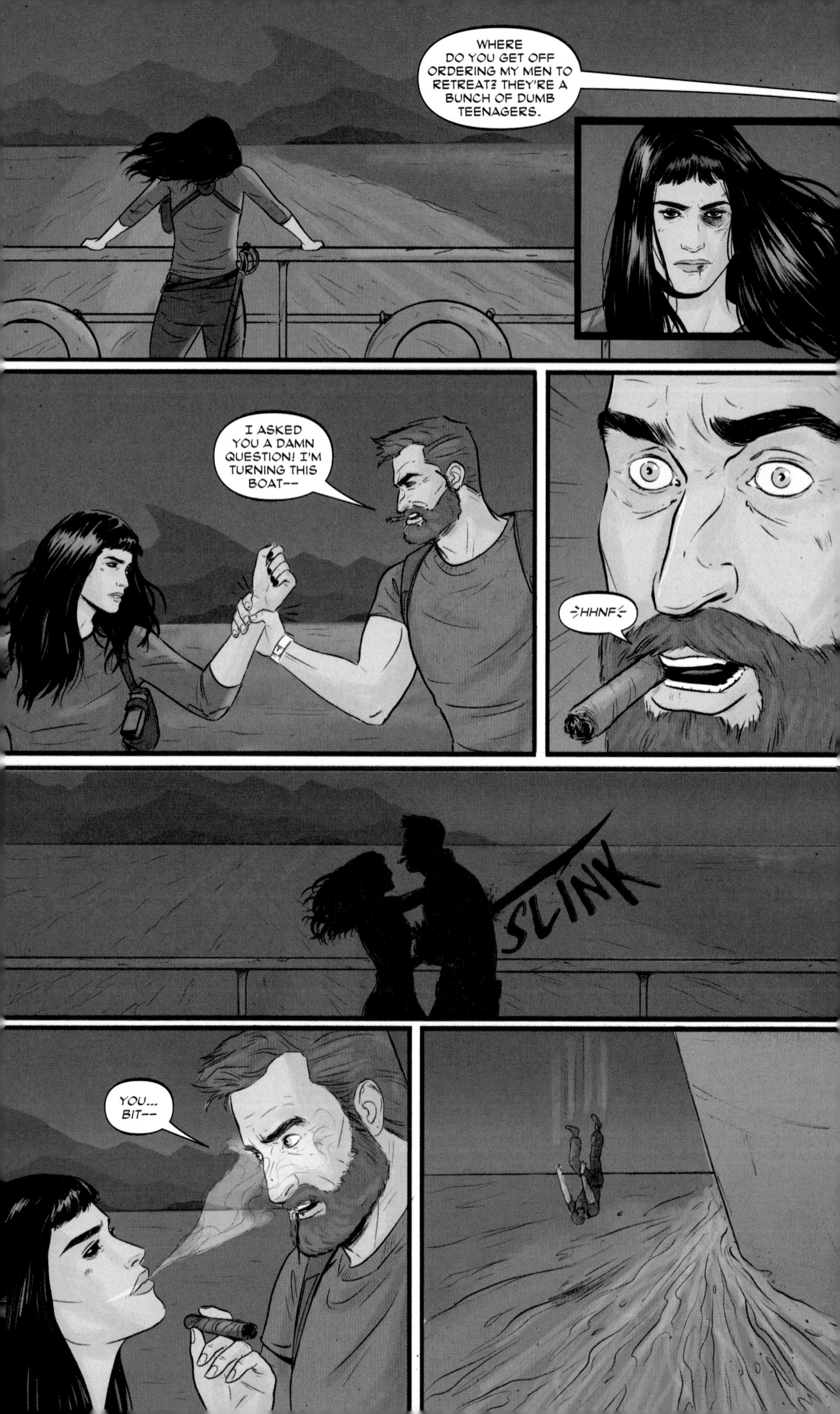

WHERE DO YOU GET OFF ORDERING MY MEN TO RETREAT? THEY'RE A BUNCH OF DUMB TEENAGERS.
I ASKED YOU A DAMN QUESTION! I'M TURNING THIS BOAT--
HHNF
SLINK
YOU... BIT--

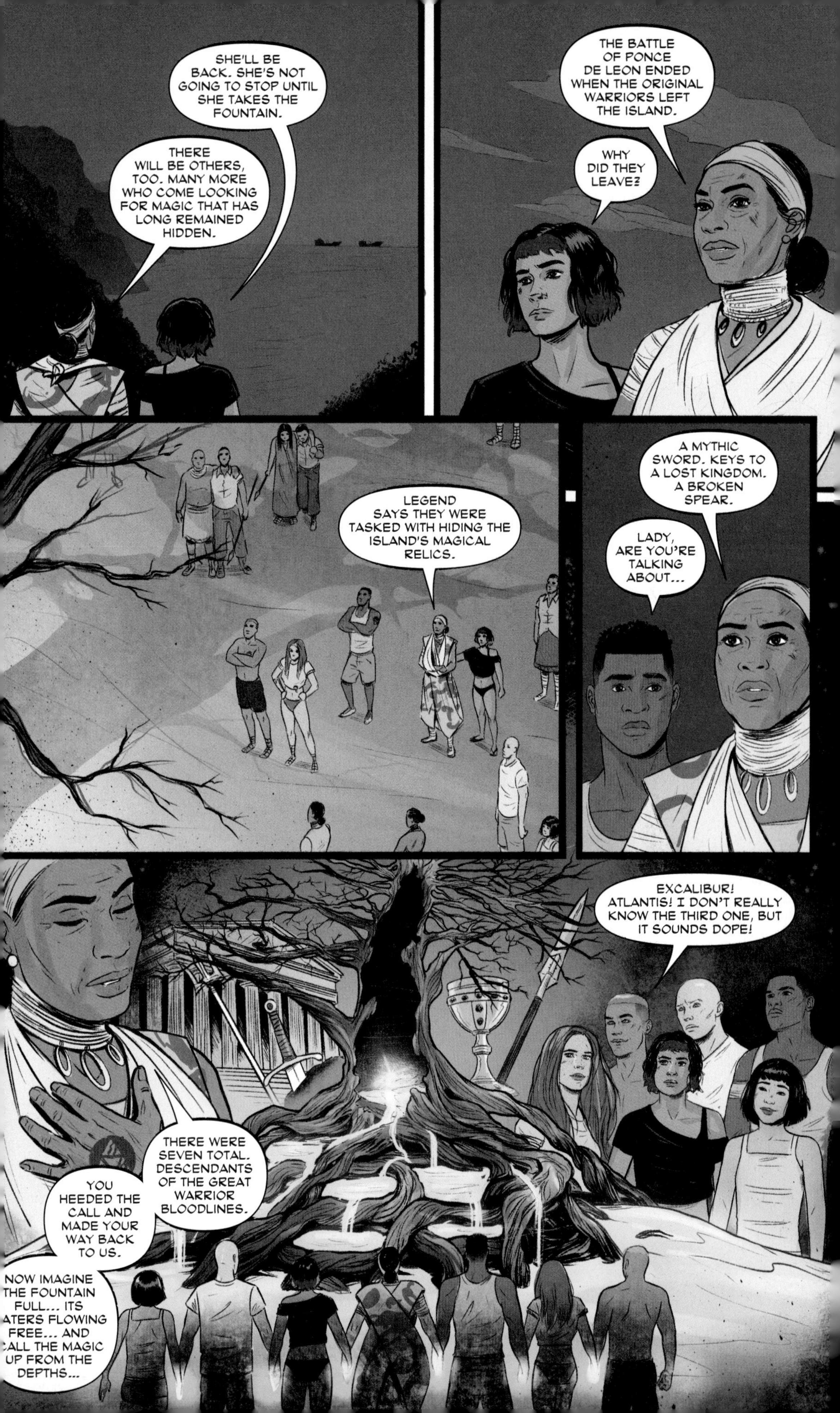

SHE'LL BE BACK. SHE'S NOT GOING TO STOP UNTIL SHE TAKES THE FOUNTAIN.
THERE WILL BE OTHERS, TOO. MANY MORE WHO COME LOOKING FOR MAGIC THAT HAS LONG REMAINED HIDDEN.
THE BATTLE OF PONCE DE LEON ENDED WHEN THE ORIGINAL WARRIORS LEFT THE ISLAND.
WHY DID THEY LEAVE?
LEGEND SAYS THEY WERE TASKED WITH HIDING THE ISLAND'S MAGICAL RELICS.
A MYTHIC SWORD. KEYS TO A LOST KINGDOM. A BROKEN SPEAR.
LADY, ARE YOU'RE TALKING ABOUT...
EXCALIBUR! ATLANTIS! I DON'T REALLY KNOW THE THIRD ONE, BUT IT SOUNDS DOPE!
THERE WERE SEVEN TOTAL. DESCENDANTS OF THE GREAT WARRIOR BLOODLINES.
YOU HEEDED THE CALL AND MADE YOUR WAY BACK TO US.
NOW IMAGINE THE FOUNTAIN FULL... ITS ATERS FLOWING FREE... AND CALL THE MAGIC UP FROM THE DEPTHS...

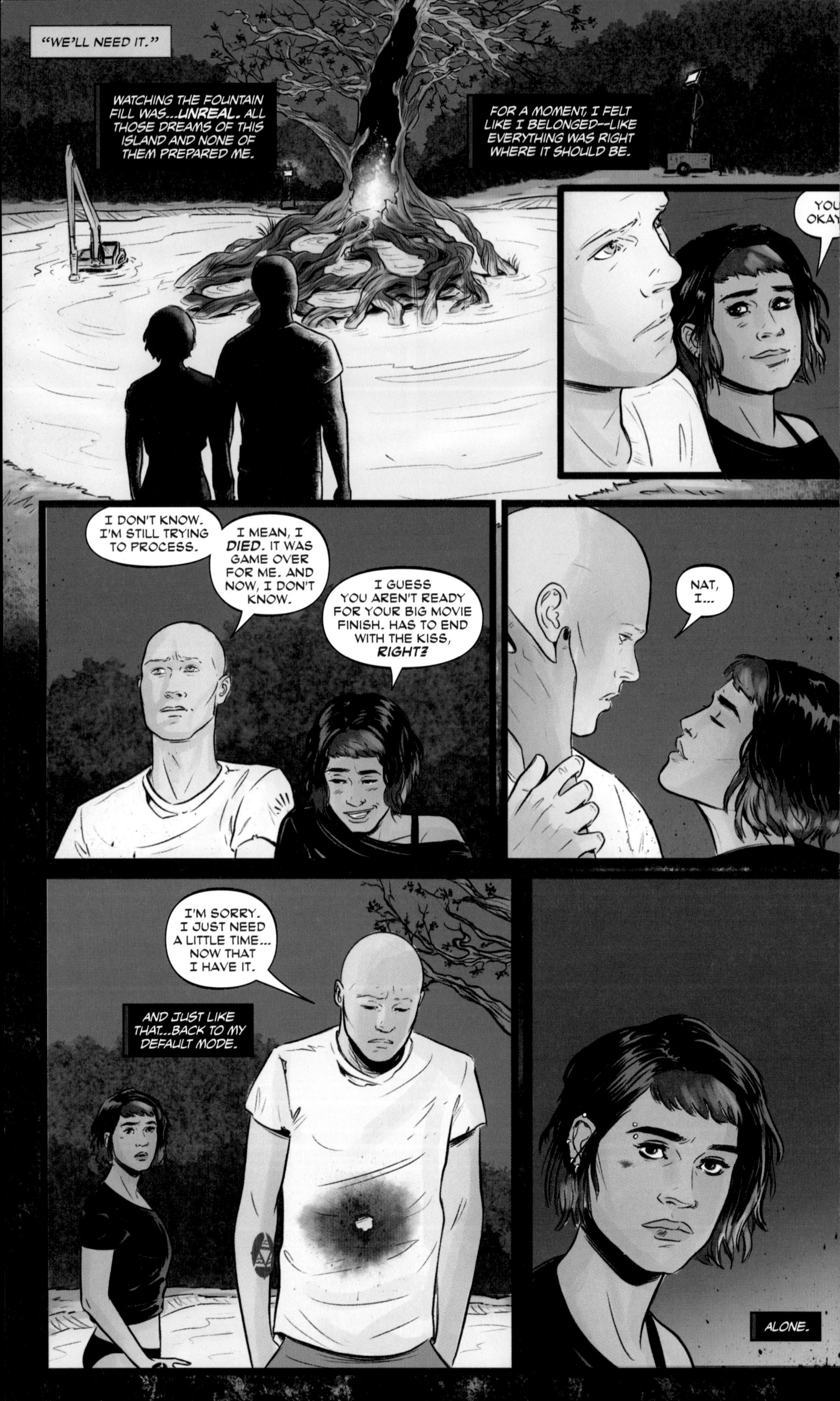

"WE'LL NEED IT."
WATCHING THE FOUNTAIN FILL WAS...UNREAL. ALL THOSE DREAMS OF THIS ISLAND AND NONE OF THEM PREPARED ME.
FOR A MOMENT, I FELT LIKE I BELONGED--LIKE EVERYTHING WAS RIGHT WHERE IT SHOULD BE.
YOU OKAY
I DON'T KNOW. I'M STILL TRYING TO PROCESS.
I MEAN, I DIED. IT WAS GAME OVER FOR ME. AND NOW, I DON'T KNOW.
I GUESS YOU AREN'T READY FOR YOUR BIG MOVIE FINISH. HAS TO END WITH THE KISS, RIGHT?
NAT, I...
I'M SORRY. I JUST NEED A LITTLE TIME... NOW THAT I HAVE IT.
AND JUST LIKE THAT...BACK TO MY DEFAULT MODE.
ALONE.

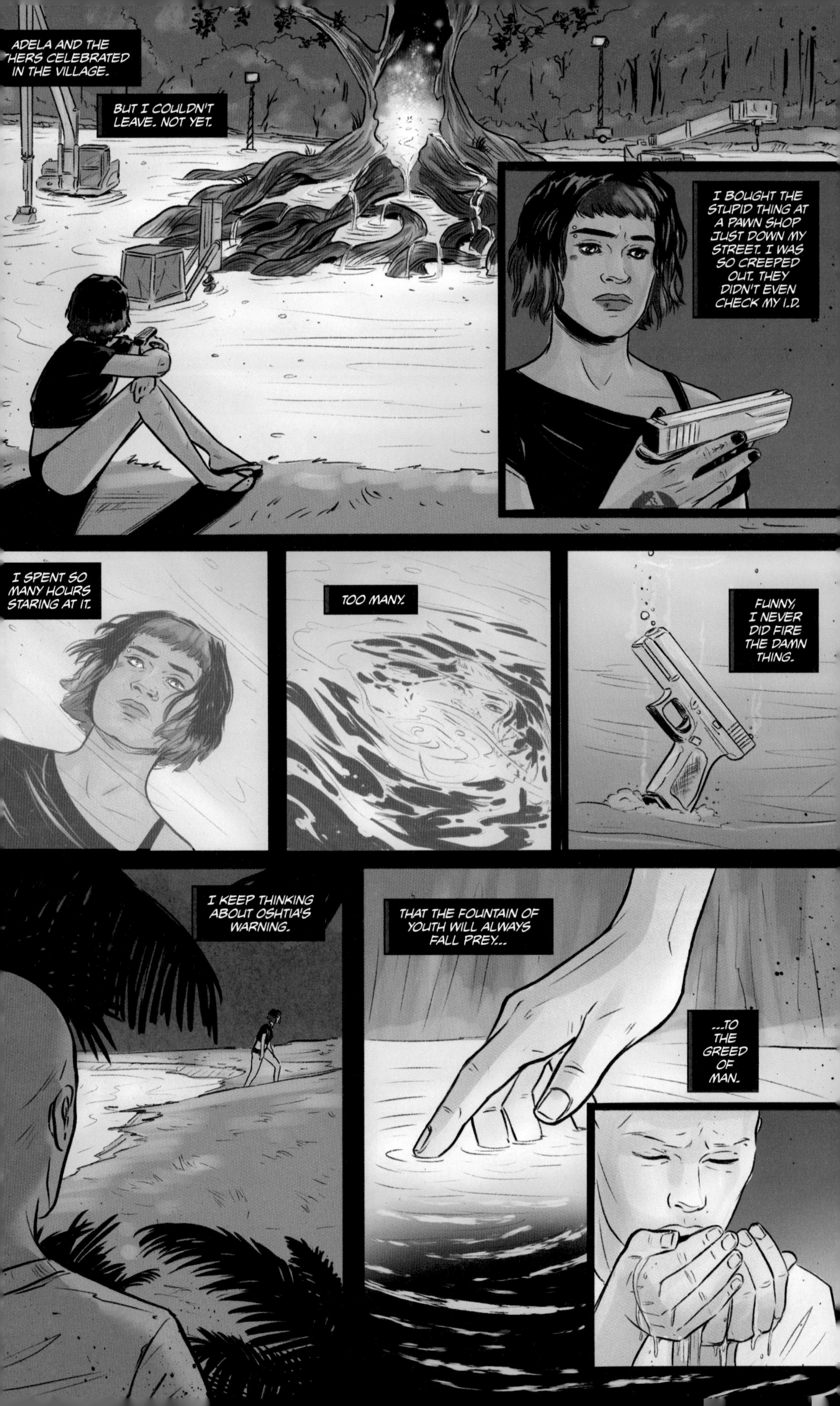
ADELA AND THE OTHERS CELEBRATED IN THE VILLAGE.
BUT I COULDN'T LEAVE. NOT YET.
I BOUGHT THE STUPID THING AT A PAWN SHOP JUST DOWN MY STREET. I WAS SO CREEPED OUT. THEY DIDN'T EVEN CHECK MY I.D.
I SPENT SO MANY HOURS STARING AT IT.
TOO MANY.
FUNNY, I NEVER DID FIRE THE DAMN THING.
I KEEP THINKING ABOUT OSHTIA'S WARNING.
THAT THE FOUNTAIN OF YOUTH WILL ALWAYS FALL PREY...
...TO THE GREED OF MAN.

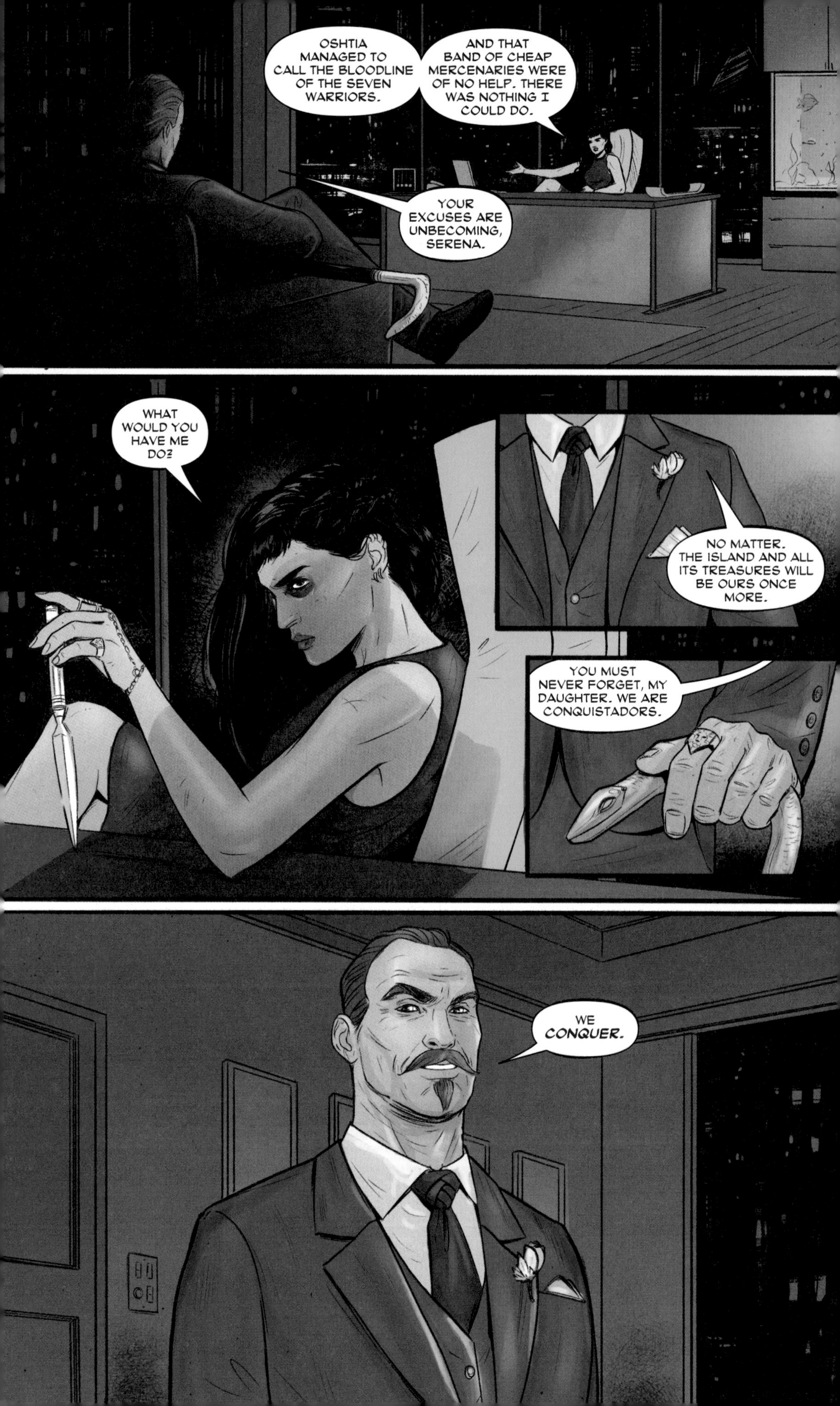
OSHTIA MANAGED TO CALL THE BLOODLINE OF THE SEVEN WARRIORS.
AND THAT BAND OF CHEAP MERCENARIES WERE OF NO HELP. THERE WAS NOTHING I COULD DO.
YOUR EXCUSES ARE UNBECOMING, SERENA.
WHAT WOULD YOU HAVE ME DO?
NO MATTER. THE ISLAND AND ALL ITS TREASURES WILL BE OURS ONCE MORE.
YOU MUST NEVER FORGET, MY DAUGHTER. WE ARE CONQUISTADORS.
WE **CONQUER.**

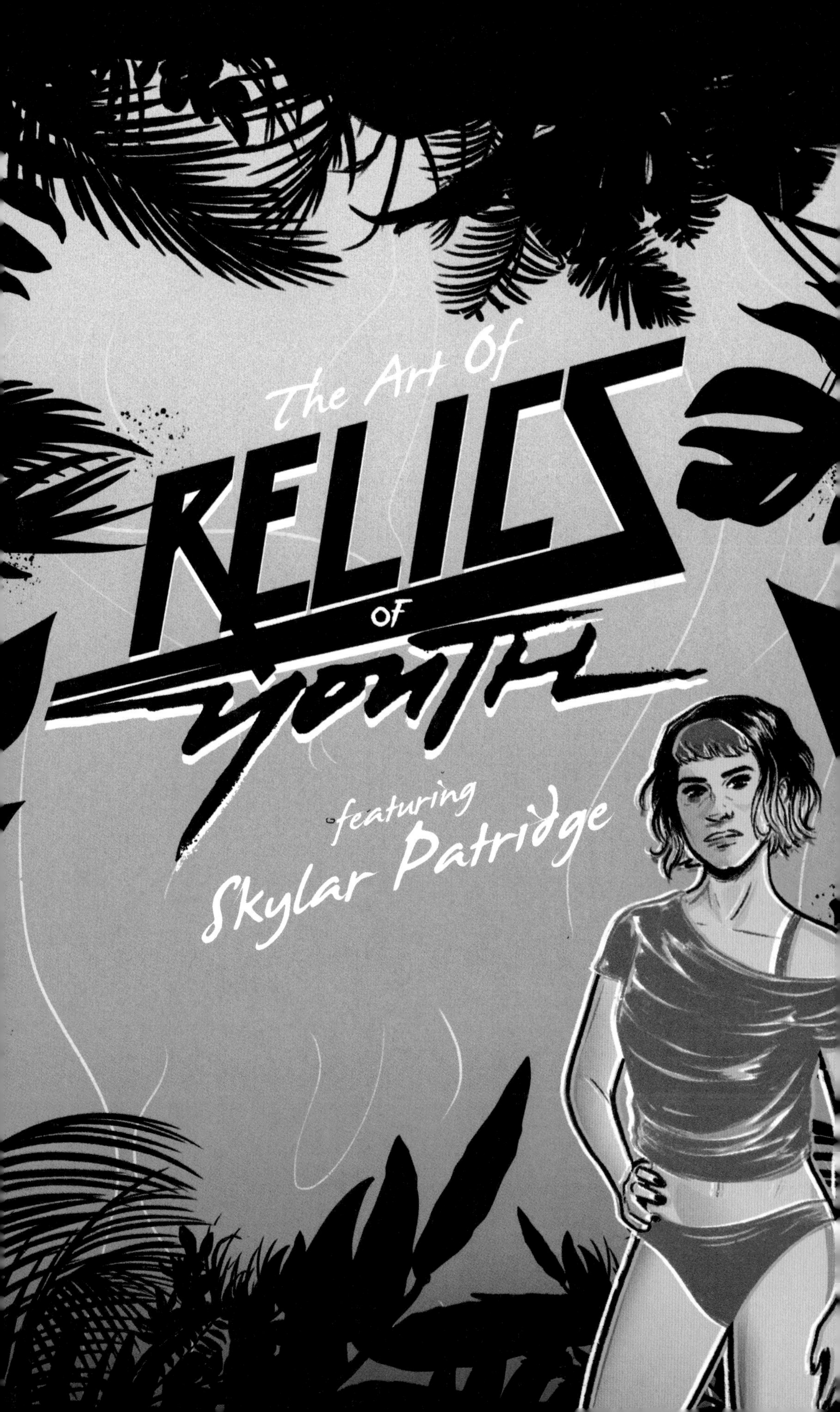
The Art Of
RELICS
OF
YOUTH
featuring
Skylar Patridge

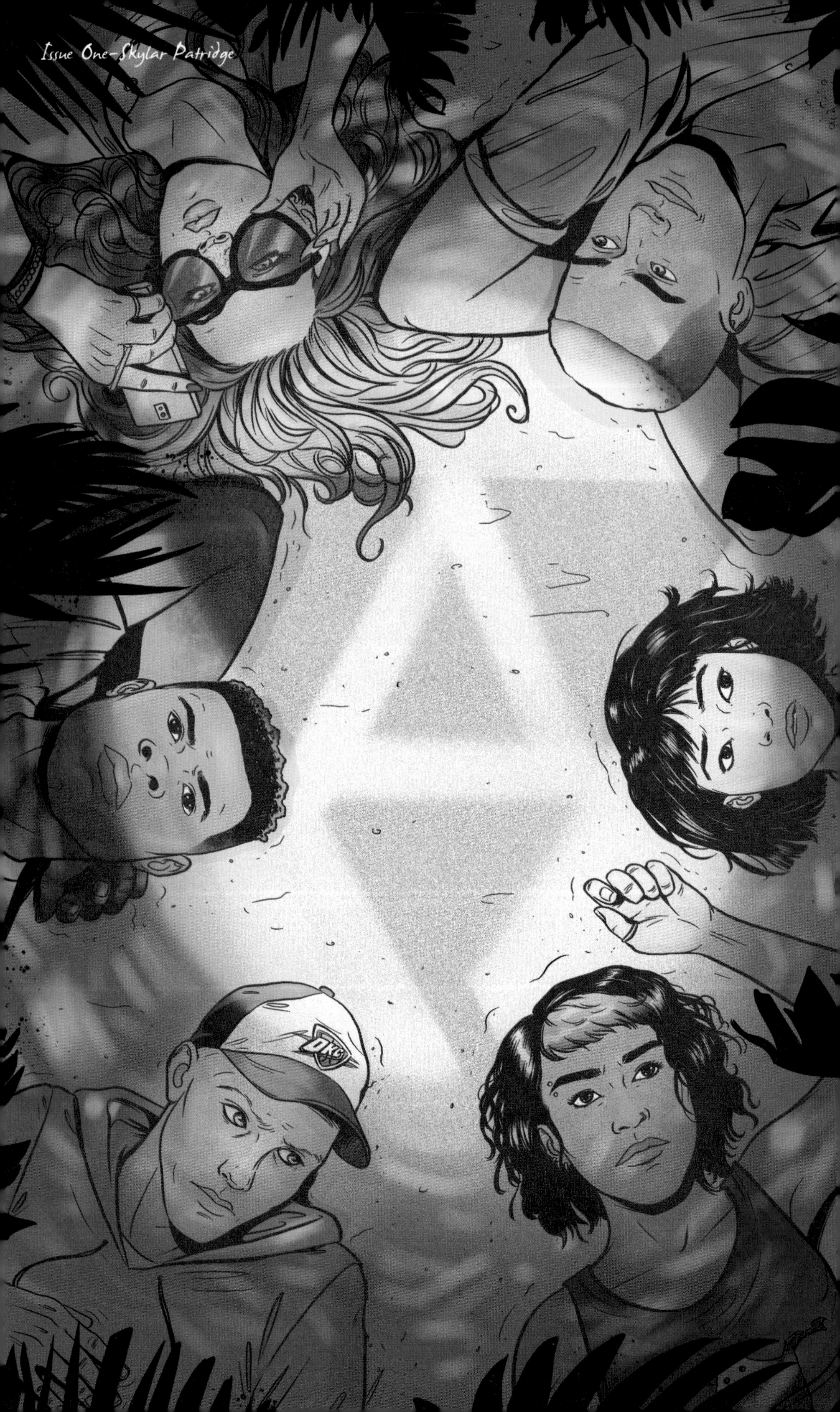
OKC

Issue One–Skylar Patridge

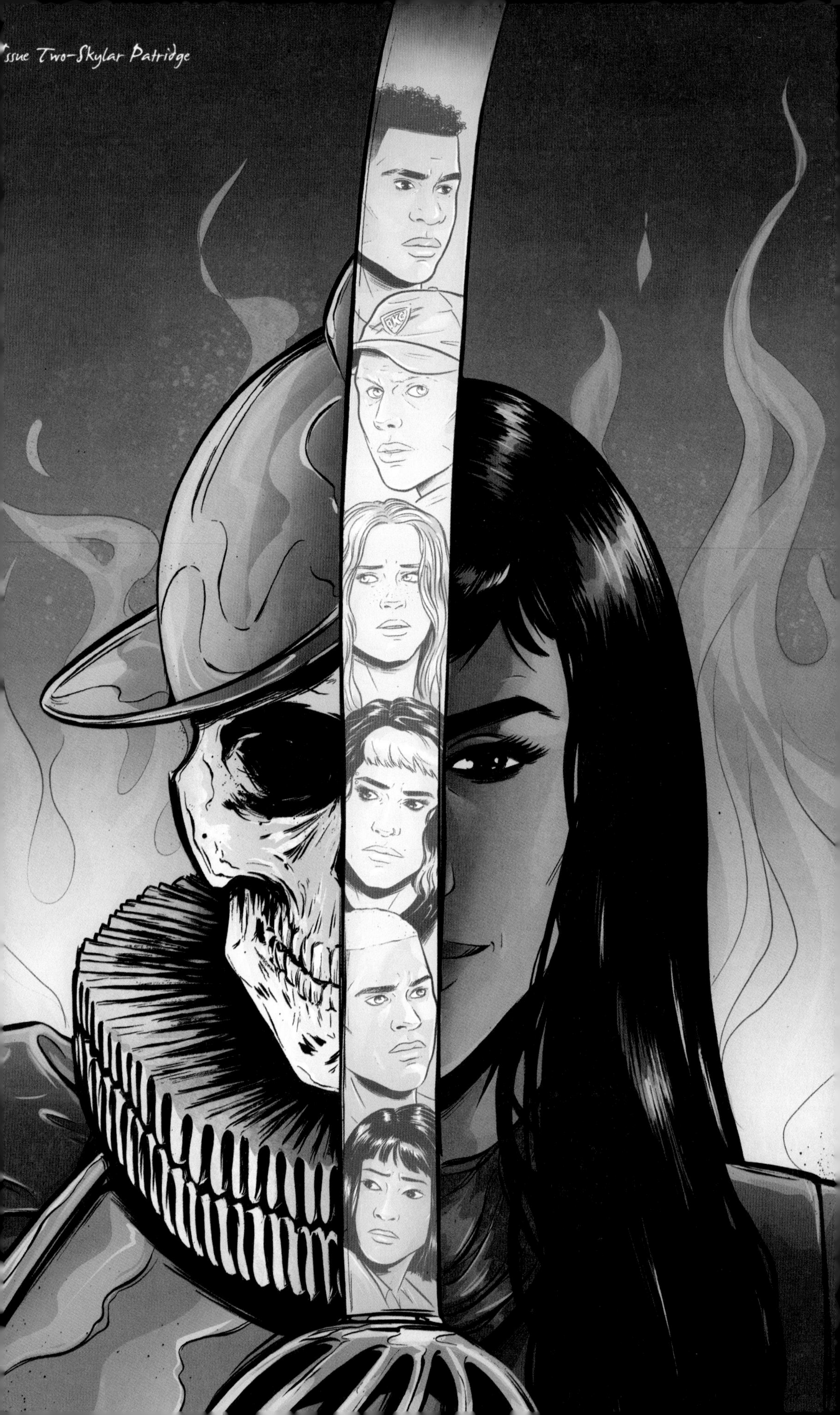

Issue Two–Skylar Patridge

Issue Three-Skylar Patridge

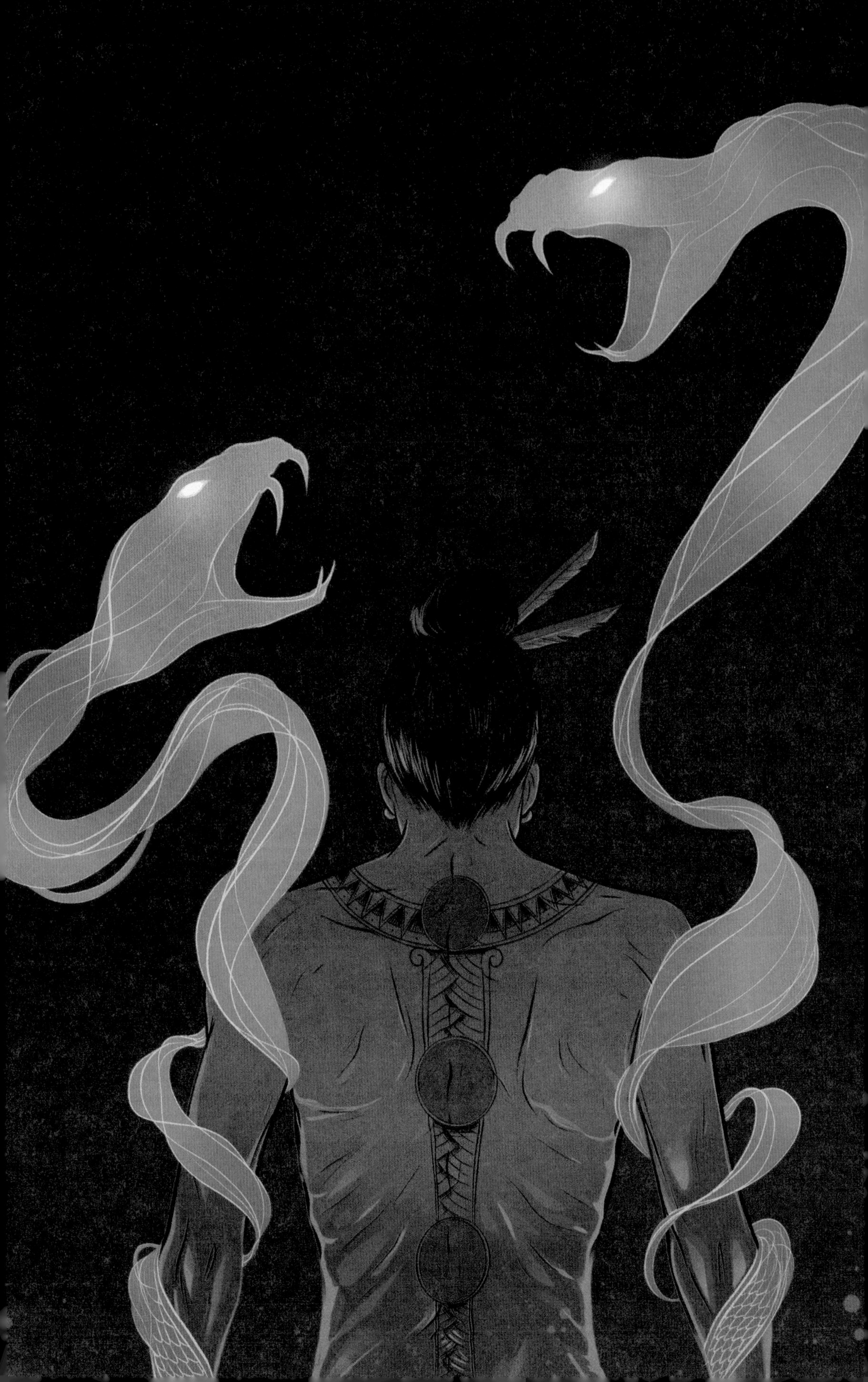

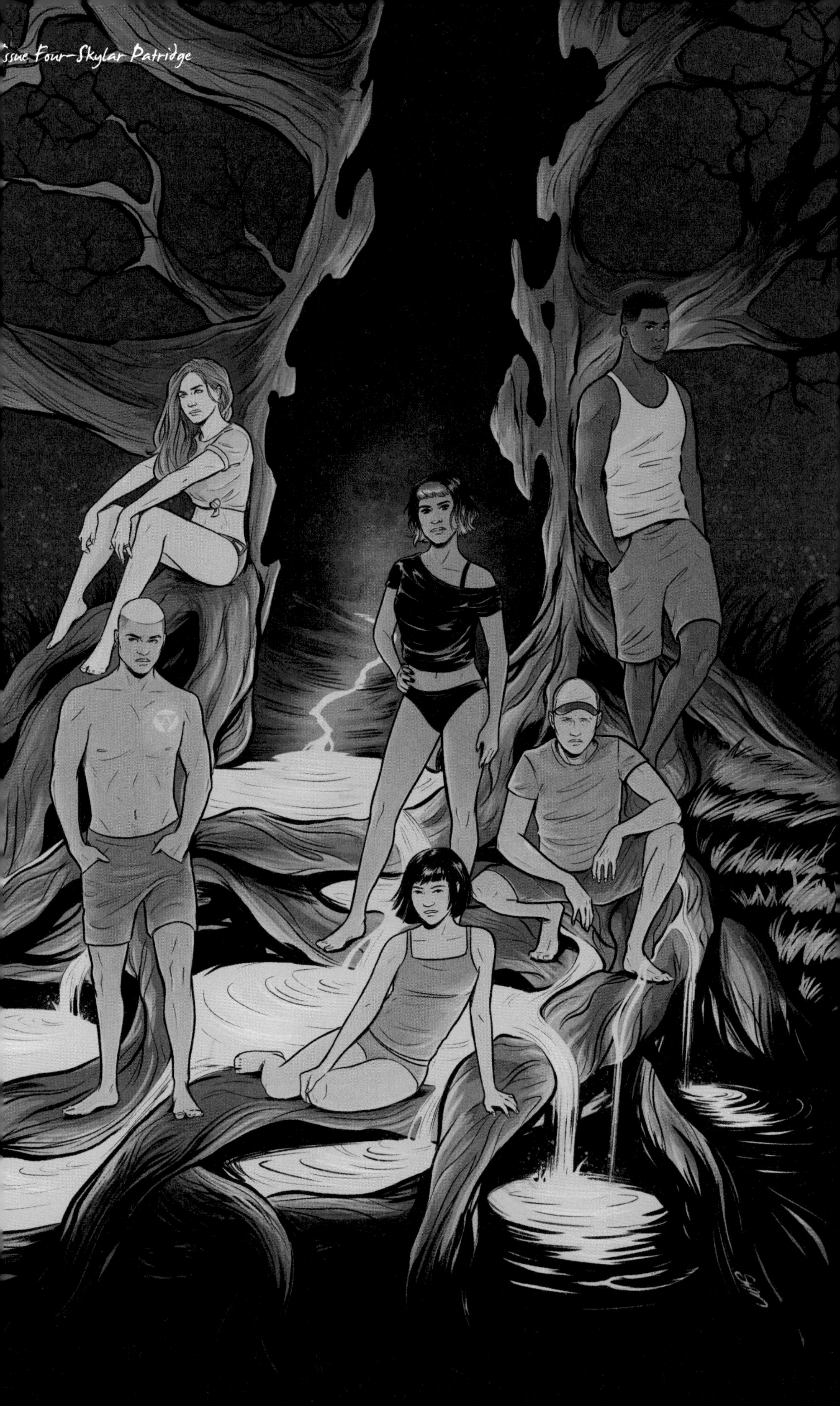
Issue Four—Skylar Patridge

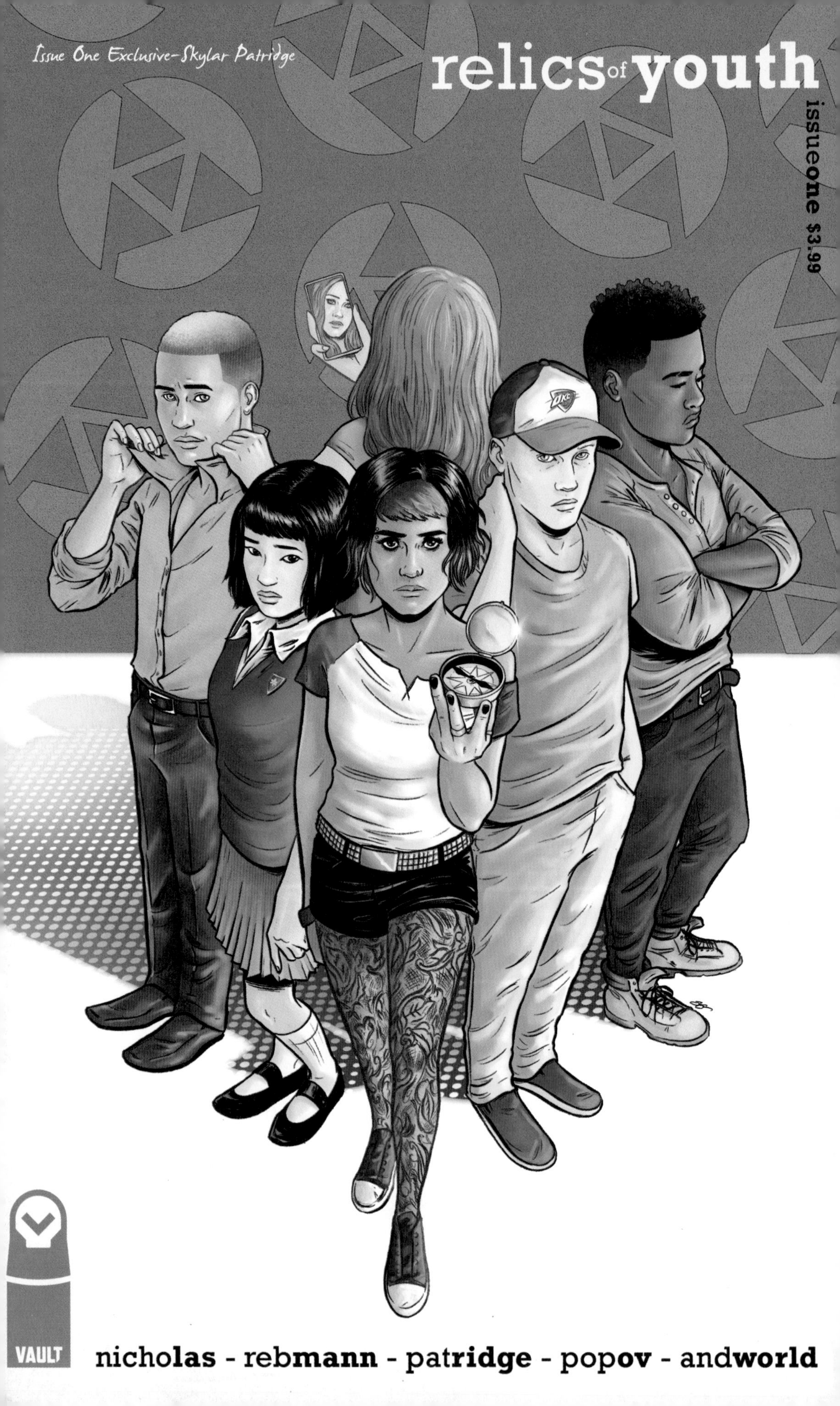
Issue One Exclusive-Skylar Patridge
relics of youth
issueone $3.99
OKC
VAULT
nicholas - rebmann - patridge - popov - andworld